MW00453796

THE WIZARD'S BREW

JORDAN REED

JORDAN REED

BLUE HANDLE PUBLISHING

For information, address:
Blue Handle Publishing 2607 Wolflin
#963 Amarillo, TX 79109

For information about bulk, educational and other special discounts, please contact Blue Handle Publishing.

To book Jordan Reed for any event, contact Blue Handle Publishing.
www.bluehandlepublishing.com

Cover & Interior Design: Blue Handle Publishing
Mahlon Rhodes

Editing: Book Puma Author Services
BookPumaLive.com

ISBN: 978-1-955058-10-0

For the four *women* who fostered my writing:

To the teacher who first got me into writing;
to my lovely wife, who pushed me to keep writing;
to my aunt, who always supported this dream as a possibility;
and to my grandmother, and her endless enthusiasm and optimism.

CHAPTER 1

A rough voice echoed off buildings and funneled through dimly lit city streets.

"Stop!"

He didn't.

Instead, the hooded thief kept running, package in hand.

Zane continued chasing the man, yelling as they dashed down alleys and cut across sidewalks. They dodged horse-drawn carriages sloshing through grimy streets, a mixture of wet ash and mud clinging to Zane's boots in a thick paste. Hot blood raced through his veins, and he felt more alive than he had in months as he reached underneath his black coat and pulled a wand from its brown leather holster.

He tried to aim as the thief maneuvered through shifting crowds of people.

Zane cursed the saints.

There was no clear shot with dozens of bystanders shielding the thief, so he slipped the wand back under his coat.

Then he started to limp.

Pain radiated from old injuries like a fire spreading over dry leaves, creeping up Zane's side until he wheezed and nearly doubled over. With his free hand, Zane fished out a flask filled with healing elixir. He poured the green liquid directly into his gullet between labored breaths, and the thick sap did its job, smothering the pain that had threatened to overtake him.

That stuff's going to kill you one day.

Zane ignored the silky voice whispering in his ear. His spent muscles found renewed strength and the limp faded away, allowing Zane to close the distance just as the thief turned down an alley. Zane passed the cane he'd been carrying into his right hand, then whirled it through the air, striking the hooded man's legs.

The thief slammed into the cold brick street and rushed to right himself like a panicked animal. Zane lunged at his prey, grabbing a handful of the man's hoodie and sending them crashing down. Zane felt half a dozen cuts and bruises forming, but he pushed aside the pain as he pinned the thief.

"Let go," the man yelled as he thrashed. "It's mine. I found it."

Zane's military training kicked in. When the thief bridged his hips and reached out to shove him, Zane sprawled out, bracing against the attempts to buck him and brushed away the push. With the thief's arm still outstretched, Zane caught it and leveraged the limb between his own arms, then yanked it away from the man's body.

"You're gonna break it!"

"Then let go."

The hooded man kicked and tried in vain to plant his feet and escape Zane's hold. With the package still in hand, he threw awkward punches into Zane's side while screaming for help.

Zane tightened his hold, ignoring the weak blows. "Let. It. Go."

He was tired, but Zane's voice remained stern, in control as he repeated his demand until the thief finally dropped the parcel next to him.

"Fine. Take it."

Zane wasn't about to trust a thief. "Push it away from you."

The hooded man spat in reply.

Zane tightened his hold.

The thief screamed in pain and again attempted to bridge under Zane's body, but he held fast. With a final yell, the man pushed the parcel as far as his free hand would let him. "There. Now let me go, dammit."

Zane released the man, stood, then grabbed his cane and slid it through a loop of string around the parcel. He raised the package to his left hand and pointed the tip of his cane at the thief. Zane verified the box's contents as the thief dragged himself to the nearest wall and leaned into it, cradling the arm Zane had held nearly broken and sobbing under his hood.

Zane felt pangs of sympathy. The man didn't strike Zane as a professional criminal.

And I thought I was cruel, the silky voice said. *That man has nothing, and then you nearly tear off his arm.*

Zane tried to ignore the voice, but it cut deep. He sighed. "Sorry things got rough, but you've been stealing for days now. My client—well, they wanted this back before you had a chance to fence it. It's not personal, but ..."

The man locked eyes with Zane, and for the first time he got a good look at the thief's face. A massive tumor bulged from his neck and his lips had a metallic rainbow sheen.

The hairs on Zane's neck stood up at the telltale signs of a potion addict after many years of abuse.

"What I drink in the gutter isn't good enough anymore," the thief whimpered between sobs. "You gotta understand."

Zane understood all too well. He fingered the outline of the empty flask in his jacket pocket.

It must be like seeing your future self.

The voice's comment left a lump of dread in Zane's throat bigger than the thief's tumor. His hand moved from his flask to his wallet, and Zane pulled out some coins and dropped them in front of the still sobbing man. Zane wasn't interested in seeing what came next; he leaned heavily on his cane as he walked away.

After returning the parcel and collecting his pay, Zane limped home, the empty flask feeling oddly heavy in his pocket.

There was only one way to remove the weight.

The thief's face flashed across his mind's eye, but it didn't stop Zane. With the pay, he bought more healing elixir. They called it troll's blood after the mythical creature, and it was one of the best healing potions one could buy legally.

On the first floor of his building, Zane ran into his apartment manager, Mrs. Mose, who was stooped and sweeping the floor. "How are you today, Mr. Vrexon?"

Zane gave a polite bow, holding the small box of troll's blood at his side. "I am doing well, thank you."

She eyed the crate under his arm. "I hope you didn't spend all your money on that."

He laughed nervously. "Of course not. I am merely restocking out of occupational necessity. Being a private detective can be dangerous."

It was a well-rehearsed lie he told everyone—including himself.

She pushed her lips together. "I worry about you, Mr. Vrexon. You are either on a job or you spend all day in your room waiting for one to walk through your front door. When was the last time you spoke to a friend?"

He deflected. "Well, it *is* hard to talk to friends when one has rent to pay."

She eyed the box again. "Lack of community drives the bottle to the hand. You can't heal what you ignore."

Zane winced and quickly bowed once more to Mrs. Mose. "Thank you for your time."

He walked up three flights of stairs and entered his flat, which doubled as his office. He turned up the gas lamps on the walls and lit them with a match. A small stack of bills on his desk seemed to both mock him and beg for his attention. Zane set the crate next to the paperwork and relaxed in his chair. But the bills kept staring, so he sighed and sifted through them. All but the last month of rent could be covered with the night's earnings.

With what he had left, that is.

Zane would give all he could to Mrs. Mose, and she would let him stay so long as he paid her back in full later.

He could feel a headsman's axe hanging above him, and he started looking for an escape. The bottles of green liquid on his desk seemed to pulse like beacons guiding him to safety. They reflected Zane's face, but all he could see was the addict's tortured gaze. In the end, Zane's inner addict won, and he opened one of the bottles with a resigned sigh.

He sipped the troll's blood as he shuffled through the other letters. Most were from people soliciting money and trying to sell him the latest fad in clothing or medicine, but one letter stood out. It was from his old friend from the war. Dennis.

He was surprised by the letter. They'd last spoken when Zane was released from a military hospital many years ago. Most of the letter was a lengthy greeting, but it appeared Dennis—who now went by Dennis Zel—lived in the same city as Zane, Alviun, where he owned a potion shop and was married to a woman he described as *heaven sent*. He loved her so much he'd taken her last name. But the otherwise sweet letter ended on a sour note. In rushed handwriting at the bottom, Dennis—at least, he assumed it was Dennis—had written:

> *Zane, the real reason I'm writing is to tell you my wife, Vana, is in danger. I dare not explain it here, lest it fall into the wrong hands. But I ask you, old friend, please keep her safe if anything should happen to me.*
> *With saddest regrets for not reaching out sooner.*
> *Your old friend,*
> *Dennis Zel.*

Zane frowned and looked out the window, wondering what Dennis had gotten himself into.

CHAPTER 2

Fex lived in a small room that was part of a larger workshop, a space so tiny many humans called them gnome closets. Inside, he had a full-length gnome mirror with a silver edge that ran the length of the wall. It was Fex's prized possession and had cost him a month of pay. He stared at himself, dressed in his work clothes, the leather apron stained by his current trade: potion brewing.

He breathed deep and fidgeted with his hair. "You got this," he mumbled. "You have been an apprentice for three scores and across four trades. You know as much as any human. Just go in there and ask. No. Demand a promotion to Journeyman."

Gas-fueled light gleamed off the silver frame, and Fex smiled. He'd bought the mirror from a gnome shop, one of the few he could find. He was told that the etching was gnomish, but he wouldn't know. "Maybe ask to be made a partner. You are skilled, you are good, and you deserve this."

A bell rang from outside his closet, followed by the creaking of floorboards. He took one last nervous look at himself. "You got this."

Fex stepped out into the workshop, myriad vials and beakers surrounding a central brewing apparatus. Fex knew the home of every bottle and the formula for every potion. He filled his chest with pride. *You got this*, he thought one last time as he crossed through the workshop and through the threshold leading to the front of The Wizard's Brew.

The Brew's shelves were lined with ointments and cures for small ailments, while the room's centerpiece was a large table featuring a stack of potions made for adventurers and soldiers alike. The Wizard's Brew served anyone who could pay.

But the man who'd entered was no customer.

It was Fex's master, Dennis Zel.

Dennis looked rough. Under his eyes sat the heavy bags of a haunted man. He'd also failed to shave again, leaving him with a scraggly beard. Dennis was nose deep in a textbook, one of many he cradled. He mumbled to himself as Fex climbed onto a stool behind the counter that had been custom built for his height.

"The safety runes set the parameters for the spell." Dennis bumped into a table but continued mumbling. "Without such runes, the spell shall fill the room with its magic. Depending on the volume—"

"Good morning, sir."

Dennis jerked his head out of the book and took a step back, causing the pyramid of bottles on the center table to rattle. He dropped his books and steadied the potions before turning to Fex, his face twisted in a scowl. "I could have broken these."

"No, sir. Remember, those are made from reinforced glass. For adventurers to use."

The bottles were the result of Fex's effort. He had negotiated with the glass blowers by selling them potions at a discount, and the bottles were selling well.

Dennis grumbled under his breath and picked up his books. He found his stool next to Fex, placed the tomes on the counter—the stack was half as tall as Fex—and smiled. "Right. This shop would have fallen apart without you."

"Only because you've been distracted by your test for the Institute."

"Still, thank you for taking care of everything for the last three months."

Fex beamed, but Dennis shifted uncomfortably and rubbed his eyes. "Fex, I have something to discuss with you."

The gnome's small heart pounded. In the last forty years, Fex had experienced moments like this. He had been traded. His master's shop had closed. He'd been forced to apply for new apprenticeships. Fex heard Dennis turn toward him, but he didn't look up at his master. "You are selling the store, aren't you?"

Dennis paused before answering. "No. Well, yes. It's complicated." He scratched his head and leaned against the counter. "I took out a loan a while back. The shop is— I put it down as collateral. Somewhat."

Fex's mouth turned to sand and one of his small hands tightened into a fist. "Somewhat? What does that mean? Either it's collateral or it isn't." Fex stood on his stool. "How much did you borrow?"

Dennis blinked in shock at his apprentice, who was now standing over him thanks to the stool. Fex realized his position and relaxed back on to the seat. "Sorry about that sir. I—"

"I took out a loan of a thousand—"

"A thousand?" The words felt weird and unreal. "That's more than the shop is worth. Who would—"

"The Green Thumb Loan Company."

Fex felt dizzy. Loan companies in Alviun had bad reputations. "Why not go to the bank?"

Dennis rubbed his neck. "They wouldn't give me the loan. They said the shop isn't worth much as collateral."

Fex pointed at Dennis. "That should have been a clue that something was wrong."

"I needed the money for the shop. But it'll be okay. I'm going to leave here and meet with the loan company before the test."

Dennis looked to the front door, as though waiting to see if anyone would step through. "I didn't use all the money. I hope I can bribe my way to a passing grade if needed."

Fex's eyes nearly popped out of his head. "Bribing? Bribing?! I considered you a person of integrity. I've seen the work you put in.

All the studying. Why would you need to stoop so low?"

"The Institute is all about results. If a bribe works, it works. It would showcase my ability to formulate several strategies to achieve a goal."

Dennis looked crestfallen, and Fex felt sorry for him. In the last three months, Fex had not once asked his master why he was trying to get into the Institute.

Fex put one of his small hands on Dennis's shoulder "What is going on?"

"It's complicated." Dennis smiled. "It's always complicated when women are involved."

Unsure how to take Dennis's comment, Fex opened his mouth to fish for more information but stopped when the bell above the door rang.

Fex turned to see Dennis's wife.

Vana Zel pulled off a scarf covering her head, and the ash covering it and her black cloak fluttered to the ground as her blonde hair fell in cascades around her beautiful face. She walked into the shop and removed the cloak, revealing a green dress and blue tattoos that swirled around her arms. Vana brushed golden strands away from her amber eyes, which glittered in the shop's light as she smiled at Dennis. "Ready for today?"

Dennis walked over and kissed his wife before taking her cloak and hanging it on a nearby coatrack. "Ready as I'll ever be. I just needed to stop by here for a minute before I head out."

He disappeared into the back. Vana looked excited and happy. Fex thought about asking if she knew about the loan but decided against it when his master came back in good spirits.

"But I don't know why I even worry," Dennis said. "Fex has been running this shop more or less by himself for the last few months."

Fex swelled with pride, but he still felt confused and betrayed by Dennis's shady dealings.

Vana hugged her husband and kissed him again. "I'll help around the shop while you're gone. Now get your things and get over there. No reason to tempt fate. She might not lend a favorable ear to your pleas if you're late."

"You said fate was three ladies haggling over the future."

She smiled. "Yes, but no woman likes a tardy man."

Dennis collected his things and hugged his wife one more time before slipping on his jacket and stepping into the street.

Vana smiled at Fex. "What can I do to help?"

Fex jumped off his stool. "Well, I need a hand moving a barrel out into the shop."

They walked into the back of the shop and finished preparing for the day. But all the while, Fex's mind replayed the conversation with Dennis. The loan. The shop. Where it all might lead. He sighed deeply when he realized Dennis had told him enough to worry but not enough to understand.

He remembered an old gnome saying: *Humans are one statement filled with infinite questions.*

ALYSSA'S TIRED EYES mirrored those of Dean Tatius-Lasome, who stared at her from across the table. She and the older gentleman had been sitting there for hours, poring over hundreds of applications for acceptance as guild wizards in the Institute of Sorcery and Science. They'd made a shortlist, and all that was left were the interviews, which would start as soon as the third member of their group returned.

"I'm going to the break room," Alyssa said. "Want anything?"

Dean smiled, wrinkles rippling across his face. "Yes, Ms. Benedictus-Lasome. Some tea would be lovely."

Alyssa smiled at the old man. "I have told you to call me Alyssa or

Ms. Benedictus. Archmage Benedictus-Lasome is my grandfather. I haven't earned that name yet."

"We both know you will earn the name before long."

She yawned. "If Agwen gets back, have him send me a spell if he wants anything."

"Thank you, dear."

Alyssa walked through the twisting halls of the spell-charmed Institute building. Her innate sense guided her through the enchanted maze until a door gave way to a kitchen break room. She brought the tea to a boil with an eldritch word, her lips tingling as the syllables rolled off her tongue.

As she filled two cups, a young man stepped into the break room holding a compass and a black robe, marking him as a new student. Alyssa smiled and watched as he tried to get his bearings. After a few more seconds, he gave up.

"I'm sorry ma'am, but I am lost. I took a left on a staircase but now I am here. I thought this would lead me to my dorm room."

She closed her eyes and felt the flow of the room. Instinct caught the ebb and flow of the charmed halls and she pointed to a closet at the edge of the room. "Open that door three times, and on the fourth you should see your room."

He looked from her to the door. "How do you know that? Is that a skill I could learn?"

Alyssa shook her head. "I was born in the building, so my senses are attuned to it. It's like how birds know to fly south in the winter. Now hurry. Your path will change soon."

The student thanked her and she navigated back to the meeting room, where Agwen sat with his back to the door and his hood pulled tight over his head.

"Sorry, Agwen. I didn't get you anything."

He turned and she caught a glimpse of his Fey ears beneath the hood.

"It's all right. I'm not thirsty." Agwen watched as she walked around the table to her seat. "I apologize for stepping out. I had some business that needed wrapping up."

She handed Tatius-Lasome his tea and the aged archmage blew on the billowing steam. "I hope it went well."

Agwen pulled back from the table, his eyes lost in thought. "I believe so. Some things came to my attention, mostly of a private nature, but they should be resolved now. I suppose that is the way of things."

Tatius-Lasome raised his cup. "Yes. I think the last great philosopher wrote that perfection is so far removed from life, the act of seeking perfection is itself heretical—"

Alyssa put a soft hand on Tatius-Lasome's arm. "Sir, it is late. Perhaps we should finish up."

"Yes, yes. So, where are we?" The archmage looked at the paperwork strewn across the table. "Right, we finished with the student applicants and have moved on to new guild wizards. We had narrowed it down to three possibilities for sponsorship."

Agwen raised a hand to halt the discussion. "I must first point out that we are acting on a low budget. We might be better off not sponsoring anyone."

Alyssa sorted through some of the papers. "That shouldn't be. Didn't the grant go through?"

"It did," Agwen said, "but we are still stretched thin. The charms of storage rooms had to be reapplied. We have one of the largest basements in the Institute. Perhaps, if I am allowed to give away—"

Tatius-Lasome cut him off. "We have been through this. The relics of the old Fey world are safest in our basement. We don't know what half of those objects do. It's too dangerous to release such unknown magic into the world."

Alyssa understood Agwen's position. It was his heritage stored down there, out of sight and out of mind. This conversion was the fifth—no, the sixth—time the group had discussed the Fey relics in the last month.

The Fey and archmage stared at each other. Alyssa knew neither would budge on the matter, so she spoke, hoping to cut through the tension. "I am not getting any younger and would desire to save any lingering beauty through sleeping well, but I won't have the opportunity if we don't make a decision."

Tatius-Lasome chuckled. "You're the youngest professor on staff and your youthful beauty is still like a fresh rose, but I agree with your point. I, too, would like some rest. Let's hear from the first of these candidates at least." The old man looked at Agwen. "Shall we?"

The Fey drew back into his hood. "Fine. But remember, our budget is limited."

Tatius-Lasome nodded and turned to Alyssa. "Will you get them?"

She turned to leave. "Of course."

An hour passed before Alyssa stepped into the waiting room for a third time. Their last applicant was a middle-aged man, his hands stained from alchemy or potion work.

"Are you Dennis?"

He stood, nervous, which was to be expected. "Yes. Is it my turn?"

Alyssa nodded. "Follow me."

She led him through the twisting halls and down long staircases. She watched Dennis as he looked on in wonder. "Are you going to ask?"

Everyone asked.

"I'd heard about the moving halls of the Institute," Dennis said. "But to see it…"

"Yes, it's a wonder created by—accident."

His face drew inward for a moment as he processed the information. "I suppose I shouldn't be surprised. The history of arcane and natural sciences is filled with such events. Strength-enhancing solution was discovered by accident."

"Indeed. The Institute was originally enchanted by Fey to double the structural capacity. But as time went on, we outgrew the space we had, so an attempt was made to expand it further. It succeeded, but we now have this issue."

He asked a few more questions before they arrived at the interview room. Alyssa was about to open a door when Dennis stopped her. One of his hands was stuffed into a pocket and she could hear paper rustling around. "Miss Benedictus, could you offer me some advice?"

She smiled. The other two interviewees were too prideful to seek her counsel. "What type of advice?"

He eased his hand out of his pocket. "What would cast me in the best light to be picked?"

"Well, the current problem is that our budget is … tight. But if you could show that you won't cost us extra, then perhaps you'll have a better chance"

"Extra?"

She smiled. "Yes. Like paying for housing."

He looked away in thought before turning back. "My family and I have a place to live, so we won't need any assistance."

"Good. That will already put you in a better spot than the last two. They both had expensive requests and were turned down. Fortunately, they had interviews with other departments. But I am sure you will be fine."

The color drained from Dennis's face as they stopped in front of the interview room door. "This is the only department that would interview me," he whispered.

This struck Alyssa as strange. Almost every working wizard who passed the test had at least two departments interviewing them. But only drawing interest from one wasn't unheard of, so she dismissed it. "Again, I'm sure you'll be fine. Are you ready?"

Dennis nodded, so she opened the door. He brushed past her and took a seat at the far end of the table. Agwen leaned back and crossed his arms, uninterested; he hadn't bothered to read any of Dennis's paperwork. Tatius-Lasome flicked through the parchment as Alyssa took her seat.

"Tell us about yourself," Tatius-Lasome said. "Who is Dennis Zel?"

"Well sir, I have studied arcane subjects since my childhood. Now I'm a licensed alchemist and run a successful shop down on Potion Lane. I also served during the war as an alchemist, medic, and sometimes as a diviner—"

Tatius-Lasome stopped him. "Diviner? Tricky field. Some have been known to go mad. Any issues?"

"No sir, madness is a side effect if one tries to look into the future or past. If you deal only with physical locations in the present, madness is highly unlikely."

Tatius-Lasome nodded. "That could be a helpful skill. We could use that to find and track things in the field. What do the rest of you think?"

Alyssa spoke first. "I can see a few ways we can use Mister Zel's skillset. He could help us replicate Fey potions and use his divining skills to track locations of new artifacts."

Agwen scoffed. "Divining is a party trick not suitable for modern magic. Any of us could learn it, if needed. Or better yet, we could set up a device to do it for us. And alchemists are a dime a dozen."

Tatius-Lasome mumbled something under his breath, but Alyssa couldn't hear it. She waved a hand. "Mister Zel, please continue."

Dennis made eye contact with Alyssa. She nodded, giving him the signal to differentiate himself from the other two candidates.

"My wife and I are somewhat self-sufficient. My family has some property where we will stay without the need for housing assistance."

Tatius-Lasome snickered and looked at Alyssa before turning back. "Well, that is an element worth consider—"

"No," Agwen shouted. "We don't need you, Mister Zel. Alyssa, please take him back."

Before Alyssa could process Agwen's request, Tatius-Lasome slammed a greying hand onto the table. "I will not stand for this! You have denied two perfectly good candidates. Over what, your perceived budget concern?"

Agwen stood, towering over everyone else. "Yes. I care for the continuation of our department, but hard decisions like this must be made. Alyssa please take—"

Tatius-Lasome snatched up his iron staff and struck the hardwood floor with the end. "I am still the Dean of the department, and will be for years. I call for a vote right now, and I say yea to Dennis Zel joining us, effective immediately."

Agwen gestured dismissively. "I vote no. We don't need him. Give us a season or two and we can find a better, more qualified candidate."

All eyes turned to Alyssa. She looked at the others and weighed her options. No matter which way she voted, one of them would be angry, which could be problematic in such a small department. Should she side with the Dean or with Agwen, her fellow professor?

Alyssa looked across the table at Dennis, who pleaded silently.

"I vote yes."

STANDING IN THE middle of his shop, Dennis marveled at his new silver badge, with its four rings and square center. On the back, a string of numbers was printed—physical proof that he was now a State Institute Mage and that he would start work at the Institution of Sorcery and Science next week. He had studied night and day for the exam. Even after passing he couldn't find a department willing to interview him, so he'd bribe a clerk to get an interview with the Fey Studies Department.

But now he could provide a better life for his family.

There was a knock at the front door. It was well into the night, and The Wizard's Brew had been closed for hours now. Fex was already asleep. Dennis stepped into the back of the shop, ignoring the knock. *Probably just a junkie trying to get a late-night fix.* He stepped lightly to avoid waking the gnome in his closet.

Dennis poured the last batch of potions for the night, the bubbling green liquid of a healing elixir, and transferred it into a barrel. He then loaded it onto the dolly and rolled it to the front.

The street entrance door clicked loudly, then it swung open.

"Hey, we're closed," Dennis shouted. "Leave before I call for a guard—"

Dennis's wife held in her hand a cloth sack of groceries. Vana's blonde hair was up in a bun, forming a reflective halo. When she smiled at him, Dennis's heart fluttered even though it had been four years since they were wed in front of the ancient monoliths of her ancestral homelands.

Vana walked across the room with an undeniable grace. "How are you?"

He fixed his hair. "I'm good. Why didn't you come through the back?"

She smiled again and shrugged. "I thought I would use the front."

Dennis had slipped the badge behind his back and met her beside a table stacked with potions for joint pain. "Guess what?"

Her face brightened like the dawning sun. "You did it. You really did it!"

He brought out the badge. "Everything is ready."

Vana placed the groceries on the table and held the badge. As she admired the badge, Dennis admired her. *She has not aged a day.* His eyes fell over her hands, and he was surprised she'd taken off her gloves.

There was something wrong about her bare, white skin. As he realized what was missing, Dennis froze, and the world with him. He thawed quickly, forced himself to hug Vana, then walked over to the counter.

Dennis couldn't keep his voice from shaking. "I— I think we need to celebrate."

He slid his hand under the desk and searched for the wand he kept for self-defense. It was his service wand, issued to him during the Ghoul War. Dennis hadn't used it in five years, but he made sure the spell wicks were kept in working condition.

Dennis's hand found the wand. He brought it out and leveled it at her. "Don't muh— make any sudden muh— moves."

Her beautiful face was drawn tight. "I had been told about you and *her*. You are the problem that needs to disappear."

From the back of her dress, she pulled a green knife, its curved blade dripping with liquid.

Dennis's hands shook. "Puh— please don't make me do this." He took a deep breath. "I swear I—"

She charged him, forcing Dennis to pull the wand's mental trigger. But he flinched when she threw the badge at his face. A flash of blue came from the tip of the wand and slammed into the wall behind her. He fired two more times. She ducked and dodged. He tried to fire a fourth time as she dove over the counter, but she slammed into Dennis with the weight and force of someone twice her size. His wand slid across the floor and out of sight. The potions on the counter crashed down around him and stained the ground.

She brought the dagger down to his chest, but Dennis grabbed her wrist, stopping the blade. He pulled a sweat-soaked hand free and punched her. It felt like hitting a stone. The dagger jerked closer, and he desperately tried to stop it again with his free hand as his heart raced.

Dennis pushed with all his strength, but his military training did not come to bear. With one swift movement, she knocked his hands free, and with another cleared them away.

The dagger plunged deep into his chest. His lungs burned, but only for a moment. Dennis's senses were fading.

The last thing he heard was the roar of a beast.

CHAPTER 3

Z ane awoke before the first bell rang out across the city of Alviun. He leaped from his bed as if running from something. Most mornings, he fled from memories. After gathering himself, Zane smoothed the wrinkles from his sheets with care and attention. He stripped his nightwear, folded it, and placed it in an organized pile to be cleaned. From his closet, Zane selected one of his many outfits. It took no time to decide since they all matched. All were smooth, clean, and ready for a new day. He pulled his clothes on and, as he'd done with his sheets, straightened out any wrinkles.

The first bell of the day rang at seven in the morning, and the sound carried through the windowpanes. Time enough to clean before opening. Zane swept the floors of his bedroom and office, then tossed the debris out the window. He looked over his office and took pride in not only how clean it was, but how the little office was his. The bill on his desk, though, told him a different story. It said he was a month behind on rent.

When the second bell sounded at eight, Zane sat at his desk, taking the seat across from the office door. He sat there through the third and fourth chimes of the day, his mood growing darker with each hour. He frowned at the lack of customers for the day and pulled a bottle out of his top drawer, it's dull green liquid reflecting the light from outside. To make the potion last, he poured only a third into a metal flask. Zane took two measured gulps from the bottle and laid back as a warmth washed over him. After a few more moments, he enjoyed a release from the untangling of knots in his right shoulder and left leg.

Zane stared at the bottle, then picked it up and swished the lovely green liquid back and forth. It spun, fell, and rose slowly. The texture was like that of sludge, gripping the sides of the bottle. He enjoyed the scene, like watching the tides in some bottled ocean. It would be just the old man and the sea today. He sat it down and laughed. Half a year as a detective, but still so little work. If Zane didn't find some soon, he would be forced to leave. He smirked and again reached for the bottle.

Shadow whispered from the far corner. *You shouldn't drink this early.* Zane stopped short and shook his head. He disliked Shadow, but he was right. Zane couldn't let himself get wasted on healing potions. Not this early in the day.

Zane stared into Shadow's red eyes. Since the war—since he'd been rescued from the dark—the creature had haunted Zane's steps. Even years later, Shadow still disgusted him. He often wondered if it was even real. Zane had quickly realized only he could hear or see Shadow, but its voice never left him alone for long.

Zane straightened out his clothes. Their clean perfection acted like armor against the temptation of the liquid. He picked up the bottle and, with only slight hesitation, placed it back in a drawer. He ignored the three other bottles, scattered and dirty, that laid next to it.

Though it was now out of sight, it didn't leave his thoughts. The potion sung out like a siren. A knock at the office door blew away the song. Zane released a deep breath, thankful for the distraction.

"The door is unlocked. Please come in."

A woman entered, dressed in all black, leaving no skin uncovered. Her face was veiled, but her golden hair caught his attention. It gave her an angelic presence.

The veil drew his notice for different reasons. Veil-wearing was an old tradition, revealing much of her background, that of a high merchant or a low noble. His eyes drifted from her veiled face to her gloved hands. On the outside of the left glove, she wore a large ring with an amber stone bearing a crest. Low noble.

Zane extended his left palm up, and she took it with her own. She bowed gracefully and nodded her head. Zane did the same, but he focused on her ring. The crest was of a large wolf's head howling below an imperial eagle. He released her hand and gestured to the chair across the desk from his. "Have a seat, Madam..."

"Zel. Please call me Lady Zel." She took her seat with grace. Definitely a low noble.

The name sounded familiar, but he couldn't place it. "How can I help you, Lady Zel?"

"I heard that you deal with problems and mysteries. You are described as a mercenary of sorts. A detective, I believe, is the word."

Zane wished he could see her face, which would tell him far more than her words. "That is correct. It's a new profession, but supported in many ways by the courts. Especially in the North. I am paid to search, or research, and deduce answers for my clients."

She chuckled grimly. "He was right. You do speak like some schoolboy."

That description sounded familiar. Dennis.

Zane remembered that Zel was the name that Dennis had taken on when he got married. "Are you married to Dennis Zel?"

"Yes, he is my husband—"

"What a pleasure to meet you. I haven't seen him in years."

"My late husband."

"I just received a letter from Dennis. He said—"

He stopped when his brain caught up to her words, which struck him like fire from a wand. "What do you mean by late?"

Her voice was weak. "He has been murdered..."

Shadow spoke from the corner, its red eyes like two embers. *She's hiding something.*

Zane tried to ignore it, but something didn't seem right. Lady Zel was too reserved. She was sad, but there was something more in her posture. Resolve. He had seen it before in people intent on revenge.

"There's more, isn't there?"

She was silent. It was a strange type of silence that seemed to suck the air from the office. Zane could hear his own heartbeat as she gently touched the desk. "The guards plan to arrest me today. They say I was the last one seen entering the shop. They say that the witness saw me flee through the front door. But I didn't go through the front that night, and I didn't leave through it, either."

Zane stared at where her eyes were covered by the veil. "Why me?"

"Because Dennis said you could help if anything happened. He mentioned some old debt. But I am not asking you to work for free. What are your rates?"

As cases go, this one was not off to a great start. His possible client had already admitted to being at the crime scene. She adjusted herself in the seat, and her face angled up and sniffed the air.

Zane looked down at the bills on his desk. He pushed them aside. For Dennis. "We'll discuss the pay later. As I said, your husband sent me a letter. It was mostly hello and how are things, but at the end he asked me to look after you if anything happened."

She straightened her back. "Forgive the question, but why are you so willing to help me? Everyone believes I killed him."

Her voice seemed blunt. Emotionless. Zane caught a reflection of himself in a far mirror and saw himself lying on a medical cot years ago.

He and Lady Zel were little more than strangers. But Zane and Dennis had been much, much more.

"Because he asked me to," Zane said. "You could say Dennis helped put me back together."

Shadow laughed from the corner.

FEX STRUGGLED WITH a box of broken glass as he carried it out of the shop. It felt like his hundredth trip, but it was closer to the tenth. He dumped the glass into the street, where it shattered into smaller pieces. The empty box was light, yet the task still felt heavy on his shoulders. He turned back to the shop. More than half of the so-called adventure potions were shattered. *So much for being shatter-proof,* he thought. He had already made a note to talk with the glass blower.

The damage to the shop was substantial. Two barrels of healing elixir had been ruined. The green slush leaked out of one, running down the lane in the gutter. Another had flowed onto the shop's floor. The elixir had been meant for the local guard. He sighed to himself. *They even destroyed the door.*

"Ho, Fex," called a voice from behind him. "How long do I need to hold this body again?"

Fex turned around to see an old gnome dressed in a dark cloak over his undertaker's clothes. His white hair and glasses stood out in stark contrast. "Uncle Dex, sorry for missing you."

"You're lost in thought. How is the—"

"Shop?" Fex finished his uncle's thought; it frustrated humans, but gnomes had turned finishing each other's sentences into a game. "Damaged. We still have lots of brew in the back, but it will hurt us—"

"Us? Who is the shop's new owner?"

The question struck Fex hard. Far harder than it should have. This wasn't the first time a master had died before his apprenticeship had finished. Last time, he had been passed down to the man's nephew, though he stayed only for a few years before leaving. Fex was used to losing masters, and he wasn't sure why Dennis should be any different. "I suppose right now I am working for Vana Zel. She holds a rank in the guild, I believe."

The old gnome rubbed his shaved clean chin. "Really now? Is that so?" Fex's uncle made certain no one was in earshot before he spoke again. "So, is what I've heard about her true?"

Fex looked away. "What do you mean?"

"They say Vana killed her husband. The guard has been by my morgue already this morning asking questions."

Memories of the previous night burned in Fex's head. Dennis had entered the shop while Fex had been sleeping soundly—until the sound of wand fire striking a wall woke him up. There were screams, then a howl. An ear-splitting, horrid howl, like that of a giant beast. It had seemed to rock the very foundation of the shop.

"Fex, are you all right?" Dex gripped his nephew's shoulder, pulling him out of his thoughts.

Fex was trembling. "Sorry, uncle. I was lost in—"

"Thought? I would be, too, especially with the idea of advancement."

"Right, advancement—" Fex agreed thoughtlessly, then stopped and looked at his uncle in confusion. "Wait, advancement? What do you mean?"

The old gnome smiled, wit and greed in his eyes. "Old trade law. Last of a craft, I think it's called. In the event no one can inherit a shop or trade, the apprentice inherits everything. You would be instantly promoted to Journeyman."

Fex forced out a hollow laugh. "Surely you jest. There's no way this applies—"

"To gnomes? But it does. You would—"

"Own the shop? They have no one else in the guild. But—"

"But it depends on whether the misses did, in fact, murder her husband. If so, she would go away."

Dex gave his nephew a calculating look. "So, I ask again. Did she do it?"

Fex closed his eyes. He had cowered in his bed until the shop was silent. Then, after what felt like minutes, he heard sobbing through the walls. Fex got out of bed, stealthy, and exited his room. In the workshop he picked up a broomstick. With shaky hands ready to swing at an attacker he prepared himself to step out into the shop.

His hands shook as he eased the door open. From the doorway, he saw Vana Zel. Her clothes were torn and her loose golden hair cascaded around her face. She held the limp form of Dennis in her arms. Several of her blue, swirling tattoos showed through ripped sleeves, and his blood was smeared across her arms. Bruises had already formed across her fair skin. Tears streamed down her face and caught the light. His eyes drifted from the scene and took in the wreckage of the shop, where the cold fog of night had drifted in from the broken door.

Vana looked up at Fex, her expression pained. "He is dead... Why is he dead... Who was she?"

Vana cried and cried until she ran out of tears. Eventually, she laid the body aside and stood, looking every bit like the tales of banshees Fex had heard as a child. Vana walked through the workshop wordlessly and dressed herself in a set of spare clothes. While she was gone, Fex walked to Dennis.

He didn't want to look too closely but his eyes were drawn to the wound. A bloody, ragged canyon had been opened in his chest, like a dagger had plunged into him. But even in the dim light, something about the blood seemed off. A black ichor seeped from the wound.

Vana called him to the back, interrupting his inspection of the corpse. Her face was wild. "Fex, you once said your uncle had a morgue, correct?"

Fex nodded. Something in him was numb, maybe broken.

"Go call on him," Vana said. "We need a place to keep Dennis's body safe until the detective comes."

"The detective?"

"Yes. Now go."

Her voice had an edge to it, and Fex had obeyed.

He remembered running through the night to the morgue to wake his uncle, who was now standing in front of him, waiting for an answer.

"I don't know if she killed him," Fex said as he thought again of Vana's question.

Who was she?

Fex's uncle leaned in close and whispered in his ear. "You might consider the possibility of her guilt, and what that possibility means for you. All I know is that the guards are biting to make an arrest."

Dex patted his nephew on the shoulder. "I will hold on to Dennis as long as I can."

With that, Dex left his nephew holding an empty box. The shop, much like his life, was now a mess.

Fex sighed and rolled up his sleeves. There was still much to clean.

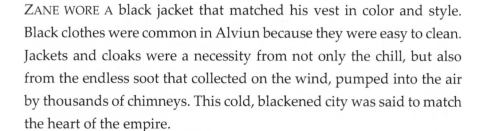

ZANE WORE A black jacket that matched his vest in color and style. Black clothes were common in Alviun because they were easy to clean. Jackets and cloaks were a necessity from not only the chill, but also from the endless soot that collected on the wind, pumped into the air by thousands of chimneys. This cold, blackened city was said to match the heart of the empire.

Lady Zel's cloak and hood lent her a gloomy beauty, rendering her a piece of living art. They spoke while navigating the dirty cobblestone streets that stretched across Alviun like a web.

"In his letter, Dennis said he took your last name."

Vana Zel nodded. "It was a condition my father had for blessing the union."

Zane noted that in his mind before resuming the conversation. "Where are we going?"

She answered, as if it was obvious. "To where Dennis was

murdered…"

Her attitude again disturbed Zane. She was almost standoffish for someone who had come to him for help. "Okay then. Where is that?"

Vana sighed. "His— my—" She paused for a moment. "Our potion shop, The Wizard's Brew."

Of course it was at the potion shop. Zane's throat tightened at the thought. He forced his mind to consider other things, like how calmly Vana was leading him to the murder scene. Zane had known people who would never return to the place a loved one had been killed. Then again, he had known others who were too eager and couldn't wait to return. Vana was somewhere in between, and her cold resolve seemed to add to her mystery.

Shadow chuckled in his silky voice. *She's single now.*

Zane ignored it. Silence clung to them as they walked the streets, eventually turning onto Potion Lane. It was too narrow for carriages to traverse, and large gutters on either side were filled with a dirty rainbow shine that flowed down and out of the lane.

Zane glanced at one of them. Despite the putrid smell, it called to him, a rough and sour siren song promising escape from pain. He hated himself for desperately craving something so disgusting.

Shadow's voice echoed in his mind. *That thief wouldn't have judged you for taking a drink.*

Vana's voice broke his concentration. "Please excuse the mess. The murder happened just last night. Fex, my late husband's assistant, is busy cleaning up."

Potion Lane and its connecting streets were always dirty with myriad stains from an indiscernible number of potions. She pointed to some of the fresher green sludge that flowed down the gutter. "That is from our shop. Several containers were broken or contaminated, so we are pouring it out."

Zane saw an opening to learn more about her and Dennis. "Why pour them out? I know several shops that would sell those at a discount. There is no law that would stop you."

"True, but Dennis always found that practice despicable. He told me he saw too many soldiers dying from bad potions. No, he wouldn't have wanted us to do that." She faced him, as if she were offering. "But there are still potions left in the shop."

He ignored the comment but stopped her in the lane, letting soldiers, adventures, and addicts pass by. He needed to steer the conversation to something else. "You said Dennis was killed yesterday?"

Vana nodded once, her voice level and calm as she elaborated. "The guards seemed unusually motivated. Dennis was killed and they sought to arrest me almost immediately. Never have I seen them move with such *efficiency*."

Zane was not on good terms with the local guards. Many thought he was trying to do their jobs, others thought him a nuisance. Zane held the guards in equal contempt. They were slow to investigate anything unrelated to a noble and quick to put the first suspect away — with or without evidence. But their quickness was still odd. As odd as a newly widowed woman carrying herself like Vana.

He shuffled in his jacket unconformably and smoothed out his clothes, trying to convince himself it wasn't too late to back out of the situation.

But he knew it was.

Zane took a breath to strengthen his resolve. This job was for Dennis. He owed the man. "It sounds like there was a struggle at the shop. Was anything stolen?"

"No, I don't believe it was an act of theft. It was… too brutal."

"Were any messages left behind? Was anything placed on his body?"

Vana shook her head as they returned to walking towards the shop. "We found no message, but there was so much damage done in the struggle…"

Zane noticed a group of people sitting in an alley sipping the nasty gutter liquid using cups and bowls. Shadow's voice never missed a chance. *Your kindred!* They were like him, but worse. Addicts. He forced himself to turn away before they could make eye contact.

The Wizard's Brew came into view. It wasn't hard to miss. A gnome was dragging broken barrels out into the street, the source of the dirty green liquid. He wore a heavily stained apron and waved them over.

"Mistress Zel, you have returned earlier than I had expected. I haven't finished cleaning, so it is still unsightly. His body is gone, but I don't think it would be proper for you to go in yet."

She held herself upright. "It's all right, Fex." She motioned to Zane. "This is Zane Vrexon, the detective Dennis had mentioned."

Gnomes lived long lives—as all Fey-blooded did—which allowed them to practice several trades, but rarely did they gain status above apprentice due to human jealousy. It wasn't uncommon for generations of humans in a trade to have the same gnome as an apprentice.

Fex looked Zane up and down. "You are not what I was expecting."

Zane smiled. "What were you expecting?"

The gnome rubbed his chin. "I was expecting more of a battle-hardened warrior. Large muscles, several scars. Master said you were a soldier from the war."

"I don't have the muscles I used to, but I have more than a few scars."

Zane inspected the front of the shop. Shards of glass littered the street, along with pieces of the door, which looked to have been shattered from the inside. Who could shatter a door? He looked from Vana to Fex. "May I go inside and take a look around?"

Lady Zel nodded and gestured to the shop. Zane crossed the threshold and immediately noticed that one of the walls was marred with scratches from what appeared to be the claws of a large beast. He removed his leather gloves and stuffed them into his jacket, replacing them with thin protective gloves that let him feel texture but kept him clean. He ran one hand over the counter. "I am going to ask you both some questions. First, where was the body found?"

Vana pointed to the ground. "Right next to you, but on the far side of the counter."

Zane peered over and saw the dried pool of blood. "And where is the body currently? I assume it is at a morgue, unless the guards took it."

The gnome nodded. "Aye, my uncle has run a morgue for years in this district. I'll write down directions and an introduction letter for you."

Zane raised his eyebrows in surprise and nodded. It was rare for a gnome to own a business. "Did Dennis have any enemies? Rivals?"

Lady Zel shook her head. "None who would do this. But Dennis has always had a rival in Atom, who owns a shop down the street."

Zane's intuition told him they were withholding something. His gaze drifted toward Fex, who was staring at Vana with concern. Zane noted it all mentally, then pointed to the giant scratches on the wall. "What caused that?"

Vana followed his finger. "It happened during the struggle, I assume."

He sighed. Unhelpful. "Anything else strange happen recently?"

Fex coughed politely. Both Vana and Zane looked at him. "Well, our adventure potions shattered. We lost about half. Maybe more."

"Adventure potions?"

Lady Zel pointed to some thick glass bottles off to the side. "It was Dennis's idea. A while back, he came up with the notion of selling potions in shatterproof bottles to soldiers and adventurers. I think it was after he listened to some of them complain about how often normal bottles would break." She turned to Fex. "Didn't you work out the deal with the glass blowers?"

Fex blushed. "Yes. I plan to go by there today and make a formal complaint."

Zane looked at the claw mark again. "Lady Zel, Fex, could I ask you both to step into a back room for a moment? I would like to look around. By myself."

Fex squinted at him. "What are you up to—"

"Of course," Vana interrupted. "Fex, follow me. You can write your letter in the back."

Zane wasn't surprised at Fex's obvious suspicion and didn't let it affect him. After both had walked into the back, Zane whispered to himself. "Now what is going on?"

Shadow rooted itself in a dark corner while Zane examined the damaged wall, which was as good a place as any to start. It looked like a claw had destroyed shelves and ripped deep into the wood. He placed his hand over the gouges and noted that there were five digits with the marks spread over an area about twice the width of his hand.

Zane followed the wall to the floor and saw a jagged piece of wood with a clump of hair caught between its splinters. He knelt and picked it up. Felt it. Smelled it. The hair wasn't oily and felt too rough to be human. It looked like fur. He pocketed it and looked up at the scratches again, wondering what could have done that kind of damage.

He turned to the entrance and stepped outside to the pile of wood that had once been the front door. Most of it was already swept to the side, but one large piece caught his eye, so he picked it up. On one side was a large burn mark. It looked and smelled like it was caused by wand fire. He flipped over the wood and noticed a footprint dried in gunk made from mixed potions. It was thin and narrow. Female. He looked through the doorway to the stained floor. The door must have broken after the potions were spilled.

He held the piece of wood and used his fingers to measure it. He let out a small whistle when he found it to be two knuckles thick. What could break a door that strong?

Zane inspected the entryway more closely. The hinges had been ripped out on one side of the door jamb and there was a gap in the frame about midway down. He looked through the broken debris and found a bent security bar. Zane flinched at the strength of whatever had done that kind of damage.

The far side of the counter was next. Zane hesitated because he didn't want to stand in the place where his friend had died. He had done that too often already. But he had a job to do, and he owed it to Dennis. Zane stepped around the counter and inspected the blood stain. It had congealed into a horrible scarlet pool, like too much paint dumped onto a canvas. Zane glanced at Shadow and waited for a comment, but the creature remained silent.

Zane had seen blood stains like this during the Ghoul War, except then it was mostly in the darkness, running through mountain tunnels, light coming only from a lantern. Like so many had during the war, Dennis had laid there and bled out. He hadn't deserved to die that way.

Burns on the hardwood drew Zane's attention. He studied the floor and noticed that the only burns in the room were near the center of the blood pool.

The counter had a bottom shelf that left a gap between it and the floor. He ran his finger underneath and found a fairly large space. He laid next to the blood stain and reached his hand into the gap, then closed his hand around a dagger and pulled it into the light.

The dagger had a green tint and was covered in blood. Its blade was almost as long as Zane's forearm, but it didn't feel right; it was too light. He balanced it on his wrist without a problem, and then plucked a hair from his head. He pressed the hair to the blade and watched as it split in half. A perfect blade. Perfect, except that it had killed his friend.

Zane took another look under the counter. The area where the knife had been was rough and grainy, as if burned by acid like the floor under the blood pool. His eyes fell on a stick-like object that laid in the back beside a piece of crumpled paper. He reached under and fished them out. The stick was a wand. He looked it over. Military grade. Maybe a keepsake from the war.

Standing over the counter, he twisted it open. Five small capsules slid out and bounced on the counter. Three were a bright blue and two were dull black. He picked up one of the darkened, spent spell wicks. He took a step back and turned slowly, the wand extended in his hand as though he intended to fire. From where he stood, he could see scorches on the far wall.

Zane began piecing together the scene. First, the door is broken through, so he fired and then... what? That didn't make sense. The killer would've been inside already, then broke the door to escape. But why?

Zane shook his head, then spread the wrinkled paper on the counter. The first things he noticed were the blood droplets in the corner. Continuing down the paper, he realized it was an estimate from a business called The Fountain. He whistled at the number written, then noticed the name written in the bottom right corner: Atom, the name of the rival shop owner.

Shadow finally spoke. *There is something under the cabinet if you haven't noticed it already.*

After leaning forward to adjust his line of sight, Zane saw a glint from underneath the cabinet. He placed the wand next to the knife on the counter and walked over. The cabinet had once contained four shelves filled with different potions. Now it was ruined, its shelves shattered on the floor along with the broken contents.

He knelt on the ground and reached under the cabinet, grabbing something cold and metal about the size of his palm. When he brought it into the light, Zane's breath caught in his throat.

It was the badge of a State Institute Mage.

The royal seal shined on its surface, and a serial number was printed on the back. He set it on the counter next to the wand and knife. Nothing had made sense before, and now it made even less.

Zane straightened his clothes and walked toward the back, where Lady Zel and Fex were waiting. Their heads immediately turned in his direction when he pushed open the door.

Vana spoke first. "Are you done, detective?"

He nodded and motioned for them to come to the counter. Fex climbed onto a stool and looked down at the objects gathered there. His face went pale at the bloody knife.

"I found this dagger, which looks to be the murder weapon, along with a military-grade wand that had been fired and a State Institute Mage badge—"

Vana gasped. "A state badge? Are you sure?"

He nodded and handed it to her. Even her veil could not hide the tears that fell to the floor. It was the first break in composure Zane had seen from her. He wished he could give her comfort or time to grieve, but he needed to know more. "How long has he been a state mage?"

She breathed deeply and pulled herself together. "He had been trying to become one for the last few months, but I never heard the result of the test."

She cradled the badge in her hands. Her frame quivered like the grieving widow she was for the first time since she'd walked into his office. Zane felt a twisted comfort watching her icy visage melt, but his next question would still hurt to ask.

"May I have the badge? It may help me in my search?"

Vana hesitated but handed it to Zane. He reached inside his vest and placed the badge inside a pocket that would button so that it would be kept safe.

He considered the knife and the wand. "To be honest, nothing here makes sense. Like the scratches in the wall. If you have claws that sharp, why use a dagger? And if Dennis were aiming at a beast big enough to make that claw mark, how did he miss?" He picked up the wand. "It might be important to the case, but I recommend that one of you take the wand. Either of you know how to work one of these?"

Fex, who had appeared genuinely shocked when Zane brought up the badge, adjusted himself and nodded. "Aye. Twenty years ago, I was apprenticed to a wizard. And during the war I rolled wicks."

Zane handed it to him. "It has three shots left. Please look after Lady Zel in case the murderer comes back."

Vana turned to Zane with an icy stare. "The killer will be back?"

Zane couldn't tell if that was a question or a statement, but he recognized the tone, filled with cold desire. Vana was eager. She wanted revenge. "I will take the knife," Zane said. "I might be able to find someone who can identify it."

Zane glanced at Fex, who was examining the wand, then addressed Vana. "Lady Zel, could you get me a cup of water? My throat is tight. Probably just the morning smoke."

After she walked to the back, Zane turned to Fex. "Can I ask you some questions about the barrel outside?"

Fex nodded and led the way. Outside, and hopefully out of earshot. In Zane's experience, husbands often keep secrets from their wives. Things an apprentice might know but wouldn't talk about in front of them. Zane spoke quickly "So, what do you know? Did Dennis have enemies? Rivals? Was into something illegal?"

The gnome looked past Zane towards the workshop. "A rival. Atom, who owns the shop down the street known as The Fountain, just like Lady Zel said. He was always coming around trying to stir up trouble and take our customers. Stuff like that. And..." Fex took another tentative look toward the back room.

Zane followed his gaze. "And what?"

Fex took a deep breath. "He needed money for the test, so he took a loan from... I think it was called Green Thumb Loan Company."

Zane's mouth went dry. "How much did he owe?"

"He said about a thousand."

"A thousand? Are you sure?"

Fex nodded. "He said he was going to meet with them yesterday."

Now Zane had a lead. "Do you have an address?"

Fex shook his head. "No, but I will look and see if it is written—"

Zane cut Fex off when he heard Vana's footsteps. "So, as I was asking, are these your healing potions? It looks like you lost four barrels?"

Fex grimaced. "Aye, it was our specialty, but it is ruined now. So..." He gestured to the street as the barrels leaked potions, forming a green river in the gutter.

When Zane focused on the filthy stream, his throat tightened. He could hear Shadow laughing from somewhere unseen.

Vana handed him a cup. He ignored Shadow and chugged the water, which caught in his throat at the sight of guards marching down the street in perfect lockstep. They wore black coats with red trim, red breastplates, and matching horsehair helmets. Hanging on the back of their left shoulders were arcane staves.

The guards came to a stop in front of the shop, then pulled their staves around to the ready and stood at attention as the runes on their weapons started to glow. One guard with mutton chops stood in the front. On his breastplate was a star, marking him as the lieutenant. He spoke with authority. "Vana Zel, I am Lieutenant Dane, and the City Imperial Guard hereby places you under arrest for the murder of Dennis Zel."

Zane stepped in front of her. The lieutenant quickly drew a wand and leveled it at Zane. "Step aside, citizen, or be moved aside. You are obstructing the rule of law."

Zane raised his arms smoothly and slowly. "I am a Zane Vrexon, a detective, and I invoke the Seeker Law."

Lieutenant Dane turned bright red, frustration creeping across his face. "Vrexon? I have heard that name. You're a troublemaker of the highest sort."

Zane thought for a moment that the man might strike, but the lieutenant only huffed. "That damn law should be thrown out."

"But for now it holds weight in the court."

The veins in the lieutenant's face looked like they might burst. "Your time will expire quickly, or you'll figure out the obvious—that she is guilty. When that happens, we will be back."

The guards put away their staves and wands and marched down Potion Lane.

Zane turned to Vana. "That was...easier than I expected. I had planned on going to a judge, but they just accepted it."

She sighed. "I will take the saint's blessings whenever I can get them."

Zane bowed to the lady and the gnome. "I have an investigation to get to. I wish you both a good day."

ALYSSA'S STOMACH HAD churned all night, and even a cup of wine could not get her to relax. The events of the previous night haunted her.

Agwen had knocked over his chair as he stormed out of the meeting room. Alyssa had voted yes, and she believed it was the right choice. But she hadn't expected Agwen to be so furious. Hurt, maybe—but not as explosive as he had been. That was the angriest she had ever seen him. After Agwen's volcanic display, Alyssa had walked Dennis to the front of the Institute and Tatius-Lasome had asked her to come by his office in the morning.

Agwen's comment about the budget still bothered her, so she looked through the department's financial ledgers before heading to Dean Tatius-Lasome's office. With each page turned, and each column studied, things increasingly looked off. The bottom number seemed okay. But the columns showed several small expenses being constantly taken out, only to be made up by large lump payments. She had no idea what these expenses were or where they were coming from. A glance at the clock reminded her it was time to meet with the dean.

The old man was stooped over the desk, his nose so deep in a book that he didn't notice her entering the room. She rolled her eyes and knocked on his open door. "Dean, you wanted to see me?"

He jerked his head up, startled. "Alyssa? Sorry, dear. It's the latest essay of a promising philosopher. He proposes—"

She flopped into a chair, interrupting his explanation before it could begin. "You asked me to come by. Also, sir, and I don't mean to be rude, but I want to discuss what Agwen was talking about yesterday."

"Ah. Yes, last night I came to a difficult decision. I think I need to bury a hatchet with Professor Agwen."

It was great news, but she was still concerned about the budget. Alyssa laid down copies of the ledgers on his desk. "Sir, I have been looking through the books. We do have money for Dennis, but something isn't quite right. I think we should start an investigation."

"That is what I think also. Do you know the last time we did an inventory on the Fey artifacts in Basement Three A?"

Tatius-Lasome turned around and laid a large tome on top of the ledgers. He hadn't heard a word. Alyssa nearly bit her tongue. Tatius-Lasome was off on a tangent that left no room for any other thought. The little old man was busy with his own project and wouldn't notice anything she showed him.

She attempted to regain control. "I will explain it from the beginning again."

The man didn't bother to look up from his tome before continuing. "All right—"

"Wait until after I am done." Alyssa's face flushed as she made one final attempt. "We need to look through the ledgers."

Tatius-Lasome waved a hand and smiled. "That sounds grand. Now where was I? Right, I would like you to take an inventory of the Basement Three A."

Alyssa sighed and nodded, then sank into her chair defeated. The old man was excited and couldn't keep still. Perhaps she could broach the subject after he said his piece.

"Not only do I think it's time to bury the hatchet as they say," Tatius-Lasome said, "but I think it's time for this department to break new ground."

She made a dismissive gesture with her hand. "And how are we going to do this?"

Tatius-Lasome pointed to the aged tome. "I would like you to start making an updated inventory of—"

"Yes, you've said that. But to what end?'

Three A belonged to their department, which would normally be considered too small to warrant its own basement. But the department was also one of the Institute's oldest, and that came with certain privileges.

Alyssa felt a ribbon of dread. Their basement was not only one of the oldest, but one of the least organized.

Tatius-Lasome leaned back. "Professor Agwen, that silly Archmage, might have a point. I have taken his suggestion into consideration. We will release and donate some of the Fey artifacts we have."

She nodded. "He does bring it up at every faculty meeting."

Dean Tatius-Lasome rolled his eyes and gave a tired sigh. "Yes. And with the saints as my witness, I have come around on the idea."

Alyssa raised an eyebrow. "This has nothing to do with last night, does it? With Agwen storming out?"

The old man nodded. "That has something to do with it. Keeping the peace is a dean's duty. But I really think this could be a good course of action for our department."

This was the heart of the matter: It would be a publicity stunt. Another show of good faith. There had been several of these through the years. As a student, Alyssa had jumped at the chance to help, but years of service had stripped her of the desire to *volunteer* for Tatius-Lasome's projects. However, she worked for him, so she had no choice but to help him with this.

But why her?

"Doesn't Agwen want to do this himself?" Alyssa asked.

Tatius-Lasome laughed. "Yes, but I want to surprise him. I want to smooth things over and to show that I've been listening to him."

I wish you would listen to me now, she thought. "Which students am I taking with me? Can I use any of the hired wizards?"

He grimaced. "Right now, I have everyone busy on other projects."

She leaned forward. "You are going to send me downstairs, into one of the biggest and least organized basements of the Institute, alone?"

He looked away nervously. "Of course not. I will also be sending the new wizard, Dennis Zel, as soon as he gets here."

She hated this plan, but rather than argue, Alyssa circled back to her own agenda. She stood over the dean and pointed at the ledgers. "Tomorrow we will go over these. Agreed?"

Tatius-Lasome smiled gently. "Yes, yes."

She picked up the dean's tome, exited the office, and walked through the changing halls, shifting stairs—and even a window— before arriving at Basement Three A. With an eldritch word, she lit gas lamps as she passed, each new light revealing more of the cavernous room. It did nothing to help her growing dread at the volume of work ahead.

The bigger and more recently discovered relics were at the front, while smaller and older objects resided farther in. Almost none of them were labeled.

Her slow, tedious work was made worse by the large room's silence. Creaks and groans escaped from dark corners every few minutes, and she jerked her head each time to check whether something was there. But no matter how hard she looked, the shadows were empty. Even with the aid of charms, all laced with eldritch words, Alyssa never detected anyone.

Until a loud bang echoed through the basement.

Alyssa turned back and forth, peering into dark corners that lamp light didn't touch. It had sounded like the door, but she couldn't remember whether she had left it open.

"Hello? Is someone there?"

No one answered. She walked in the direction from which the sound came. "Dennis? Dennis Zel? If this is a game, I am *not* liking it."

Silence was all Alyssa got in response. She turned and explored rows of shelves until stopping in front of a sphere large enough to hold a person. It was transparent and filled with liquid. The orb itself was made of a strange membrane, like that of a bubble. Connected to it was a large stone. She edged nearer, shuffling through the papers of the tome to identify the object while keeping an eye on the environment around her. She found it and stopped.

The orb was listed as a Dream Sphere. And under the sphere, Alyssa noticed marks on the brick floor, as if it had been scuffed or dropped.

She laughed, the tension in her body relaxing. "I must be losing it. It was just this stupid thing fall—"

Alyssa was interrupted by a scream.

Her scream.

She continued calling out as she was shoved violently into the sphere. Her body passed through the membrane into the putty, which forced its way down her throat and into her lungs. All sound was lost inside the strange fluid, and Alyssa's silent screams became sobs as the light faded into darkness.

CHAPTER 4

Zane didn't want to waste time. The body could wait, but a witness's memory fades quickly. The Fountain was just a few shops down and across the street from The Brew. It had a huge glass pane window in the front, and above the door was a clean sign built in the shape of a decorative fountain. A frustrated boy was sweeping the ground in front of the shop—futile struggle, as more ash fell from the sky with each sweep.

"Is Atom inside?" Zane asked.

The boy nodded without looking up from his work.

As Zane stepped toward the shop's entrance, the boy suddenly blocked his path. "Wait! I am supposed to say the thing. Um. Ah, right. Welcome ye traveler. Your journey is at an end. You have found The Fountain"—he looked at his feet, then back up at Zane—"Yup, that's it. Sorry for delaying you. If he asks, I did the thing."

Zane stepped past the boy into The Fountain without reacting. The inside was spotless. Maybe too clean for most, but Zane appreciated the level of dedication it showed. Potions of different colors were organized by function and price. A large-framed man with a bald spot was standing at the counter at the end of the room. His clothes were clean, but his apron was stained.

The man looked up at Zane and opened his arms in acceptance. "Ah, welcome, worthy seeker." His jowls bounced as he spoke. "Your long journey has come to end. You have found the lost Fountain that offers healing and youth!"

Zane crossed the floor and offered a gloved hand to the man. "Zane

Vrexon, private detective. Are you Atom?"

The man's face twitched in response. His stained hands were a clear sign of his trade. One of them had a bandage around it.

"Detective, eh? I hope the nature of your visit is related to potions."

"In a manner of speaking. I am here on behalf of—"

"Lookie here, Jef doesn't know what he's talking about." The man raised his arms in defense. "Everything I did was legit. If he's having problems, it's his own fault. I won't be pushed around."

Zane slammed the estimate down on the table without a word, then pulled his hand back.

The man's eyes rested on it. "Ah, I see something happened to Dennis Zel. I saw the guards buzzing around like flies. What was stolen? What did Dennis tell you?"

Zane looked Atom in the eye, watching for any sign of dishonesty. "Nothing was stolen, but Dennis Zel is dead."

Atom sat down heavily on a nearby stool, the furniture squeaking under him. His face was pale and, though Zane wasn't sure, he thought he detected remorse. Shadow's silky voice slithered into Zane's head. *Hah, I have seen priests with less honest faces.* Zane ignored it.

"By the saints," Atom said. "Dennis… but just yesterday I was… What is going on? Why are you here?"

"I found this in the wreckage." Zane pointed to the estimate, then raised his hand to Atom. "What happened yesterday?"

Atom looked from the paper to Zane. "Do you think I would never do such a thing. I am a peaceful—well, a peaceful-ish man."

Zane needed Atom to relax, or this interrogation would go nowhere. He shrugged and stepped back. "I doubt you're to blame, but I need to look into this." He slapped his hand on the estimate. "You offered him a substantial sum for his shop. Why?"

Atom eyed Zane with suspicion. "What if that is a trade secret?"

Zane smirked at the big man. "Fine. But it doesn't dismiss you as a suspect. Why were you interested in Dennis Zel's shop?"

Atom motioned around The Fountain. "Why not? I'm successful, but he was still a competitor. I want to expand. The more shops I have the more business I can do."

"But why his shop?" Zane tried to look nonchalant as he pointed out the door. "It's not next to yours. In fact, it's several buildings down."

Atom scratched his face, and Zane watched as a mental debate took place. "If I speak, I hope I speak in confidence. It's not a big secret, but it is a secret."

Zane looked around and nodded. "Can we speak in the back?"

Atom shook his head. "That is part of the problem. The war changed the shape of the district. They needed more potions, so they made more shops. But they are smaller now, especially the workshops. The nobles had no idea what they were doing when the edicts were made." He pointed to his own workshop with one pudgy finger. "But Dennis's shop is *three* times bigger in the back."

"Why?"

Atom shrugged his shoulders. "Luck? Dennis's shop made it through the reconstructions without the nobles getting a hold of it. Now, I'm gonna use his huge workshop to mass produce potions."

He is an ambitious fellow. Zane ignored Shadow's voice, but it was right.

Zane pointed at Atom's bandaged hand. "How'd that happen?"

Atom lifted the bloody appendage. "I cut it on one of his *adventure proof* potions."

"Adventure proof? Oh, right, those shatterproof bottles. Fex mentioned them breaking in the commotion. He thought it was strange."

"Well, I guess it's true about what they say about gnomes, they think too fast but don't act fast enough. If Fex had noticed the strange bottles in their stock, I wouldn't have cut my hand. Just like a gnome to be too lazy to fix an issue."

Zane ignored the blatant prejudice. It was fairly common, especially to those of Fey descent. "I don't understand?"

Atom unrolled the bandage to show the cut on his palm. "I picked one up to give it a lookie and it shattered in my hand."

Zane winced at the long gash. "Shattered?" He knew better than most that it was strange for even a normal bottle to break in someone's hand.

Atom smiled like he was remembering his own inside joke. "Yeah, Dennis and I talked about it. His business was going to be hit hard when people found out he was selling bad goods."

Zane nodded. "So, you blackmailed him."

Atom stood up defensively. "Hey, you can't come in here and just smear my name. I have a reputation to protect."

Zane bowed. "Sorry. Don't worry, I won't do anything to hurt your reputation." He wondered if Atom had a reputation that could be damaged in the first place. "If I have any more questions, I will stop by again. Is that all right?"

Atom calmed down. "That's fine. By the way, when would it be appropriate to speak to Mrs. Zel about the future of the shop?" His tone was casual, as though there was nothing insensitive about the question.

Zane stared into Atom's eyes and saw nothing but greed.

"You should wait." Zane's muscles tensed as he resisted a primal urge to hit Atom. "At least until after my investigation."

～

FEX EXAMINED THE shop's ledgers and books of inventory, searching for The Green Thumb Loan Company. While he was at it, he also checked to see if they had the budget for more shatterproof bottles.

More than half of the adventurer potions had been shattered, and they'd only been selling them for two weeks. Fex could hear the customer complaints about the quality of their goods. He would go by the glass maker in a few hours.

He found the address for the loan company and wrote it down as Zane walked in, leaning heavy on his cane.

"Mister Fex, sorry to bother you. Do you still have the letter of introduction for your uncle?"

Mister Fex. The gnome ran the words through his head. He studied Zane's expression, trying to decide if this man was being sincere or rude. The detective's face was stern but seemed honest.

Still, Fex couldn't bring himself to accept it. "I thought you had forgotten about it. Most wouldn't take a gnome's letter seriously." He walked toward the counter. "I have it over here."

How did a man like this get into detective work? Oh, how the saints must have toyed with him.

Zane's voice spoke over Fex's thoughts. "Thank you for being willing to write it for me."

"Why not? You are working a case on behalf of my boss."

Zane's face was unmoving. "Because gnome culture is very... tight. An outsider is only known by what another is willing to say about him. Otherwise, it's hard to trust them."

It was true. Gnomes had been abused so long that they could only truly trust each other.

Fex pulled the letter out from the counter and handed it to Zane. "Did you find out what Atom wanted? Why he came by with that estimate?"

Zane took the letter and slipped it into his jacket. "Yes. He wanted to purchase the shop. He wanted the bigger space for making more potions. Also—"

"Also? Also, what?"

"Atom implied that he wanted to save the shop's reputation. He said you're selling bad products. Claimed he cut his hand on one of the glass bottles. One of the adventurer potions."

Fex's small face got hotter than a furnace. "What does that man... Dammit. It all makes sense. Why some of the bottles shattered and others didn't. That bastard!"

Zane raised an inquisitive eyebrow. "Atom is responsible for the bad bottles?"

Fex nodded. "Everyone on Potion Lane knows about that damn worm's practice. He sabotages his competition, underselling them or buying their ingredients before the shipments come in."

Zane's face remained stern and neutral. "Do you have proof?"

"Proof?"

Fex's face remained white hot. Atom had done this to his shop. But how? The question only reinforced Fex's desire for evidence. He didn't have any proof. The glass-maker might though. "If I find any, I will let you know."

Zane nodded. "Did you find the address of the loan company?"

Fex pulled his note out of the ledger and handed it across the table. "I had never heard the name Green Thumb Loans before Dennis mentioned it. It's around the corner of Flitch and Merchants Lane."

Zane grunted and took the note. "Will your uncle be okay with waiting?"

Fex waved dismissively. "I trust Dex to wait. At least until he hears from me."

Zane bowed politely before stepping back onto the street.

⁓

ALYSSA FLOATED IN darkness that stretched eternally in all directions. Then, slowly, the coldness of the liquid evaporated and then the weightless stopped. *Am I dead?* She had studied dozens of different views on the afterlife. Alyssa didn't know which one she might be stuck in. Raw emotion overcame her like a tidal wave, and she started to cry. There was so much she had wanted to do. So much of her life was now gone.

An old memory drifted into her mind—a happy time with her parents before the accident. A candle flickered in the darkness.

"It's time to blow out your candles, dear."

Alyssa watched as the memory came into greater focus. It was the first birthday she could remember with her parents. Her younger self sucked in as much air as her small body would allow before, in one giant puff, she killed the flames. Her parents clapped and cheered. Her younger self clapped with them. It was funny to see herself feeling so happy over something so simple.

"Alyssa dear, what did you wish for?" Her father's grin stretched from ear to ear.

Alyssa brought her hands up to her mouth as she stared at her young parents. Memories rushed forward. She had asked for nothing other than her own journal, just like the ones her parents carried everywhere and wrote in constantly. The child closed her eyes and lifted up her head defiantly. "You said wishes only come true if the secret is never told."

The parents laughed. "That's right," her mother said. "It's from the story *Little Star Fairy*."

The child's face lit up at the name of the story, and Alyssa choked out a laugh at the young girl's excitement.

The mother patted the little girl's head. "Well then, how about you close your eyes and see if your wish comes true."

The child obeyed, and Alyssa watched as her parents brought out a journal. They set it out in front of her younger self. Her father smiled. "Open your eyes, dear."

The child opened her eyes, and her squeal nearly caused the room to vibrate. She picked it up and hugged it. "My wish came true! It came true!"

Alyssa laughed at herself and watched as her parents cut the cake. She reached out to touch them, but her hands passed through all three. She touched the furniture and found it solid, unmoving. For a moment, she wished she had the journal so she could take notes. *How am I viewing this? Is this what death is like? Do I watch my life all over again? Will I see other memories?*

The child beamed up at her dad. "Will you read *Little Star Fairy* to me tonight, Daddy?"

"Yes, dear."

Suddenly the world shifted and slid at odd angles. The room and the people melted away like wax, and then everything reformed itself. Alyssa marveled at her old room and watched her father reading to her by the bed. "The fairy held the fallen star. The spark asked, *Will you protect me?* The small fairy smiled and said, *Yes, I will.*"

Her father turned the page and continued. "The small star shined. *Thank you. If you keep my secret, I will grant your wish.*"

The younger Alyssa yawned and closed her eyes. Her father closed the book and kissed her on the forehead. He stood up and was about to leave when a small voice called out. "Daddy, I love you."

"I love you too, dear."

Tears came to Alyssa's eyes, and she sniffled. So much was lost, so much that would never happen again. The images changed to the family playing board games. Then to another birthday party, then her parents' birthday, and then other memories, some she didn't recognize at first. Finally, the endless, shifting sea of memories stopped. Little Alyssa was in her best dress and her parents looked like they were ready for a test.

Her father leaned over. "Are you excited to see us work today?"

Her little eyes beamed with joy. Even after all these years, Alyssa remembered the happiness of going with them.

But she hated this memory. "Please don't make me watch this..."

Through shifting halls that lead to a room divided by a thick-paned window, her younger self stood on one side with her grandfather, an archmage. "Now, little one, your parents are attempting to open a spell book written by a Fey wizard."

Her parents passed through a door as Alyssa watched in horror, her face ivory as she stared through the window.

"Please, no."

Her grandfather had a protective hand on the child's shoulder.

"Please… please don't open it…"

Alyssa banged on the glass, but it made no sound, nor did it move. She tried to grab both herself and her grandfather to warn them, but she passed through them. She cried, and her tears fell unhindered to the ground. Alyssa watched, helpless as her parents stepped inside a large circle etched into the floor. Dozens of symbols were painted all around the circle. Her mom waved to the little girl and smiled. Her father spoke as he worked. "The barrier spell has been etched. We have painted protective runes to help disperse any magic that may come from opening the tome."

Alyssa pounded on the window. "The rune circle is damaged! Don't open the book!"

Her father turned to her mother, who nodded. "I am now opening the book…"

He turned the key and fire burst from the pages. At first, it looked like a wave of light on a lake, but then it consumed her parents in a horrific flash that rivaled the morning sun.

The fire then folded back on itself at the edge of the circle, leaving a blazing cylinder that raged on as her parents' ashes settled to the ground.

FEX FINISHED CLEANING up the shop after Zane left for the loan office. The floor was beyond saving; the stains from the potions were going to stay. He stared at the floor and thought about what a carpet would look like, then he imagined the floor painted. He silently agreed with himself that a painted floor would look better before stopping. He didn't own it.

He decided to think about other things and focused on the fact that more than half of their stock was ruined. He needed more glass bottles. He stepped into the back to talk to Vana, who was brewing a new batch of potions. "Lady Zel, I am going to step out and place some new orders."

Vana nodded, her funeral veil bobbing up and down. "Will you lock the workshop door when you leave?"

He disliked the idea of leaving the shop unattended. "What about customers?"

She didn't look up from the brew. "Do you think anyone will come by today?"

Fex considered it for a moment and agreed. The shop now had a stigma that would hang over it like a black cloud, and there were the quickly forming rumors about Vana. "Probably not. I'll lock up."

He stepped into his small room, put away his apron, and grabbed his jacket. Instead of a hood, Fex wore a large-brim hat, which protected him from falling ash. The workshop locked with a click, and he was out the door and walking down the street. The neighbors watched him with a twisted curiosity, but none came forward.

He would have continued unimpeded except for a stranger.

Fex didn't recognize him, but one glance told him the man was an addict. His clothes were dirty and smeared in potion stains. The most revealing sign was the rainbow-like sheen permanently encrusted on his lips, which came from drinking the dirty potion water. "Potion gnome, I heard rumors that the mistress of the shop killed her husband."

Fex backed away from the man and kept himself out of arm's reach. "So what? Rumors are rumors."

"Aye, I guess they are, but"—the addict stopped and looked around; several people were in earshot but none he cared about—"but I saw something strange that night. Something I figured you and your new boss would like to know."

The man took one more dramatic pause.

"I saw the murderer."

Fex's stomach twisted in knots, and he didn't know if it was relief or excitement. The man looked hungry, and it was clear that his information wouldn't come cheap. "Really? What would you like for this *eyewitness* account?"

The man looked back and forth, then pointed to an alley. "Meet me over there when the next bell rings, and I will tell you—if you bring some potions."

Fex smirked, nodded, and continued down the street. The shop had several damaged potions. He could easily give the addict one of those. But first, Fex had nearly a full hour to complete his errands.

His cousin, Ler, had worked as an apprentice glass maker for the last ten years. Ler had suggested that they use Clear Through, the glass shop he worked for, to bottle their potions. Fex trusted his cousin, but not the humans he worked for.

The workshop had a small addition up front for conducting business. Fex knocked the ash from his hat and jacket before stepping inside.

A man behind the counter snarled at Fex. "What do you want? We don't need any more gnome apprentices. We got too many already."

Fex's jaw twitched, but he kept his tongue still. "No sir, I am here to review an order I placed."

The man rolled his eyes. "You mean your boss's order." The man made a comment under his breath, but Fex could hear it. "Stupid gnomes taking other people's good credit."

Fex's face twisted in anger, but he bowed politely to hide it. "Either way, I would like to speak with the owner."

The man grumbled as he stepped into the back. Alone, Fex took some deep breaths and forced himself to relax. It hadn't even been a day, and already he missed Dennis. His former master wasn't perfect, but at least he treated him as an equal of sorts.

A skinny old man stepped through the door and ran his fingers through his thin hair. "What can I do for your boss?"

Fex forced a smile. "I am here to make an emergency order of more shatterproof bottles for The Wizard's Brew."

"The Wizard's Brew…" The man walked over to a nearby logbook and looked through it. He ran a boney finger down a column until he stopped with an *ahh*. "Yes, The Brew. We can get it to you in a few days. Anything else your boss needs?"

"Well, yes. Some of our bottles shattered, which is strange since they are supposed to be shatterproof."

The old man raised an eyebrow. "What are ya saying?"

Fex could feel the tension rising between them. "I mean, we have gotten complaints that our bottles are breaking." It wasn't true—not yet, at least—but Fex continued. "Surely that is something worth bringing up."

The old man slammed the ledger closed. "I should wring your neck, gnome. You have no damn right to slander me like that. Tell your boss that I will do this job, but he better come here himself next time. Now get out of here!"

The other man stepped out from the back with a metal rod and gripped it menacingly as the older store owner again yelled for the gnome to leave.

Fex stormed off without another word. He didn't bother to linger in front of the store and instead walked a block over and waited for his cousin. Humans may have been in charge, but gnomes had a hand in most things.

And they watched out for each other.

Ler showed up a half-hour later. The balding gnome pulled out a cigarette and offered the pack to Fex, who shook his head. Ler shrugged and lit up. "Cousin, I can guess—"

"What I want to ask?"

Ler nodded. "The boss let it slip today, and now it all makes sense."

"Well, don't bury the lead on my account."

Ler blew out a cloud of smoke. "I used to make all the bottles for your shop, but I was reassigned a while back. Now some of the other boys do it. I didn't give it any thought. Then the other day I heard mention that a receipt needed to be made for Atom along with your order."

Fex shrugged. "So?"

"I seen this before, I have. The boss is double dipping. Figure that Atom paid to have something done to your order."

Fex swore and kicked a nearby wall. "Atom was the only one to complain about our bottles. I bet that fat bastard set it up to make half of my order just regular bottles."

Ler knocked some ash from his cigarette. "Worse. I seen some of those bottles. Some of them are downright brittle. Squeeze too hard and the damn things will break."

An awkward silence clung to the smoky air between them. Fex tried to think of what could be done, or what would be appropriate to ask of Ler, but his cousin spoke first.

"I will see what I can do. I cannot promise anything. But for you, cous, I'll try." He dropped the cigarette and stomped on it. "See you later."

Ler turned back to the shop, and Fex cursed under his breath as he walked four blocks to the market. The new batches of potions required more ingredients, and the shop needed a new door.

It was close to the top of the hour when Fex returned to The Wizard's Brew. He wiped ash from his jacket and hat before entering and calling out to Lady Zel as he walked in. "I have ordered a new door. I was even able to convince them to do it at a discount in exchange for some potions." He'd already made it through the shop and opened the door to the back. "I figured in their line of work an injury could end a man's career."

The workshop was empty, so he searched the rest of the building but didn't find Lady Zel anywhere inside. It was strange for her to be gone, especially with the door destroyed and the shop open to the world. Then again, there was not much left to steal.

He stepped into the back and grabbed a bottle of healing potion for the addict. It had been pulled from the shelf for being *expired*. Fex laughed to himself. He remembered all the stories of adventurers finding usable potions in ancient tombs. Despite these stories, Fex knew potions could go bad.

The bell chimed to signal the hour. Fex gripped the potion and left for the meeting. It was almost a waste to trade it away with how few they had left, but the information might be worth it. At the entrance to the alley, he couldn't find the addict. Fex sighed and told himself it had been worth the effort.

"Hey, let go—"

A sense of dread overtook Fex as he followed the addict's voice. A broken wall created a gap in the alley that he had failed to notice earlier. Through it, Fex saw an abandoned courtyard that sat between two buildings. A woman in black held the addict in the air by his throat. It didn't seem possible since he was much larger, but she choked him with one hand.

Fex watched in horror as the addict spat words through frantic gasps. "What are you? I saw you that night—"

The woman slammed the man against the wall with a sickening crack that echoed through the forgotten courtyard.

She'd broken the man's neck.

The woman in black released the addict's limp form and let it slip to the ground, the brick wall behind him cracked from the impact. The woman turned away from the slumped body, but Fex's hands shook in fear and he dropped the potion. The glass bottle shattered on the ground, causing the woman's head to whip around in his direction.

He saw her face and gasped.

Fex fled down the alley and into the busy street, darting between legs as he ran and not caring if he bumped into someone. He dared not look back until he reached the shop. Out of breath, he composed himself at the familiar sight of The Brew.

He had barely stepped into the shop when a woman's voice called out from the workshop. "Back already?"

Fex's throat clamped shut. It was the woman who just murdered the addict.

Vana Zel.

CHAPTER 5

Zane had cut his way through the city with purpose, pleased he wouldn't have to ask half a dozen loan offices to find the right one. He'd found it in less than an hour with the address Fex had found. The outside of the building looked more like an apartment than an office and matched the structures on either side.

He climbed two floors until he came to the door with a window reading *Green Thumb Loan Office*. Zane wondered about the name Green Thumb. He had never heard of them, and yet they had the funds to loan Dennis a thousand ruse. Either they were new or—and Zane found this more likely—the company was a criminal front.

Zane knocked on the door, and a voice from inside called out. "We're open. Please come in."

After obliging, he found a beady-eyed man wearing thick glasses and a suit sitting at one end of a large desk. The man had the smile of a con artist. "Welcome to Green Thumb, where we make your dreams come true. How may I help you?"

Zane crossed the room and absorbed the atmosphere. The office was simple and bare, as if they had just moved in but never bothered to finish furnishing it. One door was off to the side. Zane sat across from the con man and adjusted the chair so he could see him and the door at the same time.

"I am Detective Vrexon, but most call me Zane." He laid his cane across his lap. "I am hoping to ask some questions."

The beady-eyed man smiled. "You can call me Gene. Now, when you say detective, does that mean that our fine city guards are interested in us?"

Zane shook his head. "No, I have a private practice. I am investigating the murder of one of your clients. In his ledger, the victim had a receipt for a loan from this office."

Gene's smile faded and was replaced with a mask of sympathy. It was almost believable.

Almost.

This one is a professional, Shadow whispered.

"I am so sorry to hear that. We here at Green Thumb Loan see our clients as family, so to hear that one of them has passed is like losing my own mum. Please let us know who it was so that we can send the family flowers."

Gene was only trying to butter him up, but Zane played along. "Dennis Zel. He borrowed a thousand from you, and I am curious about the status of his loan."

Gene's face flinched. "A thousand?"

Zane nodded and slid the receipt across the desk.

Gene adjusted his glasses as he read. "I am very surprised." He set the receipt down and stood. "I'm sorry, we don't normally handle that much. Let me check our files."

He walked to a solitary file cabinet and shuffled through it until an audible *ahh* signaled that he'd found the right file. He brought it back and placed it on the desk. "It says here that Dennis Zel paid us back in full last week, which is… odd."

"How so?"

"He paid it off ten years early. I only see this when someone other than the borrower comes in to handle the debt."

It made sense. If this was a criminal enterprise, as he suspected, the interest rates were probably sky high. The only way out would be an outside source.

"Does it say who paid it off?"

Gene smiled and waved one hand. "Oh, no. We work hard to

ensure the confidentiality of our clients. We only care about receiving the payments."

"It doesn't sound like you negotiated this loan. May I speak with your boss?"

Gene flinched again. "My boss? Why? Dennis has no debt with us."

"You said earlier that loans this large are usually handled by your employer. And while the loan is paid in full, I still have questions that need answers."

Gene leaned back, his hands dropping out of sight. "I might have said that. But there is no need—"

Zane stood, holding his cane like a club. "A man has been murdered. A wizard, in fact, whose employer at The Institute might be interested in what happened."

The color drained from Gene's face. "Well, The Institute does complicate things. But that will be decided by—"

This going to hurt.

Before Zane could process Shadow's words, blinding pain exploded from the back of his head accompanied by a light flashing behind his eyes.

Zane woke up from the blackout with his head covered by a sack and limbs tied to a chair. His head buzzed like a fierce storm, and sharp pains assaulted him whenever he moved.

"I hear you are asking some questions, detective," said a scratchy voice in front of him.

Zane's mouth felt dry, and the air he breathed was hot. "That's right. But it seems you have me at a disadvantage. May I ask who I am talking to?"

There was a snap, and the bag was ripped from his head. Bright light stung Zane's eyes as he struggled to adjust. He blinked until he could tell that he was in a rough-hewn stone room. Makeshift gas lamps were mounted on the walls, their long pipes running to the floor and out into different halls. A dark green goblin stood hunched on top of one of the largest desks he had ever seen. He was dressed in an ill-fitted suit, the large jacket hanging from his shoulders.

When he spoke, a goblin accent found its way through his gravelly voice. "I am Nob. Right now, you're a… guest? Yeah, a guest in my humble home." Nob held out a cigar, and another goblin came into view and clipped the end, followed by a third to light it with a match. Nob took a big puff. "Your questions are less than flattering, hume."

"How so?"

Nob knocked the ash off the cigar. "You're asking about a client who was murdered. That leads one to think you believe we might be involved."

Zane forced a smile. "Are you?"

The goblin's face registered surprise. "That is a bold question… the kind that can carry problems for people stupid enough to ask them."

What are you doing? You are playing a dangerous game, detective. As usual, Zane tried to ignore Shadow.

"I don't think you're involved in his death. It was a real mess, as if a big fight went down in his shop, and no one mentioned any goblins that night" — Zane kept his stare level — "Also, since Dennis paid you back, you had no reason to murder him."

Nob narrowed his eyes at Zane for a long moment, until his mouth closed with a grin. He snapped his fingers, and someone from behind Zane unbound him. Nob hopped off his desk and walked over to Zane, his jacket dragging behind him. "Walk and talk with me, hume."

Zane rubbed his wrists and nodded. He looked around but couldn't find his cane, so he sighed and limped on next to Nob.

"Now then," the goblin said, "what do you want to know?"

"I would like to know why he came to you for a thousand ruse."

Nob tapped the cigar to knock off more ash. "Listen here, Dennis wanted to expand his shop. He had the idea to make shatter-proof glass bottles and needed money to start production, so he came to me. Adventurers are huge right now, especially with the empire cutting back on the military. I also saw the opportunity."

The loan made sense.

The payment didn't.

"It must have come as a shock that he paid it off last week."

Nob laughed. "You bet your ass. He gave me over two thousand. I don't know where he got that money, but I've been playing the game long enough to know not to ask."

The words left Zane dumbfounded. Two thousand ruse was an insane amount of money. Where had he gotten that? Nob didn't have that answer, so Zane asked the next question that came to mind. "He didn't leave on bad terms, then?"

"Oh, pits no. I respect anyone who can pay off a loan, especially one of mine. I gave him my card in case he ever needed me again. You could even say that he was a friend." Nob looked Zane over as if he were about to place a bet, then took a long drag from his cigar. "Truth be told, we even bought potions from Dennis."

Zane raised an eyebrow. Fex hadn't mentioned this, which meant Dennis must have kept quiet about it. "Really? Isn't that like paying off your own loan?"

Nob shrugged. "I suppose, but Dennis was one of the few people who was willing to deal with us. Not many shops will service my kind. We're seen as trash by many."

The goblin stopped walking and Zane looked up and down the long hall. "Where does this leave us?"

Nob pulled out a card and handed it to Zane. "You got any leads?"

Zane took the card and pocketed it. "Not many, but I found a dagger. It looks Fey made."

Nob stared at Zane, obviously troubled. "Are you sure?"

Zane nodded and pulled out the bloody blade. "I don't know much about Fey goods, but just take a look at it."

"Aye. The damn thing does look Fey made. Well, I think I know a guy."

"A guy?"

Nob scratched his head. "Take my card to Jweal's workshop in the old Fey district. He owes me, but he is hard to collect from. Tell Jweal if he helps ya with this, we are square. Got it?"

"Got it."

Nob knocked more ash off his cigar before returning it to his mouth. "I'd like to know who killed our mutual *friend*. When you find out, let me know. If you do that, we might become *friends*, too." The goblin removed the cigar and blew a cloud into the air between them. "Do we understand each other?"

Zane nodded. Nob smiled.

Shadow warned.

Here it comes again.

COLD SWEAT DRIPPED from Fex's face. He had simply told Vana he'd forgotten something and ran. He had gotten two, maybe three blocks away, before he felt like he had space to think. Now he was even farther from her.

He had seen Vana in the alleyway after she snapped the addict's neck. The face and voice of the two women were identical. But she had been wearing different clothes than when he saw her just moments later in the potion shop.

There can't be two Vana's, can there? Unless one was fake. A cold thought slithered into his mind. Could the one in the shop be a double? Was this some complicated plan?

Fex shook his head and looked over his shoulder in case he had been followed. When he looked back, he saw Zane.

The detective walked toward Fex from the opposite end of the street. Zane's body rocked back and forth as if he was drunk. His body leaned one way too far before collapsing. Fex ran and checked on the detective, who laid in the grime. Fex hesitated before rolling him over and patting his cheeks to awaken him. "Zane? What happened?"

The human mumbled. "Goblin mob…"

Fex repeated the words under his breath and shook his head. Goblins were dangerous, feral people. Why any sane person would deal with them, he didn't know. Fex was surprised Zane was still alive. "Are you an idiot? Did you go by yourself?"

Zane whispered, "Yes…"

"You *are* an idiot."

He scanned the crowd, checking for Vana—the version from the alley. He wanted to get out of the street as soon as possible but he couldn't leave Zane in the street. Not like a human would do.

Fex rolled Zane's arms over his small shoulders and pulled the human off the ground. Once Zane got his cane under him, he stood on his own. Fex tried to help as they walked down the sidewalk at an agonizing pace. Fex looked for a place off the street but filled with people. He found a small restaurant.

The gnome struggled to pull Zane inside and ordered water for him, followed by a meal to regain his strength. Zane ate and drank weakly at first, but before long, the man's color returned.

Fex noticed dried blood on Zane's collar. He wondered what Zane had learned from the goblins, but he waited for the human to break the silence.

"Thank you, Mister Fex."

"It was nothing. Did you get anything in exchange for your injuries?"

Zane nodded. "I found some small leads that I can follow but I fear that I lost some time. The loan company was a front for the mob, which made things a bit more complicated." He took another greedy drink of water. "How is Vana?"

Fex pondered the question for a moment. How much could he

really trust a human, especially one he didn't know? Questions gave birth to questions in an ever-growing cascade of what-ifs.

For instance, *if* the Vana in the alley had been the real thing, Fex had a chance to own the shop if he aided the investigation. But *if* it was someone disguised as Vana, he might look like a fool. Or worse, Fex could be accused of betraying her. Zane worked for Vana and held no allegiance to Fex. The man, he reminded himself, was not in his corner. Humans were never in a gnome's corner.

He had to be his own champion.

"Fex, are you okay?"

The gnome blinked and pulled himself together. He would have to handle this on his own. "Before I tell you about Vana, explain the Green Thumb being a part of the mob. The *goblin* mob."

Zane leaned forward to hush Fex. "It's wiser to keep this quiet, but I met with a goblin named Nob. He looked like he was in charge."

Fex tried to calm himself. "So, are they going to take the shop?"

"No, Dennis paid them off."

"Wait, what? Dennis paid off his thousand ruse?"

Zane shook his head. "His debt was at two thousand after interest, but someone else settled it for him."

Fex's body felt like jelly, as though he could melt into the floor. His stomach turned at that amount of money. With two thousand ruse, even a gnome could buy a shop and have enough left over to get it running. Fex had balanced the books on the shop, and he knew that they made nowhere close to that amount. "Where did he get that kind of money?"

Zane shrugged. "The mob didn't know and didn't bother to ask. It's probably related to why he died though. That sort of money doesn't come easily."

Fex let the information soak in and was deep in thought when Zane interrupted him.

"How is Vana?"

A part of Fex was afraid to share the day's events. What could be gained? He could be seen as lying. Or Vana could be arrested. He stopped as the last thought was accompanied by a touch of pain. Didn't he want her arrested? He would finally be a journeyman and own his own shop.

He needed to be his own champion. "She is…"

The words hung in the air. Zane was understanding when he finally spoke. "It's all right. Grief affects each of us differently. I remember when I found out my parents had passed."

Fex asked the question that had started to eat at him. "Is the mob involved in Dennis's death?"

"No, I don't think so. It doesn't strike me as a mob hit. Plus, Dennis paid off his loan."

Fex agreed with Zane. The mob had no motive to kill his master. Fex had known Dennis for a good while, and this all seemed so out of character. An earlier question reentered Fex's mind. Who is Zane?

That sparked a new question. "How did you know Dennis? I had never heard of you before, and I worked under the man for five years."

Zane leaned back in his chair. The shadows cast from the gaslight masked part of his face, but Fex could see the pain that rested on it.

"I fought in the Ghoul War. I was a young officer and thought that it was my national duty to serve. I performed well and was selected for a special assignment, but it was a suicide mission. I was captured, and tortured—"

Zane violently thrusted his hand through a nearby shadow. Anger shot through his pained face. After a moment, he looked back at Fex and adjusted his clothes. "No one else returned. I was sent to a field hospital. That's where I met Dennis, who was a medical officer and potion brewer. Most considered me a lost cause, but Dennis checked on me daily and I recovered in a few months. I would have lost my arm and my leg without him." Zane took a deep breath before continuing. "When the war ended, we went our separate ways. I hadn't heard from him in years. Then, less than a month ago, I received a letter from him."

Fex looked down at the table. Zane's story matched up well with what he knew of his late master. "What did the letter say?"

Zane raised an inquisitive eyebrow. "Why do you care?"

Fex's mouth went dry as he tried to come up with an answer. An answer that would satisfy himself, more so than the human.

Zane didn't give Fex a chance to respond. "He asked me to make sure Vana was safe."

It was information Fex expected, but it did little to help him. "Well, don't take this the wrong way, Mr. Vrexon, but you haven't exactly filled me with confidence."

Zane chuckled in agreement. "If this case doesn't go well, it will be my last one." He stood and pushed the chair back under the table. "Thank you for taking care of me. I will make sure to pay you back. Now, please excuse me. I need to follow up on some other leads."

Zane gave a noble bow and left as the sound of bells filled the air. Fex liked the human, but he would never be in a gnome's corner.

Fex needed to be his own champion.

But first, he needed to get back to the shop and face whoever was there.

≥

THE BACK OF Zane's head burned, and he could already feel a large knot growing. Every few blocks he had to stop and rest, leaning hard on his cane. With his free hand, he fished out his flask and sipped on it.

The pain faded as cool soothing liquid flowed down his throat, but the knot remained. It would be there for a day or two, but beneath his hair no one would notice. With renewed pep, Zane rested the cane on his shoulder and walked in long strides. Nob's helpfulness was an unexpected boon, one he wouldn't let slip by.

The Fey neighborhood was well-kept and clean, but nobody was outside sweeping—a sight reserved for this area and Alviun's upper districts. Everyone passing Zane in the street wore either large hats or hoods over their faces, all hiding the elongated ears marking them as Fey descendants.

He took a few twists and turns through ever thinning crowds until he was left standing in a small square. He continued to stroll until coming to the workshop he was searching for. A wooden hammer hung above the door, with *JWEAL* written vertically. The shop stretched half a block.

A bell announced his presence, and a Fey-marked youth stood behind the counter, obviously shocked to see a human. "Welcome to, to Jweal's workshop. How may I be of, of help?"

Zane crossed the threshold and admired the wares. A variety of tools, armors, weapons, and fine arts were scattered throughout, each imposing a level of beauty he had not expected to find in such a small corner of the city. "I am Detective Zane Vrexon. I wish to speak to Jweal. Is he in?"

The youth tried to give a calming smile, but only succeeded at looking nervous. "I am sorry sir, but the master smith is, is busy in the back engaging in several projects. If, if you want, I can set up an appointment. Or you can make an order."

Zane pulled Nob's card from his pocket and handed it to the youth. "Please take this to him. If he still won't see me, then I will leave. Can you do that?"

The youth flipped the card over in his hands a couple of times before nodding. "I can do, do that. If you would, please wait here."

Zane turned and inspected the objects around the room as the boy left for the back. On one wall was a rapier, thin and elegant. Etched along the blade were flowing patterns of flowers in bloom. The guard was likewise made to look like a collection of huge petals.

In a corner of the shop was a metal stand, each leg in the shape of different creatures—a dragon, lion, bear, and eagle ascended toward the stand's top. He reached out and touched it. Despite its sharp appearance, it was smooth to the touch.

The sudden opening of the back door caused Zane to jump.

"Sir, the master smith, Jweal, will see you," the youth said excitedly. "If you would follow me, please."

Zane reached into his jacket and fingered the wand as he followed. The workshop was dark, with hubs of light where the smiths worked at their forges. Showers of sparks accompanied each as they hammered their pieces, the air filled with the rhythmic beating of metal on metal. Zane wanted to stop and watch the smiths but instead followed the youth, who headed for a door leading behind the shop. He held open the door, which led to a small back porch and motioned in twitches. "This way sir," he yelled over the musical hammering.

Zane gestured politely. "No, after you."

Even in the dim light, Zane could see the youth's shocked face. "No, sir. After you. You are our guest."

Zane conceded, glad that the effects of the healing potion continued to keep his pain at bay. He stepped towards the door, then dove across the threshold, arms outstretched, holding both cane and wand.

A blur shot down from overhead toward him, but it was too late. Zane rolled across soft grass and recovered himself, leaping to his feet. Wand outstretched, his mind on the trigger, he leveled it at the individual in front of him.

Without moving his wand, Zane took stock of where he was—a small courtyard with a small pond, not something he had expected. The large man by the door towered over Zane and gripped his hammer stiffly, his muscles tense, skin pale but burned, ears elongated.

The man lifted his large hammer out of the grass, right where Zane was supposed to have stopped. He held the weapon in both hands and took a step forward.

Zane jerked the wand in front of him. "I am not here to cause trouble. But I am not above resolving it."

The man froze, his shoulders tense. Zane could see indecision on the man's face, so he relaxed the hand pointing his wand. "Are you Jweal?"

The man squinted at him. "It depends on why you are looking for him."

"A certain small fellow offered your service. He said you two would be square if you helped me."

The man shrugged. "So, you aren't here to collect for him?"

"No, sir. If you put down your hammer, I will put down my wand. Then we can introduce ourselves like civilized men."

The giant raised his chin to Zane. "You first."

"Fair enough." Zane lowered the wand, eased it back into his holster, and leaned on his cane. "Now then, I am Detective Vrexon. I am here investigating a murder. I have what I believe to be the murder weapon, but I would like a specialist to take a look at it."

The man leaned his hammer against the back of the building. "I am Jweal, master blacksmith and owner of this shop. Now, why did that small devil send you to me?"

Zane pulled out the dagger and sat it on a nearby table. "I am trying to find out anything I can about this."

The smith walked over and sat at the table, staring at the bloody dagger. "Look, detective, I don't know ya, and I don't want any trouble."

"Like I said, I am here trying to solve a murder."

Jweal sighed and pulled out a rag. "So, I can tell you right away that this is Fey made. I don't see any cold iron, which is strange."

Zane took a seat; the effects of the healing potion were fading. "Why is that strange? I thought that anything Fey made couldn't contain cold iron."

Jweal spat onto the ground. "That's how it should be, but old-world metal is hard to come by." He gestured to the small stone columns behind Zane. "Most of us use purification rituals."

Zane studied the nine small columns around a small circle of water. Each had runes facing the cardinal directions. "So, you would say the dagger is rare. Does that mean it's a specialty item?"

The smith picked up the blade with the rag. "Yeah. I don't know if you noticed, but it's lighter than a normal dagger of this size." Jweal held the weapon carefully. "Can I wipe the blood away?"

Zane nodded. The smith ordered an aid to bring him his cleaning kit, which he placed on the table with reverence. The smith opened it and began washing the dagger before stopping and setting the blade down with care. "I... I think this blade is enchanted."

"Like a spell wick?"

The smith shook his head. "No, it's old-world magic. Like that of true fair folk."

Fair folk were akin to myth, a group of Fey that were said to have ruled a large empire. They were once known by another name.

"Do you mean elves?"

Jweal grunted in agreement. "I don't know how much you know of fair folk history, but elves existed. In the old world, as we call it, when true magic bathed the world. It was easy to enchant things then. But all that has long since passed, and much of the knowledge is lost. We keep scraps of it alive. I only can do a purification of metals ritual... but I try to keep pieces of my history and tradition alive."

He pointed to the weapon. "This dagger has a simple but effective enchantment. It will never chip or dull."

Zane had experienced fighting with a dull edge before. The memory of deep, dark tunnels with hundreds of flailing limbs and gnashing teeth played behind his eyes. A weapon that required no maintenance would have been a blessing from the saints, but this raised more questions than answers. "Who could have made this?"

The smith shrugged his large shoulders. "I don't know. We Fey folk are far more diverse than you man folk. Traditions are varied and old. If you leave it here, I will look into it."

Zane hesitated. "You just told me that this weapon is rare. How do I know you won't steal it?"

Pain flashed in Jweal's eyes, but he quickly blinked it away. "I understand your suspicion, but I won't steal it. I am invested. Like I told you, we keep history and traditions alive. What I learn from this, I can pass onto the next generation."

Zane felt a new admiration for the smith, one of the few people Zane knew who desired to leave a legacy. He reached his hand out to shake Jweal's. "I trust you to look over the dagger."

The giant grinned as his hand enveloped Zane's. "I will return the dagger to you. I have to repay that small devil."

Zane left the shop with a limp. His body hurt. His scarred limbs tensed with every step and felt like they were filled with lead. He was ready for home.

The light of the day had started to fade away, and the city gave itself over to darkness. Wisps of smog clung to Zane's body like a lover saying goodbye. He wished he had taken the bottle of troll's blood with him, but he had left it in his drawer.

Just inside his apartment door, Zane tossed his jacket aside and dropped his cane on the floor. He sat at his desk and pulled out the bottle of potion. As soon as he saw the liquid, he felt his body yearn for it. He drank the last third of the bottle and leaned back in his chair as the warm glow washed over him, the pain that lived in his arm and leg fading away.

He had traveled a great distance on foot, but there was still a lot to figure out about the murder. Shadow took up its usual home in the corner.

So, we have a true mystery.

"Shut up, I am thinking."

Come on. What a horrible host you are.

"I never invited you."

I know, but you never would have. However, since I'm here, you should let me help you.

"You can go to hell, to its darkest pit!"

Shadow laughed, then its silky voice reverberated in Zane's head. *Let's see. Your friend was murdered sometime yesterday, but someone burst through the door from the inside after he was dead. I suspect it was the murderer.*

"Damn you!"

Zane stood up, his grip on the bottle turning his knuckles white. The overwhelming desire to throw it at the corner was strong. But he sighed, realizing he shouldn't be angry at his own twisted imagination. "Fine, tell me how you know it was the murderer who broke the door."

Because whoever did that is not someone you would want to be cornered by.

"Fair. What do you mean by *whoever*?"

You will find out soon enough. But back to the topic at hand: Why Dennis?

"I... I don't know."

Think, think! The murderer used a dagger that is probably worth more than anything in the shop itself. We're dealing with some type of big fish.

"You mean *I* am dealing with a big fish." Zane relaxed despite himself. "But you make a good point. Whoever did this must have connections."

That's right. Oh, by the way, it's time to dream. Say hello to me.

"What do you mean?"

Zane's stomach turned and his head pounded. He was about to have a blackout, something he blamed on the brew. They had been coming more frequently lately—and that was before Nob's henchmen had cracked him on the head.

Before he could react any further, Zane passed out.

Zane's shoulders ached, and his wrists and ankles were raw from the metal bars that held him to the wall. The endless blackness prevented him from seeing the ground, but he knew it was covered in dried blood. His blood. The memory of the knife, how it cut and carved at his left leg and right arm, made him shudder. *If I survive, they will probably be ruined*, Zane thought.

A voice cut through the darkness. "How is my dear guest?"

It belonged to a creature of darkness—and of the grave. A Lord of Ghouls. "Oh, please do talk. I get so few opportunities to speak with intelligent beings. The hive is filled with my animalistic cousins. All their thoughts revolve around hunger."

Zane bit his cheek so hard blood dripped from the corner of his mouth. What he wouldn't give to kill this monster, for all he had done to him. To his team. Five had been captured. Now, he was all that was left. The ghoul forced another of the countless healing potions down his throat, just like every day after torturing Zane until he wished for death. He was only alive because of them.

"Drink it all," the creature said. "You cannot die yet. Oh, no. If you die, who will *feed me*?"

The silky voice's laugh echoed off the stone walls. Zane wanted to vomit, but he had nothing in his stomach. It had been two days since he had been fed. Two leathery hands gripped Zane's head, and he felt a hot, putrid breath on his face. "This all can end, this endless night of yours. The pain, the madness, it can all be gone. All you have to do is let me in."

In a hushed and heartbroken whisper that Zane didn't know the monster was capable of using, the ghoul lord spoke again.

"You will be—no, you *are*—my escape."

CHAPTER 6

The day had left Fex exhausted, his senses heightened but his mind sluggish. He needed rest but was nervous to stay so near to a person he both feared and hoped to be a murderer.

It was a complicated situation. Fex stood to benefit if Vana really was a killer, but that did him no good if he ended up dead. He was also plagued by a tinge of guilt for his desires. Dennis had been good to him, and Vana had been nice. In the end, he stayed at the shop to avoid suspicion—though he placed one of his small chairs against the door and kept the wand near to hand.

It took time, but Fex slept and found himself wandering somewhere between a dream and a nightmare. He stood behind the counter in the shop. Newly brewed potions sat on shelves and he wore clothes specially made for the reopening of his potion shop. A young gnome came out of the back. It was a cousin of his, though Fex couldn't remember the boy's name. He was dressed in unstained clothes, a sure sign that he was a new apprentice.

"Sir, first, let me tell you how much I appreciate—"

"The opportunity? I understand. We are family. Gnomes gotta stick together." The bell rang as two women opened the front door. "It appears—"

"We have guests? Yes, I see that, sir."

The women were dressed in the blackest funeral clothes Fex had ever seen. Both wore a veil, but one kept her face uncovered. The floor echoed with their heels as they walked to the shelves and began to shuffle through different potions, but Fex focused on another sound, like dripping liquid. He ignored it and addressed the customers instead. "How may I help you two fine women?"

"You can't help us, and you can't help yourself."

The one with the exposed face stepped forward, wearing her gloom like fine clothing. She stood tense and ready, a beast preparing to attack. "I desire only one thing."

Fex scratched his ear. The dripping was getting louder. But rather than search for its source, he launched into his pitch, proud of his play on words. "Well, here at the Gnomen Brew, we know our brew. If we don't have it, we can make it."

The faceless woman stepped forward, her limbs growing and shrinking repeatedly, like the ebb and flow of ocean waves. "You desire one thing."

Fex's body stiffened. "I... I don't desire anything."

The dripping got louder as the masked woman lifted her veil. Fex saw that she was covered in dark, purple bruises. Blood dripped from her face, the sound now deafening as the women approached him. It was only then that he realized they shared the same face—Lady Zel.

Both Vanas spoke at once. "Only one desire can be fulfilled."

Fex tried to speak, but everything was drowned out by the sound of dripping water.

Fex opened his eyes. In a sweat, he switched on the gas and rubbed his eyes against the light. As his senses came back, Fex heard the dripping once more. It was coming from the workshop outside his door.

Fex picked up Dennis's wand and grimaced. There were only three shots left. He hadn't had time to make replacement spell wicks.

He had crafted many spell wicks, though he had never used a wand. One deep breath was all Fex allowed himself before stepping into the workshop. Sweat poured down his neck as he burst through the door. He waved the wand in an arc around the room so quickly that he passed over a hooded figure before leveling his aim on the intruder. His hand trembled, "Who… Who are you?"

The figure dropped its hood, and Fex could see in the dim light that it was Vana. Her face and shoulders were covered in huge bruises that were already starting to color. He blushed and turned his head away when he realized she was wearing a blanket rather than a cloak. Fex couldn't tell if there was any other clothing and turned away out of politeness. "Sorry, madam. I didn't know you were here working."

The dripping continued. He glanced behind Vana and saw a potion distilling after being brewed. Fex slid the wand into his night robe. "Are you okay? You seem to be in pain. Should I call for help?"

Vana poured some of the distilled brew into a cup. "Please, Mister Fex, go back to bed."

There was an edge in her voice, like the growl of a protective animal, which left the hair on the back of his neck standing up. Fex bowed and stepped back into his bedroom, knowing it didn't matter where he tried to rest his head.

Sleep would not come that night.

2

DIRTY LIGHT THAT filtered through the smoke of a thousand chimneys cut through Zane's window. He awoke to find himself laying on the floor, vest discarded, shirt unbuttoned to the waist.

He moaned as he stood up, wondering why he'd fallen asleep on the office floor. The last thing he remembered was passing out at the desk. Zane's shirt was filthy, and something had stained it red. He looked down and saw an open bottle of wine. Where it came from, he didn't know. A groan leaked out of him when he saw the wall. It had been carved with the precision of a painter. As he took a step back, an image came into view: Lady Zel in her funeral clothes, her hair made to look like a halo.

Zane's letter opener lay on the floor in front of the wall, its blade snapped in two. He gritted his teeth as he remembered his episode. Though he hated to give Shadow any compliments, Zane had to admit that the monster's carving was masterfully done. He hated himself for being so weak but reminded himself that his mind was on edge.

The next episode wouldn't be for days. Enough time to solve the murder.

He tossed his shirt to the side and grabbed a clean one from his dresser. As he did, Zane caught his reflection in the mirror. The countless scars covering his right shoulder and running down his arm were already irritated. He hated how deformed it looked compared to the other side, but it was a fitting match for his left leg. Even now, he could feel phantom pangs of pain from the knife that had sliced into him. Zane turned away from the mirror and pulled on his shirt, smoothing out every wrinkle before finding and donning his vest.

An empty bottle laid on his desk. He pushed it into the drawer with the others.

His jacket and cane were still where he left them the night before. He grabbed them off the floor on the way out and shook out the coat, creating a cloud of dust. At the front door of the building, Zane ran into his apartment manager, Mrs. Mose, looking especially old and haunted as she swept the floor.

She looked up. "Are ya okay, youngin?"

"Yes, Mrs. Mose. Did I keep you up?"

"I only noticed when you started to sing." She smiled. "By then, I wanted to stay up to listen to the song."

Zane hadn't sung since he was a choir boy as a child in the countryside. "I apologize for any inconvenience."

She waved her hand. "No, it's all right. I couldn't understand the words, but it was dark and mournful and beautifully sad."

Zane couldn't sing anything foreign and cursed himself silently for his unconscious rambling. "Yeah, it's a new skill. I sometimes do it alone at night."

"I think you would be an amazing singer. I bet it would be better for ya than being a detective."

Zane smiled politely. "It's not something I can share. You have a good day, madam."

He turned and left before Mrs. Mose could say anything more. He had a long day ahead of him, starting with a trip to The Wizard's Brew to check on his client.

As he walked to the shop, Zane was stopped by a woman with amber eyes and golden hair that rippled behind her. "Zane, how are you today? Have you found any leads?"

The mention of his name startled him, but he recognized Vana's voice. It was the first time he had seen her without the veil.

Something wasn't right.

"Are you going to the Brew?" he asked.

Her right eye twitched. "Yes, I forgot something. But first, please tell me what you found."

Zane gestured for her to walk with him. "After you, Lady Zel."

They walked side by side through the busy, dirty city streets as ash and soot began to cake on her shoulders.

Shadow whispered in his ear. *Are you going to offer her your jacket?*

Zane ignored it and inspected Lady Zel's face. "Is your eye okay?"

She brought a self-conscious hand to her face. "Oh, yes. I had a small accident. I feel lucky it hasn't become swollen. People would talk all sorts of nonsense if I had a black eye."

Her voice didn't sound right, like she was playing a game. Zane shifted uncomfortably next to her and looked for anything else out of place. "Lady Zel, I am sorry for being direct, but shouldn't you be at the shop or at home?"

She shrugged. "Am I not allowed to go where I wish?"

"Of course, but—"

Vana glared at him, and he looked away in embarrassment.

Shadow laughed.

"Are you all right?" she asked. "You seem distracted."

Zane hesitated but pushed past his feelings. "Yes. I was just thinking, isn't it too early to take off your veil?"

Lady Zel's right eye twitched again. "What do you mean? Am I also not allowed to choose the clothes I wear?"

"I just thought the veil must be worn for one moon's cycle."

Vana's irritation looked as though it may boil over before she stopped her eye from twitching. She didn't respond, which didn't sit well with Zane. Dennis was born in Alviun and not from the Eastern territories. The practice of wearing a veil came from the east. A practice from her family, which meant Vana was disregarding her tradition.

Zane took another analytical gaze at the woman and noticed she wasn't wearing her large amber stone ring. His instincts had been screaming, and he decided to listen. "I just remembered something and must take my leave. I will see you later, Lady Zel."

"Wait, I have a quick question." The woman's voice was marked by desperation. "What happened to the dagger?"

Zane glanced at the people who passed by on either side of them. "Sorry, but the street is busy, and things of that nature should be discussed in private. I will meet up with you at the shop and explain everything, I promise."

Without waiting for her answer, he left the woman standing alone in the crowd.

The streets widened and became cleaner as he headed to the heart of the city. At the courtyard of The Institute of Sorcery and Science, the home of state mages, Zane took off his jacket and let the sun's light rain down on him unimpeded by clouds, smoke, or smog. In the center of the wide courtyard was a three-story pillar of rotating gears, fans, and burning spell wicks. This machine was the late head archmage's greatest invention—a device that controlled the weather.

The courtyard was filled with an open-air market that only the upper-class could afford to patronize. He marched over to a large, pillared building, its gigantic doors guarded by two knights. "Stop! Unless you have written permission or an appointment you can't come in."

Zane pulled out Dennis's state badge "I have a badge belonging to a state mage. Under its power, I would like to meet with someone in charge."

One of the knights approached him and inspected the badge before turning to the other and nodding. He pulled a nearby lever and spoke into a pipe built into the wall. Orders were given, and the guard returned the badge. "Wait here."

After a few moments, the doors creaked open and out walked a short woman with cropped raven black hair and a sharp nose holding up a pair of black-rimmed glasses. "I am Cliff, Secretary to Archmage Benedictus-Lasome. He has asked me to escort you."

Zane followed her through winding hallways, up and down stairs, and out of a window that connected to another room. He saw all manner of machines and rituals underway in a half dozen libraries. They came to a stop in front of a wooden door, its red paint chipped with age.

Zane turned to his guide. "Are you sure this is the right door? I was expecting something... grander."

"We get that a lot. Archmage Harvey Benedictus-Lasome won't let anyone touch up the paint on his door."

Zane reached out to knock on the door, but Cliff stopped him. "Before you go in, a note on addressing him. Archmages often have lengthy names, considering their many titles. Archmage Benedictus-Lasome or just Benedictus-Lasome will do."

Zane nodded and knocked on the door. From inside a heavy voice said, "Come in."

The door swung open on its own, and Zane stepped inside. The room was larger than he had expected, about ten strides wide and at least that many deep. The walls were covered in books and scrolls. Spread out among them were jars filled with items Zane didn't want to ponder. At the far end of the room was a desk, its red paint matching the door. Sitting behind it was a hunched figure with thinning white hair.

The archmage looked up from papers in front of him. "Please, have a seat."

A chair slid out from the corner of the room and stopped in front of the desk. Zane took the seat. "Sorry to bother you, Archmage Benedictus-Lasome."

"Why has"—Benedictus-Lasome paused and looked over a nearby scroll—"Dennis Zel sent you?" The archmage seemed irritated as he grumbled. "He was supposed to start yesterday. Where is he?"

Zane let the old man catch his breath before answering. "He is dead. I am here investigating his murder, at the request of his wife."

Benedictus-Lasome's heavy wheezing echoed throughout the room. With a shaky hand, the old man marked out a name on one of the many pieces of paper on the desk, then set down the pen and met Zane's eyes. The archmage looked like he had taken the news harder than he should have. "Tell me what happened."

Zane gave him the same statement he'd given several times by now. "Dennis was murdered two nights ago. The guards suspect his wife."

The old man wiped his face. "Why are the guards looking into his wife?"

"She was the last person seen entering his shop before his body was found."

"What is your opinion?"

Zane looked away, collecting his thoughts before speaking. "I'm not sure, but something isn't right."

Benedictus-Lasome scratched his head, then smiled. "I can help with your investigation."

Zane squinted at the archmage. "How?"

The old man pulled out some papers and started writing "I can make your investigation an official errand of The Institute. You will be acting on our behalf, looking into the murder of a member of our guild. You won't be limited by any sort of Seeker Law. But I need a favor in return."

Zane sighed. He didn't like working under someone else's conditions. Then again, he wouldn't find a better deal. "What do you need?"

"I require your help finding my granddaughter, Alyssa."

z ⎯⎯⎯

ASHEN MUD CLUNG to Fex's black boots as he walked back to The Brew. The dream of Vana had followed him like a black cloud as he ran errands. But from now on, he'd be prepared. He patted the bag containing ingredients for the spell wicks as he approached The Fountain, the potion shop owned by Atom. Fex looked through the window, hoping to grasp a business secret to use in his own shop one day.

What he saw caused Fex to stop in the middle of the lane.

He stared as people and gnomes bumped into him in the street, his mind refusing to comprehend the image of Vana talking to Atom.

Except Vana was wearing no veil and had none of the bruises from the night before.

Fex had worked for years in the potion craft. Many could heal injuries, but none would remove the coloring. The damage to the blood vessels were gone, but the blood below the skin always remained. There was no explanation for Vana's appearance.

Who is she? What is she doing here?

"Hey! Move along or get out of the street!"

With a shove, Fex moved closer to The Fountain and stood staring through the window. Atom's face was pale as he motioned toward the back of the shop, and they began walking. Fex looked up and down the lane until he spotted an entryway to the alley.

Fex hurried down the passage toward The Fountain's back door. It was wider than the one behind The Wizard's Brew, but the walls of the buildings looked scraped, as if something large had forced its way through. The ground sagged from what looked like cart tracks. Fex wondered if Atom had arranged for secret shipments and made use of the wider back alley to transport the goods.

It was something he would have to investigate later.

Fex counted the buildings until he reached what he believed to be The Fountain. In the cover of shadows and dressed in black, he hoped no one would pay him any attention as he knelt by the door and listened.

There was a crash inside the shop. He could barely make out Atom's voice.

"What are you doing?"

The responding voice was Vana's, but something was different, as if echoing in a hollow room. "I told you already. I want to make a trade."

"Trade? Come now, haven't we known each other for—"

The wall and the door rocked as the sound of shattering bottles rang out, and a mixture of potions seeped from below the door. Fex grimaced out of habit at such a loss; he had never felt sorrier for Atom than at this moment.

Fex could hear someone—Atom, he assumed—gasping for air. The image of Vana in the alley from the previous day flashed in Fex's head. He reached for the wand and cursed himself again for having only three spell wicks.

"You will give me what I want, and out of the kindness of my heart I will give you what you want in return. I need you to set up a meeting here tonight with your backers."

"How do you..." Atom's voice was now just above whisper as he choked out the words.

Fex's free hand moved unconsciously to grip the wand. The memory of the addict's death played out in his mind. *I have to be my own champion,* he thought. His free hand moved to open the door. *What are you doing?* He had no love for Atom, but no one deserved the disgraceful death the addict had suffered. Fex pulled on the door, but it was locked and the handle jingled.

His heart skipped a beat as he heard Vana's voice.

"Who's out there?"

Saints damn me! He stood and sprinted down the back alley and cut to the exit towards the main street, into the crowd.

Fex didn't look over his shoulder until he had reached The Brew.

ZANE FOLLOWED Benedictus-Lasome into the hallway and watched as the old man dismissed his secretary before pulling out a large ring adorned with at least a hundred jingling keys. He searched until finding one that was coral green, which he slid into the keyhole, causing the office doorway to shimmer with a white light. The walls rippled out from the door and down the hall, out of sight. Zane jumped back, one hand clutching his wand.

Benedictus-Lasome laughed. "It never gets old, seeing outsiders react."

His smile faded when the door didn't open.

"Something wrong?" Zane asked.

Benedictus-Lasome's face went red in embarrassment. "I didn't expect that Tatius-Lasome would lock his door."

"But didn't you just use a key to—"

"There are physical locks, and there are... other kinds of locks."

Magic. And an archmage's magic, no less. Perhaps fighting with this door wasn't the easiest way to get what they needed. "Is there anyone else we could go to?"

Benedictus-Lasome nodded. "There is another archmage that would have the access I require."

Zane could sense something wasn't being said. "But…"

The old man searched through his large key ring again. "Two things. First, I wanted to apologize to Tatius-Lasome. Second, Agwen is… eccentric?"

Zane was starting to hate this trip. "Eccentric?"

Benedictus-Lasome held a key to the light to inspect it. "Yes. He turned down the suffix of Lasome and decided to go by Agwen instead."

"Is that odd?" Zane asked.

"Somewhat. Lasome is a title given for scholarly skill. For example, Marvin Tatius is known as Tatius-Lasome. Likewise, the title archmage is given when a wizard achieves a high level of magical skill. This means that Marvin's full title could be given as Archmage Tatius-Lasome."

Zane scratched the side of his head. "Wouldn't your title be Archmage Benedictus-Lasome, then?"

He chuckled, then fit the key into the door. "Yes, but it's a mouth full, so I prefer just Benedictus-Lasome." The room rippled again. "Anyway, Agwen is the first in hundreds of years to refuse this title. So, yes, he is seen as odd."

Zane sighed. All wizards were eccentric in his eyes, but he dreaded meeting someone even they considered off.

The door opened to an elegant room on its own. Zane forced his mouth to stay shut as he stared at a large limestone desk amid silk green curtains and curved pillars. The bookshelf behind the desk stretched from ceiling to floor. The shelves were so packed with books of uniform silver covers that Zane initially thought it was a wall. A hooded man behind the desk stopped writing and motioned for the pair to enter.

Benedictus-Lasome stepped forward. "I am sorry for disturbing you, Agwen, but I was hoping to gain access to Basement Three A. I am looking for—"

"Yes, yes." Agwen didn't even look up from his paperwork. "Dean Tatius-Lasome wanted me to go down there and look for her this morning."

The door shut behind Zane and two chairs slid out from against the walls. "Please, have a seat."

Benedictus-Lasome spoke first. "When are you going?"

Agwen ignored him and kept his head down. "Who is your guest?"

Zane bowed his head politely. "I am Detective Zane Vrexon, but please call me Zane. I am here investigating the murder of Dennis Zel."

Agwen's hand slipped, dragging ink across the paper. He looked up for the first time, showing a face younger than Zane had expected. "I am sorry to hear about Dennis, but what does his death have to do with Alyssa?"

Benedictus-Lasome looked irritated. "I offered to help Zane if he could assist in finding Alyssa."

"Why?"

The young archmage was rough and to the point. Zane watched the surprise spread across Benedictus-Lasome's face. The older man sat silently for a moment before answering. "She is in danger. I keep her under surveillance with several charms."

"That is illegal. You do know that, right, Benedictus-Lasome?"

The old archmage sighed. "Yes, but after her parents' accident, I started worrying. Now I fear for her safety, so I want to bring extra hands to help."

Zane felt like he was being sized up as Agwen looked him over. "I see you brought someone expendable." He hated the smirk that rolled over the wizard's face. "That is fine. Please follow me to the basement."

Agwen stood and searched through his own crowded key ring. The trio migrated to the hallway, and the room rippled as he turned the key. This time the door opened into a massive cold area lit by gas lamps. They stood at the top of a tall staircase, overlooking a large basement.

The younger archmage smiled at Zane and Benedictus-Lasome. "After you."

The room stretched farther than what Zane thought possible, with many of the lamps already lit. He leaned heavily on his cane as he looked over the edge.

Agwen turned to Benedictus-Lasome. "How do you even know she is here?"

The old man looked down, shameful. "Since yesterday, my spells have registered her location in the basement."

Zane asked what he felt was the obvious question. "Does it show you exactly where she is"—he paused, the confusing nature of The Institute leaving him unsure if *basement* would be the correct term— "down here?"

Agwen shook his head again. "I doubt it. Such precision would give the charm away."

The young archmage started down the steps. Zane looked to Benedictus-Lasome, whose face was flushed.

"He is right," the old man said. "My charm only shows the general area she is in. Its accuracy is good for a school, but in rooms like this, all I know is she's here somewhere."

Magic was never a simple solution, Zane reminded himself. "We should call in more people. Perhaps some students."

"I can't do that," Benedictus-Lasome said. "I already told Agwen that I came to know her location…"

"Illegally," Zane said, finishing the thought.

Benedictus-Lasome nodded. "I trust the heads of this department. But the students might tell others, and that could have serious repercussions."

Zane decided to let it go. He wasn't interested in wizard politics. "Then we will sweep the area and see if we can find her. Or a clue."

The pair joined Agwen at the base of the stairs. The young archmage looked tense as he turned to them. "Now what?"

Zane pointed to the shelves with his cane. "Let's split up. If you find anything, call out."

Benedictus-Lasome smiled and followed Zane as he started to walk the long rows of items. The relics on the shelves ranged from mundane items to beautiful works of art. He stopped in front of a jeweled bowl that looked to be made of golden vines. Zane reached out but was stopped by Agwen.

"I wouldn't do that. Not all that looks beautiful is safe. When dealing with these, it's best to wait until you know what it was designed for."

Agwen let go of Zane's wrist and turned away. The detective noticed how vast the room felt, as if all of creation had been collected in this one room. He shuddered.

As the search continued, Zane could hear the two professors walking faster than him. He shook his head and took a slow pass through his row, letting his eyes wash over every detail.

"What did you call me?"

"How dare you!"

Zane could hear the two archmages arguing where the lamps were still off. He sighed and jogged up to them, passing a corner and watching as they stood before the dark half of the basement.

"What are you two fighting over?"

Agwen turned to Zane. "I was telling this old fool that we didn't find her, so she must be elsewhere."

Benedictus-Lasome shook his head. "No, we haven't even finished searching the basement. We should keep looking."

Zane wasn't paying attention to them, but was instead staring at the walls.

"Do you see something?" Agwen asked.

The detective pointed. "The lamp is out. All of them up to now have been lit."

Agwen shrugged. "So what? She could have gotten lost in the dark."

"That could be. Try lighting it."

With a soft-spoken word, the lamp burst to life—just as Zane had expected.

He turned around, back the way they came. "We missed something. We should turn around and do another sweep."

Benedictus-Lasome rubbed his chin in confusion. "Why? We already checked there."

"Yes, but she came this way, lighting the way as she went." He pointed to the newly lit lamp. "This suggests she didn't go any further. So, the question is, why? I can think of a few explanations, but I would like to double-check our steps in case something happened on her way back to the stairs."

Zane started walking but was stopped by a frail arm. "What do you think might have happened?"

"I hope she fell, or maybe touched a magical trinket. But if someone was going to hurt her, she might have been dragged into the shadows."

"Then why don't we check over there?" The old man was frustrated, and Zane sympathized.

"There hasn't been any evidence of foul play. Let us not assume the worst yet." Zane put a gentle hand on Benedictus-Lasome's shoulder. "It's going to be all right."

The old man sighed and followed Zane back into the rows, with Agwen following closely behind. They had about given up when Zane noticed a large tome laying on the ground. The detective picked it up and turned it over. Unlike many of the items around him, it was not covered in dust. He laid it back down.

Zane inspected the area around the fallen object, trying to see if he could spot anything out of the ordinary. He saw scuff marks on the ground by a large sphere sitting atop a flower-shaped pedestal. The orb was bigger than Zane and seemed to contain a murky liquid. He squinted and stared into the sphere, being careful not to touch it. A woman with raven dark hair and a sharp nose floated inside.

"Hey," he shouted to the archmages. "I think I found her."

Benedictus-Lasome and Agwen rushed over and examined the object.

"It's a Dream Sphere," Agwen said. "They allow you to relive any memories you desire."

Benedictus-Lasome began to lose his composure. "Is it safe? How do we get her out?"

Agwen shrugged. "We cannot get her out. The dreamer has to do it. Unfortunately, if she doesn't know she is inside, she could be trapped indefinitely."

Zane shook his head in disbelief. "How could she not know?"

"I am merely stating the difficulties associated with the Dream Sphere," Agwen said, an edge in his voice. "She has been here all night. It seems obvious that she may be unaware of her predicament."

Benedictus-Lasome's face was pale, and Zane could see him sweating as he spoke. "What happens if that is the case? If she's in there indefinitely?"

In a cold voice, Agwen answered. "She will starve."

Zane laid his jacket and cane on a nearby crate, then walked up to the sphere and looked back at Agwen. "How do I get in there?"

"You simply touch it, and it will pull you in. But if you go, there's no telling what could happen. The orb is not meant for multiple people at once."

Benedictus-Lasome looked nervous. "We must find another way. There must be one."

Zane put a hand on the old man's shoulder. "This is what you brought me here for." He glanced at Agwen. "I am expendable."

The old man's voice was barely above a whisper. "I am so sorry."

Zane whispered in return. "I am used to it."

He reached out and placed his hand on the sphere. The surface stuck to his hand, then pulled his entire body through the membrane. The liquid surrounded him as he floated a few inches away from Alyssa. He breathed deeply, and the sludge filled his lungs.

Then darkness overcame him.

CHAPTER 7

A fter the first few breaths, Zane opened his eyes. He was laying on a soft feather bed with sunlight pouring in from the nearby windows. The room was familiar. He swung his feet off the bed and brushed against a bag. He looked down and it hit him. "This is my old room."

Zane had used the bag when he left to join the war. He picked the old wooden sword off the floor that he had played with as a child and moved over to the bookshelf. It was filled with books on many subjects that held his interest when he was younger. He pulled one off the shelf "My old Nana would have me write this down and repeat it to her by memory."

He placed the book back on the shelf. From outside the room, he heard yelling. Zane followed the voices that carried up from downstairs. The words were inaudible, but he had a strong guess what the argument was about. He opened the door and stepped down the creaky stairs. A familiar scent filled the air, and he smiled and breathed in the smell of his mother's cooking.

Zane stepped down and turned into the kitchen, pleased.

Then he saw his mother.

Her hands covered her mouth and tears filled her eyes. Across the room, his father was yelling. No, pleading. Zane shook his head. In front of his father stood a younger version of Zane dressed in his old officer clothes, the ones sent along with his deployment letter.

"Son, you don't have to go," his father pleaded.

"I do. As a noble, I am expected to fight for emperor and citizen."

"There are others. Stay here and help with the farm."

The youthful Zane jabbed his finger at his father. "You expect me to live like a pariah and be labeled a coward?"

"Son—"

"No! I am going!"

His younger self marched up the stairs. As he did, he passed through Zane like a wisp of smoke. With his younger self gone, the room was frozen. He walked soundlessly to his father. He saw in that moment what he could not see so many years go.

His father was heartbroken.

Zane inspected his father's hair, receding and grey. How much it had changed from his childhood memories. As for his mother, her hair was still as radiant as a field of marigolds.

Tears fell from his eyes, uncontrolled, as the world slid away and he dropped into darkness. When his crying ceased, Zane found himself standing in a tent. His younger self stepped through the tent flap with a salute. A silver-haired official sat at a large table, hunched over a map marked with dozens of red lines denoting trails, dates, and numbers.

"Sir," young Zane said. "You called?"

The commander looked up from the table. "I am up to my ass in ghouls, lieutenant. We need to find a route straight to the center of this damn mountain." He stabbed the table with one of his meaty fingers. "I am sending you and a dozen other squads on a recon mission. Each of you will be given a tunnel to try."

"Which one is mine?"

The commander sighed and rubbed his scalp. "The most dangerous."

"Tunnel sixteen?"

The commander shook his head "No. Sixteen has the most deaths, but tunnel twenty-four, well"—the commander slammed a hand onto the table, his face twisted in anger—"we don't know a damn thing about tunnel twenty-four. No one has come back. The men have taken to calling it the Tunnel of Shade."

Younger Zane raised an eyebrow. "Shade? As in the ruler of the dead?"

"Yes. I have done my best to squash the rumors, but we need to find the truth." The commander paused a moment. "I wanted to talk to you because... I need to apologize. Your team is not expected to return."

The younger Zane laughed. "My team is always up for a challenge, sir. We will bring light to Shade's realm and bring out the dead."

The commander gave a grim smile. "May the Lords of Light guide you."

Younger Zane saluted and walked out. The scenes froze yet again, and Zane walked to the map. His eyes rested on the tunnel marked twenty-four. He gave a dry laugh. Shade's realm. How close to the truth that had been.

Darkness bled into the tent and drowned everything before being broken by twelve great braziers lining a huge stone hall. Knights dressed in armor stood at attention on both sides. At one end was a large staircase leading to a robed figure on a lofty throne. A king. At the base of the stairs stood a single figure dressed in the finery of an ancient noble. He bowed low and deep. Zane could not make out his face.

The king's voice echoed through the chamber. "You have failed me."

The noble didn't lift his head. "Sire, I did as instructed, did I not?"

"Don't you dare twist my words. I wanted the darkness for myself."

"I understand, sire, but I did not know that it would bind with the one who freed it."

The king slammed a thin fist onto the armrest of his chair, and the hall shook. "I don't care! You have failed!" He stood and pointed at the noble. "You are cursed for all time to be one with the darkness. The darkness is you and you are the darkness. Forever."

The shadows poured from all corners of the great hall and engulfed the man. The scene froze and Zane walked around the room, inspecting every detail. "What is this memory?"

It's mine. Zane turned to the voice and found himself looking at two red eyes staring back from the shadows.

"Why are you here? You're only a figment of my imagination."

Shadow snickered and laughed. *I would appreciate it if you didn't probe too deeply.*

Zane reached for his wand, but it wasn't there.

This is all a memory. A dream. In an ephemeral world, no weapon can aid you. Shadow's thin arm extended from the noble to a doorway, which glowed with a clear white light. *That will lead you to the next room. After that, you can escape to find the girl.*

"Why should I trust you?"

Shadow rippled as it attempted a shrug. *Do you have a choice?*

Zane spat on the ground of the dream world, marched to the door reluctantly and took one final look back before stepping through. He fell facedown onto wet grass, surrounded by tombstones, and spotted his younger self standing in front of two graves. Pain raced through Zane at the scene of his younger self crying and cursing the heavens.

Zane remembered the day he came back from the war to find his parents had died. The sky cried a flood of water, masking his younger self's tears.

Zane noticed a faint light shining from an open grave a few steps away. He walked over and stared into a white void. "Where will this take me?"

Consider it the backstage of this device. Jump in and we can go from there.

Zane looked back at his younger self and sighed. Even if he could say something to himself, it would not help. He took a single step into the grave and disappeared.

It was as if he was passing through thick morning mist that faded into a bright space where thousands of bubbles floated around him. A memory played on the surface of each. Every memory, the good and bad, from his entire life. The sensation was overwhelming; he was lost, and he knew it.

Zane hated himself for what he had to do. "Where is she?"

Where do all bubbles go?

Zane ignored Shadow, who asked the question again. Rather than respond, Zane looked up and started to float. He didn't understand how it worked but dared not question it. He flew past hordes of bubbles until he stopped at the edge of the sea. Above him, just beyond a barrier, was another innumerable collection of bubbles. Taking one deep breath, he flew through to the next cluster.

The distance felt both impossibly long and short, as if the rules of logic no longer applied. The cloud of spheres rolled over Zane and, though he couldn't explain it, they felt both lonely and gentle. Zane stared at each until he began seeing a figure with raven hair and a sharp nose at different ages of her life. The bubbles changed too quickly for him to accurately identify her height or age.

He whirled amidst the bubbles and realized he had no idea what he was doing. He gritted his teeth and prepared again to do the unthinkable. "How do I find her?"

Oh, are you talking to me again?

"Yes, you bastard. Now take me to her."

What is the word?

"Please."

Laughter echoed in his head, then spilled out until it surrounded him. A shiver ran down Zane's spine. His hands felt clammy. A dark shadow stretched from Zane, twisting through the different bubbles, the end extending out of view. Zane focused on the path and floated past memories of family, friends, birthdays, and school.

Pleasant-looking memories gave way to more traumatic ones. Zane stopped in front of a bubble where all he could see was a sheet of fire. Finally, the end of the path came into view and led to a bubble with a wall of rain. He stared at it before reaching out hesitantly. "How does this work? Do I touch it?"

Yes, it's that simple. Do be gentle with her.

Zane was disturbed at the sympathy in Shadow's voice. He placed his hand on the bubble and was transported inside. The air was cold, and the rain passed through him. Across a green field covered in statues and tombstones, a large crowd of what looked like scholars and mages were dressed in funeral clothes.

Two caskets laid above two empty graves. Zane noticed Benedictus-Lasome with a hand on the shoulder of the raven-haired girl, who was crying, crumpled on the ground. On the other side of the coffin was an older version of the girl. The two mirrored each other, crouched and weeping, but the rain passed through the woman. Zane walked through the crowd and laid his hand on her shoulder. She jumped in surprise and looked up at Zane, then pulled away, crawling backward across the ground on all fours.

Zane took a knee and held up his hands to calm her. "Sorry for startling you. I am Zane. I was asked to rescue you."

She wiped the tears from her face. "You don't look like a mage or scholar."

"Archmage Benedictus-Lasome sent me."

She stood to regain her dignity and he did the same. He was surprised to find that she was a head shorter than him. She wiped her clothes despite their cleanliness. "So, you're not from The Institute."

He nodded. "What's your name?"

"Alyssa. Alyssa Benedictus. I am the granddaughter of Benedictus-Lasome."

Zane extended his hand, and she hesitated before taking it. He could feel a slight tremor in her grip. He would be nervous too if he was her, and he was impressed with her courage.

He looked around. "What do we do now?"

"I think I have been slipping from memory to memory"—she squinted, as though finally realizing how strange his presence was—"but how did you get here?"

"It's complicated. How did you get into the sphere?"

"I was assigned to inventory the basement. A new wizard named Dennis was supposed to assist me."

Zane rubbed his head. "I was hired to investigate his death."

The color drained from her face. "He's dead?" She looked away and sighed. "If grandfather sent you, then you must be able to help."

Zane had rarely dealt with people from The Institute. During the war, they were considered too important to be wasted in the field. The few he had met were tight-lipped and arrogant, unlike this young woman.

"Agwen said it should be easy to get out if I were able to find you."

"That would make sense. Such a device was meant for one person, not two. It's only because we are both humans that this worked."

Zane raised a questioning eyebrow, and she responded by pointing to her head. "We live far shorter lives, and so have fewer memories. That means there's enough room for each of us."

"What would happen if there weren't?"

She scratched her head for a moment while he watched. He couldn't decide if she was pondering the question or trying to remember something.

Finally, she stopped. "At best, we might exchange memories. At worst, we would exchange parts of our personalities. But such a thing would drive us both mad."

That would make things complicated. "Can you get us out of this machine?"

She looked him in the eye. "I think so, but first we need to get out of this"—she gestured around them—"this memory field."

Zane grunted in agreement. "I don't mean to pry but you seem to have recovered quickly from this memory."

She looked back on the scene. "Yes, these seems to be more than just memories. They might contain the emotions from the past, as well. It seems you being here disturbed it."

"Ah."

Alyssa squinted at him. "Ah?"

Zane hadn't meant for the sound to slip out. "Yes, it explains some things. Do you know how to get out of here?"

She shook her head. "No, I don't. How did you escape your memory field?"

Zane looked away nervously, "It was complicated…"

"Complicated?"

"I will try to get us out, but please don't ask any questions."

She began to speak, but Zane ignored her and waited for the voice to roll in.

Look in the coffin.

"You're a bastard, you know that," Zane whispered.

Alyssa gasped. "What did you say?"

Zane walked to the coffin without saying a word. Alyssa grabbed his shoulder. "Hey, are you listening to me? Don't touch that."

He stopped and turned to Alyssa. "I need you to trust me."

"Trust you? I don't even know you."

He covered the ground between them. "I know that, but I can get us out of this memory. I can't explain it, but I know that I can."

She searched his eyes but then relaxed. "Okay."

Zane nodded and walked back to the coffin. He flipped open the lid and a white light pooled out.

Alyssa stepped up next to him. "That shouldn't be possible."

It made Zane sick, but Shadow had helped. It felt disrespectful, but Zane placed one foot into the coffin, then the other. Once more, Zane drifted through the white void surrounded by thousands of whirling memories. He turned to face Alyssa, now drifting with him through the light.

"All right," he said. "How do we get out of here?"

Alyssa extended a hand, and Zane took it. She spoke eldritch words, each syllable echoing with a power that washed over him.

Zane started to sweat. "Will this work?"

She paused. "Everything around is a construct of Fey magic, so… maybe?"

"Maybe?"

There was fear in the back of her eyes. "Fey magic is based on the Fey mind, which is completely different from ours. But the Imperial True Tongue is based on Fey magic so, again… maybe."

Sweat now dripped from her forehead as Zane noticed two large clouds of memories moving toward them.

"We're running out of time," she shouted.

"What?"

"Our memories are following us! If they touch—"

"Insanity, memory loss, bad stuff. I got it. How are you getting us out?"

"I am going to force a fail-safe. If I shake the foundation of this place, I think it will kick us out. Now shut up, I need to focus!"

She shut her eyes and started chanting the syllables of power. The world around them seemed to pulse and rock with increasing intensity. Zane closed his eyes, but even through his eyelids he could see Alyssa basking in a small sun, her hair and face illuminated in a brilliant glow.

Cold water suddenly poured over him, washing away the image. The air in his lungs was replaced with water. When he opened his eyes, Zane found himself swimming in the Dream Sphere's jelly. The orb opened and poured them onto the floor. Zane slid across the surface and hit the rack of artifacts before vomiting onto the floor.

He coughed repeatedly until he could gulp in air. Agwen helped

Alyssa recover, but no one checked on Zane. He crawled over to his jacket and pulled out his flask, then sipped on his drink and raised a toast. "No, no, I am fine." He leaned against the shelves, breathing heavily. "No need to worry about me."

Benedictus-Lasome, his eyes rimmed in red, approached Zane. "Thank you. You did far more than I thought possible. How can I repay you?"

Zane put away his flask, feeling better after the warm glow of his drink. He stood up and draped his jacket over his shoulder. "I am running out of time with the Seeker Law. You can make this investigation official, as you promised."

Benedictus-Lasome looked over to his granddaughter before turning to Zane. "You said the guards believe it was Lady Zel. If your investigation proves this, what will you do?"

"Send for the guards."

"You're willing to reject your pay?" The old archmage nodded, seemingly pleased by the answer. "The Institute will officially open a case and you will act as a consultant to our agent. Is this agreeable?"

Zane had been fortunate to just get this far and he disliked the idea of having to answer to a wizard. But, if he was lucky, this might open doors for him later.

"I can handle that."

"Good," Benedictus-Lasome said. "I have someone ready to—"

"I want to be the agent."

Benedictus-Lasome and Zane both turned to Alyssa, who was pale. Agwen had been helping her off the ground, and the sphere's fluid dripped from her to the floor as she peeled the hair from her face. "I want to work with this man."

Benedictus-Lasome started to protest, but it was clear that Alyssa wouldn't take no for an answer.

CHAPTER 8

A lyssa sat across from Benedictus-Lasome inside his office, still drying her hair with a towel. Her grandfather sat scratching the paper with his pen. "You haven't been out of The Institute in more than ten years. Not since your parents…"

"I know. But I have my reasons."

"Reasons? What reasons? You are a professor. Is it that man? What did he do to you inside that thing?"

Alyssa would be lying if she didn't admit to feeling a connection to Zane, but this, she told herself, was only due to him sharing her memories inside the sphere. "He saved me, so I owe him my life, that's true. But more importantly, someone tried to kill me."

Her grandfather looked lost. He mouthed the words before scratching his head in confusion. "Who would want to kill you?"

"I don't know, but someone was down there with me. I was pushed into that device."

"What?"

"There was a sound and I followed it to the sphere. When I got close to it, someone pushed me in."

Benedictus-Lasome's face was pale. "Who would do this?"

She could feel the blood draining from her face, matching his. "I don't know. I used some charms and words but couldn't detect anyone with me. Whoever was down there must have been able to overcome my spells."

"So, it's someone that is skilled. Could it have been Agwen or Tatius-Lasome?"

"I don't think so. Agwen didn't know I was there, and Tatius-Lasome sent me. If either wanted to get rid of me, there would have been an easier way to do it. This happened the day after Dennis died. I cannot help but feel that it is connected. I don't know how, but I plan to find out."

He shook his head. "That is still not a good reason. We have professionals that could handle this. Why do *you* need to go?"

Alyssa sighed and looked away, feeling almost embarrassed to open up. "Because I owe it to him. He saved me. I don't know if I could have gotten out of there without his help. We both know how hard it is for people outside of The Institute to work with our agents. I have seen reports. It might be easier on him if I do it."

Her grandfather's half-hearted chuckle caught Alyssa off guard. "Yes, that is true. I understand where you are coming from. If I can help, please contact me."

She smiled and stood, getting ready to leave. "If you'll excuse me, I need to clear my schedule with Tatius-Lasome."

"Unfortunately, it seems that his office is locked and inaccessible at the moment."

"That is fine then. I will go see Agwen."

"Wait one moment." He shuffled around in a drawer and pulled out a thin wand with a holster. "Take this with you."

Alyssa shook her head. She had never owned a wand before. "Don't you think you are being paranoid?"

"You are going to go look into a murder you think is related to your accident. You should take it. Just in case."

She sighed in resignation; her grandfather was right. She picked it up as she stepped out into the winding halls and changing doors until she came to Agwen's office. She knocked and waited for a response. "Please, come in."

Agwen's office was still a spectacular room to stand in. It felt as though she could catch inspiration from the pages of old Fey lords from just being so close to the books. He smiled at her. "I am happy to see you are doing well. How can I help you?"

A chair slid out for her, but she shook her head, sending the chair back to the wall. "I am going to be gone for the next few days. I was hoping to take some time off. I was told that Tatius-Lasome's office was locked, so I came to inform you."

Agwen nodded. "He asked me to look over things while he was gone."

"Gone? Gone where?"

A quick reply. "Holiday"

That wasn't like Tatius-Lasome at all, she thought, but that wasn't the point. "Then I'll ask you. Is it alright for me to be gone for the next few days?"

"Yes, of course. I assume it has to do with your tragic ordeal."

"Yes, I am going to help Detective Vrexon. Someone or something pushed me into that sphere. I think it might be connected to Dennis's death. The timing is too strange."

He started to write some notes. "Understood. I wish you the best and hope to see you in a few days. I will inform Tatius-Lasome. Do be careful, Miss Benedictus."

She gave a polite bow and stepped out of his office.

z

AS SOON AS Zane was dressed, he was ushered into Benedictus-Lasome's office once again. Inside, both Benedictus-Lasome and Alyssa sat around the desk.

Zane took the free seat next to Alyssa. "How will this work?"

Benedictus-Lasome gestured to Alyssa. "That is something you will have to take up with State Mage Alyssa Benedictus. She will be our agent in this case, as she requested." He turned to face her. "You are hereby empowered by The Institute to look into the matter of the death of Dennis Zel, State Mage Sixth Class."

Alyssa raised her right hand. "I, Alyssa Benedictus, Third Rank Mage, will seek out the truth."

She stood up and stepped out of the room. Zane tried to follow, but Benedictus-Lasome stopped him from leaving.

"I don't know what you did"—the old man pointed a finger at Zane—"but make sure she comes back safe."

Zane nodded and stepped out into the hall with Alyssa. She smiled and started walking and gestured for Zane to follow through a door, into a stairwell, and out a window before entering a classroom. The detective found the whole building a work of insanity.

Alyssa talked as they walked. "Since we are working together, will you bring me up to speed?"

Zane explained how the case had come to him, and what he had found in The Brew, including the bloody dagger and Dennis's badge. "The body is being kept in a morgue right now. I am going to see it after this."

Alyssa said. "What about the dagger?"

They passed another set of students who were climbing up the stairs below them. Zane watched them pass and shook his head. "It's Fey made and it's enchanted."

She stopped and turned around. "Fey-made and enchanted? That should be in our care. How did it end up with you?"

Zane shrugged. "I don't know, but I dropped it off with a Fey smith. He told me he would look into it."

She looked deep in thought for a moment before speaking. "Such a thing is worth a lot to The Institute, but what about the Ironbark family?"

Zane stared at her, confused. "Ironbark family?"

"They recommended Dennis to take the examination. They should have been informed about the outcome of the test. If you want, we can go look at his file. It should have more information on them."

The existence of a new lead made Zane relax a little. "That would be perfect."

She nodded and lead the way. As they continued through the maze, another question struck Zane.

"Are the Ironbarks related to Vana?"

"I don't know who that is. Is she related to Dennis?"

"She is—was—his wife."

Zane had forgotten Alyssa had not met Lady Zel. He made a mental note to ask Vana about it later.

"Are recommendations needed?" Zane asked. "Can anyone apply to be a state mage?"

Alyssa thought about it for a moment. "Yes and no. Anyone can apply, but we can and do deny applicants. Many self-styled mages are partially, if not fully, insane. To avoid that, we like to have wizards recommended to us by respected groups or people."

The Ironbarks must be part of the upper class. He had stopped in thought until a group of students pooled behind them, waiting for Alyssa and him to move. Zane apologized and followed her into a large dorm room. Students entered and exited through doors that filled the walls. At the center of the room was a large circular desk with clerks sitting behind it. Zane followed Alyssa closely as she stepped up to the desk and spoke with a small woman.

"Could you please pull up the paperwork on a new State Mage, Dennis Zel?" Alyssa asked.

"One moment."

The woman stepped to the center column that Zane realized was a large file cabinet. A few moments later, the clerk came back with two papers. "I am sorry, but this is the only information I have about Dennis Zel. I see nothing on him being a state mage."

Alyssa frowned and looked over the two pages. Zane leaned close and did the same. Very little information was written, and the papers said Dennis hadn't passed his exam. A note at the bottom of the page read *The Ironbark family has been notified*.

Alyssa looked up from the papers, confused. "This information is wrong. I was there when Dennis was given his badge."

The clerk shrugged her shoulders. "I am sorry ma'am. All I know is what's on these pages."

Zane looked around at all the clerks. "Is it possible for us to speak to the person who filed this?"

The clerk thought for a moment, nodded, and stepped away. Alyssa set the papers down. "This doesn't make any sense. Some of this information is even different from the file I saw just a few days ago."

"Such as?"

"They dropped his address, as if they didn't want anyone to contact him. The only address listed is for the Ironbarks."

"Can you write down their address for us?"

She nodded and made a note of the Ironbark address. The clerk came back with a young man with a long nose who bowed his head. "Hello, I am Derk. I filed Dennis's paperwork. Is there a problem?"

Alyssa pointed to the documents. "Can you explain these?"

Derk examined the pages. "There is not much to explain. I was working that night. He came here after the exam, and I told him that he had failed. He was sad and left."

Zane and Alyssa looked at each other in confusion. She turned back to Derk. "He passed the exam. I held the documents in my hand the other night. Not only that, but he was also given a position in the Fey department."

Derk started to chuckle. "That is impossible ma'am. Like I said, I filed the documents early yesterday..." He stopped mid-sentence, staring slacked jawed at the desk. He blinked a few times as if he was collecting himself. "No, that isn't right. I filed them on the night of the exam."

Derk picked up the papers and looked them over, one hand holding his head. "I don't remember this. No... I, I remember him passing. Also"—he staggered for a moment, then waved for the two to lean close—"Mr. Zel passed the exam but didn't qualify for any department, which is weird. I've never seen that." Derk began to whisper. "I felt bad for him, and when he passed me a bank note to get him into one... Well, I set him up with the Fey department."

"Why that department?" Alyssa asked.

Derk opened his mouth and immediately closed it, holding his head. "I don't remember. I am sorry, but I think I will be taking the rest of the day off." He started to turn away but stopped. "Please don't tell anyone about the bribe."

Then he left, leaving Zane and Alyssa dumbfounded.

"That was strange," Zane said. "Do you understand what just happened?"

"No. Magic that affects the mind is rare, and illegal, besides being a complicated field. It could just as easily be that the young man is taking something that has impaired his mind. Or he's lying."

Zane nodded and made a mental note about the conversation. "At least we got the Ironbark address. Was there any other information you gleaned from all of that?"

She shook her head. "Shall we go?"

He nodded and the two of them stepped out of a door and into a hall. From there, Alyssa lead them through the bizarre paths. Before he realized it, they were outside. He turned back to look at the large metal gates that he had entered through, which were still wide open. "How...?"

"I'd rather not go into detail right now. We have a case."

Zane was starting to think that this was going to be a long day.

Sunlight felt nice on his skin. He had missed it since he moved to Alviun and enjoyed the small pleasure before they returned to the pile of work to be done. "Alyssa, I need to stop by the shop. I had hoped to be there sooner but..."

She nodded. "I understand. It will give me a chance to inspect the scene and meet Vana Zel."

They walked to the edge of the courtyard, where the bright sunlight abruptly ended in a wall of smog. Alyssa wore neither cloak nor hat but stepped right into the gloomy weather. Zane shook his head at the woman who was about to be covered in ash and mud, something generally reserved for the poorest of people who could not afford protection from the skyborne filth.

As they walked down the street, however, he could not find a single hint of soot on her face or clothes. The ash seemed to swerve away from Alyssa on its descent. The raven-haired woman didn't speak or even look at Zane, but her face betrayed her emotions. She acted like she wanted to be home.

He didn't blame her.

They turned onto Potion Lane, its stained bricks overflowing with new colors. It was in full swing. Soldiers, adventures, and servants all crowded the street, collecting potions of various powers and effects. Alyssa's face showed discomfort at being surrounded by so many people. The door of The Wizard's Brew was still missing, but the inside had been cleared of debris.

Fex met them at the door. "Hello Zane." He looked up at Alyssa and asked with suspicion. "Who is she?"

Alyssa introduced herself in gnomish. Fex could not hide the surprise on his face, but he bowed and responded in kind. The two passed words in whispered hushes, the syllables sounding soft and fluid. The pair seemed to have forgotten Zane entirely until he coughed awkwardly.

"This is Alyssa Benedictus—"

"She prefers Alyssa. Her grandfather is Benedictus-Lasome."

Zane raised an eyebrow to Alyssa. "Yes, well how—"

"Am I? I'm fine." Fex's face looked grim, lines on his face pulled tight, bags under his eyes full. "Have you talked to my uncle yet?"

Zane shook his head. "No, I haven't. I've been—"

"Busy looking into the loan, I know." The gnome seemed angry. "But isn't checking the victim a basic part of being a detective?"

"It can be, but I had some other leads that I wanted to follow first, so I—"

"Came here? That makes no sense."

Zane took a steadying breath and leaned heavily on his cane. "I am here to check on everyone. Also, I need directions to your uncle's morgue."

The gnome seemed surprised, but he nodded his head and went over the directions twice. Zane repeated them to him and said goodbye. Alyssa made certain to say goodbye in the gnomish language before they both turned to Potion Lane. She was careful not to step in any of the liquid that poured out of the many shops. "How can people stand this? Don't they know that the mixture of these potions can be toxic?"

Zane shrugged. "I don't know. I don't think they care. All that matters to these shops is money and disposing of bad batches this way saves time. I can't blame them. Times are tough, and the city said they couldn't pour it into the sewer system directly."

"But officials are okay with it mixing in the street before it pours into the sewers on its own?"

Zane shrugged again as Alyssa continued to dodge the rouge liquid. In the spaces between the shops stood several hunched and lonely-looking people. Their clothes were rugged, stained, and their eyes focused on the dirty liquid in the gutter. She forced herself not to look at the addicts.

Fex's directions were easy to follow. The morgue was a short building with a flat roof. Unlike all the nearby buildings, it did not have a chimney. The door was locked, so Zane knocked and waited until a metal plate slid open. He bent down to meet the gnome's eyes.

"What do you want?"

Zane handed a letter through the slit. "I want to have a look at Dennis Zel's body."

The gnome took the letter through the opening. Zane could hear him opening the letter. It was a moment before the gnome spoke. "I am Dex. My nephew told me you would be coming, detective. Is she with you?"

Dex's eyes moved to Alyssa, who leaned down and spoke to him in gnomish. The metal plate slid shut, and the door opened. Dex was bald with a wrinkled face. His white apron and gloves were stained in red and brown. A horrible smell drifted from inside the building.

"You will want these." The older gnome handed them each a heavily perfumed mask. Zane placed one on his face and handed the other to Alyssa.

Her face was already pale. "Do we really need to do this?"

Zane was sympathetic, remembering the first time he watched a dissection. "Yes, but if you want, you can wait out here."

Alyssa looked up and down the street nervously. "No, I'll go." She took the mask and held it tight to her face.

The ground floor was a single large room with wide halls that lead to a pulley elevator, which they took down to the basement. Zane marveled at the device, and Dex chuckled at the obvious fascination on Zane's face. "It was expensive, but worth making it easier to move bodies. The basement temperature helps keep them preserved until the Medical Guild comes to pick them up."

"Do they do business with you often?"

Dex nodded. "I even had to deny a rather large amount for Dennis's body. I would have sold it if it weren't for my nephew."

The selling of bodies to the Medical Guild wasn't surprising. Many schools needed cadavers. It felt like a lifetime ago, but Zane had worked on such bodies as a medical student before the war.

Dex looked up at Zane. "They wanted to buy the body because it's in decent condition, with no sign of tumors like many of the ones found near Potion Lane."

The smell was far worse down in the basement. Alyssa held the mask closer, but Zane could see the edges of her face turning green.

Dex pointed to a bucket in the corner. "If you're going to throw up, do it over there."

Zane neither watched as she went to the corner nor made a comment when he heard her expel the contents of her stomach. Instead, he spoke to Dex.

"I never introduced myself. My name is—"

"Zane. I know." The gnome looked at his gloves. "I would shake your hand, but it wouldn't be clean."

Dex gestured for him to follow through the rows of bodies. Most were fresh, but some were bloated, and many had the large tumors Dex had spoken of around their stomach and throats. The memory of the thief from several days before chilled Zane.

The gas lamps casted long, thick shadows, one of which pulled away from the wall. Two red eyes shimmered in the blackness. *How does your death look to you?*

Zane tried to ignore it, but he, too, could see himself years from now, his throat so engorged that he could not eat or drink, his stomach so painfully large that he couldn't walk. One day, he would die a painful death in a gutter with no one around him.

Shadow laughed. *Maybe it's begun already.*

Zane turned away from the tumor-riddled bodies as Dex stopped in front of him. Dennis laid there on a table, his clothes stripped away. A deep knife wound had been opened in his chest, the veins around it black. The man who had helped him all those years ago was gone. The view sickened Zane much more than even the image of the tumors. His self-pity was replaced with heartbreak for Dennis.

Alyssa finally rejoined them, her sickly face matching the corpses in the room. She held the perfumed mask tight to her face and whispered to Zane. "How can you stand this?"

Zane was pulled from his thoughts and realized that he was no longer covering his face with the mask. He attempted a lighthearted shrug. "I am used to the smell."

Memories of the war came to him in that dim room. The stench of the dead was always strong, and it had long since ceased to disturb him. An awkwardness lingered in the air, which Dex attempted to break with a cough. "So, what are you looking for?"

Zane sighed. "Anything that might help me."

The old gnome gestured for him to continue. Zane pointed at the gaping wound on the body. "What can you tell me about this?"

"A dagger looks to be what killed him."

"Yes, but I noticed some unusual burn marks around the dagger on the floor. The spot where Dennis's blood had pooled was also burned." Zane pointed to the veins. "Now look at these. I am wondering if the blade was coated with something."

Dex rubbed his face with his arm. "That is a possibility."

Zane continued to examine the body and noticed a cut on the left hand that leaked a green liquid. He inspected the other hand and saw scrapes on the right knuckles. Zane recognized those marks from his own hands after a fist fight. Someone might have a black eye. He turned back to the liquid seeping from the left hand and reached out to touch it, but Dex stopped him.

The gnome looked up at him. "You surprise me. It took me a full day to notice that stuff coming out of him. But whatever that stuff is will burn you."

Alyssa spoke through her mask. "Could it be some form of acid? Maybe a byproduct of potion abuse?"

Dex shook his head. "I have seen it all when it comes to potion addicts, but this is different. It burned the skin around the wound and entered the bloodstream. It seared anything his blood came in contact with. If he had survived the stabbing, that stuff would have done him in."

Shadow slithered from one dark corner to another to get a closer look. From the new angle, the red eyes appeared to be watching the body. The thought sent a shiver through Zane's body. It was easier to ignore Shadow's comment when it—he?—was dismissed as a part of Zane's damaged mind.

Shadow sounded almost amused. *I have seen this before. It is a poison made from mushrooms of the Eastern Forests. I think it's called Last Death.*

Zane looked up from Dennis's body toward Shadow. "How would you know?"

The glowing eyes moved in a motion that Zane took as a shrug. *It was a favorite of my peers when it came to torture. Injecting a small amount will cause a burning sensation all over the body. But too much and the person will have holes burned through its flesh before bleeding out.*

A knot formed in Zane's stomach, and memories of his dark cell in the war flooded in. He wanted to tear the shadow limb from limb.

"Hey, are you okay?" Zane felt Alyssa's hand on his shoulder. "You were talking to yourself."

His left hand held a white-knuckled grip on his cane, and both Alyssa and Dex looked concerned. Zane coughed and smoothed out the wrinkles in his vest. "Yes, I am okay. I was just thinking that it's a poison."

Dex frowned and scratched his head "Poison? How would you know?"

"I was"—Zane looked to the body, to the gnome, to Alyssa, and then at Shadow—"I was in the war. Let us just say I have heard of it."

Dex pulled a glove off and stroked his cheek. "I have heard some nasty things were used in the Ghoul War."

"Yes. This stuff was used in small doses to torture people, to burn them from the inside out. I think it was called Last Death."

Alyssa gagged while holding her mask tight to her face. "That's horrible."

The gnome went to a table and picked up some tools. "Aye, it is, and there is a way to test this theory."

Zane turned to Alyssa. "You may wish to stand elsewhere."

"You can't mean…"

"Yes." Zane laid his cane against the wall, handed his jacket to Alyssa, and rolled up his sleeves before looking to Dex. "Before the war, I was a medical student. Can I assist you?"

Dex handed a pair of gloves to Zane. "I won't turn down help."

Alyssa walked away, and Zane heard her throw up again. He hoped his jacket would stay clean as he and Dex cut through flesh and clipped bones.

Dex pulled his gloves off and picked up his board with his notes. "Are you okay with me taking some medical notes?"

"Go ahead. Just tell me what you need."

Zane stared down into Dennis's chest cavity. Zane and Dex had opened up his former friend's torso. An hour after they'd started, the heart was gone, along with the edges of the neighboring organs. They all looked burned. Even the inside of the ribs had suffered.

Dex wrote on his notes. "It looks like what you said was right." The gnome tapped the board with his pen. "I've never seen anything like this. Where does stuff like this come from?"

Zane cursed Shadow silently before answering Dex. "I heard it came from forests of the Eastern Territories. From some type of fungus."

"You sure?" Alyssa asked from behind them. "I still think it could be some type of acid."

She was sitting in a chair inside the elevator, putting as much distance between her and the body as she could, her face still pale.

"It's a hunch," Zane said. "But if you would like, I'm sure we can test it."

She looked unconvinced. Dex took a sample and placed it in a glass beaker.

Zane handed the gloves back to Dex. "Thank you for holding the body."

The gnome set his papers down. "It was for my nephew. This wizard took good care of him, much better than most humans would." He smiled and extended his hand to Zane. "Also, I can use this information to publish a paper at the medical schools."

Zane shook his hand, then joined Alyssa in the elevator and prepared to head up. Dex rushed over to catch them. "I must confess, I hope Vana Zel is guilty of this murder."

Alyssa's surprised gaze wandered to Zane as the gnome spoke. "Why?"

Dex looked away and sighed. "It would be for the best for my nephew. If she is guilty, there's a good chance he would inherit the shop. I have checked the law and the records. The Wizard's Brew would legally pass to him upon her conviction. All the same, I wish you well in your investigation."

Z

ALYSSA'S MOUTH WAS dry and her stomach empty after vomiting in the morgue. The smell of death clung to her even after leaving the building. She glanced at Zane, who seemed unfazed even after sticking his hands inside someone he obviously cared for. *Is this what it takes to be a detective?* she wondered.

Zane broke her train of thought. "Are you okay?"

She needed to be okay, regardless of how she actually felt. "Yeah. I have never been in a morgue or seen a dissection. Do you normally do this during an investigation?"

"No, my jobs are normally catching thieves or runaways. Sometimes I spy on cheating spouses." Zane straightened his clothes. "But I guess I am accustomed to bodies. I attended medical school for a short while before and after the war."

Though she'd had her share of traumatic experiences, Alyssa's life had been mostly sheltered. "But still, he was a friend, you know? How could—"

"I have buried, burned, and put down more friends than I would like to count." Zane's expression was dark as he cut her off.

"Put down?"

Zane looked up at the cloudy sky as if searching for answers. "During the war, some of the undead carried an infection. If they bit you then you would, well, you would join their side."

She brought a hand to her mouth. "That's horrible."

Zane waved his hand to dismiss the idea. "I don't need any sympathy, but thank you."

Embarrassment rose to her cheeks as she asked her next question. "Will all this help me find whoever tried to kill me?"

Zane took his time to answer as they walked. "It should, if they are connected. But we need to gather more information."

This was not the answer Alyssa had expected. "What type of information?"

He laughed weakly. "Any and all."

"That seems strange. Don't you need some kind of theory first?"

Zane shook his head. "Once you have a theory, you want to prove that theory. You begin to interpret all your evidence differently to make it fit."

"That makes sense. How do you approach it, then?"

"I collect as much information as I can, see where it leads, then make a decision."

It seemed so simple, and yet... not. Slight regret over volunteering for the investigation sat in Alyssa's empty stomach, but she was already involved. "I can test the blood, to verify your theory on the poison."

"That's a great idea."

He stopped on the sidewalk, reached into his pocket, and pulled out a small clump of hair. *No*, she thought. *It's fur.*

"Can you test this?" Zane handed it to her. "I found it in the shop by the giant claw marks."

"Claw marks?"

He scratched his head. "At the scene, there was a giant claw mark in the wall, and this fur was laying on the ground next to it."

"Why didn't you look into that?"

"Dennis died from a dagger wound."

Alyssa opened her mouth to speak but decided against it. Instead, she shook her head.

What have I gotten myself into?

CHAPTER 9

Zane and Alyssa arrived at the doorway of The Wizard's Brew, where a new door had finally been fitted into place. From the street, they could hear arguing from inside.

"I was nothing but supportive," a deep male voice shouted. "He failed."

Vana Zel's voice was clear and unflinching. "He passed and he was murdered—"

"A murder that you're suspected of. The guards will be by later today—"

"How would you know that?" Vana asked. "Detective Vrexon has invoked the Seeker Law. They can't come until tomorrow."

"They're coming, and it doesn't matter how I know. What's important is that I have made bribes at every major gate. We can be out of the city in an hour. In two, we will be long gone."

"Detective Vrexon will lead me to the murderer."

"He is a fraud."

Zane had heard enough and opened the door. Vana was wearing her funeral clothes and veil, quite different from what she'd been wearing that morning. The man stood a head taller than everyone in the room, wearing a cloak of bear fur, the animal's head made into a hood. His bare arms bulged like logs and were covered in swirling blue tattoos that reached from his wrist to his face.

"This is a private conversation." He glared menacingly at Zane. "Leave!"

"I am Detective Zane Vrexon. And I am not a fraud."

"I said—"

"What have you found?" Vana asked.

"Dennis had formed connections with the goblin mob."

The bear snapped at Vana. "Which probably killed him. All the more reason to leave."

Vana waited for the giant to finish before turning to Zane. "Mr. Vrexon, please continue."

Zane could see the burning anger in the large man's eyes. "The mob considered him a friend. Dennis paid off his loan sometime before passing the exam and being hired by The Institute."

The big man made a dismissive gesture with one of his large arms. "More talk of passing the exam, but where is the proof? Vana, doesn't it matter that you're being targeted?"

Alyssa entered the conversation with a bow. "I am Alyssa Benedictus, a member of the Institute of Sorcery and Science. I have been sent to investigate the death of Dennis Zel. I apologize, but I couldn't help but overhear your conversation. If you know when the guards are coming by, I can give them the official paperwork."

The large man went pale, like a cold corpse. He also seemed nervous. "I must still insist that we take you to safety, sister."

Vana let out a low growl, a bestial sound that sent a chill down Zane's spine. His hand instinctively drifted to his wand.

Lady Zel's brother took a full step away. "I will be back to check on you."

He marched out the door, forcing Zane and Alyssa to move to avoid being bowled over.

"Good work, Mr. Vrexon," Vana said after he was gone. "What else have you discovered?"

Zane sat on a barrel by the door. It felt good to take the weight off his bad leg. "This morning I decided to check Dennis's status at The Institute. They didn't know that he had died."

"Any idea about who might have done this?" Vana asked.

"All I have is that dagger. I know it is Fey-made. I have an expert looking into it." Zane scratched his head. "But the autopsy..."

He glanced to Vana and waited a moment, trying to gauge her reaction. But reading Vana was like trying to interpret hieroglyphics on a brick wall, so Zane continued. "The autopsy showed that Dennis died from a single dagger wound. However, the dagger was coated with a poison possibly called the Last Death."

Alyssa stood in the corner, her eyes searching for a seat. "Zane believes it was a poison, but it could have easily been a type of acid. I am taking a sample to the Institute to have it analyzed. We have scholars of toxicology, so we should be able to deduce what it is."

Vana went stiff at the name of the poison. But she recovered, approached Alyssa, and unfolded her arms into a small hug. "Thank you for coming."

She let go of the confused Alyssa and extended a hand to Zane, who took it and smiled politely. "Thank you."

Zane winced when her hand tightened around his. Vana's grip was strong. Far stronger than her frame would suggest. Unbelievably strong. He feared she would crush his hand before she relaxed hers and retracted it with an apology.

She started for the back room but stopped at the doorway and turned. "I would like to ask you both to stay awhile, at least until the guards arrive." She shifted her focus to Alyssa. "I will have a stool brought out for you ma'am."

Zane rubbed his hand, trying to stimulate blood flow. "Of course. By the way, how was your walk this morning?"

"My walk?"

Zane could feel the nerves of his hand spark back to life. "This morning I saw you on a walk. Near my office, just a couple of streets over. You seemed... unusual."

"How so?"

He pointed to his forehead as he closed the distance between them.

"Your veil was pulled up."

Vana leaned in close as though she was about to whisper something, but Zane was shocked when she started smelling him. It was like a bloodhound hunting for scent.

"Today has been long," she said, still sniffing Zane. "Could you remind me exactly where this was? I'm afraid it's easy to get lost near your office."

He felt uncomfortable and took a step back. "I wasn't looking at the street signs."

"I see. Sorry to bother you this morning with my unusual appearance."

Vana called for Fex and asked him to make drinks for everyone. A stool was also brought out and Alyssa took a seat in another corner of the room. Zane adjusted his clothes, taking time to smooth out all the wrinkles, real and imaginary. Vana had set his nerves on edge, reminding him of the time he faced a pack of undead hounds in the Ghoul War. Even now, a primal urge wanted him to flee somewhere high and far away from the beasts.

Zane's hands started shaking and his throat tightened. The watered-down healing potion had worn off more quickly than he'd expected. He reached for his flask and swished it around. What little remained would not give him the sweet release that he craved.

Zane watched as Alyssa struggled to find a comfortable spot on her stool. She pulled a slim book from her pocket and started to read. Zane closed his eyes and tried to push the pain from his mind.

Fex gently tapped on his shoulder. "Here is some tea. Was the morgue any help?"

Zane took the cup and blew on it. "Yes. Your uncle is extremely professional."

"Good."

The gnome handed Alyssa her cup and the two exchanged some words in gnomish. Zane stared down at his tea until the two were done.

"Fex, do you know much about Lady Zel's brother?"

The gnome looked toward the back of the shop before leaning in. "I have seen him a few times." He took a moment to think before answering. "He started to come by a lot after Dennis decided to take the exam."

"Can he be trusted?"

Fex's eyes narrowed and, for the first time, Zane could feel a distance between them. "Can any human be trusted?"

The gnome stepped into the back room while Zane sipped on his tea, which was warm with a hint of honey. He enjoyed the taste as he leaned back again, watching the world outside through the window and trying to take his mind off his aching arm and leg. Lady Zel returned with a cup and offered it to Zane, but he smiled and held up the tea he'd already been served.

"Please drink this," Vana said. "It will help you."

She must have seen how tired and sore he was. Zane didn't want to drink anything other than the tea in his hands, but he didn't want to be rude, either. Zane took the glass and stared at his reflection before drinking it. With that first sip, he could feel a faint warmth wash over his body.

He drank the rest in one gulp.

The pain lost its edge, and the knots in his muscles began loosening. Zane looked to her face, hidden behind the veil, and felt a sudden flash of shame. He calmed himself with the idea that this shouldn't be a surprise. Many people treated old injuries with potion work.

Zane handed back the cup. Vana began to turn away, but he stopped her and pulled out his flask. "Could I ask you to fill this up for me?"

Vana nodded and took it into the back. He met Alyssa's questioning eyes and shrugged. "It's good water."

Vana returned with the flask, then went to work in the back. Zane gestured his thanks. He patted the potion, now deep in his pocket, and closed his eyes. As a veteran of battle, he knew the value of good rest.

Zane dreamed of a dark crypt, and the court of the strange king. From the corner, Shadow brought one dark hand to his face to hush him. The ground gave way and he fell through darkness before landing in an open grave. Looking down were two Vanas, one masked, one unmasked. He rolled rover to gather himself and found that he was looking into the cold, pale face of his friend, Dennis.

Alyssa shook Zane awake and tried to pull him to his feet. "Wake up! The guards are almost here."

He rubbed his eyes and stretched his back. Six guards, each dressed in black cloaks hemmed with red, arrived and opened the door without knocking. The commotion drew Vana from the back.

The guard in front had a polished helmet with a plume of horsehair and a mustache that wrapped around to his sideburns. It was the lieutenant he'd spoken with before.

"Vana Zel, we are here to arrest you for the murder of Dennis Zel," the lieutenant said. "Come with us. Now."

Zane stepped in front of Vana and raised a hand to stop him, but another guard removed a wand from under his cloak and held it rigid at his side. "Stand down, or we will beat you down."

Alyssa pulled a letter and a badge similar to Dennis's. She extended the letter to the lieutenant. "Excuse me, sir. This matter is being looked into by The Institute of Sorcery and Science."

The guard looked at her badge with disgust. "We are here to apprehend a dangerous criminal. If you keep trying to interrupt us, we will be forced—"

He stopped speaking as Alyssa allowed the letter to unfold under its own weight. The sigils of The Institution burned with an arcane light that filled the room. "As I said, The Institute has taken an interest."

The guard closed one eye at the light and took hold of the letter with his free hand. Annoyance washed over his face as he read it. "Why? This is a murder of some alchemist."

Alyssa nodded. "We have a history of looking into the murders of our members."

The lieutenant looked up from the paper in surprise. "What? That third-rate alchemist was a state mage?" He looked over to Zane, and his grip on the wand tightened. "What about him?"

Zane caught a hint of mischief in Alyssa's eyes as she responded. "He is acting as my assistant in an official capacity."

The guard folded up the letter and pointed it at Zane. "You're going to use this meddlesome fool?"

"Yes."

Dane shoved the letter into his belt. "I will be keeping this."

She bowed politely. "I have copies."

"When the disgraced Lady Zel is found guilty, let us know." He slammed his wand back into its holster. "We will come to collect her."

Zane smirked. "I will let you know whatever truth we find."

The lieutenant spat on the floor before storming out of the shop. The five other guards followed him back into the gloomy streets. Alyssa breathed out and fell back on her stool, droplets of sweat sticking to her face. "That was scary. I thought they were going to shoot me for a moment."

"You almost buried the lead," Zane snickered. "But you did a good job,"

He called to Fex, who came running from the back. "Could you let Vana know that the guards should leave her alone for now? Also tell her we are leaving, please."

Fex nodded, but for a moment the gnome looked disappointed.

Zane turned to Alyssa. "Whenever you're ready."

She stood. "Where are we going?"

"To see a smith about a dagger."

⟋⟍‾‾

FEX WAVED GOODBYE to Zane and Alyssa before locking the front door. The carpenters had done a good job. He had paid extra to get it reinforced this time. The gnome was almost interested to see if anything could break it, but Fex sincerely hoped it wouldn't happen again.

Unlike the front entry, the door to the alleyway was open after Vana stepped out. Fex pulled up a chair to the exit and waited. Like when her brother, Evan, had left, Fex had slipped out the back and paid a kid to follow his late master's wife. The urchins were only as good as the money that he'd handed them. Now he waited for one of them to return. Fex hadn't decided what to do yet, but perhaps he would follow them himself once he knew where to go.

Fex bristled as he remembered the first time Evan had come by the shop to convince Vana to leave with him, back to the old country. The big man seemed to ignore Fex, as if he was a piece of furniture. He referred to Fex as *Vana's gnome*, like he wasn't worthy of a name. If he were eight feet taller and two hundred pounds heavier, he would have shown Evan a thing or two.

Fex pushed the fantasy aside as one dirty urchin turned down the alley and ran to him. The boy's hair was matted and covered in an ash paste, its color lost in the filth. His clothes were worn and stained by ash and smog. Fex waited for the kid to catch his breath before asking what he'd seen.

"Well, sir, I saw the big man with the blue tattoos walk to the guard post. I watched him through the front window, I did. He sat a stack of bank notes on the desk, then the lieutenant smiled and carried them off. Words were spoken but I couldn't hear them."

Fex waved the boy on. "That is okay. Where did he go next?"

"He marched out down the street. He didn't care about his nice clothes being ruined by the ash or smog. I followed him for blocks, then he walked into a bar, he did. I tried to go inside, but I was kicked out, so I watched for a while. Other people went in, rich and poor."

Fex shrugged. "So what? Is that worthy of note?"

The boy smiled and extended a filthy hand. "There is more. But I need to be paid."

Fex smirked and handed over the agreed upon coin. "Now, what happened?"

The boy pretended to count the money before putting it away. "I noticed them people all had swirling tattoos. Blue, like on the big guy."

Good observation, Fex thought. The tattoos were a tradition from Vana's ancestral home. It had been explained to him that the shape of the swirls told the family history, marking one clan from another. Fex had always known Vana and Evan to have those tattoos.

Saints, what should I do? "Where can I find this bar?"

The urchin gave Fex directions to the bar. The place sounded run down. Fex waved the boy off. "If I have another job for you, I will find you."

The boy smiled and ran away with his newfound wealth. Fex sat for a moment, scanning the alley while waiting for the second boy. He shut the door after a few minutes and was about to leave when he heard a knock.

Fex found the second boy gasping for air, so he waited until the kid had regained his breath. "Where did Vana go?"

The boy smiled as he broke into his story. "The lady? She went down to Merchants Lane and Trader Avenue."

"What did she do?"

The boy shrugged. "Nothing. She just walked around. For blocks. Made me nervous 'cause I couldn't see her face. So, I, being smart, ran up close to her. No one notices kids like me." The boy was pointing at his nose, just above a grin of accomplishment. "She was sniffing the air."

It was strange and Fex didn't know what to make of it. Then he remembered Zane's address. The detective had mentioned that he had seen Vana that morning. *She's looking for the double*! Fex knew it was important information, but it didn't tell him if Vana was working with Dennis's murderer or not.

The boy was still staring at Fex, now with an opened hand. Fex sighed and paid the boy, who took off without a moment's notice. The gnome made his decision. He was going to follow Evan.

Fex locked up the workshop and started down the alleyway. If his legs had been longer, he would have kicked himself. An old gnome proverb came to mind: Chase two rabbits and you go home hungry. The path to the bar was simple and straightforward. Fex kept to it, until he arrived at a pub with a filthy sign above the door that read *Foolish Noble*. Fex couldn't make out the picture, only the words below it. He opened the door and was greeted by a rolling wall of smoke. All who lived in Alviun were used to smoke, but in the Foolish Noble it seemed to have replaced the air. The thick cloud left much of the room obscured.

Fex's height had often been a problem, but it was an advantage in the Noble because, while others navigated through it, Fex walked under the nearly opaque smoke. To a gnome, the inside of the shop was nearly identical to the outside, the only difference being that the humans and their tobacco acted as the chimneys.

Fex scanned the room, and even with the overhanging ceiling of smoke, he located the bar. He yelled up through the cloud. "Is there a meeting here today?"

The bartender called back. "Aye, several in fact. Which one are ya with?"

Fex wasn't sure what to say but decided to be direct. "I am with Evan."

"Evan?"

"Big guy with fur and tattoos."

"Oh yeah, him. They are in the basement. And make sure to tell them to clean up after themselves. I get enough questions."

"Thank you."

Fex was happy for the wall of smoke; no one questioned who he was. The stairs led to a single hallway. The door at the far end was wide open and the smoke continued to float well above him. Despite the noise from above, all sound in the basement was drowned out by a drumming echo from the room. The walls seemed to vibrate.

The gnome felt an overwhelming sense of primal force emanating from the room, but he forced himself forward. He needed to know. The room past the door was huge, its edges lined with boxes. At least ten people were cloaked in animal hides, their faces coated in paint of varying colors. They chanted ritualistically in a language Fex couldn't understand. He wanted to freeze on the spot, but a mixture of fear and curiosity pushed him onward to the large stacks of crates. Fex scrambled up one of them until he looked down on the group of people. As he gathered himself in a crouch on the highest crate he could reach, Fex looked back in time to see one of them close the door to the basement.

A cold chill ran down his spine.

From his vantage point, Fex could see a dozen men standing around a large brazier that burned with a ghoulish fire. He noticed for the first time that four wooden pillars stood at the corners of the room. The twelve men gathered at the edge of the light, then Evan emerged from the shadows, wrapped in a robe of wolf fur.

He carried two fistfuls of colored powder and stretched his head skyward. "We brothers have gathered here. But why?"

"To reclaim our inheritance," the others shouted.

"Yes! Our inheritance! Long has it been denied to us. Our ancestors lived as instructed by the spirits."

With a gentle toss, Evan released one fistful of powder into the fire, which grew and turned green. Smoke rolled out of the brazier and spread to cover the entire floor. Evan ignored it and pointed with his free hand to the pillars. "The spirits blessed us with strength, but we turned our backs on them. The Moon's Chosen was not there to protect us when the empire came knocking. But the Moon's Chosen are here, and we shall follow them into battle!" He tossed the other handful of powder into the fire. The smoke turned yellow, and the air had a smell of nature. "Tonight, we will join the ancestors!"

Fex's head felt light as the smoke poured out. The room began to spin, and he lowered himself onto the crate. His vision blurred, and the last thing he saw was shadows dancing across the walls.

CHAPTER 10

"How long had I been asleep before the guards arrived?"

"About four bells."

Zane looked up at the rolling clouds as he and Alyssa entered the Fey district. Memories of the sun in the countryside, where the time of day could be determined by its position in the sky, flooded his mind. Zane felt uncomfortable as he walked the Fey district. Many of the people who lived here gave him a strange look as they passed by. He ignored them. After stepping into Jweal's shop, the young boy from before recognized Zane and directed him to the back patio.

Jweal sat at a table, the dagger resting in front of him. Zane and Alyssa took seats across from him.

"Hello, again Jweal. Have you learned anything about the dagger?"

"Yes, but only about the symbolism of the enchantment. Not a thing on who made it." He tilted his head to Alyssa. "Do you trust this woman?"

Zane nodded. Alyssa stood, bowed her head, and spoke in an almost musical language. The smith smiled and returned the gesture. They both sat, and Zane looked back and forth between them. "What language was that?"

Alyssa beamed with pride. "It's a variant of the Fey tongue, mostly used by traders and diplomats."

Jweal smiled. "She is well-cultured. Do others of The Institute speak so well?"

She shook her head. "No, I am somewhat specialized."

Zane adjusted his clothes uncomfortably. "Now, what about the symbolism?"

Jweal covered the dagger with a cloth. "It's bad luck to discuss a blade while it's out in the open." The smith brushed his hair back. "It is forged from Fairy ore. I have only seen this metal twice in my life. It's light and durable and was made to be imbued with magic." He traced the edge of the dagger under the cloth. "The shape of the blade is symbolic. It tells us that it was made for bloodletting. To cut the ties of bonds. This usually means ending a life." He tapped the handle "The wrapping around the handle also holds meaning. This weapon is meant to be used out of sight of others."

Zane had dealt with a few enchantments during his time in the military, but most of those were practical, such as lighting an area, starting fires, and adjusting temperature. All of the objects were covered in runes with simple ways to activate them. "So, it's an enchanted dagger meant to kill in secret, but how? What does it do?"

"Fey enchantments are a bit different, but I can't rightly explain how they work. I can explain several rituals that create enchantments. I know how to do it, not how it works."

Zane got to the point. "So this dagger was specifically crafted for murder. Or, more accurately, assassination. This makes it sound like a Fey killed Dennis."

Jweal spat on the floor and cleared his throat. "I know." He sighed and rubbed his face as he gathered himself. "I ask you, sir, not to bring this to the authorities. We are already a burdened people. They would use this as an excuse to add to it."

Zane's mouth hung open, stunned, but Alyssa spoke up.

"No evidence will be given for the purpose of presenting your community in a poor light. We only want the truth—"

She continued in the musical language from before. The smith argued with her in the same tongue.

The two went back and forth before Jweal admitted defeat with a sigh. "I understand. As I've said, this dagger was specifically designed for murder. There are other markings, but I don't know anything about the tribes or clans who use them."

Zane cursed to himself. It was an answer, but it only gave him more questions. The dagger was obviously the tool of an assassin, but why would someone want to have Dennis killed? And where did Fey fit in? "Thank you for your help and your time, but I must ask, do you know anyone who could have more information about these enchantments?"

The smith nodded and pulled a letter from his pocket. "I figured you would want to know more. This is a letter of introduction to Khmer. Even with this, it might be difficult for you to get an audience with him, but you can try. He is an elder of the local community, and no one knows more than him. You can find his home in a library just off the square, in an abandoned storefront."

Zane reached out for the letter, but Alyssa grabbed it first, smiling. "I will take the letter. I am leading the investigation."

Zane could see playfulness in her eyes and decided to let it go. "If it is all right, Jweal, I would like to take the dagger."

The smith folded up the knife in the cloth. "Fine with me. Such weapons should not be found here."

Zane shook Jweal's hand and they departed. Per his directions, it was a short walk to the rundown library. "What did you two talk about in that foreign tongue?"

Alyssa brushed her hair back "Old Fey ideals. You see, Fey came from a place so strange calling it foreign is an understatement. There, things could change on the whim of the master or a courtier. Finding the true state of something for them is both a constant endeavor and cherished goal. It means finding something pure and immovable."

"I... see." Zane didn't understand the idea at all, but he'd never been well-versed in the internal workings of philosophy. He placed the information in the back of his mind. "Is this the place?"

If Jweal hadn't told them, they wouldn't have guessed that a library was there. The windows were covered with boards and the walls with graffiti. Zane couldn't discern their original color, as a mixture of words and pictures overlapped with more recent images. It was as if one artist ignored those who came before.

Zane reached for the door and looked back over his shoulder. "So, I am the assistant?"

She smirked and held up the folded parchment. "I have the letter."

Zane gave a weak laugh and opened the door. Light spilled out, cutting through the dark room. Books were scattered throughout the building in piles, varying in condition from pristine to little more than frayed bundles of paper. In a shadowy corner, stacked books were made into a chair upon which sat a withered elder. The pair approached the man, who seemed steeped in age.

Alyssa held out the letter. "Sorry Khmer, but we need to speak with you."

A white beard rolled out of the darkness, but the old man's face remained hidden in shadow. His long, slender fingers seemed too long to be human, so Zane assumed Khmer was of Fey descent also. His hands looked like parched paper as he took the letter and read it before placing it in his lap.

The old man pointed to Zane but addressed Alyssa. "Are you with him?"

"Yes. This is my assistant, Detective Zane Vrexon."

It was the third time she had referred to Zane as her assistant. He assumed it was a running joke, but he didn't yet know her well enough to be sure. Zane made a note to discuss it with her later.

Khmer gestured for Zane to come closer, then looked him over for a long minute before speaking. "Young man, I have not seen your kind in many long years."

Zane looked at Alyssa questioningly. He was not sure what the old man meant, but it made him feel like he was not the one the comment was directed towards. The old man wheezed, and Zane feared that the old man was dying until he realized that he was laughing. "I care not who you are. You have been spoken for."

Zane bowed his head, confused. From the corner of his eyes, he caught sight of Shadow briefly. His red eyes flickered in and out for a moment then vanished, as if Shadow decided to flee. If it bothered Shadow, then it was a good reason to be here. "I am sorry, Khmer. But what do you mean?"

The old man frowned. "Are you not aware of what you are?"

"I am Zane Vrexon, a detective."

The old man sighed. "I see. It seems I spoke in haste. Please forget my words. If I say any more, I will tip the scales of chance. Only know that there is always a third choice. Take this advice as you will."

"Thank you?"

All were silent until Alyssa got the conversation back on track. "We are looking into a murder. Can you help us?"

Khmer extended his trembling arm, and Zane placed the wrapped dagger in his hand. The old man pulled the cloth from the weapon and traced its lines. He turned the knife over while he examined it, light from the open door reflecting off the blade.

Zane pulled out his flask and brought it to his lips, but nothing came out. He brought his eye to the opening and saw only his reflection. He shook the flask and listened to the sound of the liquid inside.

"I don't allow liquids that could hurt my books," Khmer said. "This rule applies even to you, dear guest."

Zane stared numbly at the old man before moving to cap his flask. But Alyssa stopped him. She brought a finger to her lips, put on her glasses, and stared inside the flask. With the flask in hand, she brought it to her mouth. Alyssa seemed intrigued by the magic and grinned like a child at market day.

The old man laughed. "You're a scholar?" He laughed again, clearly enjoying her curiosity. "I will permit you to study my art."

Alyssa's smile faded as she realized she was being watched. She bowed politely and continued examining the liquid. The old man set the dagger in his lap. "You brought a dangerous object to me."

Zane nodded. "It was used in a murder."

"More like murders. This has seen much blood in its life."

"How much?"

"How does one measure? No, you only need to know that this is an ender of lives."

Zane's skin became gooseflesh. "How common are these?"

The old man gestured to the books scattered around in his aged room, which felt like a swamp of books. If one was not careful, they could be bogged down in endless information. "The Fey culture is as wide and diverse as it is old. There have been plenty of reasons to murder throughout history: in defense, in the name of faith, in the names of our Lords and Ladies."

The old Fey folded the cloth back over the dagger. "The lines on the blade show the signs from one specific group of Fey, who were masters of this craft. They were called Alver, but they no longer exist."

Zane looked to Alyssa, who returned a shrug; she clearly hadn't known this either. Khmer wheezed and coughed before starting again. "Alver are, or rather were, a group of assassins. The whole clan was trained in such dark arts, but they were bound by spells and magic that kept them in line. Their actions were detected only if they were spotted, or evidence was left."

Zane pointed to the dagger. "Like this?"

He could not see the old man's face, but he could hear the smile in his voice. "Yes."

Alyssa handed back his flask, now interested in the new subject. "What can we expect?"

"Expect? The Alver are gone. Never to return, which is for the best. They were tools of violence of the Courts and Lords."

Zane sighed, desperate to keep his one lead from falling apart. "But a murder has taken place with this weapon. Isn't that unlikely?"

"No. Such objects are bound to get caught up in such acts. It is the fate crafted for them."

Zane didn't understand what the Fey meant but made a note to perhaps ask Alyssa later. He felt anger rise in him as his eyes scanned the corners of the room, looking for where Shadow was hiding. The creature wasn't watching as he normally would. He called out in his mind, but Shadow refused to answer. Under normal circumstances, Zane would have enjoyed the internal silence. But he needed answers and Shadow hadn't led him astray in this case. It figured Shadow would disappear when the leads dried up.

The old man's beard swished side to side as he handed the dagger back. Zane placed it at the bottom of his jacket pocket and bowed to Khmer.

The Fey waved one arm. "It's my honor to help. I do pray that this action is not related to Fey kind. May the Courts rise again."

Once Zane and Alyssa stepped outside, the door closed, as if by a gust of wind. He slipped off a glove and lifted a finger to check the breeze but found none. Zane slipped the glove back on as Alyssa smiled at him. "The magic in there is incredible. True magic, I think!"

Zane raised a hand to stop her. "This is out of my depth. I need to eat. The Zinny district is nearby. How about we go there?"

"You mean the Western Islands?"

"That's right, they have a district where many immigrants from there live." Zane motioned with his head. "This way."

She stopped and looked toward The Institute looming in the distance.

"Are you okay?" Zane asked.

"Yes, it's just that I haven't eaten outside The Institute in years. I mean, I should be fine, right? But what if I'm allergic or get sick?"

Zane watched flecks of ash fall from the sky. The ash of thousands of chimneys keeping people warm, combined with the fires of industry that burned within hundreds of factories. "It will be fine. The Zinny district is one of the cleanest places in the city. Their food is said to be entirely healthy."

It took her a moment, but Alyssa regained her confident gaze. "Okay."

Zane gestured the way and started walking. Bells rang out across the city, signaling that it was near the evening mealtime. Zane was hungry and he could only guess that Alyssa was too, especially after she'd emptied her stomach at the morgue. "Do you have a restaurant you like?"

She shook her head "No, I haven't left The Institute since..."

He remembered the burning and the yelling coming from a memory of hers. "Since the fire?"

She nodded and looked away, watching the buildings as they walked past. "Do you have any suggestions?"

"Yes. I was thinking of a noodle shop I enjoy."

Zane took Alyssa across two different districts before they reached the Eastern Sun Cross Street, which had long stretches of red and yellow cloth that made a canopy covering the intersection. This was enough to protect most of the district's patrons from the city's constant stream of ash. Alyssa watched with interest as workers with brooms swept any ash that slipped past or blew in. The workers moved, one after another, between the crowds as they shopped from vendor to vendor. "Why do they—"

"Sweep?"

She nodded.

"It's part of their religion. The High Lawgiver decreed that cleanliness is what separates the civilized from the uncivilized."

"Fascinating. Is that why you like to eat here?"

Zane met her gaze and chuckled at himself. "Yes, I have an appreciation for their cleanliness."

He guided her through the crowd. Low-burning lanterns produced light at tables under a tent. The people inside sat and talked over steaming bowls of food as Zinny waitresses moved from table to table in their colorful clothes, their hair pulled back in the traditional style. Zane and Alyssa took their seats at an empty table. One of the waitresses came up, speaking quickly in her native language. Alyssa smiled politely. "I am sorry but I—"

Zane talked over her in the Zimmian language, his accent rough and forceful. The waitress nodded and left.

Alyssa raised her eyebrows in surprise. "You can speak Zimmian?"

"Only enough to order food."

She smiled. "Well, it's always another surprise with you."

Zane studied her. He knew so much, and yet so little about her. He had shared and seen her memories. He had experienced firsthand her sorrow and heartache, but they remained little more than acquaintances working a case together. Mrs. Mose's earlier concern reverberated in his mind and touched his heart.

She was right. Zane needed a friend.

"Any thoughts on the investigation?" he asked.

She sighed and rubbed her eyes in frustration. "Several, but nothing concrete. It could be a Fey assassin."

"Which, if true, would cause even more hatred for Fey people."

She rubbed the bridge of her nose. "Yes. And what about the poison?"

"You're going to test it, right?"

"Yes, but if it is from the Eastern Territory, who could have gotten it?"

Zane crossed his arms as he thought. "The Eastern Territory joined the Empire generations ago, but much of their culture is not understood outside their border. However, I think Vana and her family come from there."

"How do you deduce that?"

Zane raised one finger. "First, there's the veil that Vana wears."

Alyssa shrugged. "I have seen many women wear veils. It's an old tradition."

"One that originated in the Eastern Territory. I know only a little, but it holds a different meaning when done in the empire than it does for the people from the East. This by itself doesn't say much, but when combined with my second point, I think we can draw some strong conclusions about their family's heritage."

"And what is your second point?"

"Evan's tattoos. I've seen soldiers with similar ink. When I asked them about it, they told me it was what the warriors of the East wear. They claimed it protected them from evil."

Alyssa shook her head. "That may be, but even both of those facts combined don't prove anything."

Zane smirked and held up a third finger. "Yes, but the poison is from the East also. Don't you find that suspicious? Together, it all starts to paint a picture. What that picture is, I am not sure yet."

"Is it of Vana as the murderer?"

Zane stopped and thought for a long minute before responding. "I don't think she did it. But..."

"But what?"

"Well, she acts strange. Like she is more interested in revenge than justice."

Zane stopped and remembered his unease that morning. "Also, I ran into her once in the street, and she wasn't wearing the veil."

"So she took the veil off."

Zane removed his leather gloves. "Like I said earlier, the meaning for Easterners is different from the empire. Their custom is for the mourner to wear the veil to hide their grief—and anger."

Alyssa looked away in thought. "I can understand that."

"Also, the Fey-made dagger doesn't fit. I still don't know where that would come from."

"The dagger bothers me, too. Something like that should be in my department, not in the street."

The flow of the conversation came to a stop. Not wanting to sit in silence, Zane decided to broach another subject. "Why do you keep telling people I'm your assistant?"

Alyssa looked confused. "I have the letter making this an official investigation. So, legally, The Institute is looking into the murder of one of its members."

"Yes, but it's my case."

She nodded to him as though she had just pieced something together. "I am sorry for causing a misunderstanding. We are in this together."

Zane smiled. "It's okay so long as we are on the same page. I am the one that should apologize."

"It's fine."

Zane felt embarrassed for bringing up the issue at all, and an awkward silence came over them until the waitress came with two bowls of steaming noodles and two pairs of chopsticks. Zane pulled some coins out and handed them over before thanking her in Zimmian.

Alyssa ran her hands over the chop sticks. "How do I eat with these?"

Zane showed her how to hold them and use the utensils. As they ate, he considered Alyssa the stranger.

What he needed was Alyssa the friend.

"So...how long have you been at The Institute?"

They traded life stories over the meal. Hours passed, and they sat at the table long after the food was gone. Finally, they left the shop and made their way to The Institute. All the proper and respectable shops had started to close for the day as they walked the cobblestone streets.

"You believe that the fire was intentional?" Zane asked.

Alyssa nodded, her face tight and grim. "I checked the records years later. The safety runes were marked through and the circle was broken, but I have been told that it was unintentional. A workplace accident."

"Would such a thing be possible?"

She was silent for a moment. "It can happen. It was a thirty-four-rune array. At that size, a small mistake can have... disastrous consequences."

They stepped into The Institute courtyard's clear night sky. The moon was just beginning its journey across the horizon.

Alyssa turned to Zane. "I will run some tests tonight on the poison, and I will see you in the morning."

Zane nodded. "I will be here."

"Meet me at the second bell?"

"Of course."

She walked through The Institute's large iron doors. He waved once more and then turned back towards his flat. In the reflection of the windows of the shops, he noticed Shadow's eyes following him as the creature spoke.

Such a charming mage!

Zane ignored him and sipped his flask.

Oh, the cold shoulder now. Shadow's image started to vibrate in laughter. *I suppose that's all you have left since I ate the other one! But come now, I was of help, was I not? That poison, for example.*

With one large gulp from the flask, Zane leaned hard on his cane and picked up his pace. He had questions for Shadow, but he was too tired to deal with Shadow's voice.

Z⎯⎯⎯⎯

ALYSSA HAD ENJOYED the dinner and the walk home. Zane could be a gentleman when he wanted to, it seemed. She blushed, then pushed her thoughts to the side. Her task was not to be some swooning maiden, but to find who tried to kill her.

She was tired, but needed to get something done. The rooms and halls she passed through seemed randomly arranged. One connected room led to another, each offering no prediction as to what the next might be. Some believed there was a complex order to the arrangement, but no one could prove it. Instead, she let her instinct guide her to the room she desired.

She ended up in front of an old janitor's closet. Past the door was a lab where half a dozen students, scholars, and wizards buzzed around running tests throughout the night. A young lady with round glasses approached Alyssa from a table in the middle of the room and bowed. "Welcome to the testing laboratory. My name is Frame. I am free to run any test you need."

Alyssa responded with her own polite bow. She hadn't seen this student before. "I am Alyssa Benedictus. I need two tests conducted."

Alyssa handed over a tube with poison residue from Dennis's body. "First, I need you to test this. There is some blood and possible flesh mixed in. It may be an acidic poison found in the Eastern Territories. I think it was called The Last Death."

Frame took the beaker and held it up to the gas-powered light as she studied it. "This is an unusual request, but I think I can do that. Some of the people here are specialists in alchemy and toxicology, so we should be able to discern the matters. What is the second test?"

Alyssa handed over the hair Zane had given her. "I need this examined. If you can, I need to know if this is human or animal."

The young lady took the hair. "That should be easy enough. The zoologists keep strange hours themselves, so I will examine it and then take it to them for analysis. Will that be all?"

"Yes. If you can please have it ready by morning, I will come by and pick up the results." Alyssa began to leave but stopped and turned back. "No one else is to know of this or retrieve the results."

"Understood. I will have these ready for you in the morning, Ms.

Benedictus."

Alyssa stepped through the door, back into the ever-changing halls. She kept a continuous path, always forward, and came to a long hallway that stretched into odd-angled turns. There was a single door, which she knew would lead to her personal room.

But a figure blocked her path.

Agwen stood outside her door in his normal robe, hiding his Fey ancestry. "Alyssa, I am glad I was able to catch you. How are you feeling?"

Alyssa had purposefully left her quarters unfixed, letting it drift among the shifting labyrinth of The Institute, which made it almost impossible for two people to run into each other when looking for the same room.

He had been looking for her specifically.

Her eyebrow arched slightly. "I am well. Thank you for helping rescue me earlier. Also, thank you for doing the paperwork for my absence. The detective has been considerate. I even think he must have been trained as a noble once, so—"

"Why are you helping that man?"

The question cut through the conversation and took Alyssa by surprise. It was not like Agwen to interrupt someone. She took a moment to collect herself before responding. "At first, I wanted to help him because he saved me. It would be easier to work with me than one of The Institute's agents. But now I have another reason."

Agwen raised an eyebrow with genuine interest.

"There is a dagger from an allegedly extinct Fey clan. Besides that, I have met local Fey decedents and even had an opportunity to study their magic in person. There was an old man casting spells without words of power, hand signs, or runes—things I have read about and studied but never seen in person. This case might provide even more opportunities for me to learn."

Agwen cleared his throat. "You will need to keep me informed.

Anyway, I am merely concerned. You seem different since being freed from the Dream Sphere."

"I am nervous." Alyssa felt a measure of release telling Agwen the truth. "I could have died."

He stepped closer. "The Institute has more than enough resources. You don't have to be the one to help investigate this murder. It's unlikely to be connected to what happened to you."

"Maybe, but if the killer is here in The Institute, I may be safer out there."

Agwen offered a hollow smile. "Safer? The world outside The Institute is filthy and dark. Filled with undesirables. It is far safer here."

She turned the question over in her head. He was probing her for something, but she could not decipher what it was, and Agwen's face was unreadable.

"Like I said, I am returning a favor. It has been a long day, and I would like to get some rest. Goodnight, Agwen."

"Good night, Ms. Benedictus." He bowed and disappeared past a turn in the hall.

Alyssa entered her room, pulled the door tight, and bound the door shut with eldritch syllables. As far back as she could remember, Agwen had always been direct, but something had changed. She set some magical alarms and got ready to sleep.

Morning would come early and Alyssa needed to be ready.

CHAPTER 11

Zane's key slipped soundlessly into his flat door. It was too late for his elderly apartment manager to be up, and he didn't want to wake her. Shadow had stopped trying to make conversation, and Zane relished the silence. He was still not ready to contemplate what it meant for Shadow to have its own memories.

The light from the gas lamps gave the carving of Vana a foreboding feeling. But Shadow's handiwork was an impressive painting of death. Fitting, since it came from a creature of death.

Zane hung his coat next to his wand holster, the ash and soot flaking and falling from his garments to the floor. He tossed his gloves onto his desk and pulled out his flask, which held what was left of the liquid that Lady Zel had given him. He took care when tossing it back, making sure not to waste a single drop.

Tomorrow would be rough. But that was tomorrow. Right now, he would try to relax.

Shadow stood in the corner where the lamp's light didn't reach. *You're relaxing too early.*

Zane sighed. He knew he had to face the truth, whatever it was. "Why do you say that? No, better question: Why do you say anything? I mean, saints be damned. I saw a memory. Your memory!"

Zane threw his flask at the creature, but it bounced harmlessly off the corner before stopping on the floor. He was on his feet in a flash of rage, frustration slipping out with each ragged breath.

Shadow's red eyes were unblinking. *You have a guest in your bedroom. By their breathing, I assume that it's an assassin.*

Zane froze. He hated Shadow and didn't trust him, but he couldn't risk ignoring the creature's warning. Zane eased across his office back to his holster, which held his wand. The floor creaked as he stepped toward the coat rack and picked up his cane. His eyes didn't leave the door to his bedroom.

The knob turned from the inside.

Zane stopped and held his breath until the knob returned to its normal position. He sighed—a moment too soon.

When the door burst open, pieces of the frame scattered across the room. Two knives came from the darkness and Zane rolled toward his jacket. A figure cloaked in black sprang from the door, their face obscured by a mask. The skin of their arms was grey, like the bark of a burned tree.

The assailant drew back their right arm, ready to deliver a punch as they ran toward him. Zane pulled his wand free just in time and aimed it at the assailant. Before he could pull the mental trigger, the attacker's right arm grew to twice its original size and closed the distance between them. Zane raised his cane just as the grotesque fist connected with the force of a warhammer.

The cane buckled as his feet left the ground. Zane's body slammed through his office door and was only stopped by the opposing hallway wall. The attacker's swollen arm grew again, the open palm like a net that enveloped his body and pinned Zane to the wall. From behind the mask, Zane heard the assassin's hollow voice. "Where is my dagger?"

Zane struggled against the inhuman grip, which kept him from bringing his wand to bear on the assailant.

The grip tightened around him as the masked figure punctuated every word.

"Where. Is. My. Dagger?"

Zane felt like his bones might start to crack as he gasped, unable to breathe. He heard a door open and tried to shout but the assassin's vice grip trapped the air in his lungs.

Then the top corner of his front door exploded.

Both Zane and the attacker looked in the direction of the blast, confused. Mrs. Mose held a staff and, with steady hands, ran her fingers along runes etched in the wood.

"You got three seconds to let go."

The staff hummed with power as the assailant froze.

"One."

Zane winced as the grip around him tightened.

"Two."

Mrs. Mose leveled the staff at the assassin's masked head, and the tip began to glow.

"Three."

In an act of survival, the attacker broke away and shot down the stairs. A blast exploded from the staff and struck precisely where the creature had stood just an instant before, tearing a hole in the floor. Zane heard the front door of the building break open.

He looked up at Mrs. Mose and thanked her. "Where did you get that thing?"

"It's a souvenir from when I met my husband."

"Your husband?"

"Third brigade of the artillery mages. All I know is how to use this one spell wick"— Mrs. Mose flashed him a grin, which would have been toothy a few decades earlier—"but it's all I need." She examined his door, which was missing a chunk of wood. "Mr. Vrexon, I will pay for this door. You will cover any damage in your room. Sound good?"

Zane nodded and pulled himself to his feet.

"Yes, ma'am. You have a good night."

z

ALYSSA DID NOT dream. Her sleep was a calm sea of darkness, but the surface was disturbed by the ripple of a scratching sound. It was faint and rested in the back of her mind, until one final creak finally woke her. With an eldritch word, she lit her gas lamps. The light would not carry out to the other side of the door, a side effect of the room lacking a fixed location in The Institute.

She pulled on her robe and used another arcane word to see the other side of the door. Sparks caught in the air as she spoke, a sign that her charm had failed. Her eyes went wide, and she felt her hair stand on end.

That should not have been possible.

The spell she placed on the door was being undone. She tried to lock it again, but the charm failed. Whoever was out there was a far greater wizard than she was. Her lips and tongue were almost stunned. She had not been prepared for her spell to be countered.

Alyssa had one final spell left in her. She focused on the door handle itself, and instead of locking it, she wove a charm to keep the lock from moving. It worked, which means she had guessed right; the counter charm was specific to the door being locked but didn't prevent her from affecting its movement.

Then the door handle started to glow.

She cursed at herself. Whoever was on the other side of her door was working to undo her charm. Alyssa fought her anxiety and searched for a solution. *The chair!* She grabbed it and jammed the back under her door handle before shoving her body against the door. Though the door wasn't tied physically to any part of the building, it still could be stopped by normal means. The knob started to spark, but Alyssa threw the last of her power into it, speaking a locking charm until her tongue was numb.

The knob glowed hot, then cooled. The scratching stopped.

The room went quiet.

Alyssa's face hurt, but she seemed to be safe. Just to be sure, she dragged her desk in front of the door. Her body quivered as adrenaline pumped through her and stress-fueled tears rolled down her face. Someone powerful was out to get her.

She tried to speak a word to snuff out the gas light, but couldn't, so she turned them off manually and crawled back into bed.

Without the use of a charm, sleep did not come easy.

Z

ZANE LIMPED THROUGH his door and pulled it flush, dropping his useless cane on the floor as he walked across his violated office.

Shadow watched. *What, no thank you? We could have died.*

The word 'we' hung in Zane's head another unpleasant reminder that Shadow was more than a figment of his imagination, that the two were connected and that the creature needed him alive, like a parasite on its host.

Zane hated himself as he spoke the words.

"Thank you."

He shut the bedroom but could not turn off his mind. Would the assassin return that night? If so, how would Zane defend himself? He set the wand next to his bed, not wanting to be caught without it again.

Shadow's voice whispered in his ear. *Relax. I will keep watch for the night.*

Just yesterday, Zane would have scoffed at his imagination offering to keep him safe. But now he wondered. Was it his imagination? Either way, it deserved a scoff.

Exhaustion took over and sleep consumed him. Perhaps it was dealing with Shadow that evening, but Zane dreamed of the first time they met.

A younger Zane wore the standard black armor adorned with the traditional red and white Imperial Manticore. On his hip was a heavy sword, designed more to crush than to slice. Zane's unit was comprised of seven men—three with wide shields and maces, three with spears to strike from behind the shields, and Zane himself, who also held a spear and shield. In addition to leading the men, his job was to fill any holes that opened in their small line.

Zane had only selected volunteers. All were aware of the reputation of this passage and that no others had returned. After entering the tunnel, the men started to whisper, discussing how it was cursed by the Lord of Creation, or that the Shade—the shepherd of the dead—wandered its halls. Zane squashed this talk; he wouldn't let it affect morale.

They traveled slowly down the cavern, which was so narrow only two of them could fit shoulder-to-shoulder. Zane ran one gloved hand down the wall and found that it was rough and covered in scratches, as if the stone had been dug into by thousands of hands. Zane pulled his hand free and ran his bare fingers over the wall. His fingers easily fit the grooves, and the image of his own hands digging onto the stone sent a shiver through his soul.

Their lamps illuminated some of the tunnel, but past the edge of their light came the sound of thundering footsteps. The echo shook the ground beneath them.

"Shields up," Zane shouted. "Let them try and break our wall."

The two men in front raised their shields and braced themselves, their spiked boots digging into the stone. The horde of rotting flesh charged blindly into the light, clawing and growling with every step. A loud crunch reverberated down the tunnel as they slammed into the shields.

Zane gave the commands. "Spears! Tear them down!"

Two spearmen jabbed, batted, and broke into the withering corpses. At any break in the siege, the shield men would strike with their maces. Their training kicked in and the soldiers moved as a seamless unit for what seemed like an eternity, the men ready to relieve one another on the front line, while others stood watch for a surprise attack from behind.

When the last decaying body stopped moving, Zane checked the gauge on his lantern. It showed that this skirmish had cost them half an hour. They prepared to advance when the sound of another wave echoed down the tunnel.

One of his men spoke up. "Sir, I think we should fall back. We have already driven farther..."

Zane knew the words he left unspoken. *Farther than anyone has before.* The tunnel was long and narrow and could be guarded from the entrance without too much trouble. Zane was tempted to keep moving forward but shook his head and dismissed the idea. *There is no value in this tunnel.* "Yes, let's fall back. We will send sappers or mages to seal the path. No one can win this route."

No words needed to be spoken among the men. Their training kicked in again as they fell into lockstep at a steady pace. The thundering of the undead stayed outside of the edge of the light. Zane counted the seconds and waited to give commands to counter a charge, but it never came. The sounds of the undead pursuers kept Zane's nerves tight, but he kept the bile down. He was the commander and couldn't show weakness.

Halfway back down the tunnel, the front guard called for a stop. Zane turned from watching their rear back to them. "What the..."

The words were lost on his lips. No more than a couple of feet in front of them was a wall of darkness, their lamps' light failing to pierce the shadowy veil. The guard who called a stop looked to Zane for an answer. "Sir, what should we do?"

Zane looked forward at the black void, then back toward the sounds of clawing and growling ghouls. He cursed himself, realizing he was trapped. He asked for a lamp and stepped inches away from the darkness. Zane inspected the black hole before throwing the light into it. The lamp disappeared, but no light escaped.

And the ghouls were closing in.

Zane looked over his shoulder, but the stretch of light didn't help his nerves. There were no good options.

"Weapons out and shields up," he ordered. "Forward!"

Blackness surrounded the unit as it waded into the deepest dark Zane had ever experienced. He looked over his shoulder and shouted to his men, but the veil swallowed all sound. He whirled his spear around him. It should have connected with the wall of the tunnel, but it touched nothing.

Zane's head was light and his legs threatened to give out, but two cold hands steadied him. He looked behind him for the friendly face of a fellow soldier.

Instead, he found two red eyes.

"Welcome to my home."

CHAPTER 12

T he room was pitch black, but Fex's eyes, having retained Fey attributes, adjusted far faster than a pair of human eyes would. Fur skins laid scattered on the floor along with a burnt-out brazier. There were stains on the pillars, but Fex's head hurt too much to ponder what they could possibly be. It took him a moment to remember where he was. The final puzzle piece clicked into place when he remembered the colored smoke.

He reached into his belt and pulled out Dennis's military wand. He checked it, ejecting three unused spell wicks. They bounced on the crate, and he cursed at himself for dropping the wicks before sliding them back into the wand and sealing it with a twist. Convinced he was alone, Fex dropped down onto the next crate, then the next. By the time he made it to the floor, he had full control over his limbs again.

Fex was sore but happy to be alive. What had he been thinking going there alone? Being closer to the ground, he could smell the residue of the smoke. His trained nose picked up some of the ingredients used to make it. *Who needs this many psychedelics?* Fex staggered over to the door only to find that he was locked inside. He cursed to himself and leveled the wand at the knob. "I hope no one hears this."

He pulled the mental trigger and both the door and the knob cracked. The door swung open, but the force caused it to bang into the adjoining wall and carried it back to a close. Fex cringed and pushed the door open with his free hand, keeping the wand level as he stepped out into the hall. Fex hoped the noise from the bar on the ground floor was loud enough to mask the sound of his actions.

As he climbed up the stairs to the bar, Fex allowed the wand to rest at his side, hidden by the sleeve of his jacket. The smoke was just as thick as he had left it. If anyone noticed him, they didn't care, so he made his way to the door and stepped out into the ash-covered streets.

Fex started walking the long way home on empty streets. He was two blocks away from the bar before he allowed himself to relax and enjoy the freedom of the open lane. So often he would get pushed around as he walked, but now the streets were for him alone.

It was late and dark, the light from myriad gas lamps reflecting off the clouds, giving the city the feeling of an exotic land. The flames in the lamps seemed to flicker in strange colors. He shrugged it off as the waning effects of the drug. It was pleasant at first, but soon each shadow seemed to grow. The light seemed to have turned against him, adding to the menace of the darkness.

He gripped the wand with a sweaty hand.

"Meow!"

Fex's hand shot up and he pulled the mental trigger. The blast tore apart the darkness of a nearby shadow. A cat jumped and ran down the street. He cursed himself for wasting a spell wick on a cat, then shook his head and laughed. His laughter ended when heavy footsteps approached him from behind.

The figure was dressed in black, their face covered by a black mask. It had a feminine shape, but something was not right. The joints seemed unnaturally long.

One of its arms mutated, growing inhumanly large. The grim image of the addict from the other day came to mind as Fex imagined his own body crumpled in the street. The figure's measured walk turned into a run. The gnome turned and fled, but the heavy steps followed close behind. He twisted back and fired the last of the spell wicks. The figure raised its engorged arm, using it as a shield.

Fex's shots hit the creature's arm, splitting open its clothing and revealing grey skin underneath. The figure slowed for a moment but continued chasing and regained full speed in seconds. Their longer legs brought them within reach, and the gnome realized he had no hope of getting away. Fex tripped and raised the wand at his attacker, but it was empty.

The figure raised its arm like a mallet and Fex was about to be the nail.

The arm swung down. Fex closed his eyes and covered his head. At the last possible moment, a shadow passed over him and the figure vanished in a sound of gnashing flesh and crunching bone.

Two monsters fought in the street, ripping and tearing at each other, one clad in fur, the other swinging its elongated limbs. Their feet cracked the street's bricks as they slammed into each other. With one smooth motion, the figure that chased him threw the furry monster against a nearby lamp post.

The pole bent and gas hissed from the open crack. The creature stood and dove again at the masked monster just as a pillar of fire ignited. Fex covered his eyes again as the sounds of bone-shattering blows echoed in the darkness. Fear finally overtook him and he stood up and ran, leaving a trail of ash and the carnage of battle behind him.

The sounds of the fight followed him, so Fex ran without looking back until the potion shop came into sight. He panted as he locked the doors and jumped into his bed.

Fex's body seemed to vibrate with adrenaline as cold sweat dripped from his skin. From his bed, Fex grabbed the components to make spell wicks, and with shaking hands assembled one after another.

No more empty rounds.

CHAPTER 13

A lyssa's jaw was stiff when she woke up. Her desk and chair were still pushed up against the door. With a word, she ignited the lights. The arcane word worked muscles still sore from last night. Whoever had countered her charms was powerful.

She got dressed and moved the furniture out of the way. The door looked normal, but from this side it would. She twisted the knob, but it wouldn't move, even using all her weight. She sighed in frustration, slipped on her glasses, and studied the door. Strains of magic had been tightly woven into it that had not been there the night before.

She pulled at the invisible threads as she studied the spell. Whoever had been at her door had changed tactics last night. Her door now had a powerful charm placed on it to keep it from moving. They had reinforced her work. *Clever.*

It was a pain, but she could fix it. Her charm was the core of this spell and she forced her power into it. The doorknob glowed bright before she heard a loud click. She touched the knob. It was hot, but the door opened effortlessly.

She pulled her door tight as she closed it behind her, then stepped into a water closet followed by a stairwell. Turning to face her room, she weaved strands of arcane power, backed by eldritch words. As soon as she finished the final syllable, her room vanished, now hidden. Feeling secure she marched upstairs, out windows, and through doors until she came to the labs.

Many of the students and scholars from last night had left, but Frame was still at her workstation with heavy bags under her eyes.

Alyssa felt for her, remembering her own long hours working overnight in labs. "Do you have my results?"

Frame smiled. "It took all night, but yes."

The student pulled papers from a file cabinet and straightened them before handing them over. Alyssa read them as Frame explained the results.

"That black liquid was not much to go on, and you were right, there was decomposed flesh mixed in. A lot of it. Another student who was assisting me couldn't stomach it and threw up. It was a huge mess, he had eaten—"

"The report please." Alyssa had neither the time nor patience for such details.

"Right, sorry. It took some digging, but it looks like you were right. It was poison from the Eastern Territory. It is very rare. If you hadn't suggested where to look, we probably would have never even figured it out. I cannot pronounce the proper name for it, but as you said, some call it Last Death."

Being an expert on Fey history and magic, Alyssa had heard her fair share of poetic names, but Zane had known it almost immediately. He didn't strike her as an academic. "Any reason for that name?"

Frame shrugged. "We couldn't make sense of it. We think it has something to do with religious beliefs. Based on what little information we could gather, it is called Last Death because, given enough time, it can completely eat through a person until nothing is left."

The image of Dennis's melting innards carved its way through her mind. Her stomach felt like it was on a rollicking ship as she tried to push the memory away. "What are the odds of someone being able to just... know that, without doing the research you've done?"

Frame scratched her head. "I am not sure. Maybe an expert, or someone who has seen it used before, but it seems unlikely. It acts more like an acid than a poison."

Who are you Detective Vrexon? "Thank you for looking into it."

"Ma'am, don't you want to know about the hair?"

Alyssa had forgotten about the fur she'd dropped off. It seemed inconsequential compared to the poison. "Yes, sorry."

"This is quite a fine specimen. A dozen students are already asking to study it."

Alyssa flipped through the papers to the section on the hair. She read it over, then looked it over once again, doubting her eyes. "Is this true?"

Frame smiled with excitement. "Yes, it's polymorphic hair."

"That cannot be. Not even we can make that. Who" — Alyssa looked up at Frame as it hit her — "Unless it's natural?"

"Yes. From what we can tell, it is naturally occurring polyhair. We have only a few on record."

Alyssa was aware. It was possible for some creatures to change their shape, but to change their very nature was another thing entirely. Whatever the hair belonged to could not only change shape. It could shift its very being. "Do we know how many natures are in this polymorph strain?"

Frame smiled. "It's human and canine. But that is all we can determine."

"Great work. I will write you a letter of recommendation for this."

Alyssa turned to go, but Frame held onto her hand. "Actually, ma'am, I was hoping you would consider giving me the hair to continue studying. I could write a paper on this. It would go a long way for me in my studies."

She looked Frame in her eyes and could see passion and ambition. *This girl will make an excellent wizard.* "Do you have the paperwork?"

Frame's smile almost split her face in half. She pulled out the prepared official documents. "Just sign here and here, please."

Alyssa complied and handed back the papers. Frame was bouncing in place, clutching the documents close to her chest as she thanked

Alyssa profusely.

"Please let me know if you find anything else," Alyssa said.

"Absolutely!"

Alyssa committed Frame's name to memory and left to meet Zane at the front door.

Z

ZANE WOKE UP in a cold sweat that had soaked through his blanket. He rose and looked at the bed in disgust. He didn't have time to clean it. The dull light peeking through the window told him he was late.

Zane washed the sweat from his body and put on fresh clothes. He kept his wand ready as he stepped out into his office, which looked just how he had left it last night. Both the door to the hallway and his bedroom door were broken beyond repair. The mess begged to be cleaned, but he reminded himself that he had no time. Zane gave the wall carving of Vana one last look and kicked his broken cane in frustration on the way out.

Mrs. Mose stepped into the room just as he reached the front door. Splinters fell from the hole she'd made. He froze as she looked around the room, her eyes stopping on the carving. "I thought I would check on you..." She tilted her head as she pondered it.

He could feel heat rise to his cheeks. "Thank you, but you didn't have to do that."

She pointed at the wall, her face a mixture of frustration and admiration. "It's well made, almost haunting... but it has to go. Either I will fix it and add it to your rent, or you can fix it yourself."

He sighed. Late on rent, and now this. "Understood. I will get it fixed after I get paid."

She nodded and held open the door she had blasted the night before. "You're a good man, but I need the money. Just make sure to pay your rent."

He grabbed his jacket and squeezed by. "Thank you, ma'am, for fixing my door."

Mrs. Mose shrugged. "I blasted the door. It would be better if I fix it. Good luck on your day."

Zane buttoned his jacket and headed down the stairs. As he stepped out into the world, he took one last look at the building. Zane knew his apartment manager and her son would be busy fixing the door today, and he felt guilty for being the cause of the damage.

His muscles grew tired with each step. Thankfully, few people were out, some going to work, others going home. In the courtyard in front of The Institute, the clear sky above was beautiful and the stars were almost all gone. The air wasn't any cleaner, but seeing the sky made it feel like it was. The bells from churches and clock towers rang out as the sun's long light stretched overhead.

Alyssa stood on the steps of The Institute just outside the large iron doors. Dressed in black scholar's clothes, she called out to Zane as he walked up the stairs. "I was waiting for you. Something happened to me last night." Her eyes fell on his injured leg as he limped up each step. "Where's your cane?"

"I also had an interesting night," Zane began as he explained the attack.

Alyssa's face went from cheerful to pale as the story went on. By the time he finished the story, her eyes were filled with fear. She seemed to hesitate for a moment before sharing her own story. Their experiences were different and there was no proof that they were related. Still, he anticipated her question.

"Are we safe?"

Zane shrugged. "It depends."

"On what?"

He took a seat on the steps and watched the coming light of day, a rare sight in the shadowy city of Alviun. She took a seat next to him and looked out in the same direction.

"We know this was a preemptive murder," Zane said. "And that the assassin is related to Fey kind."

"So, Lady Zel isn't the murderer?"

He thought about that for a moment. Lady Zel was still hiding something—something relevant—but he didn't know what. "I'm not sure." He looked over to her bag. "What did you find out?"

She removed the documents and handed them to Zane.

He nodded as he read. "So, it was Last Death."

"Yes, but I don't know how you knew. Even our experts had to look it up. Its use is incredibly rare in the empire."

Zane heard the faint words in his head. *You're welcome.*

He brushed the air with his hand, as if trying to wipe away the sound.

Alyssa watched him intently.

Zane cleared his throat and read the results on the hair. Some were human and others canine. How had a dog of some sort gotten into the shop? He worked the thought over in his head but couldn't figure it out. The memory of the claw mark came to mind.

As if reading his mind, Alyssa spoke up. "All the hair is the same texture, but it's a mixture of human and canine."

Zane pointed to the paper. "What does it mean here by polymorphism?"

"A polymorphism is a dual being. One who is either fully, or partly, two beings and can shift from one to the other."

Zane's training in anatomy and medicine was working against him. What she'd described seemed impossible. "Could you explain it in another way?"

She thought about it for a moment. "Are you familiar with the older stories? Some of them speak of shapeshifters."

"Right, like a child being swapped for a changeling."

Alyssa shook her head as she struggled to explain. "No, that would be different. This type of shapeshifter is limited but, in some ways, greater. Though it has been mostly theoretical, the only explanation comes from Fey history. It is thought that their body holds two spirits. We believe it only occurs naturally."

They were a step closer, but the solution hadn't revealed itself yet. "I don't know how this connects, so for now I think we should move on."

She raised an eyebrow at him. "Where to?"

"I say we go to the Ironbarks. Perhaps, if we know why they supported Dennis, we can make more connections."

She registered the idea. "I can see that."

Zane stood and offered her a hand up. She accepted it, and the two took off toward the Ironbark estate. Zane hoped the address in the file was trustworthy. They were forced to stop a couple of times to make sure they were on the right path. Eventually, the streets started to become cleaner, a sure sign of an upper-class neighborhood. The Ironbark home was rustic and practical, not at all what Zane expected of a wealthy family. It looked more like a large hunting lodge that had been dropped into the city, then halfheartedly made to blend in.

The gates to the Ironbark property held the family crest, an ornate image of two wolves standing on their hind legs, facing each other and holding axes, a tree between them.

Alyssa touched the wolves thoughtfully. "This isn't a coincidence, is it?"

Zane examined it, remembering the emblem on Vana's amber ring. The image of a wolf. "Doubtful."

They pulled a cord that rang the bell above the gate. It took a few minutes before a metal slit slid open. "What is your business here?"

Zane was about to answer but was cut off by Alyssa. "I am Alyssa Benedictus, here on behalf of The Institute. This is Detective Zane Vrexon. He is assisting me in an official capacity. We are here to ask questions about Dennis Zel's death."

The man on the other side of the gate sounded confused. "Death?

We heard from him just two days ago."

The day of the murder. Zane spoke up. "Sir, we just need to get some information."

The old man's voice was weakening. "Why is The Institute investigating his death? Unless..."

Zane and Alyssa shared a glance before she answered. "He became a state mage right before he died."

"This has to be a joke. Who put you up to this?"

Alyssa pulled out her badge, along with a folded document, and passed them through the opening. "Here is our official authorization for the investigation."

They heard the wrinkling of paper, followed by a grunt. "Give me a moment." The metal slit slid shut.

Zane looked to Alyssa. "You mentioned that Fey could be polymorphs. Would this ability be hereditary?"

She corrected him. "Polymorph*ic*, but yes. The stories show generations would share this ability, then other times it would lay dormant."

He pointed at the crest, noticing for the first time that the hands of the wolf were human. "It might be a stretch, but an Ironbark could have been the source of the hair and claw marks."

Alyssa nodded, reexamining the crest. "Who are the Ironbarks to Dennis and Vana, then?"

As he considered the question, the front gate swung open and an old but well-dressed servant bowed and waved them in. "I am Giles, the head butler. The master, Noble Ironbark, will see you now. He seems eager to hear more of the news you carry."

Giles escorted Alyssa and Zane into the house through a grand hall. The walls were lined with a legion of hunting trophies, many of them large game. Zane had hunted in his youth, but even he would have never dared to seek out such beasts. They followed Giles up the stairs to the bedroom door, where he stopped and turned to them. "Please, be delicate with the master. He is old, and his health is on the decline."

He led them in and closed the door behind them. At one end of the room was a desk with a bookshelf, and at the other end was a large bed. An old man laid there with a bear fur blanket pulled tight around his shoulders.

When he sat up, even with the fur around his shoulders, Zane could see blue swirling tattoos covering his arms. The aged noble's intense eyes looked them over. He had been a person of great physical strength but was now bowed with age like an ancient tree. On his finger rested a large amber ring.

The noble's grey hair shook as he coughed and motioned Zane and Alyssa to his bedside. "You come bearing news…" He handed the folded papers back to Alyssa.

Zane bowed in classical fashion. "I was originally hired by Vana Zel to find Dennis's killer and prove her innocence."

The old Ironbark coughed. "My daughter is suspected? This is the first that I have heard of this. It appears my idiot son is not telling me everything. Go on."

Zane's mouth dropped open. Daughter? Even as Zane responded, his brain made connections. "I am sorry sir, but you are the head of the Ironbark family. Vana's surname is Zel, and I know that Dennis took her name."

The old man smirked, as if remembering an inside joke. "Our family once had many enemies, but we have wanderlust in our blood. It is in our very nature to explore, so hiding away would never suit us." The noble Ironbark let loose a phlegmy laugh. "If I had time, I would tell you both the many stories of my family. But suffice it to say, to keep our identities under cover, we change the surname our children are born with every couple of generations. But always—always—we are members of the Ironbark family."

Alyssa's face was twisted in thought. "That makes no sense. I mean, people talk. The moment your family changed names, the word would get out. There would be some delay, but that's hardly a reliable solution."

The old noble waved a hand. "Aye, and many a family story will prove your point, but traditions die hard. Now it's done more out of respect to the old ways. But that is in the distant past. Tell me of the present."

Zane cleared his throat before he began. "While searching the crime scene, I found a State Mage badge. Later the next day, I took it to The Institute." He gestured to Alyssa.

She smiled. "When it came to our attention, an official investigation was ordered."

Old man Ironbark looked across the room to his desk. "I am shocked to hear about Dennis getting a state badge. I had received word in a letter that he had failed."

Alyssa frowned and gave an apologetic bow. "A letter with incorrect information was sent. We believe someone tampered with his file."

Ironbark seemed to age by the moment, and death seemed to loom over the man. "But I heard about him failing before I ever even received the letter."

Zane pressed. "Who told you that?"

"My son."

Zane frowned. Evan was becoming increasingly suspicious, but his actions didn't make sense. Why the need for deception? "Sir, when we met your son in passing, he made it sound like your daughter was being hunted."

The old noble's face grew grim "Yes. I cannot explain it all to you, but she might be in danger. Evan heard rumors that she is being targeted by the old families who still reside in the Eastern Territories."

Zane looked for a chair. He felt uncomfortable standing while the old man laid in the bed and his leg ached. "Why would they want to hurt her?"

The old man's grizzled face was twisted as if caught between fear and frustration. "I can't say." He grabbed some folded papers off his nightstand and handed them to Alyssa. "Can you look at these for me?"

She took the papers and read them, then read them once more. "Where did you get these?"

"I was told they came from The Institute."

Alyssa furrowed her brow. "When did you receive them?"

"Yesterday. Are they real?"

Zane reached out to take the documents, but Alyssa pulled away.

"They're signed by Tatius-Lasome, but that can't be right," she said. "I need to take them back to The Institute." She looked up from the papers, her face nearly white. "Is that okay?"

The old man coughed and nodded. "You have already told me the truth, which is more than I can say for some."

Zane let the comment hang in the air. He could feel the awkward turn the conversation had taken but forced himself to speak. "It's off subject, but what is the meaning of the wolves on your front gate?"

The old man's eyes narrowed. The veins across his body seemed more defined, as if working harder. "Why are you asking about the wolves? You are here about a murder."

Zane chose his words carefully and kept his face still. "I am interested in the crest, that's all."

The old noble sighed. "There are old stories of warrior wolves in the Ironbark clan. What exactly they mean is uncertain, but there are many such legends in my family's homeland. I wish not to speak more about it."

"Understood." Zane said, but continued to stand there waiting.

Ironbark met Zane's eyes. He had obviously expected his words to have ended the meeting. "You require more?"

"Can I speak to your son?"

"Why?"

Zane felt the old man's accusing glare of suspicion, which was common in his profession. "I wish to follow up on some leads."

The old man sighed again and looked out the nearby window. "You can find him at his favorite pub, The Foolish Noble. Giles will give you the address for it. Now, I want to be left alone."

They bowed and left. Just outside of the room, the Ironbark butler was waiting. He showed them to the front gate and gave them directions.

"I hope you will keep my lord, Noble Ironbark, informed on your investigation," Giles said. "Dennis was a good man who loved Vana. He never asked for anything. I think that's why the master helped him."

Zane cocked his head. "What do you mean, helped?"

Giles looked back to the house. "It is improper to speak of my master's activities, but he will not speak of it. He would find it improper. He paid off a debt that Dennis held. That is all I can say."

"Thank you," Zane said. "I wish you and your master well."

By the time they were a block away, Zane was already deep in thought.

Alyssa cut into his silence. "So, it looks like that answers the question of who murdered Dennis."

"Who's that?"

"The Eastern families."

Zane shook his head. "Why would they kill Dennis? Especially if their target is Vana."

DIP THE INK, *write the spell, wrap the tube, then inspect.* Fex repeated the steps over and over. He didn't know how long he had been there, but he had made more than two dozen spell wicks. His eyes ached, and his head spun, but he continued. The tubes now took up a large section of his small bed.

A gentle knock at the door disturbed him.

"Fex, are you all right?"

It was Vana's voice. Fex picked up the wand and started to load the wicks. "Yes, one moment, please."

With the wand's cap firmly tightened, he cracked opened the door, keeping the wand in the other hand, behind his back. "Sorry, I just woke up. What can I do for you, Lady Zel?"

Vana was dressed in her mourning clothes—all black, with her face hidden behind a veil. Not an inch of her skin could be seen, but Fex would have bet that she was still covered in bruises.

"It's already four bells into the morning," she said. "Normally, you'd be out opening the shop." She stopped, a touch of concern in her words. "Your face is pale."

Fex hadn't looked in a mirror, but he imagined seeing a man with a hangover. "Sorry. I am not feeling well."

Vana sniffed the air before speaking. "Take your time, Mister Fex. I understand you had a long night. I will run the shop until you are well. Do be careful."

She turned and walked into the front of the store. With a breath of relief, Fex shut the door. The hand holding the wand was damp and seemed to twitch. Fex stared at it and wondered if it was the wand or his hand, though he knew wands didn't shake. Not wanting to risk firing a shot, Fex dropped the wand on the ground. He left the unfinished spell wick on the desk and collapsed onto the bed. The pile of wicks rolled and pooled around him.

He ignored them as he stretched out and closed his eyes. Sleep rolled across his exhausted frame.

He never even bothered to turn off the gas light in his room.

CHAPTER 14

Zane and Alyssa found The Foolish Noble wedged between two older, yet somehow nicer buildings. The pub was a filthy, soot-covered mess that seemed to have never been washed, not even by a rare rain. Inside, the air was little more than smoke so thick it somehow surpassed the city's smog. Alyssa stayed close to Zane as they waded through the fumes to find the counter.

Zane looked over to Alyssa. "Would you like to ask, or…?"

He could barely see her face, but she was smirking. "I will let you handle this, Mister Vrexon."

Zane tapped the counter, getting the bartender's attention. The man was dressed in a dirty vest over a shirt with sleeves rolled up to his elbows. Zane couldn't make out his face, but the barkeep's beard made him look older.

A raspy voice called out through the smoke. "What can I do for ya?"

"I am looking for a friend and hope you can point me in his direction."

"Sure. Who is he?"

"Evan Zel. I'm told he's a regular here."

The bartender waved one arm to instruct them to follow him deeper into the building. As the fumes thinned, Zane could see that the man had greying hair and a handlebar moustache. Zane stared at his clothes, which were horribly stained from catching countless spilled drinks, and couldn't help but think about how to clean them.

"I had thought all of his friends were already here," the bartender said.

"We're running late. Thank you for showing us the way."

"Part of the job." He pointed to stairs that descended into a basement. "Here it is."

The air was clear down there. He pointed to the door at the bottom, then gestured to his post. "I need to get back up to the front. Remind them to take it easy. They might pay a lot, but I still don't like fixing doors." He hurried back into the smog.

The doorknob was new and locked. He waited until the bartender was out of earshot and turned to Alyssa. "Do you have any spells or charms that might help?"

She gave a small smile and pulled out a thin horn, traced three runes on it, placed it on the door, then got on her knees and listened. Zane bent his knees beside her. He stared at the sticky floor and hated the idea of having to clean the filth off his pants. His jacket was already dirty with ash, so he removed it and carefully laid it on the floor and placed a knee on its corner.

Alyssa focused on listening and repeated what she heard.

"The clans won't reunite without the Moon's Chosen. Is our revolution at an end? No, the plan must go on. ...But we haven't seen a Moon Chosen in hundreds of years. Are we not forsaken? ...No, I have consulted the bones and I know for sure. The Chosen has returned in our time. ...Will they join us? ...Yes, the Chosen is marked by destiny to lead our homeland. We will clear a path."

There was a large slam and even in the hall Zane could hear the shout.

"No more secrets. I won't stand for it. I want to meet the Chosen."

Alyssa adjusted the horn and continued repeating the conversation.

"Fine. I am about to head there now. Follow me, my comrades."

She stood suddenly and pulled the horn from the door. "I think they are coming to the door. What should we do?"

Zane tripped on his jacket and Alyssa helped him up. He swore at the sticky floor and swiped his jacket from the ground. They hustled up the stairs and into the dense smoke, stopping at a small table by a window.

He turned and spoke in a low voice. "We'll blend in and wait for them to leave. Then we will follow."

They were concealed by the haze when a stream of men entered the pub's main room. One by one, they walked straight for the door and out into the street. Zane managed to wipe a window clean enough to see through. He watched each person, taking note of what they looked like. The group wore normal clothing for the city and didn't stand out.

Except for Evan.

The big man wore a large wolf fur cloak, a large sword, giving him the look of a wildman. Evan took the lead and walked down the sidewalk. Treading carefully, Zane and Alyssa exited the bar and trailed two blocks behind.

Evan was a giant among men. Crowds seemed to part in front of him and his group. The cobbled streets became progressively filthier as they passed into lower-class areas, finally turning into a mixture of stained colors and mud as they neared Potion Lane.

Zane recognized where they were going and leaned over to Alyssa. "I think they are going to The Wizard's Brew."

"But why? The only ones there are Fex and Vana. I thought they were looking for the *Chosen One*?"

Zane nodded. "Exactly."

They watched as the men turned onto Potion Lane. Members of the crowd were forced into the nearest shop or alley until they passed. As Evan marched out in front of his followers, Zane recognized the noble air with which he moved. When they stopped in front of The Brew, Zane pulled Alyssa closer until they stood at the edge of the men, who kept their focus on the shop's entrance.

Evan raised a hand to bang on the door but stopped short. Instead, he knocked with an air of respect. Vana opened it. Her veil was pulled up, revealing a smirking face. Some of Evan's men gasped and pointed. Murmurs spread throughout the group.

Evan coughed. "Sister, your veil is up. That is, well… not appropriate." He looked over his shoulder to the increasingly agitated men. "But that's not important. Sister, may we come inside? We have some important conversations before us."

Vana's right eye twitched. She bowed, but with none of the grace or poise she normally had. Zane's hand drifted to his wand.

Alyssa tugged on his arm and whispered. "What is going on?"

"I don't know, but my gut says something is wrong."

"Your gut?"

She sounded confused, as though she'd never heard the term. "My instincts," he said, realizing Alyssa's extended stay inside The Institute for so long had interesting consequences.

Vana spoke, but her voice lacked its usual strength. "I am sorry. I didn't expect any guests. Please give me a moment to clean up."

She stepped back into the shop. The men whispered among themselves, and some even started to break away.

Evan turned back. "Please wait. I promise"—he paused, straightened his posture, and spoke with bold confidence—"no, our ancestors promised us a future purchased from the Fates themselves." He cleared his throat, as though preparing for a grand speech. "This will be a day to rem—"

A sharp squeal rang out from the street behind them, like broken glass being dragged over another sheet of glass, followed by a scream of pain. Everyone turned to the sound. On the far side from Zane and Alyssa stood several goblins, their faces painted red, each armed with knives, bats, and even short swords. A man from Evan's group laid on the ground bleeding, his cry for help cut short by a goblin's cudgel.

Zane pulled his wand and pushed through the crowd as his years of military training took over. He knew he needed space for a clear shot. Some of the men broke and ran. Others pulled hidden weapons. Evan removed his sword from its sheath and cried out in a language that Zane didn't understand. His followers returned his cry as they prepared for a battle.

Zane fired into the cluster of goblins. They fought back with a fanatic vigor, and even those without weapons would not give ground. Everything seemed to blur, and Zane felt like he had been here before.

A twisted sense of peace settled over him. Zane was back in the Ghoul War.

His wand emptied, Zane reached into his coat for more spell wicks. He turned as two weak hands grabbed the back of his jacket and Alyssa pulled close to him. Her lips moved, but the words were lost in the commotion, so he ignored her and loaded his wand. Spent spell wicks bounced against the bricks. He loaded the wand and tightened the cap, but the remaining goblins rushed off down multiple alleyways. Cold sweat clung to Zane's body as he came back to his senses.

He turned to ask Alyssa if she was okay, but a whistle cut him off. He cursed at the source.

The City Imperial Guard rushed in from both ends of Potion Lane. The runes on their staves hummed and glowed with power. The same mustachioed lieutenant stood out front, his wand in one hand. "Everyone drop your weapons!"

Zane dropped his wand and checked to make sure Alyssa was unharmed. She was sobbing, but before he could even attempt to comfort her, a man from the crowd pointed a knife at the guards. "We were attacked! Who are you—"

The lieutenant blasted the man's leg with wand fire. The man dropped, holding his ruined leg.

The lieutenant leveled his wand again. "Everyone drop your weapons and prepare to be arrested."

The remaining crowd complied. Members of the guard rushed forward, clamping cuffs on everyone. Zane kept his voice smooth and reassuring as he spoke to Alyssa. "Don't resist. Things will be all right. Just listen to me."

She was still crying, but she nodded. Alyssa had never seen war and didn't realize the battle was over.

Zane turned to the nearest guard. "Are we being taken to the local house?"

The guard punched Zane in the face. "Shut up! We are asking the questions here!"

The City Imperial guard was not known for civility. He spat on the ground just as Evan was moved alongside him. "Is this your fault, *detective*?"

Zane shook his head. "I don't even know what's going on."

Evan's veins bulged against his skin, but he remained in control as the guards led them down the street. Zane kept an eye on Alyssa, who was being handled with care by the guardsmen.

For this small blessing, Zane was thankful.

⌇

ALYSSA'S TORRENT OF emotions were wrapped tightly with fear. Her cheeks burned with tears that streaked down her face, not yet wiped because her hands were cuffed and attached by a short chain to a similar pair of manacles around her ankles. The guards had left her in a small, solitary room, her bag resting beside her on a soft couch across from a desk. Alyssa wished she could have stayed with Zane, even if he was in a dark cell.

A grey-headed officer entered the room, wearing a breastplate showing an emblazoned star below a thin line. "Hello, I am Captain Bersk, and I am in charge of this district. To be honest with you, we have looked over the scene and all we can determine is that some goblins attacked."

She couldn't detect any form of question in his speech. "I am sorry, but I am not sure what I am doing here?"

The captain stared at her. To Alyssa, he looked like a man trying to solve a puzzle. "Fine, let's start with this. What is your name?"

She cleared her throat and tried to speak clearly. "I am Alyssa Benedictus, third class mage and a professor at The Institute of Sorcery and Science."

Captain Bersk's face paled at the words, but he kept calm. "You do know that impersonating a state mage is a crime punishable by The Institute. So, if you're lying, I recommend coming clean right now."

She shook her head. "I am telling the truth. I even have documentation I can show you, if you take off my cuffs."

His eyes narrowed, but at last he sighed. With a single thin key, he unlocked the wrist restraints. "Any funny business and I will see that you're behind bars for a long time."

She nodded and pulled her badge and some paperwork from her bag. The captain left the badge on the desk as if it might bite him and looked over the paperwork. "Fine, but what is a member of The Institute doing down here in this pit of the city?"

Bersk handed back the paperwork and badge, and Alyssa, her hands now free, finally wiped the dried tears from her face. "Have you heard about the murder of a man named Dennis Zel?"

Bersk nodded and tapped his desk. "It came up in a report. Something about an alchemist's death, with the main suspect being his wife. A private detective stopped my men from arresting her."

She narrowed her eyes in confusion. "Is that all you know? I spoke with some of the guards yesterday."

He stopped tapping his fingers. "No, I haven't heard anything else. Will you go over the details with me?"

She pointed to the papers on his desk. "With the help of Detective Vrexon, I am investigating Dennis Zel's death, as he was a state mage employed by The Institute."

The man rubbed his temples, eyes closed in frustration. "Did you get the name of the guard you told this to?"

"I am sorry, but he didn't say."

"Bastard knew not to say that much at least," Captain Bersk muttered before opening a pair of newly bloodshot eyes. "I need you to fill out some paperwork."

z

ZANE TASTED IRON. His shoulder and leg throbbed, but he refused to let the pain control him. The swelling around his left eye was growing, threatening to blind him on that side. He raised his right arm in self-defense as Evan's hammer of a fist slammed into him again.

"You accuse me?" he screamed.

Asking questions in a small cell had not been a good idea.

"I am only following up on my leads—"

Another meaty fist hit him. The world spun, and Zane was forced to steady himself on the wall. "Let me finish, dammit." He spat on the ground. "I am trying to help Vana."

Evan's bright-red face was drenched with sweat and his breathing heavy after the continuous pounding he was serving Zane. "Help? You are clueless for a *detective*." He spat on Zane and turned away to a nearby bench, where he sat and looked through the bars out into the hallway.

Zane let himself slump to the floor. His body throbbed and the agony threatened to overtake him.

Shadow settled into a corner, its red eyes staring at Zane while remaining silent.

The detective took a deep breath before speaking again. "Can we start over?"

Evan took a deep breath and leaned away. Despite his savage look, his demeanor shifted toward civility. "What do you want to know?"

"You told your father that Dennis failed his exam at The Institute."

Evan nodded, his face stiff like leather. "That's right. He even has a letter about it. You saw it, right?"

"Yes."

"Then why are you asking me? You have your proof!"

Zane sighed. This case was not going in the direction he'd hoped. "But you didn't tell him that the letter was wrong." Zane studied Evan's face, fishing for information, waiting for any change, no matter how small. "Why?"

The leathery face crinkled. "No need to worry him. I can handle the family business. If the letter is full of lies, it's my job to find out why."

Zane spat out a small pool of blood. "Fine, but did you do anything with that information?"

The muscles on the big man's arms bulged. For a moment, Zane thought he was going to get another beating, but Evan sighed and relaxed. "No. I have more important things to do. Any other questions?"

Zane cracked a small smile. "Only if I don't get beaten down again."

Evan didn't so much as twitch, but Shadow laughed from its corner.

"I suggest you keep quiet," Evan said.

Zane used the wall to stand. "I want to know about *wolves* and the *Chosen*."

Mistake, Shadow whispered.

Evan leaped from his bench, but Zane was too tired to react. Evan slammed Zane into the wall and gripped his throat. "Pits! Who have you been talking to! Tell me now or I will snap your neck!"

Zane struggled to breathe. "Would you kill me in this cell?" he coughed out.

"Damn right!"

Evan's civility was completely gone, his savage fury on full display. "I own most of the guards here. Now talk!"

Shadow was yelling in his ear. *Talk, detective. Talk or we die.*

Zane hated himself. He hated Shadow. He hated not knowing if Evan was bluffing or not. "Fine..."

Evan released him and shoved him back into the wall. "Talk."

Zane wheezed, forcing air into his burning lungs. "We found some strange hair—fur, really—at The Wizard's Brew. It's not my area of expertise."

He looked at Evan to see his reaction. The big man's stern face was torn by a large grin, his demeanor completely different. "Fur? Like that of a wolf?"

Zane nodded. "The Institute ran a test. It's both human and canine in nature."

Evan started to laugh so loud it roared out and down the hall. He grabbed the bars. "The moon truly has descended. I had doubts, but now I know our work is blessed."

His thunderous laughter was met with cheers from his followers in neighboring cells. Their enthusiasm put things into perspective, and an image began coming into focus.

Evan turned back to Zane. "What do you know about the Chosen?"

Zane shrugged his shoulders. "Only the phrase *the Moon's Chosen*... and one other thing."

"What's that?"

Don't push it, Shadow warned.

Zane turned his head to the corner and smirked at the creature.

"I know who the *Chosen* is."

Evan's grin turned into an aggressive scowl. He stepped closer and Zane flattened himself against the wall of the cell. "How would you know that?" he growled.

Zane glanced at a guard who watched dispassionately. "Because I followed you from The Foolish Noble to The Brew. Only two people are there now, and I doubt you were talking about Fex."

Evan was only a step away from him with murderous intent in his eyes.

You went too far, Shadow whispered.

Just in time, a commanding voice echoed down the hall that stopped the large man short of wringing Zane's neck. "Where is the detective?"

The guard ran down the hall to answer the voice. "This way, sir."

Zane heard hurried footsteps until a grey-haired man stood on the other side of the bars. Evan backed away to his bench. Zane spotted the breastplate with the star and a line above it. "I am Captain Bersk. Follow me, Detective Vrexon."

The jailer unlocked the cell and stepped to the side. Zane limped out of the cell, then looked over his shoulder to Evan.

"We'll talk later."

z

ALYSSA GASPED AND covered her mouth when the door opened and Zane walked into the captain's office. She reached out to his face but stopped short of touching it. It was swollen, and large bruises were already forming. "Are you okay?"

He forced a smile. "I will be alright. How are you?"

She didn't answer but motioned toward a spot on the couch. She waited for him to sit before taking her place beside him. Bersk followed him into the room and sat behind his desk. "So, I understand both of you are working a case. A case my men said nothing about. Tell me what you have found."

Zane's words were muffled as he spoke with thick, cracked lips. "Sir, we are still in the middle of the investiga—"

The captain slammed a hand onto the desk. "My men have either lied to me or are being insubordinate, neither of which can be tolerated. Now tell me what you know so I may start an investigation of my own."

Alyssa looked to Zane. As disreputable as the guards could be, they were still professionals, and she liked the idea of getting their help. She nodded to Zane, hoping he would understand the gesture.

He sighed in resignation and nodded back. "Can you explain it? My mouth hurts."

She turned back to the captain. "First, thank you for releasing Zane. At this time, we don't know much. Dennis's death was only two days ago. At the scene, we found his state badge, the murder weapon, and some fur."

Bersk grunted and opened his notebook with a pen in hand. "I don't care about fur or badges. What was the murder weapon?"

"It was a rare Fey-made dagger, magical in nature, smeared with a poison known as Last Death."

The captain frowned. "Could some Fey gang be involved? We just witnessed goblins attacking people in the middle of the street."

Alyssa shook her head. "We don't know. It's true that we have found some Fey-related elements, but the poison used is something rare, from the Eastern Territories."

Bersk sighed. "Of course, it would be."

Zane sat up straight. "What's that supposed to mean?"

"Most of the men we took from that goblin attack are Eastern folk, one way or another."

"How can you tell?"

He pointed to his arms. "The blue tattoos. All of those hardcore traditionalist bastards, even their women, will tattoo themselves."

Zane covered his face with his palm and shook his head before leaning back.

Alyssa turned to the captain. "What does that have to do with anything?"

"Some lieutenants have been talking, and mind you, it has been some time, but word is a group of Easterners has been paying off guards to look the other way. For small things mostly, nothing on the level of a murder."

He stood and pointed to the door. "You two are free to go. My men shall look into this matter further."

Alyssa offered her arm to Zane, who stood slowly. "Sir," she said, "with respect, we are still gathering information."

Bersk waved his hand. "It's obvious that the Eastern gangs are working with or fighting with some Fey gang. This Dennis Zel must have been caught in the crossfire. I will let you know when we have concluded our investigation."

Alyssa and Zane were escorted from the office into the lobby of the guard station. Zane's voice was weak. "I am sorry, but could you help me walk?"

She nodded. Zane reached his arm around her shoulders and she gripped him around his waist, surprised at how heavy he was. "Where are we going?"

"To The Wizard's Brew. We have work to do."

CHAPTER 15

A banging at the front of the shop reached deep into Fex's sleep. He thought he'd heard yelling earlier, but now he couldn't tell whether he had dreamed it. The gnome rolled out of bed. His clothes—the same ones he'd worn the day before—were a mess, and his hair stuck to his head in odd shapes. He shook his head and wrapped his hand around his wand.

The workshop was the same as he'd left it, except the back door was open. He pulled the door shut and stepped into the front. Papers were spread across the floor behind the counter and the knocking was even harder now.

"Vana, are you there?" A woman's voice.

"We are closed," Fex yelled. "And no, she isn't here."

The knocking went on.

"Look the door is locked and we are—"

The voice called again and this time Fex recognized it.

"It's Alyssa and Zane, could you please let us in?"

Fex called back as he walked to the door, wand in hand, just in case. "One moment, I got to unbolt it."

The gnome finally swung the door open and gasped at what he saw. Leaning against the doorway of the shop, Alyssa held up Zane, whose face was swollen. "Oh saints, man! What happened to you? Come in, come in!"

Fex pointed to the back of the shop with the wand and locked up before retreating with them. Alyssa struggled to help the man limp his way to the workshop. In the back, Zane leaned against the table.

"Thank you, Mister Fex, but could you please put the wand away?"

The gnome almost jerked his hand in surprise before placing the weapon on a nearby counter. "Sorry, I have been busy. I had a long night. I think... maybe... I don't know." Fex shook his head to clear his thoughts. "That's beside the point. What happened?"

Zane coughed. "It's complicated. Can I have a healing potion?"

Fex grabbed one from the shelf and handed it to Zane, who drank it in one gulp and took a deep breath before speaking. "We went to the Ironbark family's estate and—"

"The who?"

"The Ironbarks," Zane said. "They sponsored Dennis for his exam and paid off his loan."

Fex looked incredulous. "Why would they do that?"

Alyssa answered. "Vana and Evan are Ironbark born. Their father is the patriarch."

Fex looked from Zane to Alyssa, expecting one of them to crack a smile in jest. He could understand that Zane was not thinking straight, with all the damage to his head. But Alyssa, too?

"Their name is Zel..."

"She's right," Zane said. "Zel and Ironbark are one and the same. Vana's father told us that Evan's favorite place to drink was The Foolish Noble. Sure enough, we found him and his followers there."

Fex felt the blood drain from his face at the name of the bar. "I... I have been there."

Zane and Alyssa looked to each other and then back to the gnome. The detective raised an inquisitive eyebrow. "The Foolish Noble didn't strike me as a place a gnome would go."

"I followed Evan there. Well, I hired a kid to follow him, then I went there myself. You won't believe what he was doing in that basement. No, wait, I am getting ahead of myself."

Zane made direct eye contact with Fex to silence and calm him. "It's all right. Start from the beginning."

The gnome relaxed and ran his hand through his messy hair and summarized the previous day's events, then eased himself down to the floor. A weight had been lifted. "I think I was drugged because on the way home I saw a monster who could... shift and inflate its limbs. It attacked me. I ran out of spell wicks and thought I was dead, but then a giant wolf saved me."

He closed his eyes, expecting to be called insane, but Alyssa's response was immediate.

"Did you say wolf?"

Fex looked up at Alyssa, who held a hand near her mouth. "Zane, could it have been?"

The detective stood quickly, almost collapsing under his own weight before leaning against the table. "Fex, where is Vana?"

"I don't know. I saw her early this morning. I had stayed up all night rolling wicks so she told me to go to bed."

Zane sighed. "I guess you slept through the goblin attack?"

Fex jerked his head to Zane. "Goblins? Where?"

Alyssa crossed the room to the gnome. "We followed Evan and his followers here. At the door, we saw Vana. Evan seemed upset her veil was pulled up, but before we could learn anything more, goblins attacked everyone."

Fex's mouth ran dry. "What did her face look like?"

Zane shrugged. "Normal. Just like I saw her yesterday."

The gnome shook his head. "It shouldn't. Her face was covered with huge swaths of bruises, at least on the night of the murder. Later, I saw her face completely clear, but that couldn't be."

Alyssa looked confused and looked to Fex and Zane for an explanation. "Why couldn't it? You work in a potion shop. It wouldn't have been difficult to fix herself up."

Zane answered first. "No healing potion or elixir I know of can get rid of bruises. They can mend wounds, but they can't remove the blood that has already pooled beneath the skin."

Alyssa caught on. "So, someone with an unblemished face couldn't be the same person."

The three stood in silence until it was destroyed by the turning of keys at the front door. A female voice carried to the back. "Fex, are you here?"

He called back without thinking. "Yes."

The footsteps carried across the hardwood floor. Zane rested his hand in his jacket. Fex realized the detective was reaching for his wand, so Fex grabbed his own off the table and held it behind his back.

The door swung open to the workshop. Vana was dressed in black. And wearing a veil.

"Oh detective, Ms. Benedictus," she said. "I didn't realize you were here. I was out for a walk."

She faced Fex. "Do you know what happened out front? There are blood stains on the pavement."

It was a cold way of speaking, lacking any depth of emotion or concern. Was she the bruised or unbruised Vana? Whichever she was, the Vana sniffed and walked to the back door. She laid her hand on it gently, then slammed her palm into it with surprising force.

She turned back to the others, fidgeting with her clothes. "I am sorry. It's been a long day. I seem to have forgotten myself. Fex, do you remember where I said I was going?"

Fex opened his mouth to answer but froze in fear. He didn't know what to do.

Zane spoke up. "Lady Zel, I have some questions. I don't know how to ask this but..."

"But what?"

"Will you please lift your veil?"

She gave off a low growl, and Zane rocked for a moment as if he would take a step back.

"Do you know what you're asking?" Her voice was fierce but controlled.

Fex felt smaller than ever before, as if standing in front of a large predator. Zane looked undaunted, and Fex wondered how.

"I probably don't," the detective answered. "At least not as well as I should. But when it comes to you, I find myself having to ask such blind questions. So, again, will you please lift your veil?"

The growl faded and she stood rigid. With her left hand, the one with her amber ring, Vana Zel lifted her veil.

Fex's stomach turned as he took in the sight.

Vana's face was bruised, as he remembered. But in the light of the workshop, he could see that her delicate cheekbones were twisted and deformed, as if she had been beaten with a club, healed, then beaten again.

Alyssa gasped and stepped forward. "Vana, you need to see a doctor. That is not something a healing potion can fix."

"I know." The comment was dry and matter of fact. Vana dropped the veil back down with the same hand. "I hope this satisfies your questions, *detective*."

Even Zane's face seemed green, as though he might get sick at any moment. "Yes, thank you. Alyssa, if you please?"

Alyssa approached him and let him place an arm over her shoulders. The detective looked at her but spoke to Vana. "I am sorry Vana. We are making progress, I think. If you will excuse us."

Vana stepped to the side as the two stumbled out. Lady Zel turned back to Fex. He couldn't see her face, but he could feel the glare.

"What is going on?"

CHAPTER 16

D o you understand?" His voice was even more stern the second time.

She studied his face and tried to read his expression but nodded slowly.

One less thing to worry about. "Follow me."

Zane leaned heavily on the rail next to the stairs as he walked up. The door was locked so he gave a lazy knock. "It's Zane, the detective. I need to talk."

A human voice called back. "Detective? I was not expecting you back so soon. I don't think this is a good time."

"I don't care! Open it!"

Hushed voices argued, but Zane couldn't make them out. The hair on the back of his neck stood on end. "Fine," the voice said as the door clicked open. The clerk, Gene, was prim and proper, just as he remembered. He looked Zane over, not even a flinch at his injuries, then glanced at Alyssa. "Who is she?"

"A partner in the investigation. I have questions."

"Can't they wait?"

"No."

Gene sighed and stepped to the side. "Come in then. Be careful what you say. The boss is not happy."

He limped in with Alyssa in tow. Four goblins stood around the desk, each sitting on a stool. Nob sat in what would have been the clerk's middle chair. The goblin boss snuffed out his cigar and eyed Zane. "Detective hume, I hope this is of importance."

Zane attempted to give a polite bow but his body resisted. "My partner and I had a run in with some goblins on Potion Lane."

A large goblin with deep facial scars snarled. "Did they wear red paint?"

"Yes, all over their faces. Do you know this gang?"

Nob wiped his head. "That would be the Red Tusk Gang. They have been a pain in our arse for a while. But dammit" — Nob slammed a fist onto the table — "they have crossed too far into our territory this time."

Zane limped to the wall and leaned against it. Alyssa stood somewhere behind him, out of his sight. "They are related to my case. What do you know about them?"

A one-eyed goblin picked his fingernail with his knife, his one good ear flopping as he spoke. "They mainly sell and run drugs, but they do some… *enforcement* work for the right price. Need someone gone, they hit them fast and hard, with too many goblins for the hume guards to arrest."

"So, was this related to drugs or did someone call for a hit?"

The goblins exchanged glances and talked in their native language, which was like listening to a mix of barks and screeches. Nob leaned back when they stopped. "We think it's a hit, but we're not sure. Rumor is, the Red Tusk have a seller on Potion Lane who might know more, but there's no telling who it is."

Zane sighed. He was tired, and this case was not getting any easier. "But this seller might know who hired the goblins? And what merchandise they are moving?"

"We know the answer to your second question," Nob said. "Ambrose."

Zane's face twitched. Ambrose was of one of the strongest — and most dangerous — of the healing potions. He heard legends of people almost regrowing fingers before their bodies shut down from the rapid strain. Ambrose was highly controlled by the state, so Zane thought he'd never encounter the stuff. "How did they get ahold of something like that?"

Nob's eyes went wide, and Zane could see jealousy in those grey globes. "If I knew, I would be selling it. Not them." With one of his long fingers, the goblin drummed on the table. He seemed tired and bothered. "Is there anything else I can help you with, detective?"

Zane turned to face Alyssa. The state mage was white as a sheet and she fought the rigidity of her face as she mouthed, *can we leave*? Zane let out a nervous chuckle. The detective was exhausted, and all he wanted to do was climb into a potion bottle.

"No," Zane said, answering Nob. "Thank you for your time."

He tried to bow again, then turned toward the door. Alyssa led the way to the exit and stepped through ahead of Zane. She waited until they were down a floor to blurt out the question that appeared to have been eating her insides like the Last Death. "Was that the Goblin Mob?"

Zane smirked. "Yes. The short version is that Dennis had taken a loan from them, but the Ironbark family paid it off."

Once outside, Alyssa looked up and down the street before turning to Zane. "Where to now?"

Zane was panting. "Somewhere to sit down."

FEX SAT ACROSS the workshop from Vana as she brewed potions. She hadn't spoken a single word since Zane and Alyssa left. He couldn't blame her; they had asked her to commit a cultural taboo.

But the silence was too much for him to bear. "I am sorry."

The blurted words forced Vana to look up from her work. She set down the potion and turned off the valve of her Bunsen burner. When she spoke, her voice was calm. "Why did you need to see my face?"

Fex looked at the floor. "I saw you, or someone who looks exactly like you, murder a person. I saw your face, but it had no bruises. I needed to know who was real."

"And it wasn't for the ownership of The Brew?"

Fex shivered.

"No reason to be surprised, Fex. I have heard what people are saying. They call me a monster. Were you hoping to get me put away so you could take over the shop?"

Fex fumbled for words. "No. Maybe. I don't know. I … I don't know."

Vana breathed out and her frame seemed to shrink. "Make no mistake. I am a monster, but not the kind they are making me out to be." She was quiet for a moment. "I didn't kill my husband."

Fex watched as she stepped toward the back door and touched it, lost in thought. "I can smell the thing that killed Dennis. I think it can change its shape. I have followed it when I could, but it's clever. It would double back on its own trail. Hiding in the shop, or even in my own home. I thought I would kill it last night."

"Last night?"

Vana let out a twisted laugh, one Fex could only imagine coming from someone losing her sanity. "It found you in the street after you walked out of the bar. It looked like it was about to crush you."

The blood drained from Fex's face. Images of the beast that came out of nowhere flickered in his mind. "But that would mean…"

"Yes."

"How?"

She spoke to the wall like it was a faraway audience. "There are family legends of men who fought like wolves. I have always thought that they were exaggerated, but now" —she turned to Fex with eyes glowing like embers— "after what has been happening since the night of Dennis's death, I know at least some of the stories are true."

"The claw marks in the shop. You were fighting the thing that killed

Dennis."

Her body trembled, then she sobbed, tears dripping from below her veil. "Everything hurts. Everything. My body feels like it is being ripped apart."

Fex jumped up and tried to comfort her, but he was out of his depth. "It's all right. We, we can find help. Let's go see Alyssa. Maybe she could—"

"No! I will find who killed my Dennis!" Vana expanded, her clothes straining to contain her form. "I will use this power and rip the life from their body."

"Then why hire the detective?"

"I can follow the creature's scent, but it's smart. I can never pin down this monster. I keep getting close, but always just out of reach."

Fex stepped back. He wanted to run, but he stayed—against his better judgement.

"Now," she growled, "tell me everything you know."

CHAPTER 17

T he iron doors of The Institute welcomed Alyssa. The shifting halls and rooms were a comfort when compared to the static world outside. She wanted to relax but decided to do some research first. At her command, the halls gave way to a large library.

The Institute's was the empire's largest, containing several floors organized by subject. She stepped out onto the fifth floor of the room. A tired-eyed boy sat behind the clerk's desk. "Welcome to the religion and philosophy floor. Can I be of help?"

Alyssa couldn't contain a smile. "I thought you were supposed to say, *How may I help you?*"

The student sighed and rubbed his temples. "That is what I thought, but Archmage Palo-Lasome came by—"

"He argued that you can't offer help since you can't help yourself."

The student looked up and nodded. "Yes, that's right. Does this happen often?"

She remembered her time working at that desk. "Yes, anytime someone new sits in your seat. I am looking for information on the religious practices of the Eastern Territory."

He stood and stared across the room, then pointed to different volumes bound in leather. "These are not replicas, but originals handwritten by priests who traveled there years ago, so we ask you to be careful. Is there anything else you need?"

Alyssa pointed to the books. "Are you familiar with this culture?"

He shook his head. No easy answers. She thanked the young man, who bowed and walked away.

Alyssa grabbed the thick volumes and carried them to a nearby desk. The handwriting was rough and several pages were stained, with much of its content dedicated to simple day-to-day activities of the priest. She thought it was amazing how little was written about the territory that had been part of the empire for a few hundred years. She pressed on with her research.

As the hours passed, the gas lights never wavered, nor did she.

Alyssa looked up to find someone staring down at her. She gave a polite smile.

"Agwen, I am sorry. I didn't see you there. Please, have a seat."

He nodded and, with an almost inhuman grace, he took his seat. He smiled pleasantly, the first one she had seen from him in days. "How are you?"

She didn't know how to answer.

The day had been stressful, starting with the attack in her sleep. Then there was her imprisonment after the goblin assault. She hadn't noticed how tired she was until Agwen disturbed her studies.

"I am feeling weak at the moment, but I see no other choice but to press on."

Agwen leaned forward, and her old friend's presence felt reassuring. "Can I be of help?"

She thought it over for a moment. "I need a sounding board if you have time?"

He nodded and leaned back, his hands covering his lap. "Of course."

Alyssa opened and pointed at several of the texts. "I am looking into what is referred to as the Moon's Chosen. From what I can see, it is a religious practice of the Eastern Territory. The priest who wrote this book doesn't say much, but he claims the Chosen is a high priest of sorts, one that is reborn into their role."

"It sounds similar to the belief of the great spiral of the Fey, that the great souls are sent back to help lead."

She hadn't thought of that, but that didn't fully explain it. "There is more. It seems there is no specific personality or physical trait that is desired in the Chosen. Instead, the wording is unorthodox."

Agwen had seemed more interested from the moment he had made the connection to his own culture. "How so?"

"Well, they are reborn into this rank. The priest comments that they must be able to bear something called the *moon's marking* to be the Moon's Chosen."

Agwen smiled. "Essentially, the Moon's Chosen is one who can physically become a Moon's Chosen. It seems circular in nature. There must be more."

Alyssa was thankful to share her thoughts with someone of the same mind. "That is what I thought, so I started searching more broadly, and I think I found it. Every Eastern clan has a common symbol—the wolf."

He shrugged. "What does the wolf mean?"

Right, she reminded herself. He didn't know about the details she had found during the investigation into Dennis Zel's death. She needed to bring him up to speed. "We found some interesting things…"

She looked around, searching for anyone who might be in earshot. Agwen understood and spoke arcane words, causing the air around them to ripple with power—a spell that would keep their conversation private.

Alyssa felt safe to continue. "We found scratches in the wood like claw marks, and the other day I ran a test and found that the hair discovered at the scene was an example of polymorphism."

Agwen's composed face seemed to break down. "No, that can't be."

"But it is. It's a cross between human and wolf."

"So, the Moon's Chosen is a person capable of becoming a wolf. Is that what you're suggesting?"

"Yes."

He nodded, his face lost in thought. "That is fascinating, but how is it related to the case? Is this Moon's Chosen the murderer?"

"No, but we ran into a group… worshiping the Chosen is maybe the best way to put it. But it doesn't make sense for them to murder her husband."

"Could the client, this Moon's Chosen, have lost control?"

"I don't think so. But Zane had a run-in with an assassin." Alyssa couldn't control her face, and Agwen leaned in closer in response to her obvious distress.

"What happened?" he asked. "Are you okay?"

"It's all so horrible. Did I mention we were attacked by goblins?"

"Goblins? Why?"

Alyssa held back tears. The whirlwind of violence had been quick, but it had left a lasting impact. "We followed the group of worshipers to the client's shop, then a gang of goblins came out of nowhere. The guards think there is a conflict between them, but that still doesn't make sense."

Agwen's face flickered between emotions for a moment. She couldn't read it, but he seemed kind when he spoke. "I am sorry. Maybe you should spend the rest of your vacation here at The Institute, perhaps end your *vacation* early? Tatius-Lasome and Benedictus-Lasome would understand."

They would understand, and Alyssa appreciated that, but she wasn't ready to give up. "I need to see this through to the end. Is Tatius-Lasome back yet?"

Agwen relaxed. "No, but he might be back tomorrow. Are you sure you won't stay here, away from this dangerous enterprise?"

Alyssa shook her head. "Thank you for your concern, though."

"No," Agwen said with a grin. "Thank you."

ZANE LIMPED AWAY from The Institute after dropping off Alyssa. Each step seemed to jolt his body. He needed more troll's blood, but he couldn't afford any, especially since he needed the money to repair his apartment. Zane focused instead on what he could control. Each step carried him closer to the Fey district and back to the smith.

Once inside the shop, Jweal escorted him to the back and an apprentice brought him a cup of tea. It helped relax his throat, but it wasn't enough to take the edge off.

Jweal looked as if Zane had put him in an awkward position. "You look like hell."

"I feel like hell." Zane sipped the tea. "I have a couple of questions."

"I assumed. What do you need this time?"

Zane could tell Jweal was irritated with him and his questions. The smith probably felt like Zane was picking at things that would incriminate the Fey, but that wasn't why Zane was there. "I need one more thing and our business will be done. Then I will tell our mutual *friend* that you are squared away. Is that fine?"

Jweal rubbed his chin. He had the look of a man trying to avoid a scam but relented. "What do you want?"

"I need a cane that can conceal a blade."

"That's it? We can do that for you. Wouldn't be the first one of those we've made."

"There is one more thing, though."

CHAPTER 18

It was early, but Fex was already on the brink of exhaustion. The last few days had stretched him to his limits, and he didn't know if he could keep dealing with this much stress. At least he had clear orders, which helped take the burden of making decisions off his shoulders.

The duty guards at the desk frowned at his approach. "How can we help you?"

Fex pulled out a letter written and sealed by Vana. The guard refused to even reach for the envelope. "Look here, if this is not important, then you better get out."

Of course. I should expect such laziness from humans. "This letter was written by the daughter of a noble house."

The guard banged on the desk so hard it shook his inkwell. "Do not lie to me, speck. If this is a letter from a noble's daughter, where is her servant?"

Fex gritted his teeth and tossed the envelope across the desk. "Maybe you should read it."

The guard's face was beet red with veins quivering against his skin. He tore open the envelope and bank notes fell onto the desk. The guard seemed confused, but he started reading the letter with vigor.

Fex had spent the previous evening running errands for Vana, mostly to her family estate. The old butler, Giles, helped him greatly, never questioning him. Fex appreciated that.

The guard's throat sounded dry when he finally spoke. "I am sorry. Please wait one moment." He stood quickly, knocking his pens over.

After grabbing the bank notes, the guard hustled to the lieutenant's office. The bang of a slamming door carried through the air, and yelling could be heard inside the small space. The door flew open, and the lieutenant marched out to Fex. The imposing man stared down at him, and Fex could see his own face in the polished metal of the lieutenant's breast plate.

"What the hell is this?"

Fex gave a small bow, trying to come across as polite. "It's a letter written by a noble house wishing to pay for the release of Evan—"

"Saints damn you! I can read, speck. But why?"

Fex played the idiot. "How am I, a speck, to know such things?"

The gnome could have cooked breakfast on the man's head, judging by how red his face was. Fex was nervous that the lieutenant would start to beat him, but he shoved the letter into one of his pants pockets and turned to a nearby guard. "Go get Zel."

"But sir..."

"I said get Evan Zel," he yelled. "Now."

The lieutenant knelt until he and Fex were at eye level. "After I turn Evan over to you, I never want to see you again. Understood?"

Fex nodded and the lieutenant stormed back to his office. The gnome whistled until Evan came out front with the guard, who looked at him doubtfully. "You and your employer are in charge of this man. His friends will be staying here until we are satisfied with their stories."

He turned back to Evan. "I hope to never see you again."

The guard walked away and Evan met Fex's gaze. "Did my sister send you?"

Fex nodded. He hated the self-assured look that washed over Evan's face. The man looked as if everything was in his control.

"Let's go greet her then." Evan pointed to the door. "Open the door, gnome."

Fex was done with the disrespect and disregarded the request entirely. "I will see you at The Wizard's Brew."

Before Evan could react, Fex was out the door with the nimbleness of a rabbit. The massive man followed but couldn't catch up despite his long strides. The pedestrians slowed Evan down while. Fex darted from opening to opening, avoiding people as they walked—as he'd done for decades.

Vana met Fex inside the shop, standing regally in her mourning clothes. Her words rushed out from behind her veil. "Was Evan released?"

"Yes," Fex forced out between breaths. "He is almost here."

Fex hid behind her before the door opened and Evan stormed in, staring down at the gnome. He masked the anger as he looked up at his sister and spread his arms. "Thank you for freeing me from that unjust imprisonment. You could have acted sooner, but—"

"I did it for myself, not for you."

Vana's words left her brother speechless. Fex climbed up to his seat and watched with interest from behind the counter. Evan's face was streaked with shock, but he recovered and stepped toward her. "Sister, I come bearing good news. News of your future. I know you are going through... changes."

If Vana was affected by Evan's words, Fex couldn't tell. She was unmoving and cold, as if carved from ice. The gnome could feel the growing tension in the air the longer the siblings bickered.

"Sister, what is going on? We used to be so close. Let me show you something about yourself. Something you don't know..."

She turned away and placed a gentle hand on the counter. Circling the center table, Vana stopped short of passing her brother, then paced back the way she came. She prowled for a few more unnerving moments before snapping her fingers.

"Fex, please tell my brother what you told me."

ALYSSA SAT WITH Zane in a small café in the late morning. Over the course of coffee and breakfast, Alyssa shared everything she had learned about the Moon's Chosen. Zane nodded along and seemed to absorb all the information.

When Alyssa finished, he set down his cup. "So, about this polymorphism thing, are there physical signs?"

She cursed herself for not anticipating his question. "I am not a specialist in this field. In many Fey stories, the short answer is no, but their biology is different from ours. If I had to guess, I would say the change would be physically painful. *Very* painful."

The dark blue of bruises now seeped down Zane's cheeks like a leaking dam. It looked painful, and Alyssa had to resist the urge to grimace while addressing him. "Are you feeling better?"

He nodded, still staring into his cup. "Yes, just thinking. This case has become more and more convoluted. We need to figure out where the dagger came from."

She was about to reply when a letter with no outside markings slid across the table. No one had been standing near them, and even without touching it Alyssa could tell that the letter was charmed. She tore it open and read it.

Each word brought more frustration.

"What's it say?" Zane asked.

Alyssa looked up to see his concerned expression and realized she had crumpled the paper. "I am sorry," she said while smoothing out the wrinkles. "It's from The Institute. A review board has been called. They want to see me immediately. Something about dereliction of duty. It makes no sense. I mean, I took official leave of absence." She stood up, laying some money down on the table for their breakfast. "I am sorry detective, but I must leave."

Zane followed her out the door. "I am going with you. It's the least I can do after dragging you to the goblin mob."

They were still in the courtyard of The Institute, and with a short walk stepped through the large iron gates. Alyssa and Zane had just turned a corner in the building when a door opened and out stepped Archmage Benedictus-Lasome, out of breath. "I heard that you are being summoned."

Alyssa nodded. "Can you tell me what is going on? Who called for this?"

Benedictus-Lasome looked away as though searching for the right words. The lack of confidence struck Alyssa, and she felt her stomach drop.

"Grandfather, who called for it?"

"Archmage Tatius-Lasome."

Confusion struck like a heavy mallet. "Tatius-Lasome? But..."

Zane's gaze bounced between them. "Tatius-Lasome. He is your boss, right? Why would he summon you?"

She had known him for years. Tatius-Lasome had even been friends with her parents. *Was this something he would do?* Alyssa turned the question over in her head, but it made no sense no matter how she looked at it. "I have no idea."

Benedictus-Lasome waved them on. "I don't know either. The Archmage Tatius-Lasome is an odd man, but no more than any other archmage. This is very unorthodox. They should have waited for a report from you."

Alyssa felt a chill run through her. "Has it started?"

Her grandfather nodded urgently. "Come now, or you might get discredited without getting a word in."

The old man shuffled down the hall to the nearest door. He pulled out a giant ring and placed a heavy black iron key in the door. "We don't have time to find the proper door, so we will go straight to the room."

With a turn and click, the door opened. The room on the other side held a row of elevated benches, all filled with archmages in eccentric clothing. Alyssa recognized several of them, but she could not remember the last time she had seen so many in one place.

Tatius-Lasome's stooped form stood on the ground level. His voice carried through the door. "Deputy Wizard Alyssa Benedictus has abandoned her duty to the Fey Research and Rediscovery Department. She left to play detective with a shady—"

Principal Arch-Lasome knocked his iron staff. "Archmage Tatius-Lasome, please wait a moment. It seems your professor hasn't abandoned her duties entirely."

Arch-Lasome stood regal and tall with his flowing white beard. "Alyssa Benedictus, thank you for making it on short notice to this... unusual meeting." He pointed to a spot nearby. "You and your party may sit over there. We will call upon you in a moment."

Alyssa and Zane followed the man's long slender finger to a desk.

"Who was that archmage?" Zane asked.

"He is the head of The Institute, Principal Arch-Lasome."

Benedictus-Lasome climbed a set of stairs and joined the other aged wizards on the bench and Tatius-Lasome began again, droning on in a monotonous tone that Alyssa had never heard.

"We know nothing of this Zane Vrexon or his work, but somehow our glorious organization decides to partner with him. What does this say? It only makes sense that he has done something unforgivable to Alyssa under the guise of helping her. He has taken advantage of her. We should sever all ties, arrest him, and send Alyssa out for psychological evaluation until she can recover enough to fulfill her responsibilities."

There was a murmur among the archmages. Arch-Lasome brought it to a stop. "This is highly irregular. This was called to discuss Alyssa, not the detective."

Tatius-Lasome bowed. "Of course, but I believe if I question Mr. Vrexon, I may bring some things to light."

Arch-Lasome nodded. "I shall humor this request."

Tatius-Lasome stepped away and Arch-Lasome waved a hand.

"Deputy Wizard Alyssa Benedictus, you may come to the stage."

Alyssa took a deep breath and stepped past Zane onto the raised platform. "I volunteered to take on this position as an investigator for The Institute to repay Detective Vrexon, who rescued me from a device known as a Dream Sphere." She grew silent and guilt washed over her for a moment. "It was my vote that allowed Dennis Zel to join our ranks. For that reason, I felt... responsible for the man. The day he became a State Mage was the day he died. The following day, I, too, was attacked. I believed that this couldn't have been a coincidence."

A murmur rippled through the audience. She watched as confusion registered on their faces.

Arch-Lasome tapped his staff against the floor and the room fell silent. "This is the first time that we have heard anything about you being attacked. Why is that?"

All archmages should have been notified of the event as soon as it was discovered. Someone in The Institute was working against her, the same person who had buried Dennis's true exam results.

"I don't know," Alyssa said. "But archmages Agwen and Benedictus-Lasome were there. I was told Tatius-Lasome was out of town."

Alyssa scanned the crowd but couldn't find Agwen, which was not a good sign. "Through Archmage Agwen, I applied for a leave of absence. I have more than a few vacation days accrued, so I sought to use them to see if the murder was related to my attack. After helping Detective Vrexon, I know my attack and Dennis Zel's death are related."

Arch-Lasome nodded and stroked his beard. "Tatius-Lasome, what do you have to say about this?"

Tatius-Lasome mumbled to himself and his eyes scanned the archmages before resting back on Arch-Lasome. "I received no such information, nor did I receive any account of Alyssa asking for time off. This is the reason I have called you here. She claims she has *abandoned* her station for a noble goal, yet there is no proof that she asked to leave."

Arch-Lasome shook his head. "That is not enough for such a meeting to be called. If that is all, then I don't even know why we are here."

Alyssa searched the hushed audience. When she spoke, her voice echoed in the chamber. "Agwen, are you here?"

No one raised their voice to answer the call. An archmage sitting beside Arch-Lasome shook his head.

"Alyssa," Arch-Lasome said. "Do you have any other evidence?"

"No," she said. "The matter is simple. My friend Archmage Agwen said he would handle it all, but he is not here at the moment. May I ask for a temporary extension until he can testify?"

The bench of archmages broke into whispers and Tatius-Lasome snickered, something she had never seen the old man do.

Something was wrong.

A dull-eyed archmage, whose name Alyssa couldn't recall, stood. "I call for the case to be decided presently, and Alyssa to be evaluated. Dennis Zel was not even here a day. He does not warrant our attention. Furthermore, this Zane Vrexon, this *detective*, should not be associated in any way with The Institute.

"But," the archmage continued, "he should be questioned before being dismissed."

⁓

FEX WAS ON the verge of panic as he finished recounting his night at The Foolish Noble.

"I saw strange things. Evan was performing some heretical ritual, wearing animal skins with dozens of people. He tossed this powder into the fire. It induced some hallucinations."

Evan's eyes bulged in rage. "You followed me, you little waste of air! How dare you speak of the Mysterious. Shut up now!"

He panted, his shoulders rising and falling in rhythm. Under Evan's gaze, Fex shrank away in fear as his hand reached for the wand.

"I can explain all of this, my dear sister."

She stood still, regal. "Please do. I want to know why you invoke the Mysterious."

He smiled and made a symbol with his hands as though he were praying. "Times have changed, and I plan to correct the wrongs of the past. Our clan betrayed our ancestors, but I will save the motherland. The bones have spoken, though I am not the only one who sees it. Others have read the portent and know the stars are aligned for the clans to reunite. I have checked over and over."

Vana shook her head. "You did not answer my question. But no matter. What Mystery do you invoke?"

Evan smiled, as if he were aware of a joke that no one else knew. "I asked for the moon's guidance. And for the pack to run again."

"Why?"

The big man lunged forward at his sister, his body charged with an insanity that Fex had seen only in addicts. "I told you, the bones have spoken! The time for the Moon's Chosen is now!"

Vana pushed his arms away as he reached out to grab her. She continued to put distance between the two of them.

Then she stopped.

"Oh, now I understand."

"I doubt it," Evan said. "But I can teach you something of your destiny that you don't yet know. I am here to show you the way."

Vana stepped half a foot closer to Evan. Fex pulled back, making himself as small as he could in a room with two giants.

"Oh really," Vana said. "Tell me, how important is this destiny to you?"

Evan laughed as Vana took several measured steps closer. "I doubt you can grasp it. If you could, you would be jumping at my offer to leave for the ancestral land. This will be of the greatest importance. It will shape this age."

"Is it important enough to murder my Dennis?"

Fex watched, frozen by the growing tension. A low, mournful growl entered the room, rising the hair on the back of his neck. Fex looked for the source of the sound until he noticed Evan's imposing visage was white with pure fear.

CHAPTER 19

Z ane stood from his comfortable seat. His muscles argued against the action, but he pressed on with the help of the new cane he'd picked up the day before. Tatius-Lasome glared at him, a youthful light flickering in his dim eyes. The room had devolved into chaos, everyone talking over everyone else, No single voice was able to take control of the conversation. Zane and Tatius-Lasome looked at each other. The archmage's face was still.

Then, with one tap of Arch-Lasome's staff, the room fell into silence.

"Professor Alyssa Benedictus," the principal said, "would you please step off the stage? Archmage Tatius-Lasome will you please step forward, and Zane...?"

Zane bowed with respect. "You may refer to me as Detective Vrexon."

The old man nodded. "Detective Vrexon, please stand before us."

While stepping up to the raised platform, Alyssa stopped him. "You don't have to get up there."

He smiled. Given the circumstances, it was nice to have a friend. "Thank you, but I think I need to."

Zane stood on the stage alongside Tatius-Lasome. Light seemed to pour down on him from some unseen corner, and over his shoulder, in the dark hallway, stood a lone figure.

Tatius-Lasome laughed, and the sound seemed to rattle inside Zane's head. "May I start my questioning?"

Arch-Lasome raised a hand. "Questioning? What position do you think you are in?"

Tatius-Lasome ignored the archmage and turned to Zane. A dim glow came from the figure in the hall. It was enticing and lured Zane's focus astray.

"Detective," Tatius-Lasome said, "you stand before a trial of archmages, accused of extortion. Now beg for forgiveness."

Arch-Lasome stood up, banging his staff against the floor. "Tatius! You've gone too far!"

Another archmage stood, pointing at Arch-Lasome. "Let him finish!"

"You can't say that to the head of the assembly!"

"Pay your respects!"

The archmages descended into arguing.

As Tatius-Lasome repeated his demand, Zane could hear a faint sound. It grew into a distant roar. Then his senses were overwhelmed by the light and sound.

It seemed so simple, such an easy thing to give.

"I ask the court for forgiveness."

"Forgiveness for what?"

Zane's body grew heavy, his mind light, like existing between sleep and awake.

Tatius-Lasome's voice seemed so kind as he prompted the detective. "Forgiveness for your crimes, right?"

Zane nodded slowly. "I ask for forgiveness for my crimes."

Tatius-Lasome chuckled and circled Zane, his heavy staff clicking against the floor. With it, he pointed to Zane while speaking to the squabbling archmages. "In asking for forgiveness, this rogue has admitted to his faults."

Tatius-Lasome continued to talk, but Zane couldn't hear him. He was too preoccupied with the light from the man in the hallway. Tatius-Lasome kept walking around Zane like a wild animal waiting to go for the kill. The sounds of the room seemed to grow further and further away.

Why was he here? What was he doing? Zane couldn't remember.

Shadow appeared before him, a tall pillar of darkness, his blood-red eyes locked on the detective. *Oh my. My poor Zane, you are in some trouble. Do you need a hand?*

Did he? Zane didn't think so, but he knew he had been doing something important. But what was it? He was barely aware of Shadow as it made a clicking sound. *Really? This is what you have been reduced to? Fine, I will help you. Remember, we are in this together… You are still my only hope of escape.*

Tatius-Lasome stepped through the fading pillar of darkness. "Detective Vrexon, I have laid out the reasons you are a rogue, but we have other options other than arrest. You have shown a degree of usefulness. I offer you this one-time-only deal. Give up this case and come work for me."

Zane started to move his mouth, to form words, but a different voice rolled out, one that used to belong to the beady-eyed creature in the corner.

"No," Shadow said.

The figure in the dark hall rocked back and forth, then crumpled to the floor, picked itself up, and walked away. Tatius-Lasome was incredulous. Even at such a short distance, his voice was just above a whisper, "How? What…- What did he do? Who is he?"

Shadow stretched Zane's face into a smile. The mist in the detective's mind cleared as some type of spell faded, and Zane struggled to take control of his body.

The silky voice of Shadow whispered to him. *I helped you out; shouldn't you let me drive for a bit?* Zane pushed Shadow away from his mind by force of will.

"No."

This time, the voice was Zane's.

The detective stood on the stage, his breath coming in heavy gasps.

Tatius-Lasome stepped away confused, his eyes darting around the deathly quiet room.

Arch-Lasome leaned over his desk. "Detective Vrexon, could you explain yourself?"

2

UNDER THE COUNTER, Fex gripped the wand. Next to him were more than a dozen spell wicks ready for use. He had even bought a quick loader. If a fight broke out now between the siblings, he was ready to stand his ground. But he had other worries.

It sounded like Vana could easily tear Evan apart, and with each breath, her body grew. At first, Fex thought his mind was playing tricks on him—until he noticed her clothes had started to strain at the seams.

Evan took a full step back, his hands raised in defense. "Let's talk about this. Do we have a reason to fight?"

Vana took half a step forward. "It depends on how you answer my question."

Evan slipped his sword from behind his back and carefully placed it on the ground. Then, in an act of submission, he took a knee. "The Mysteries are deep, their truth profound. They demand much. Let them strike me down if I lie to their Chosen."

Her voice was rough and bestial, as if her body struggled to produce human sounds. "Did you kill my husband?"

Evan held her gaze. "No."

Fex saw the weight of burden and ambition in his eyes, yet they remained bright and clear. He believed Evan. Vana's body was tense, as if her form was ready to explode, and he couldn't tear his eyes away.

"Did you move against him?" she asked.

Evan was silent as sweat dripped down his face, a quiet fear in his eyes. Vana raised an arm into the air, her sleeve slipping down, revealing muscles far larger than should have been possible. Vana's entire body seemed to ripple with power, ready to tear into the man with a fury that Fex had never seen before.

Evan raised his arm up in defense. "I didn't ask for his death. I asked for someone to stop him from getting into The Institute. That's it." He shook with fear. "But he still got in! What I wanted —"

A thud at the front door interrupted Evan's begging.

⟶

ALYSSA HAD FELT the faint strands of magic from her seat. It was a beautiful and complicated charm, like listening to a master musician. If Tatius-Lasome had performed the magic, he had done it without any words or gestures. The archmage she knew couldn't cast spells like that, and Alyssa wondered why the others allowed Tatius-Lasome to continue.

Alyssa addressed the bench. "Principal Arch-Lasome, I would like to approach."

"You may."

Alyssa stepped up as Zane wobbled in place. She reached an arm around him and steadied him on his feet, then whispered, "Are you all right?"

He tried to speak but settled for a quick nod. Zane seemed completely exhausted, like he had just run a marathon. Alyssa recognized the tell-tale signs of resisting a powerful spell, but she still wondered how he had done so.

Finally, Zane recovered enough breath to speak. "I think the archmage was doing something to me, but I had some help to repel him."

Help? If she had noticed the charm, then all the archmages above must have also noticed.

"What is he after?" Zane asked.

"I don't know, but I am going to find out."

Tatius-Lasome looked around as if he were lost. Principal Arch-Lasome had regained control of the crowd and fixed his anger onto the old man.

"Tatius-Lasome, what is the meaning of this? You know that charming someone is against everything that The Institute stands for. His admission would have meant nothing, even if it were true."

Tatius-Lasome looked over his shoulder, his focus gone. He nodded as if having a silent conversation. He turned to the crowd. "I will leave for now. Good day, fellow archmages."

"Now wait a moment—"

The same archmages burst into argument again. In the confusion, Tatius-Lasome bowed and stepped off the stage. Each weak step was met with the metal knock of his staff. The folds of his cloak flowed around as he passed through a doorway and disappeared. The other archmages grew quiet, stepped away from their benches and began to shuffle off to various areas of The Institute.

Benedictus-Lasome joined Alyssa and Zane on the stage. "Good job, Detective. If you had not fought back, Tatius-Lasome would not have relented."

"Relented?" Alyssa was on the verge of yelling. "He should have discredited himself by using a charm like that."

Her grandfather looked away. His eyes glanced up at the benches that still held some lingering archmages, who were close enough to overhear them. "Let's take this back to my office."

The three of them walked to a nearby door. Benedictus-Lasome placed the key to his office in the keyhole and opened the door. Zane was the last through and pulled it tight, and Alyssa retrieved a second chair for him to sit in. He thanked her and laid his cane across his lap.

Benedictus-Lasome dropped down into his soft chair, and the old man rolled his hand over the arm of it.

Alyssa waited for both men to get comfortable before beginning. "Grandfather, what did you mean earlier?"

VOICES BARKED ON the other side of front door before yet another thud reverberated through The Wizard's Brew. Fex watched as the door burst from its frame and red-painted goblins rushed in, yelling slurs in the imperial tongue. "Death to the blue skins! Death to the blue skins!"

The first goblin sprinted toward Evan. He reached for his sword, but to Fex it was obvious that the goblin's small cleaver would carve through him before he could defend himself. But Vana's hand flashed down, crushing the goblin. Evan scrambled to his feet, sword in hand, ready for the next attacker as more of the Red Tusk Gang crowded the room, each goblin yelling war cries in their native language.

Fex hesitated for only a few heartbeats before he fired from the desk into the doorway. Shot after shot rocked the entrance until the wand ran empty and he jammed more spell wicks into the quick reloader.

Evan acted like a barbaric hero of old, hewing through the mob of goblins as they poured into the room. Vana's hands acted like claws that savaged the goblins as they approached. Every slash and grab shattered their bones, but still more flowed in, each armed with makeshift jagged knives and cleavers.

One lanky goblin with a knife leaped at Fex but was slammed into the counter just shy of the gnome. The blade slashed the air, inches from his face. Fex jerked the wand in front of his assailant's face and pulled the mental trigger. The wand tip flashed the white light of wand fire, and the smoking goblin flew back into the pile of corpses. Again, Fex unloaded every spell wick into the charging horde.

A firm hand grabbed his shoulder, causing Fex's mind to jerk free from his mental loop of firing. He turned to see Vana, her veil still firmly hiding her face, but sections of her torn clothing revealing a mixture of swirling blue tattoos and dark purple bruises.

Evan roared with laughter, his cloak stained with goblin blood. He stabbed into the floor and swept his arms around wide. "How thrilling! This is what the Mysteries spoke about. It's what our blood craves, the glorious honor of battle. And just *look* at you, dear sister!"

He pointed at the bruising that marked her skin. "You bear the mark of the most holy one. The chosen child of the moon, and the protector of the clans. I can show you the truth of your fate."

Vana crossed the floor with inhuman speed and lifted the mountain of a man by his cloak. His feet dangled helplessly.

"Shut up," Vana roared. "You speak and speak, but I don't care about any of it. I want the thing that killed my husband."

She dropped him carelessly. Evan landed on his feet, but to Fex he seemed weaker. He dropped to his hands and knees and stammered in disbelief. "Si-sister, I am speaking of the future, not the past."

The growl that erupted from Vana's throat silenced Evan, so she turned to Fex. "I am going to change clothes. Please fetch the guards."

Fex nodded numbly as Vana walked past him. The gnome stepped carefully around corpses on his way to the door. He looked to Evan, who grinned like a man who had come face-to-face with a deity.

A shiver inched down Fex's spine.

BENEDICTUS-LASOME WIPED his head with a handkerchief. He had just explained to Alyssa and Zane that someone at The Institute was using psychological magic. Many people had been affected by the spell, which Alyssa's grandfather discovered after investigating Dennis Zel's application to become a state mage.

But psychological magic was broad in scope.

"What type of magic are we talking about?" Alyssa asked.

Benedictus-Lasome rubbed the arm of his chair. "The type that alters memories. I have found a half dozen faculty members who couldn't remember Dennis ever applying."

Zane taped the desk. "Wouldn't someone altering memories on a mass scale be... noticeable?"

Benedictus-Lasome's eyes looked worried, which filled Alyssa with dread. "It should be," he said. "Such magic needs preparation and specific tools. The mind is a complex labyrinth. Often, it requires the subject to have a desire to be affected for it to work in the first place. But..."

His eyes fell on Alyssa, who sighed and finished her grandfather's thought. "Fey magics can affect the mind in ways that our magic cannot. It's something about how the Fey mind works. It's alien to us."

Zane narrowed his eyes. "Can someone who isn't a Fey use this magic?"

"Yes," she said. "The basis of all magic is altering the state of mind. If we studied long enough, even we could use Fey magic. But it takes many years to master."

The lines on Zane's face seemed to deepen as he considered her words. "So that leaves a short list, yes? It must be someone who works with matters of the Fey."

Alyssa knew more than a dozen wizards who had worked in the Fey department, but none had ever shown the aptitude for performing Fey magic, nor had they studied it long enough. "Besides myself, there are only two who might have that kind of skill. One is Agwen, who you've met. The other is Tatius-Lasome."

"What is his connection to Dennis though?"

Benedictus-Lasome shook his aged head. He looked old, even older than he had before the day's inquisition. "I don't know. Anyone who remembers anything about Dennis mentions Tatius-Lasome, but it seems a little too obvious."

Alyssa nodded in agreement. Something wasn't adding up, and she felt again like the scared little girl she'd seen in the Dream Sphere. "Why has he not used that magic on me?"

"Only you can answer that," Benedictus-Lasome said. "Your knowledge in that field is greater than mine."

Her mind raced over the basics of the magic. Then she realized the answer was in front of her. Her thoughts and mind had been shaped by her studies. It had made her mind more akin to that of Fey, enough that this magic might not work on her. She kept her thoughts to herself as she turned to her grandfather. "What should I do?"

With a weary hand, he scratched his head. "It might be best to leave. Whoever is doing this is powerful and cunning."

Zane stretched and rubbed his left leg. Though he was in obvious pain, he also seemed to be searching for the words he wanted to say.

"It might not be safe, but you can stay with me."

Alyssa blushed at the thought of being invited over to a man's house, but immediately scolded herself for being so childish. His offer was about her safety, nothing more.

Zane stood, and she noticed that he leaned harder than usual on his cane. "It's time for me to leave this place. I have had enough people messing with my mind."

He moved for the door but stopped short of opening it and glanced over his shoulder.

"Are you coming?"

CHAPTER 20

The sun felt warm on Zane's skin as he and Alyssa stepped out of The Institute into the courtyard. The clear air helped lift the remaining fog from his mind, and he was grateful Shadow had remained silent about his newfound power. The creature had freed him from the strange psychological magic that had assaulted him, but Zane had more questions about what Shadow was, several of which he was scared to ask. He hated to acknowledge his unwelcome guest, but Zane had to admit the creature deserved it this time.

"Thank you."

"For what?"

Zane had almost forgotten Alyssa was next to him. He quickly thought of a response. "For helping me with the case."

She looked exhausted. Understandably. Her job was on the line, and her boss might be trying to kill her. Alyssa was about to say something but stopped to point out a grey goblin racing up the steps to them.

He stopped and lifted a finger, gesturing for them to wait while he caught his breath. "Humes, are you Detective Zane Vrexon?"

"Yes. Did Nob send you?"

The goblin's large ears flopped up and down as it nodded. "Aye, the boss needs you to head to The Brew."

Zane knelt and placed a gloved hand on the small goblin's shoulder as it turned. "The Brew? Slow down. What's going on?"

The goblin snapped his head back and bared his needle-like teeth. "Get your mitts off me, Hume! The Brew has been attacked by Red

Tusks!"

"What? Why?"

The goblin spat on the clean ground. "Damn humes don't need to know goblin business. Just follow me."

He broke free from Zane's hand and started running. Zane looked back at Alyssa. "I should have stopped by the shop today. Sorry, but you should—"

"You are not going anywhere without me." Her pale face showed nothing but resolve. "I am already too deep into this."

He nodded and started to chase the grey goblin. With their long strides, they caught up quickly and ran through the streets and on sidewalks taking the paths of least resistance. Muck and ash clung to Zane's boots and pants and seemed to coat the goblin's clothes entirely, but the filth slipped off Alyssa like water from a roof. Zane repressed his jealousy.

The detective limped as fast and as hard as he could. His injuries strained his muscles, and with every step his throat tightened. The need for troll's blood consumed his thoughts, but his stride was still enough to keep up. They turned onto Potion Lane, which was uncharacteristically empty. People clung to the sides of buildings or peeped through the shop windows.

The goblin pointed to The Brew. "All right, I am gonna split. You humes go take a look. When ya get done, go to The Green Thumb. The boss will see ya there."

Alyssa turned back to him. "Wait, why are you leaving?"

The goblin spat on the ground. "There was a Red Tusk attack, and ya want me to go up there? Pits no. The guards would arrest me in a beat. Naw, see ya later." The goblin took off, his grey ears bouncing on the sides of his head.

Alyssa turned back to Zane. "Would the guards really do that?"

He had seen it before. Not just with goblins, but the guards often arrested first and asked questions later; the faster a crime was resolved, the better they looked. "It wouldn't be unheard of. Let's go take a look."

Standing in front of The Brew was a city guard, who stopped them before they could go inside. His black and red uniform stood out against his breastplate. A staff rested in his hands, the runes humming with power. "This is an official investigation by the City Imperial Guard. Please move along."

"I am Detective Vrexon, and this is my client's shop. I need to talk to her and make sure she is safe."

The guard's leather gloves tightened on the staff. "No. I said move on." When they didn't immediately walk away, the guard gestured down the street. "Now!"

Alyssa pulled on Zane's sleeve to keep him from doing something rash. "Let's wait."

Zane grunted in assent and pulled out a bank note for the guard. "Okay, but will you let her know that Zane is here?"

A greedy smile spread across the guard's face. "I suppose I can do that for you."

Zane and Alyssa stepped back, giving a wide berth from the doorway.

That's when Shadow's silky voice finally touched the detective's mind. *This has taken a different turn. What do you think?*

This time, Zane answered internally. *I don't know. A goblin attack is rather obvious compared with the threads we've pulled so far.*

Shadow chuckled. *You're right. This strikes me as panicked. Someone's getting nervous.*

Zane felt revulsion for needing Shadow's help, but he'd be in a lot of trouble without it. *Thank you.*

A silence hung in his head before a surprised voice said, *You're welcome.*

Alyssa leaned in close to keep her voice low. "What do you know?"

Zane was stunned. "What?"

Alyssa searched his expression. "You have that look on your face, like at the morgue. You have some insight you didn't have before."

Zane grimaced, upset he'd let his thoughts slip across his face. "I think we are getting close. Whoever is behind this is feeling pressure. Attacking The Brew doesn't seem organized at all. It's sloppy."

Alyssa stared across the street, but Zane kept his eyes on her. How much did she know? Should he tell her?

The guard in the doorway leaned in and yelled something. Fex pushed past him. "Detective. Get in here."

The guard stared at them without a word as they walked into the shop. It looked like a battle zone, and even the Ghoul War veteran was taken aback as he saw a room filled with the corpses of green-skinned goblins with red paint scattered over the floor. Blood spatter coated the walls, and most of the bodies showed signs of sword injuries and wand fire.

But some of the goblins appeared to have been crushed by someone's bare hands.

At that, Zane remembered his companion. "Alyssa, don't look—"

It was too late. Alyssa's eyes were locked on` the pools of blood on the floor. Her face blanched and her body wavered. Zane reached out and caught her, then eased her against a wall. Fex was already there beside them with a cup of water.

"I thought that would happen," the gnome said.

Zane passed her the drink. He was sorry for her and angry with himself for not warning her sooner. He was glad that she hadn't thrown up; he might not have kept his own stomach in check if she had.

"Fex, will you look after her for a moment. I need to talk to Vana."

Fex pointed to the door to the workshop. "She's in there with her brother and Lieutenant Dane."

Zane thanked him and walked through the doorway, keeping his new cane from touching blood-soaked floors and bodies. He would need to clean his boots later.

In the back corner of the room, Lieutenant Dane was talking to Vana and Evan. "Mister Zel, I understand you are a gentleman and all, but I can't let this slide. My captain wants answers. He is coming down on me hard."

Evan motioned to the bodies on the ground. "I am not asking you to let it slide, I am saying that we are not involved. These bastards rushed in and attacked us. Remove the bodies and go looking for the goblins' nest."

The lieutenant's red plume waved as he shook his head. "I understand that. Vana, you are already suspected in a murder, and now this happens. Evan, I have to take her in. I have to follow regulations on this."

Evan started to raise one of his meaty hands to argue but was stopped by his sister. There was a strange weakness in her movement. "No, I will go with him. Perhaps, under the watchful eyes of the lieutenant, I will be protected."

Dane said nothing but allowed her to be in front as he escorted her from The Brew. She stopped in front of Zane on her way out. "Detective, I hope you will follow this to its source."

He gave a slight bow. "Of course."

With that, Vana left with the lieutenant and Fex returned to the workshop. "My uncle will be by soon to pick up the bodies. He will be coming through the back entrance."

Zane turned to Evan, the larger man's face showing a storm of conflicting emotions. "Mister Zel, what exactly is going on?"

He shrugged. "How should I know? These goblins attacked us without warning."

Fex stepped closer, his wand pointed at Evan. "No, I am done with this. I have seen your *followers*. Who the hell are you?"

Zane joined Fex in pressing Evan. "Are these *followers* part of the revolutionary group you run?"

Fex stared at Zane, confused, but kept his wand levelled at Evan. "What are you talking about, detective?"

Zane's eyes never left the larger man, his disgust for Evan pouring out. "Evan Zel wants to free the Eastern Territories. He believes Vana is some type of *Chosen One*, a religious figure for his group."

Evan's eyes were those of a cornered animal. "Let's talk about this. We can come to an understanding."

His big hands twitched toward his sword but a burst of static repelled his fingers from the handle. Alyssa stood in the doorway, pointing one finger at Evan. "Please— please don't touch your sword."

Alyssa's face was still pale, but Zane watched as she forced her eyes from the bodies. He turned back to Evan and pulled his wand. "I have had a long day already, so I'll ask you again. How are you related to all of this?"

Evan's large frame seemed to deflate a little as he resigned himself to coming clean. "I am the first-born to a failing noble family. We have been sinking into poverty for the last two generations, but I know we used to be something grand. We were the Lords of the Forest Hills and the Cavern Mounts, where my line had ruled gloriously for ages. But my forefathers betrayed both land and kin." He breathed deep, straightening back to his normal height. "I want to free my blood from this cycle of shame. It's not my destiny to do so, but to unite the clans, I need a symbol. I need the Moon's Chosen. The bones told me it would be of my blood. My father is far too old, which left only my sister. I had started to doubt the bones, but you have reassured me, detective."

Zane remembered how Evan and his followers reacted in the jail cell. The information he gave Evan sent them into a frenzy.

Evan smiled and balled his hands. "Everything was within my grasp, but I had some problems."

Zane raised his eyebrow. "Like what?"

Evan's vigor seemed to have fully recovered. "Like Dennis trying to get into The Institute."

The warrior let the statement hang in the air before continuing. "If Dennis were accepted, I would have never convinced him and Vana to move to the homeland with me."

Fex squinted in confusion. "Why would he move regardless? He had a successful business."

Evan laughed and shook his head. "Successful? Do you know the debt he is carrying? The damnable goblin mob practically owned this place. Why do you think these damn creatures attacked?"

Zane's eyes flicked to the goblins' bodies. "Dennis didn't owe anything. His bill has been squared with the mob. Not only that, but they also saw him as a friend. These goblins are part of a rival gang."

Evan waved a dismissive hand. "So what? Goblins are beasts, little better than gnomes. They changed their minds."

"Can I shoot him in the knee?" Fex asked Zane with no hint of sarcasm.

The detective smirked but shook his head. "No, he isn't worth the wick. Evan, what did you do to Dennis?"

The big man rolled his eyes. "For the last time, I didn't kill him. He was a soft coward, but he made my sister happy. He even did a job for me once. After that, he refused to work for me and he started studying to join those imperial mages. But I'd never ask for him to be killed. Didn't need to. I had a connection in The Institute."

Alyssa cut in. "Who?"

Evan shrugged. "One of my followers told me about him. Didn't name him, but I know that he sells black-market items. I had my followers set it up. If this guy didn't keep Dennis out, we would reveal his illegal dealings."

Zane's mouth tightened. "But Dennis did get in, and now he is dead."

Evan thought about this until the realization lit up his face. "So, this professor at The Institute might have... You know."

Alyssa's voice was weak, as she struggled with the information. "You're saying someone at The Institute caused Dennis's death? Who?"

"I don't know. Like I said, my follower knew the guy, not me."

"Do you know where this follower is?" Zane's anger at Evan's casual, and self-important attitude was slipping into his voice.

Evan laughed at the question. "Why would I keep track? He's his own man."

"When was the last time you saw him?"

"A few days ago."

Every curse Zane knew danced through his mind, and many tried to escape out his mouth, but he settled on just one. "Dammit!" He lowered his wand and stormed away to the shop.

Fex hesitated but followed. "What's wrong, detective?"

Zane shook his head in disgust. "Evan's insider is cleaning house."

Fex raised an eyebrow, the wand limp at his side. "What?"

"His Institute contact is tying up all the loose ends. He's going after anyone related to this pit of a mess."

Fex touched his chest. "Wait, are we in danger?"

Zane pointed to the bodies on the ground for his answer. "What do you think, Fex?"

The color drained from the gnome's face. "So who's this inside man?"

$$z$$

ALYSSA'S STOMACH WAS in knots. This was far worse a sight than what she witnessed inside the morgue. The air was filled with death, and the floor was sticky with it. She had followed the conversation and it had led to only one thing.

"It has to be Tatius-Lasome…"

The others turned to her. Evan and Fex looked confused, but Zane nodded. "So it would seem. Why else would he try to get you removed from the case?"

That was certainly the most direct reasoning, but other things troubled her. Tatius-Lasome had acted so strangely in the last few days. Yes, he'd sent her down into the basement after she had been the deciding vote admitting Dennis to The Institute. And his instructions had directly led to her being attacked,.

Still, some things just didn't make any sense. "Why goblins?'

The others looked around the room, each considering an answer. Zane offered his thoughts. "Maybe they were used as a cover."

Fex's face was white with fear. "I overheard Vana, the unbruised one I mean, talking to Atom. They mentioned goblins and something about tusks. At the time, it didn't make any sense, but now…"

Evan looked at everyone in confusion. "Unbruised? What do you mean?"

Zane sighed, and Alyssa noted how he looked more exhausted by the second. "Vana is covered in bruises. It looked like her bones had been broken, healed, and rebroken."

Evan smiled, with some hidden knowledge. "Mark of the Divine. A sign that she changes as the moon changes."

Alyssa spoke up, her mouth dry as a bone. "She is capable of polymorphing. She can shift from human to wolf."

Evan's large hand jerked and pointed an accusatory finger at her. "That is sacred knowledge! Only those steeped in the Mysteries should know that!"

Zane lifted his wand in warning. "Let her finish." He nodded to her to continue.

"Humans are not meant for such things. Such rapid changes would tear and break the body every time. It's amazing she hasn't crippled herself by now."

Fex looked pale as he stared at the floor. "Then, the potions... the pain she must feel..."

Alyssa gave no answer as she, too, imagined the agony Vana must have been experiencing. The memory of her parents' fire burned in Alyssa's head, and it fueled a growing anger on Vana's behalf.

Silence clung to the air until Evan spoke. "So, what is this gang you speak of?"

Zane answered. "They are the Red Tusk, a goblin gang."

Alyssa felt like she had been immersed into icy water. And the confusion and misdirection, the constant threat of violence, made her feel as though she couldn't tread that water for much longer.

They needed answers. Fast.

"So... which Vana went with the lieutenant?" Alyssa asked.

"The bruised one," Fex said.

"The real Vana," Zane clarified.

Alyssa probed her mind. Shapeshifting appeared in ancient lexicons of black magic, and such spells would twist the mind and ruin the body.

But it also showed up in Fey legends.

"Maybe Tatius-Lasome knew something," she said. "In Fey culture, there is a creature known as a changeling that can shapeshift."

Zane seemed to understand where she was going. "We should split up and cover more ground. Alyssa, Fex, please check out Atom. I am going to see what the mob knows."

Alyssa and Fex started strategizing.

"Do you have a wand or know some type of fighting magic?" Fex asked.

Alyssa pulled a thin wand from her clothes. "I have a loaded wand. Also, just for future reference, fighting magic is called War Charms. Unfortunately, I know only a couple of charms for self-defense. You think we will run into trouble?"

Fex shrugged. "I'd be surprised if we didn't at this point, but I almost hope a fight breaks out. I have a few strong words for that man."

Evan spoke up, drawing everyone's attention. "What about me?"

Frustration showed on Zane's face as he pointed at Evan with his cane. "What do you mean? You are the problem. We wouldn't be here if it weren't for you."

Evan gritted his teeth and cast his gaze down in shame. "I didn't care for my spineless brother-in-law, but he was part of the clan. It is my responsibility to take care of him and my sister. What can I do?"

Zane leaned on his cane and sighed. "Go ensure that Lady Zel is safe. That is what you can do. Take care of your sister."

Evan tracked blood through the shop and stomped out into the street, and Fex looked ready to murder him for the mess.

Zane addressed Alyssa and Fex. "I am heading out next. Let's meet back at my office when we are finished."

FEX'S CLOTHES WERE filthy and he was exhausted. His home had been attacked twice in a matter of days, and the only saving grace was that his room was still untouched. He had been lost and confused for what seemed like an eternity, but now all he felt was anger. And it was focused on one person.

Atom.

The fat man had cheated Fex and, in his mind, ruined his reputation. And now Atom was connected to the attacks, too.

Fex pulled himself from his rage to look up at Alyssa, who was still pale, her eyes drifting to the bodies and then quickly away.

"Miss, we should get a move on," Fex said. "I will meet you outside.

I need to leave the back door open for my uncle. He will take care of this mess."

She nodded and left. He unlocked the back and turned to leave but was stopped by a knock. He opened the door to see his uncle, Dex, standing on the other side. The old gnome looked worried, his face quickly turning as green as the goblins in the other room. "What have you gotten into?"

"As always, it's complicated when humans—"

"Are involved?" Dex pointed to the bodies as he cut his nephew off. "Yes, but goblins? That—"

"Is beyond reproach, I know. They were sent to kill us—"

"By whom?" Anger burned across the older gnome's face.

"I don't know but Atom, who owns The Fountain, is involved."

Fex's uncle spat on the ground and kicked a nearby wall. "What a fat, worthless human."

It appeared Atom's reputation stretched further than even Fex believed. "Yes, I am about to go over there and confront him."

Dex yelled as he stomped the ground. His uncle's wild rage worried Fex. "Uncle, please calm down. Take a seat. I will be right back."

Dex huffed but did as his nephew asked. Satisfied, the younger gnome stepped through the workshop and into the front, where Alyssa stood gazing over the lines of potion bottles that sat on the shelves, purposefully averting her eyes from the corpses. She didn't seem to notice him enter the room.

Fex threw his apron onto the counter and began to inspect the wand to ensure it was in good repair. He broke it down into its rod, cap, and wicks. The rod itself was dirty and filled with ash residue. Fex had not checked its condition, assuming Dennis had kept it up to snuff. That was clearly not the case. Fex cursed as he banged the powder out, not having time to clean it properly.

"What are you doing?" Alyssa asked.

"Cleaning it. That silly man Dennis did not take care of this wand, and now my life depends on it."

She watched with interest and pulled her wand out. "I borrowed this from my grandfather, but I don't know much about them. I know more than a few words of power that I can use in self-defense." She held out the wand to Fex. "Would you like to use this one instead?"

It was a civilian model, made for those that needed something simple to defend themselves. With it in hand, Fex compared it with Dennis's. His was used and needed repair, but Fex felt he would need the stronger fire it provided. "No thanks, these military wands are made to be abused." He chuckled and shook his head with grim humor. "Just like us gnomes, I guess. But thank you for the offer."

Alyssa took the wand back and placed it back into her holster. "Are you ready to head over to Atom's place?"

"Almost. Let me put this damn thing together and say goodbye to my uncle."

A few clumsy movements later, Fex had reconstructed the wand and slipped it into his jacket. Fex found his uncle still sitting where he had left him. He looked much calmer than before, so Fex pointed toward the door over his shoulder with his thumb. "I am about to head out."

Dex went to his cart and pulled out a shovel. "Let me go with you, nephew. I will beat that human until we can see things eye to eye."

Fex grabbed his uncle's shoulder to stop him from marching off. "No, I will handle Atom. You will be more helpful here. If you would, please remove the bodies and send me the bill. I will—"

"Give Atom a slap or two for me." Dex set the shovel to the side. "If you're a good nephew, that is."

Fex chuckled and walked through the shop, doing his best not to spread the gore. At the door, he puffed out his chest and led Alyssa into the street, which was once again filled with pedestrians, several curious onlookers having stopped in front of The Brew. "What happened in there?"

Fex stomped past and yelled back, frustrated. "Goblin attack."

He and Alyssa waded against the growing tide of people, who ignored them and worked their ways closer to glimpse the carnage. The pair slipped through the crowd and down the street. When they arrived, they found that the windows of The Fountain were covered from the inside and the door was locked.

"Is this shop normally closed?" Alyssa asked.

"No, I have never known this place to close for any reason. Rain, sleet, blazing hot summers, these doors are always open. Even during his third wife's funeral."

She brought a hand to her mouth in surprise. "No..."

"He even had a funeral special. Buy two, get one free. Atom never misses an opportunity."

"Until today, it seems."

Fex looked around the entrance but couldn't find the shop boy, Jefferson. Fex had often walked by only to spot the kid cleaning the front steps. But he wasn't here, and the pile of soot and ash in front of the door was higher than normal.

He knocked on the door with all his strength. No answer came from inside. He banged with his small fist again, then kicked the door with all the force his body could produce. When that didn't work, he reached into his jacket and grabbed the wand.

Alyssa knelt, stopping him with a gentle hand. "Let me try."

Arcane words rolled off her lips, and Fex's Fey senses felt a wave move through him, like a faint tingle of static, followed by the sound of an unlocking door filling the air.

Fex smiled and pulled the door open. "Thank you, Miss Benedictus."

The lamps were turned down low, leaving the room cloaked in shadow. The Fountain was a mess, with broken bottles scattered across the room and the rainbow shine of dozens of mixing elixirs bubbling beneath their feet. Fex's chest tightened. This was every brewer's worst nightmare.

Even the damage to The Brew wasn't this bad.

He and Alyssa turned at the sound of a whimper coming from the back. Fex pulled his wand and kept it by his side as he stepped through the sticky mess. A light escaped from the crack of the back door, and the whimpering grew louder. The gnome turned back to Alyssa, who held up her own wand. He could see her hand shaking, but she nodded. She was ready.

Fex eased the door open, taking care to keep his wand leveled at the opening. The gas lamps were on, and their light reflected the broken apparatuses scattered across the floor. It was mixed with ingredients and watered-down potion mix. Atom was on his knees, shuffling through the broken pieces of his workshop, his back to Fex.

Fex lowered his wand. Atom, the large human who was nothing more than a bully, now looked so small. "Atom... Atom, are you okay?"

The potion maker's shoulders jerked in surprise. His bulk swayed as he tried to stand but stopped and rocked back. Sitting on the floor, Atom turned. His face was swollen to twice its size, already turning black and blue.

Fex's chest tightened and he couldn't move, but Alyssa stepped forward. "Sir, are you okay?"

Atom waved her away. "I don't know who you are, but I don't need ya sympathy or ya help. I have work to do. Get out of my place."

Fex shook his head and slid the wand back into his jacket. "I can't do that, Atom. And you know why."

Atom looked past Fex to the floor. "What do you mean, speck?"

Atom's insult was the last straw. Fex stepped forward and slapped the man's face. He snarled, but Fex slapped him again.

"Saints! My name is Fex!"

Slap.

"Not gnome!"

Slap.

"Not speck!"

Atom eyes sagged closed as he covered his head with his hands. "What do you want spe—"

Fex held up his palm again.

"What do you want, Fex?"

It was progress, and now Atom was softened up and ready to answer Fex's questions. "You know why I'm here. The Brew, my home, is almost as bad as this"—he gestured around the broken workshop—"and I know you're involved."

Atom started to laugh, but it was cold and strained. "It ain't my fault. No, no, it's your damn mistress' fault. That bit—"

"Sir!" Alyssa's face was stern as she cut him off.

Atom pointed out the door. "That *woman* came here, poking into stuff that was none of her business. She blackmailed me and now" — he looked around the room—"now I am ruined. Those damn beasts can't walk through a shop without recking it." Atom slumped even more. "I'm tired, and I would like you both to leave before I call the guards."

Fex remembered that day, remembered Vana's threatening tone as he listened at the back door. "Did you see her face?"

"What?"

"Did you see Vana's face? Was she wearing her veil?"

Atom's face twisted into frustration. "What the pits do you mean? Of course I saw her face. Came in here all dolled up in her funeral garb."

Fex waved his hand in front of his face. "Was her face covered in bruises?"

"No, why would it be? Did that Dennis beat her?"

The gnome relaxed with a sigh. "No. You didn't speak with Vana. She has been covered in bruises since the night of murder. You should know better than most that no potion will make those go away. Speaking of potions, I have another matter to discuss with you regarding a batch of bad containers."

Atom glanced at Alyssa, then turned his big eyes to the gnome. "What do you know, spe— Fex?"

"My damn adventurers' bottles. You paid the glass blowers to give me a different order."

Atom's eyes shifted away. "I don't know what..." He trailed off, as though the action of lying was too exhausting. "Fine. I did. It was a good idea, those potions. Wished I had thought of it first, so I needed to cripple it. How did you know?"

"Gnomes talk."

Atom didn't say anything but nodded in understanding.

Now it was Alyssa's turn to address the potion maker. "Are you selling Ambrosia?"

Atom's face was pale, his tears mixed with sweat. "I... I don't know what you're talking about."

Alyssa's face was colder than Fex thought possible, but a slight quiver in her jaw betrayed her warm heart. "So, you think a goblin attack on your primary competitor from a gang that deals in drugs is just a coincidence?"

Atom's voice was just above a whimper. "Do the guards know?"

She shook her head. "Not yet."

Atom was on the verge of tears. "Yes, I sell that stuff. Never pure though. I always mix it. That's how I keep the quality of my potions up. It's the only way I can outsell others. The more shops that pop up, the more rivals I have." He turned to Fex, pleading. "Ambrosia is the real reason why I wanted The Brew. I needed a bigger workshop so I could produce more legitimate potions. I wouldn't need that blighted stuff anymore."

Atom's big frame sagged like a balloon losing air. The man seemed more pathetic now than when they had entered the shop. Fex had another question, and he took a moment to consider it before speaking. "What did *Vana* talk to you about?"

"She wanted to meet with my seller, with the gang. I don't know how she knew. She was so strong, and I thought she would kill me, so I set up a meeting." He paused. "Look, I don't care anymore. Tell the guards, my business is already ruined."

Alyssa asked the final question of the defeated potion maker. "We won't rat you out if you tell us about these goblins. What are the Red Tusks doing?"

The big man spat. "I made a deal with a devil." He stood up in the small space and kicked his broken tools out of his way as though mentioning the painted gang had given him a shot of adrenaline. "Red Tusk is a damn freak of a goblin. Years ago, he loaned me some money at a very low rate. Then he offered me protection, so I took him up on it. Why not? They are the meanest damn creatures that I have ever seen. But now I am ruined."

A voice like a cold wind blew in from in the rafters.

"You broke your word."

———

ZANE KNOCKED ON the door to the loan office with his cane. A voice called from the other side. "We are closed. Please go away."

"I have been called here for a meeting with the boss. May I come in?"

The door clicked and Gene opened it. "Mister detective, follow me."

He led Zane to Nob's office and welcomed him inside, where goblins worked around the room. Many were in the middle of sharpening their weapons, while some checked the condition of crossbows and wands. One big goblin held a military-grade staff.

Behind the desk sat Nob, sucking in big gulps of cigar smoke. "Detective, I am glad you decided to join us."

Zane watched the room around him. He could still feel the lumps from a couple of days ago. "I apologize for the delay."

Nob took a slow drag on his cigar, the smoke flowing up his face like a river. "I assume you know about the Red Tusk attack?" Zane nodded as Nob leaned back into his chair, gesturing to all the other goblins to come nearer. "Now would you care to explain what the pits is going on? Why would a rival gang try to move in on me?"

The goblins stared at Zane, who felt like a piece of meat in front of a pack of dogs waiting to be given the order to eat. "I have reason to believe Dennis Zel's murderer is connected to the Red Tusk gang."

Nob grunted thoughtfully. One long pudgy finger tapped the desk. "And who is this murderer?"

Zane shuffled in place, looking back and forth between the menacing henchmen. "I am not sure. We know that they can control their limbs in strange ways, such as enlarging them, and they can make themselves look like my client."

Nob raised an eyebrow. "Who is the client to Dennis again?"

"His wife."

One of the goblins leaped to his feet, yelling and barking in his native tongue while pointing at Zane. Others joined what the detective could only interpret as a violent threat, but all were silenced when Nob slammed a fist on the desk.

"I apologize about that. It sounds like the *shapeshifter*, and my men hate him. He is a hitman of great renown in the underworld, mostly in league with the government and nobles."

Excited by a new lead, Zane decided to press the goblin boss. "Are you sure it's the same one? I have heard stories of changelings in Fey stories."

He hadn't, of course—not personally—but Alyssa had mentioned it, so Zane figured it was good enough to go on.

Nob grinned. "You know your stuff hume, I'll give you that. This might be possible, but we doubt it. This changeling... well, he is known for wearing the guise of a loved one."

Zane raised an eyebrow. "Loved one? To get close to his target?"

Nob raised a hand of uncertainty. "Somewhat. We think it's more of a personal preference because this guy has a twisted mind. He takes the loved one's shape so he can see the despair and confusion on the victim's face. You said the wife in your case had been seen on the street before the murder, right?"

Zane nodded as the goblin took a long drag. "I bet you have even run into the wife, except something wasn't right. That would also be the shapeshifter. He has been known to hang around to take care of loose ends or to make more evidence so his double gets arrested."

Shadow's silky voice cut in. *Whatever attacked you doesn't fit the mold.*

Zane agreed. "Someone—something—attacked me the other night. It was able to enlarge its limbs and it had the strength of an ogre. It was looking for the murder weapon. Does that sound like your shapeshifter?"

Nob shrugged. "Not to my knowledge, but maybe it was a rush job and he couldn't do it like usual. What's the deal with the dagger, anyway?"

"The smith was of great help. The dagger is old, enchanted, and was used by an order of Fey assassins."

Zane expected Nob to be concerned, but the goblin just looked confused. "There is no order of Fey assassins in this part of the world. I know. I have looked."

Another goblin spoke up, but Zane didn't understand what he said. Nob grunted his agreement. "There is a seller of Fey artifacts, mostly trinkets and such, but once in a while something big comes up."

"Like the dagger?"

Nob smirked, and Zane thought it over. "Can you set me up with the seller? I would like to meet him."

The goblin scratched his face quizzically. "I could do that, but why?"

"I am following every thread. I am not much use in a gang fight, but I can chase leads. If I am lucky, the seller will point me in the direction of the shapeshifter."

"All right, I will set it up and let you know when it's done."

ALYSSA WATCHED A leathery, muscular form drop from above. A red hood trailed from his head and he was armed with a long, wicked knife. Its voice crackled like wood being crushed. "You had simple rules to follow, but those loose lips of yours..."

The goblin clicked its tongue chidingly.

Alyssa snapped out a charm, but before the words could be finished, the goblin folded her with a kick. The air in her lungs expunged in a violent burst.

Fex screamed. "What do you think you're doing?"

Wand fire slammed into the wall above her, and Atom's scream split the air. Alyssa's lips were numb and she coughed and hacked, trying to refill her lungs. She frantically scanned the room to find Fex pinned to the ground with one arm twisted behind his back. The goblin only needed one hand to subdue the gnome, while his other handheld his knife at Atom's throat.

"Now ain't this something here? Two rats with loose tongues. First, I am gonna cut the fat man's tongue out. Then I am goanna kill these—"

The goblin's words dissolved into a cry of pain as Alyssa's wand fire struck him in the shoulder. He hissed and rolled to the side, a small trail of blood dripping from the wound. The wand shook in her hand, and her mind groped for the mental trigger.

"Run!"

She stood in terror, the wand shanking. A pair of gnome hands pulled on Alyssa's clothes and urged her toward the door. She turned and ran with Fex. Atom's large hands pushed her from behind, his panicked voice yelling. "Faster!"

The lunatic goblin called out like something from a runaway nightmare. "Don't run from me!"

Alyssa was almost across the room and through the open door of the shop when Atom cried out in pain. Her head snapped around to see the little grey goblin riding on one of Atom's shoulders, with its knife lodged in the other shoulder. "Where do you think you're going?"

Alyssa spoke an eldritch word, putting all of her will into it. An invisible wall slammed into the goblin, sending him sailing across the room. She tugged frantically on Atom's sleeve. "You're almost there!"

He heaved and lunged through the doorway, one arm holding his bleeding shoulder. Alyssa turned in the doorway to see where the goblin had gone, then fire began coursing through her body. She looked down at a knife that had been plunged into her stomach. The grey goblin stood across the room with its arm outstretched. "Not so fast."

She fell into the street. Air came in painful breaths, like something heavy was on her.

Fex came into view, his face twisted in panic. The gnome's voice seemed so far away. "It's going to be okay. Don't worry..."

The voice drifted off as black curtains shut on her vision.

CHAPTER 21

F ex's heart pounded, and the gnome wondered if he would ever live a simple life again. He wanted to turn back the calendar one week, to when his biggest concern had been asking for a promotion.

Alyssa stirred under the silk bed sheets. Tight bandages clung to her side and a large blood stain peeked out at Fex. Her head tossed and turned, then her cloudy eyes opened. This beautiful sight sent waves of relief through Fex as faint tears came to his own tired eyes. She was trying to sit up in the bed, but he put a light hand against her shoulder. "You're all right now, Ms. Benedictus. Just relax. The potions are still doing their work."

She grunted her understanding and laid back down. Fex got up from the bedside stool and grabbed a cup of water. "Drink this. Slowly now. Good."

The groggy look in her eyes was already fading. "Thank you. Where am I?"

Fex's eyes rolled over the meticulously clean and organized room. "You've been sleeping in the detective's bed."

Her face looked startled and turned a shade of crimson as she looked at her clothes. "What am I wearing?" She sat up with a loud groan, one hand hovering near the bandage. "Why do I hurt so much?"

Fex held up both hands to calm her. "The worst is over, and you're doing much better. What do you remember?"

She closed her eyes in concentration. "I used true words of magic to push the goblin away, and it took more strength than I expected.

Atom fell through the door. I turned around, and—"

Alyssa's face turned as grey as a corpse. Fex placed a comforting hand on her arm. "Easy. You need to stay calm."

"That monster threw his knife at me! The same knife that Atom…"

"The goblin's gone. I got you outside and the guards at The Brew came running over. One of them caught that goblin in the shoulder with his staff and chased him back into the shop."

Her eyes were still two pools of fear. "Is Atom okay?"

Fex shook his head and said nothing. He had no sympathy for the fat man, but even Atom hadn't deserved to be hurt like that. He lived but was severely injured. If Fex was going to see that man off, it should have been by driving him out of business or at the hands of the law, not by some rabid goblin.

Alyssa sat in silence and looked smaller somehow, perhaps even smaller than Fex. His emotions spilled over, and he forced out all the fear he'd been keeping inside. "I didn't think we were going to save you. I had to use all the best potions the shop had to offer, even some different methods of application." Fex placed a hand on her arm. "My uncle and some other folk helped me carry you inside. Dex isn't a doctor, but he used to work for one, years ago. He made sure everything was in the right place."

Her eyes widened. "What do you mean, everything in the right place?"

"You really don't want to know. Trust—"

"I do want to know. *I need to know.*"

The gnome nodded. "The knife was obviously made to make sure the person on the business end didn't walk away. My uncle Dex made sure the blade was removed safely and put your… insides in the right spots again."

Alyssa nodded for Fex to continue.

"Then we soaked bandages in the elixir and applied them straight to the wound. I kept pouring healing potions down your throat, as well. I would have kept going, but my uncle stopped me. He said that too many potions could kill you just as easily as the injuries. We— we were there watching over you until the detective came back."

She still looked so pale and weak, so Fex got her another glass of water and waited until she drank it all before continuing. "He offered his flat and his bed, which, compared to the shop, is a step up. My uncle used his cart to move you. Of course, he cleaned it as best as he could before putting you in it. He put you in the front even."

She cleared her throat. "My clothes?"

"Mrs. Mose, the apartment manager, gave you some of her old clothes. Yours were covered in blood. She cleaned and dressed you. Wouldn't let Zane help. She kept going on about how it already wasn't proper, with you sleeping in his bed."

Alyssa smirked. "Where is he, if I am using his bed?"

Fex pointed to the patched door in the corner. "He is sleeping on his desk."

He eased her back down onto the bed. "You need your strength. Sleep now. In the morning, you will be doing a lot better."

She followed instructions and rested her head on the pillow without a response. Even with her eyes closed, Fex noticed that she searched for something. The gnome knew that neither of them would have a pleasant night. He turned down the gas lamps and walked over to a corner, where a pile of clothes and a blanket had been laid on the floor and made into a small bed.

Fex closed his eyes, and sleep came over him faster than he thought possible.

⌇

ALL THAT KEPT Zane company in that dark cell was constant pain. Every day someone—*something*—had been force-feeding him a healing potion. He resisted at first, but soon he lapped at the potion greedily every time it was brought. He hated himself. His weakness. But the last dose had been what felt like days ago, and his body and mind yearned for it unceasingly. His lips were dry, cracked. Bleeding. The horrific pain that had been suppressed with regular draughts of healing potion had begun to consume his mind. His arm and leg burned like pit-fire.

The sound of a door opening echoed through the darkness, and the glow of the first light he'd experienced in weeks fell on him. Zane thought that he was experiencing a pain-fueled dream. But then, human figures materialized in the gloom.

"We have a live one! Get the medic team ready!"

A group of men started bashing on the chains that bound him to the wall. Each blow radiated up though his bones.

The pain washed over him and drowned all else.

"Detective!"

Zane awoke in a cold sweat.

Alyssa stood over him in the dim light. "Are you okay?"

He sat up, his back stiff along with everything else. It wasn't anything he hadn't lived through before. "I am all right. Thank you for asking."

Zane was happy to see her alive and moving. He had cursed himself for putting her into danger after promising her grandfather she would be safe. He looked into her eyes and only found worry.

"Zane... you were crying."

The detective was still. Motionless. Finally, with great effort, he waved away the concern. "Like I said, I'm fine. In fact, I think I will go for a walk."

Zane stood but his leg gave out immediately and he tripped into Alyssa's arms. She grimaced as she caught him. "I think you should lay back down."

Pain clawed at him, but Zane was resolute. "No, a walk will be good for me." He looked around his office. "Where is my cane?"

She eased him back until he sat on his desk and picked up the cane from the floor. It had been right under his feet, and he hadn't even noticed.

Zane could hear the gentle care in her voice as she handed it to him. "Would you like me to go with you?"

He felt slight embarrassment at his own weakness, but he pushed the thought away. "Thank you, but you need your rest. I just need a little fresh air."

He stood and stepped out into the night. As he walked, Zane pulled on his jacket. The streets were empty and cloaked in a thick blanket of fog. The cold seemed to pierce deeper into his body than normal, so he pulled the coat tighter with his free hand. Zane gritted his teeth as he stopped to regain his breath.

Two red eyes stared at him in a darkened window. *You should go back.*

Zane ignored Shadow and pushed through the tendrils of cold fighting to drown him, but the silky voice followed him. *You need rest, Zane.*

"Shut up."

Oh, you're speaking to me today? How unusual.

"I don't need this. Not right now."

Why is that?

Zane swung his cane through the fog but lost his step and fell. The ash and muck clung to him. His breath came in ragged bursts. "Because of you, I live in this world of pain!"

The voice seemed sympathetic. *True, you are the victim of my desire. But such is the way of the world.*

The word *victim* hung in Zane's mind, and he thought of Alyssa. She hadn't deserved to be stabbed. Zane stood back up and started to wipe off the ash. His clothes were not torn, but it would take time to clean them. The disgust at the filth was a relief to his mind, a slight distraction from his injuries.

He walked on for another two blocks before Shadow's voice spoke again. *Where are we going?*

"To Atom's shop. I am going to see if there are any clues about the goblin that stabbed Alyssa."

Why? I doubt you will find anything useful.

Zane glanced at Shadow's eyes. Grim determination laced his voice. "I need a distraction from you."

The lack of lamps on Potion Lane left it shrouded in darkness. Some of the stores had a single light to fight through the fog. Heavy locked doors kept the shops safe. Zane waited a moment to see if he spotted the lamps of night guards on patrol. Once he felt secure, Zane made his way up the alley to The Fountain.

The alleyway behind the shop was wider than Potion Lane itself. He found the broken door with the lock hanging uselessly. In the doorway, Zane questioned what he should do.

Shadow's eyes materialized in the darkness. *You came this far. The door is open. Why wait?*

Zane hesitated in fear of the unknown. Was the shop truly empty? He collected himself and stepped through the doorway, using his cane as a guide. The workshop was smaller than The Brew's. Its floor was stained with broken glass, spilled potions, and what looked like dozens of goblin footprints. He followed them into the shop and looked with disgust at the blood by the door. He lit a nearby lamp, hoping none would take notice.

The room looked worse in the light. He knelt and looked for clues. There wasn't much to see, but he noticed a trail of blood leading away from the front door. The droplets had fallen from the weapon, Zane guessed. He followed it until it stopped in the middle of the room.

A dead end? No. A larger spray stained the floor before the trail disappeared, as if it had dropped from higher ground. Zane looked up and spotted a small hole in the ceiling big enough for a goblin to fit through.

Zane clicked his tongue. Now he had reached the end of the trail. He was too tired and it was too late for him to crawl onto the roof. With a sigh, he turned off the lamp and stepped back into the workshop. On the way to the back door, his eyes caught the glint of unbroken potion bottles.

I might have some suggestions to help with your pain. He ignored Shadow, but it continued. *You could take those potions.*

Zane stopped in his tracks. "What do you mean?"

You can borrow those elixirs. Pay the store back later if you like. After all that has happened, no one will notice if a few go missing.

Zane was tempted. The physical pain he felt was so much worse than normal, and his stash was depleted.

Shadow whispered like a serpent in his ear. *If you look hard enough, you might even find ambrosia...*

Shadow was right; no one would suspect a theft, and the idea of ambrosia left his throat tight with longing. Zane stood and made his way through the dark room.

A noise from the alleyway drew his attention. "Hey, was that door open before?"

Zane shuffled into what he assumed was a closet just as lamp light filled the room.

"I thought I saw light coming from here a moment ago, but it looks like someone has broken in."

"I told you I heard something. We should have come here sooner."

The light shone under the closet door. Zane put a hand to his mouth, which muffled his breathing, but his heart pounded in his chest. "Wait, is that blood? It's everywhere! By the saints, we should get the others!"

"Wait. I think this is the shop that was attacked by goblins. I heard Red Hood was here, but didn't have time to stain his hat..."

"Red Hood?"

"The bloodiest, most violent goblin ever seen. Willing to work for anyone with the money to pay him. They say he dyes his hood red with the blood from those he kills. Rumor has it, he likes to camp out in an area for more victims."

"We… we should leave this place."

"Scared?"

"No. It's just not a great idea to hang around. This door must have been broken by the goblins."

"That would make sense. All right, fine."

Zane listened as the floor creaked and the light vanished. Their voices disappeared, but he didn't move. Finally, he sighed and slid to the floor but bumped the wall and a heavy bag landed in his lap. Curious, he slipped the bag into his pocket.

He had waited far longer than needed for the guards to leave, so he left the closet and shuffled through the dark until finding a match. He lit a low flame and, in the dim light, Zane opened the bag. Inside was a small yellow bottle with liquid that moved like molten steel. His breath caught in his chest.

Ambrosia.

Zane's hands drifted over the bottles he'd noticed before. He grabbed three off the shelves, filling his jacket pockets.

Shadow's eyes pierced through the darkness as he whispered. *They are gone, detective.*

Zane ignored him as he walked to the back door and pushed on it with his cane. It made a deafening creak as it moved. He saw no lantern light, so Zane took a deep breath and stepped into the gloom.

With long strides, he made his way back to his office. Every shadow along the way made him tense. With a free hand, he checked to make sure the bottles were still in his pocket. As he walked, he filled his flask with one of the potions, then, for good measure, threw the bottle down a nearby alley.

Zane wasn't even in his office before he started drinking. The warmth washed over him, and he found new strength in his limbs as every ache faded away. It was the greatest drink he had ever had.

He walked softly through his front door, putting away his coat and cane. Zane sat behind his desk, placing his flask under his hat after one long swig. With the potion coursing through his veins, the old chair was comfortable.

Sleep gently fell over Zane.

Shadow watched from the corner.

CHAPTER 22

F ex woke up hours before either Alyssa or Zane, who had moved from the desk to the chair. The gnome was quiet as he stepped out of the office. He had several things to do, the first of which was checking on Vana. He hoped she was safe, having spent the night in jail. It was a silly fear—considering how she'd saved him in the street—but he still worried.

The morning light had just started fighting against the clouds and the ash, but people were already out in the street, setting up for another day. He walked with purpose as horse-drawn carriages sloshed through the streets of Alviun. The guard station was already active with people bringing their problems to the authorities, so Fex waited his turn. When he got to the front of the line, the guard behind the counter addressed him in an even tone. "How can I help you today?"

Fex could see the faint look of distrust that every human carried for gnomes. "I am here to see Vana Zel. She was placed under this station's watch yesterday after her shop, The Wizard's Brew, was attacked by a goblin... raid? Is that the word?"

The guard grumbled and opened a logbook. He scanned over one page, then another, until his index finger came to a stop. "Ah, here it is. Yes, she was here yesterday, but was released into the care of her brother."

Of course she is with Evan.

He thanked the guard and left. There was only one place he could think to find Vana.

The Ironbark estate.

ALYSSA WAS HAPPY Zane's apartment manager had given her some spare clothes, along with a hat and jacket. She tried them on and looked at herself in the mirror. She thought them sweet and homely, but simple and not cut for her. At The Institute, Alyssa had custom clothes with runes woven into them to help with temperature and cleaning, but now those were a ruined, bloody mess.

She looked at the stack of bandages laying in a large pile on the floor. While changing, she had noticed a large, fading scar. Her whole body still ached, like she'd exercised all day. The pain had been intense, but she had trouble remembering it.

Her mind turned to her situation. Alyssa was unsure of her job and home at The Institute, the only place she had ever known. She considered her options. *Maybe the detective needs assistance.* She imagined the two of them around the office, reading the paper and drinking coffee, discussing cases, softly touching hands. She watched the slight blush come to her cheeks in the mirror and shook her head.

She hardly knew the man, and she had bigger issues to consider, like why Tatius-Lasome had called a meeting to push her out of The Institute. Just last week, the two of them had argued over the translation of a book as respected colleagues. But now, he saw her as the problem.

Alyssa heard a knock at a door in the other room. She reached for the hat and jacket on the bed and stepped into the office. Zane sat behind his desk, sleeping soundly. Alyssa was glad to see him resting peacefully. She had been troubled to find him crying and whimpering in his sleep. It was a side of him she had never seen before. But they had known each other for only a couple of days. *Perhaps he always cries in his sleep.*

She heard the knock again. It was still early, and she wondered who it could be. Alyssa stepped lightly across the room and opened the door only to discover an empty hall. She looked left and right until she heard a cough from below. She looked down to see a green goblin, who had taken his hat off and held it tight to his chest.

"Eh, sorry to bother, ma'am, but is this the office of Detective Zane Vrexon? I see his sign on the door."

Alyssa nodded and looked back over her shoulder to the sleeping detective before answering. "The current case has been tiring. Could you give him a moment?"

The goblin gave a toothy grin. "Of course. Thank ya, ma'am."

She shut the door gently and walked toward Zane, past the carving on the wall. It was quality work. Amateur, but still good. The woman seemed familiar, but Alyssa couldn't quite place her.

Zane's head rested on his chest, his feet crossed on top of his desk. She pushed on his shoulder gently. "Detective Vrexon, you have a guest." When he didn't budge, Alyssa was a bit more forceful. "Detective Vrexon!"

His head jerked and he blinked in the light of the room. "Ms. Benedictus, what is going on?"

"You have a guest. A goblin."

He rubbed his eyes and looked down at his clothes. "I seem to be a mess."

She nodded in agreement. It looked as if he'd rolled through the muck of the street. "If you want to freshen up, you're welcome to, but your guest is waiting."

Zane cleared his throat and attempted to smooth out his clothes. "Thank you, Ms. Benedictus." He sighed and met her eyes, still dissatisfied with his clothes. "This will work. Please let him in."

Alyssa smiled at playing Zane's assistant. She walked across the office and opened the door. "The detective will see you now."

The goblin hurried toward Zane but stopped at the carving in the wall. He twisted his head as if trying to make up his mind, then he snapped his long fingers. "This is in the style of Debroven, right?"

Zane scowled at a corner of the room. "I think so." The expression turned into a soft smile as his gaze returned to the goblin. "But it is hard to remember for sure. Remind me who Debroven is?"

The goblin closed his eyes as if reading from the back of his eyelids. "Debroven is believed to be a minor artist of unknown background from two or three hundred years ago. The exact time is still debated, but I personally believe it comes from the Pox Plague era. I am impressed that you have seen his work. Then again, those who have seen his work rarely forget it."

Zane raised an eyebrow. "Why is that?"

The goblin pointed at the carving. "A person represented in this style is meant to be haunting, as if they were a living ghost. This is how many diaries and histories described many people during the Pox Plague."

"You certainly have an eye for art."

The goblin chuckled. "Art is seen as an unusual skill for a goblin, I know, but Nob finds it useful in… certain fields."

Zane smirked. "I imagine so. Speaking of Nob, what can I do for him today?"

The goblin climbed into the chair across from Zane. "The meeting with the Fey dealer is on for the eighth evening bell. I will be acting as the buyer. It will be in Dock Area B, by the warehouse."

Zane nodded and pulled out a pen and paper and wrote the address down before looking up. "Will any of Nob's friends be there?"

The small goblin nodded, his ears flopping. "Actually, Nob will be in the area with you in case the Red Tusk group makes a move."

"Why would they do that?"

"That area has always been a sort of neutral zone, but now both gangs are moving in. Unfortunately, that is the only place the seller would meet. I assume it's because the Tusks are nearby."

Zane made some notes. "Can we meet here before heading over?"

The goblin chuckled. "Yes, that's fine. I will bring a carriage for us to ride in."

Zane stopped and looked up. "You have a carriage?"

The goblin pulled off his round glasses and cleaned them. "Oh, yes sir. It isn't only Mister Nob who appreciates my skills in the arts. I have several patrons throughout the city, though many won't admit it. Some prefer my more... discreet services."

Zane grunted his acknowledgement. "It seems we have an arrangement. Anything else, I can get you?"

The goblin shook his head. "No, I will be here by the seventh bell. You have a good day, sir."

He jumped back to his feet and headed for the door as Alyssa held it open. "Sorry sir, but I never got your name."

He placed his hat back on his head and smiled. "Most don't bother with asking, so thank you. My name is Neub. That is the closest it can be pronounced in this language, anyway. Thank you again, ma'am."

Alyssa closed the door behind Neub, then took a seat across from Zane. "So, we are a step closer to finding the truth. Why are we going to a meeting tonight?"

He smirked and pulled out his flask. "We? You are still injured."

She had always wondered what was in the flask. *Alcohol? Tea? Clean water?* It was part of the man's mystery.

"Never mindN my injuries," Alyssa said. "I have lost too much, suffered too much, to sit still. I am more a part of this than ever. So, as I said, why are we going to this meeting?"

Zane looked down at the desk and tapped his fingers in thought. "The goblin mob informed me of the underground dealing of Fey goods, like the dagger we found. I believe the trafficking is coming from The Institute."

Alyssa had heard rumors of professors doing such things before, but always dismissed them. "What makes you think that?"

"Do you know other ways to have a regular trade of Fey goods? Especially here in the center of the Empire?"

She thought of more than a dozen ruins within a day's ride of Alviun, but they were watched closely by not only The Institute, but also the Imperial Army.

Only a few people in The Institute would have access to Fey artifacts. *If Zane is right ...* Alyssa's eyes widened with the realization. "There is only one basement in The Institute with Fey artifacts. There is a log for those who access it and a registry of what's down there."

Zane's face lit up with excitement. "Let's follow up on that tomorrow. I hope to get an idea of what they are selling at tonight's meeting. We can compare the dagger and whatever else they're moving to the registry of items."

He stood and grabbed his jacket and cane. "I have some errands to run beforehand, especially if we are going up against an Institute mage." He picked up his hat and slid it on his head.

Zane was already heading out the door when Alyssa noticed that he had forgotten his flask on the desk. She looked to the door and smiled as she raced to catch up with Zane.

She wasn't going to be left behind.

CHAPTER 23

It was late morning before Fex reached the Ironbark estate. He pushed open the ornate gate and went through, surprised to find that the courtyard was filled with people. By their dress, he surmised they were of varying social classes. They sat around fires, drinking freely from barrels. Others attempted to sing together in a drunken stupor. In a corner, a group was fist fighting.

Fex walked undisturbed through the courtyard. None of the people seemed to notice him, occupied as they were with their own activities. He had already started up the stairs to the front door when he was stopped. "Gnome! What are you doing here?"

The man swayed back and forth drunkenly as Fex pointed to the top of the stairs. "I am looking for Vana Zel. Is she—"

The man became frustrated and loud without bothering to allow Fex to finish. "Who are you? Do you work for the government?"

His voice carried to others outside the house. As if called to action, they followed their friend's voice. One of the men pulled out a meat cleaver. Fex took a step back. His hand twitched. Every instinct told him to reach for the wand in his jacket, but if everyone charged him, even the wand wouldn't help.

A gentle voice cut through the crowd. "Is that you, Mister Fex?"

He turned to see the old Ironbark butler, Giles. He had only met the man twice, but he'd never felt more relieved. "Yes, it's me! Is Vana here?"

The butler nodded and raised one hand to the approaching crowd. "It is all right, good men. He is Fex, the gnome that works for Vana and Dennis Zel. He is not a government agent."

The one with the meat cleaver hesitated. "How do we know that? Wouldn't it be safer if we simply got rid of him? He is just a gnome-."

"Are you suggesting that Vana could be working for the government?" Giles asked.

The man backed away. "No, I just mean—"

"We cannot question the guidance of the Moon. She knew that Mister Fex would come to see her."

The man dropped the cleaver and bowed his head. "Sorry."

Giles looked down with a smile. "Lady Zel was expecting someone, but she did not know who. Please, follow me."

The house was a mess. Everything looked like it was in the process of being moved. Large trunks and boxes lined the halls. At the first landing of the stairs stood several men in a circle, laughing. Evan Zel led the chorus.

"The fates are with us. Now nothing can stand in our way. We have the blessing of the Moon."

Evan's eyes fell on Fex and Giles as they approached, and he pointed at them aggressively. "Why has he been allowed in here? I thought that I made it clear that none should disturb the wake."

Fex caught the word and wondered who had died. Giles gave a slow bow. "I am escorting our guest to Lady Zel."

One of the men jammed an ugly finger in the air at Giles. "You call her Holy Mother or Moon Mother, understand?"

Evan placed his hand on the man's arm and forced down his accusatory finger. "Forgive the old butler. He is not of the faith and had known my sister long before her destiny was made clear." Evan turned back to Fex and Giles. "I thought I had given the strictest orders. My sister, the Moon Mother, was not to be disturbed. Was there something you were unclear about?"

"I am sorry, sir. I have received the strictest orders from Lady Zel, I mean, the Moon Mother, that if Mister Fex arrived, I would escort him to her."

The men behind Evan started to whisper amongst themselves. Evan glared, and they flinched at the bonfire of his fury. At their silence, he turned back to Giles. "Fine. Let me take him the rest of the way."

Giles was unmoved. "I am sorry Master Evan, but she was very clear."

The burly man looked like a kettle about to boil over. "That might be, but I am the master of this house and your employer, so you will let me escort this gnome to the Moon Mother."

"Sir, the will has yet to be read."

Evan marched across the hall. His muscles rippled under his funeral clothes as his hand reached for his sword. "You dare question my honor?"

Fex didn't like where this was going. He reached into his jacket and searched for the wand.

His nervous hand found it as a voice cut through the tension.

"Fex, thank you for coming."

Everyone looked up to Vana on the staircase. She was dressed in black and white robes, a dark veil covering her face. She exuded an unearthly air. When her sleeve slipped down, Vana revealed a beautiful silver bracelet with red gems embedded into it. "Thank you, Giles, for escorting Fex to me."

"Of course, Lady Zel. I am here to serve."

The men who surrounded Evan bowed their heads in reverence. Evan was the only one who looked upon her.

"Sister, I wish you would have told me this gnome was coming." He grimaced at Fex with frustration. "He is from your false life."

"I can arrange my own meetings. Now, please move aside so my guest may come up."

Evan gave Fex another disgusted glare but moved to the side with the other men. The gnome pulled his hand away from his wand and climbed the rest of the stairs, not daring to glance back. Vana waved for him to follow, and they walked alone down the halls until they came to a bedroom.

There was a large bed with a single figure lying beneath the sheets. A white cloth covered its face. Vana answered before Fex could ask.

"It's my father. He passed away yesterday. Shortly after the detective came by, it would appear."

Z————

ZANE WAS ALREADY growing tired of the conversation.

"This is a nice carriage, Mister Neub."

The goblin smiled politely, hiding his teeth. "Thank you, Ms. Benedictus. I bought it at an auction. You see, it belonged to a collector of sorts, but his children didn't see the need to keep it. Or perhaps they were unaware of its value. I was able, through a proxy, to buy this for what would easily be half its price."

"Why is it worth so much?"

Neub and Alyssa continued talking as Zane leaned back and tuned it out. He had tried his hardest to rest for the night's mission. With his errands completed, Zane felt prepared for whatever might happen. But dealing with a fully trained wizard was never easy. The military recommended catching the target off guard, or a frontal assault with a dozen men, though Zane doubted he would be dealing with any military wizards.

His hand went to his flask, still filled with a quarter of the health potion mixed with some Ambrosia. He had been a little nervous when Alyssa rushed after him with it, but apparently she hadn't looked inside it. He told himself that it didn't matter. This, of course, was a lie.

Shadow's eyes stared at him from a nearby reflection. The creature didn't say anything, which aggravated Zane more than if he had spoken.

"Detective, did you hear me?"

Zane looked turned to the goblin. "Sorry, what was the question?"

Neub's lips turned upward in a smile that looked thoroughly practiced. "I asked if you are ready? The iron glows hot, as they say."

Zane furrowed his brow but nodded. He shifted in his seat, making sure he had his flask, wand, and his custom cane. Alyssa continued her casual conversation with Neub as though it was a normal night. Zane took a few sips from his flask and let them talk uninterrupted. The fresh warmth was welcome as ever on such a cold night. More than that, Zane believed that he would need the extra strength.

Neub glanced at his pocket watch and collected his briefcase filled with banknotes. Zane stared unflinchingly at it. More money sat there than he had seen since coming to the city.

The goblin took a deep breath and put on his hat. "Well, here I go. Please keep an eye out for me. I know the boss will try to pull me out of the fire if things get too dangerous, but I would appreciate it if you two would help. I mean, you two will be closer."

Alyssa placed a comforting hand on Neub's shoulder. "Don't worry. We will come to your aid."

He gave what Zane believed to be a real smile this time, needle teeth and all. "You are all right for a hume."

Neub stepped out into the night. The warehouses loomed over him like old, decrepit mansions and streetlamps colored the growing fog. A figure walked into an umbrella of light wearing a large hat and a cloak that encircled him. Neub appeared out of the shadows, joining the figure under the lamp. The goblin gestured, and the figure pulled an object out from his cloak. It reflected a golden and silver sheen.

Alyssa leaned across him, looking out the window. "It's a bowl, I think."

Zane nodded in agreement. He had never asked what the goblin was going to buy, knowing only that it was Fey in nature. He glanced at Alyssa. "Will you be able to tell if the bowl is authentically Fey or not?"

"I believe so. There are several markers that are very hard to fake."

Some good news for once. Now they just needed to secure the bowl.

Neub pointed at the bowl, but the figure shook his head and extended his hand, palm up. The goblin nodded and started to hand over the case.

The deal was interrupted by an ear-piercing squeal.

The cloaked seller kicked Neub in the chest, knocking him to the ground and grabbing the case.

Zane burst out of the carriage into the night air. Down the street, wand and staff fire filled the air along with barking voices.

Alyssa followed tight on Zane's lead. "Neub, are you all, right?"

"Yes! Quick, after him!"

Zane didn't slow down to check on Neub. He kept running, unsure of what Alyssa was doing behind him. He turned the corner to see the cloaked figure a block away. Zane pulled his wand from its holster and chased the figure as he cut down an alleyway.

The straight line of the alley gave Zane a clear shot. But, against his better judgement, he yelled out a warning. "Stop!"

The figure tossed a hand in his direction. Zane fired, but the air around the dealer's hand rippled as a charm took form. Zane kept shooting as he ran, but each time the figure twisted around to block the wicks.

The figure slipped in the muck of the alley and the golden bowl rolled away. Zane was almost on top of him when the dealer raised both hands, and the air rippled into a transparent surface. Zane was thrown to the ground a few feet away. His body ached, as if he had sprinted into a wall.

By the time he got to his feet, the cloaked figure had disappeared. Zane's body had burned through the potion and Ambrosia mix. He leaned hard on his cane as he crossed the alleyway, searching until, in the dim light, he found the bowl covered in ash and mud. He picked it up with one gloved hand and started the long walk back to Neub's carriage. Even from here, he could hear the echoes of the fighting goblins.

Zane walked through darkness until he found Alyssa. She was breathing heavily, and her hair was disheveled as her head swiveled, as if looking for someone. Zane waved the bowl over his head to get her attention and answer her question before she could ask.

"He got away, but he dropped this."

A DULL LIGHT that matched Fex's mood pierced the window and fell over the body of old man Ironbark. The room had a pungent odor that stung the nose, but Fex had adjusted to it after the first hour. He could have left a long time ago, but he didn't want to leave Vana. She was a good... whatever she was, and Dennis had been a good human.

Maybe humans can be in a gnome's corner, he thought. Vana sat as silent and still as her father. At times, he worried that she had died, but he would notice the slow rising and falling of her chest.

But this late, Fex was the one who was nearly dead asleep. With Vana's gentle touch, Fex was stirred from his half-sleep. "It is time for you to go."

He stretched his stiff muscles and adjusted his clothes. "I am sorry. Is it rude to fall asleep during a wake?"

"You did what no one else here would have done. You treated me like a human, like a person. Thank you."

Fex's mouth hung open. He knew he should say something, but he couldn't think of anything worthwhile. Vana stepped away to the nearby desk. From one of the drawers, she drew out a large envelope and handed it to Fex. "Take this. Go back to the shop and open it there."

He slipped the bulky paper into his jacket. "I shouldn't leave you."

"I didn't want this life, but it's the one I have been given. You can still go and live for both of us."

Vana looked out a nearby window. Fex stood there, feeling torn.

"Is there anything I can do for you?"

She sighed. "I would have wished to see justice for my Dennis, but I will probably be long gone by then. He'll always be the love of my life." Vana turned back to him. Her veil hid her face, masking all but her voice. "Go now. Everyone should be drunk to the point of sleep, as it is so often at these wakes."

"But—"

"I can't protect you here forever." She was sharp with him this time. "My brother would one day come to me, telling me you have disappeared, or that he has found you dead. Leave now, while you can."

Vana pointed to the door. The gnome felt like he was staring up at a statue. No, he corrected himself, *it's like she's something more than mortal*. He bowed and left. Down the stairs, people lined the sides of the main hall, every one of them was sleeping off their liquor. Fex found Evan by the stairs with a woman on each arm.

He could no longer contain his hatred for the man. Fex spat on Evan on his way out, his saliva mixing with the beer stains on the giant man's shirt. The small fires that had been burning in the courtyard were now low and fading. One or two of the people were still awake, poking sticks into the flames.

Giles stood by the opened door as Fex came closer. "Leaving us so soon?"

Fex nodded. "I am. But first, I must apologize. It was never my intention to get you into trouble. I also wanted to thank you for caring after Lady Zel."

Giles waved the concern away. "It is all right. She will make sure that I am fine. Even Evan wouldn't try to get rid of me." The butler looked back and forth and gestured to go forward. "I am well aware of who my employer is. I know what's in the will."

Fex shook his head and stepped through the gate. "Tell Vana I am sorry."

The gate closed like an old door of a crypt. Fex bowed politely even though no one could see him, then made his way through the streets. His mind drifted along with his feet, but before long, Fex was standing in the Brew's workshop.

He pulled out the thick envelope. Fex had never been given anything like this before. His small hands shook as he fumbled with the heavy envelope. As he unfolded the parchment, the first words he could read were *Deed to The Wizard's Brew*. His heart pounded faster than he thought possible.

Fex scoured every page. Once he started crying, he couldn't stop.

The shop is mine!

The thought played over and over in his head. His lungs worked like great bellows as he breathed between sobs. With his dirty sleeve, Fex cleaned his face and picked up the papers again, confirming one last time that he was the shop's sole owner.

Fex wasn't his only champion.

CHAPTER 24

Alyssa rubbed her eyes as she dressed in front of Zane's mirror. Again. *There is nothing inappropriate about it*, she told herself. She wasn't a naive girl, and such emotions made her feel silly. The detective had slept outside in his office again after another day of excitement, which she was not getting any more used to.

After smoothing the wrinkles out of her clothes, Alyssa tapped on the glass with a musical rhythm, then with elegant movements of her fingers she traced out runes on the mirror. She empowered the markings with a few eldritch words, and the mirror rippled.

The aged face of Archmage Benedictus-Lasome came into view. He looked up from his desk of paperwork. "Alyssa? Is that you?"

She forced a smile. "Yes, grandfather."

Benedictus-Lasome adjusted his mirror, then his glasses. "Dear, I have been working on getting you back into The Institute. It has been difficult, especially since Tatius-Lasome has ignored all my requests. In fact, he has refused to talk to anyone since the hearing, but I have made sure your room was still out of reach. All is safe and sound." He coughed. "But until this is resolved, I think you should find more appropriate living quarters. I have even looked into an apartment building not far from here. You could stay—"

"Grandfather, I need your help with something else right now."

He stopped and adjusted the glasses on his wrinkled face. "What do you need, dear?"

She pulled out the golden bowl. Zane had spent a good amount of time cleaning it. In fact, she had never seen someone wash something that long or hard. It now shined with an almost unnatural glow, and Alyssa didn't know if it was because of the Fey metal or Zane's dedicated scrubbing. "I need you to check the inventory list for Fey artifacts to see if there's a match for this bowl."

"Why?"

This was the important part. "We believe someone is stealing artifacts from The Institute and selling them on the black market."

Her grandfather raised a finger to his lips. Standing up, he spoke arcane symbols, causing the air to ripple with power, then sat back down. "Now you can continue."

"There is an inventory in the basement. I had dropped it down there during the incident with the Dream Sphere. It should contain a description of every object. The bowl, if it is from there, should be listed with the following major features. Do you have your paper and pen ready? You might want to write this down."

"Always, dear."

"An eye sits at the bottom. Looks to be either a hand washing or scrying bowl. It seems to be of the second era and of high Fey tradition." She continued to describe the bowl and the small details that marked it.

Her grandfather wrote it all down. "Is that everything?"

She stopped staring into the bowl and met his eyes "Be careful. I don't know what's going on. But—"

"I am an old archmage. I still remember when dueling was allowed in The Institute. I will be fine. Now, you stay safe, okay? I will reach out to you with a charm letter if I find anything."

The mirror rippled, then his image faded away. Alyssa took a deep breath and tried to relax, but she couldn't ease the tension. It was late in the morning and now she was forced to wait. She walked into the office, where Zane sat behind his desk. "I didn't mean to eavesdrop, but the walls are thin."

She walked around and set the bowl on the desk. "It's all right. All we have to do is wait."

Minutes passed like hours. Alyssa sighed knowing she needed something to keep her busy. "Is there a bookstore nearby?"

Zane thought about it for a moment before answering. "I believe I saw one around the corner, maybe a couple of streets over."

She grabbed her things to leave when a tap came to the window. Zane looked up from his desk to see a paper stuck to the glass. Alyssa knew immediately what it was and sighed in relief. She opened the window and took the note. "That was faster than I had expected. It's a message from my grandfather."

She unfolded it and read. It was simple, asking her to contact him by mirror. Alyssa motioned for Zane to follow her. At the mirror she once again traced the runes and empowered them. Zane leaned over, whispering. "Will this damage my mirror?"

As the mirror rippled, she laughed. "It won't. I could explain how it works, but I would need a chalkboard."

"I will take your word for it then."

Archmage Benedictus-Lasome came into picture. He looked pale. "Dear, thank you for contacting me."

He nodded to Zane. "You too, detective."

"Of course," Alyssa answered.

"I have found some... unsettling things."

Alyssa and Zane glanced at each other. Zane asked, "What have you found?"

Benedictus-Lasome scratched his head, his face marred by sweat. "I found the inventory log and an object that matched the description. According to the ledger, it had been moved to a lab a week ago."

This concerned Alyssa. She should have known about such a transfer. The department was small and word would travel fast. At the very least it should have taken weeks to get approval, but no one had made such a request. "Do you know which lab?"

Benedictus-Lasome's glanced past them to the office. His actions made Alyssa nervous. "It has an address, but when I checked it in the records, the address came up to be an old warehouse. No lab is listed there."

Zane shrugged. "Are there some labs that are not listed?"

"No legal labs. All arcane labs must be registered with The Institute, but there are still several such labs throughout the nation run by hedge mages."

Zane raised an eyebrow, and Alyssa answered the question. "Self-taught mages. Such people can be dangerous due to gaps in knowledge."

She shook her head. "If it was an illegal lab, then it would not be able to get any help from The Institute. So if we sent the bowl to a lab, it should be legal and on record."

Zane nodded in agreement but still looked a little confused. Benedictus-Lasome tapped on some paper that sat in front of him, just outside of the image of the mirror. "I noticed something else. Several objects have been sent there, over the last few years. However, none have ever been returned."

Zane stepped away and grabbed the Fey dagger. "Did you see anything about a dagger?"

Benedictus-Lasome adjusted his glasses and ran his finger over the papers. He came to a stop. "Yes, an enchanted dagger with several markings over the blade. The blade is green in color..."

The description went on, and Alyssa listened carefully. As far as she could tell, it was a perfect match. That was their connection, then. "Who signed off on it?"

Her grandfather sighed and looked around. "That's what makes me nervous."

"Who?"

"Tatius-Lasome. He signed off on all the transfers, but—"

"But what?"

"The handwriting doesn't look right."

Zane crossed his arms and leaned back onto a wall. "So, what now?"

"Grandfather, can you secure a meeting with Tatius-Lasome?"

He nodded. "I would expect an invitation as early as tomorrow."

"Good. While you work on that, I need to eat."

Benedictus-Lasome's image disappeared from the glass, and Zane pursed his lips. "I don't have enough for two."

She smiled. "That's all right. I would like to get out and walk for a bit."

ZANE WAS HAPPY to be alone in the office. He smiled as he pulled free his flask and placed it on the desk. Ambrosia was the strongest healing potion in existence, and the idea of getting to taste it again excited him. Zane didn't like the idea of drinking an illegal substance, but his desire overcame his conscience. He brought the flask to his lips and sipped slowly, wanting the drink to last as long as possible.

Zane's injuries felt truly gone, and he wondered how he ever managed with normal brews. Shadow materialized in the corner and watched. Despite having no face to show emotion, Zane could feel it judging him. He set his drink down on the table, his blood pumping like fire.

I am watching you.

Shadow's voice wracked Zane's nerves. He slammed one hand on his desk. "What are you? How can you have memories. Your own memories!" Zane stood and marched to the corner. "You have been in my ear since I was in the field-hospital. I have ignored you, humored you, and I was close to accepting you as part of *my* broken mind." He took a deep breath. "But you're not a part of me. You're something else. Someone else. And dammit, I want answers!"

Zane stood eye-to-eye with Shadow. His injuries felt like they had never existed. Shadow's red eyes seem to stare deep into his own.

You really want to know?

"Yes!"

An arm of darkness shot out and gripped Zane's collar, and the familiar feeling of a blackout creeped up his spine. An inky face stretched from the corner.

"Fine." The face's mouth moved, but it looked wrong, as if it were a puppet on the arm of a ventriloquist. "I will show you."

A wave of darkness washed over Zane. His last thought was that those words were spoken with his own voice.

Zane floated on a sea of darkness, as if night were given the form of a vast ocean. He tried to force his eyes open, but they did not budge. A voice called out over the surface of the blackness.

I remember being a noble of some esteem.

The world around Zane shifted like morning fog. Zane stood in front of a mirror, looking back at himself. But it wasn't his face. This man had taut, pale skin and long black hair pulled back over his shoulders.

But his eyes were red, like two pools of fire.

They were Shadow's eyes.

Zane tried to talk but no words came out. Instead, Shadow spoke and Zane watched as the reflection's mouth moved. "This was my face— or rather, it was my *favorite* face."

Your favorite?

Shadow smirked. "Yes."

Zane's heart fell into his stomach as he realized that their roles were reversed. Shadow could hear Zane's thoughts, but he couldn't speak. Zane wondered if this was how Shadow lived or existed; he was unsure which word to use.

"I have been around a long time. I have also had many names, such as Debroven, as the goblin guessed. I don't think there are many others today who would recognize my art."

Why did you carve that image of Lady Zel?

"Her elegance in that moment deserved to be immortalized, and I couldn't keep myself from doing so. It reminded me of better times. Such good times those were. Until"—the face in the mirror looked troubled, as if haunted by some painful recollection—"until the quest started for..."

The image changed to a pool of inky black water in an underground cave. The walls and ceiling were all natural stone, untouched by any hand. The ring around the pool, though, was elegant and smooth, with strange glyphs etched into it.

"The pool of...The pool of..."

Zane watched as Shadow studied himself in the reflection of the water and touched his mouth.

The pool of what?

Shadow shook his head. "It seems that the old charms still hold power over me. I cannot speak of the pool. Just know that it was what I long sought for my Lord."

The scene shifted once again. He stood inside the large throne room; the same one he had seen in the Dream Sphere. The memory played out again, with the old king cursing Shadow. "I found it, but it wasn't what I or any of us expected. That fool king punished me unjustly."

The final scene came into view. As the world faded away, a man laid crumpled on the ground, chained to the wall and floor. His beard was ragged, and dried blood covered one shoulder and leg. It took a moment for Zane to process the image, but it struck him like a lightning bolt.

That's me.

"Yes. The Ghoul War, as you call it, was something I was forced into. I had grown tired of my curse, my prison, so I was going to use you in a forbidden ritual. But it went wrong, and now I am a part of you."

Uncertainty now colored Zane's thoughts, but he raged inside at the monster that had tortured and now lived within him. The image faded away and he returned to darkness. When he cooled off, Shadow spoke. "Any questions?"

Are my blackouts you, or is it the brew?

"Both. I think."

Why me?

"You had spirit."

The darkness rescinded and he stood in his office again. His body felt heavy and tired as if he had run for miles without rest. He looked at Shadow in the corner and stared into the two red eyes.

"Why should I trust anything you say?"

Shadow's silky voice sounded remorseful. *You shouldn't.*

"Why?"

Shadow was quiet for a long moment before answering. *Because of my failure, we are merging. One day, we will be one person. One entity. Our individual selves will be gone.*

"What?" Zane's blood had turned from molten lava to ice. "Why would you let us die?"

As I said, the ritual went wrong.

z

ALYSSA HAD SPENT the afternoon walking around the city surrounded by the dirty air. It felt different to be covered in the ash that fell from overhead, like being touched by the sky. She and Zane were waiting for her grandfather to let them know when to return to The Institute. At most it would be one more day, and she hoped that it would finally bring the case to a close.

She stepped into Zane's building and was almost to his door when the apartment manager, Mrs. Mose, stopped her. Her face showed a mix of fear and concern. "I am sorry to bother you dear, but—"

She hesitated, but Alyssa pressed her. "Is everything okay?"

Mrs. Mose grabbed Alyssa's sleeve with one bony hand. "I heard strange noises coming from Mr. Vrexon's office. I knocked on his door, but he said everything was all right. That should have been it, but his voice... it didn't sound right. Would you please make sure he is okay?"

Alyssa nodded and rushed toward the stairs, then stopped for an instant, not wanting to be rude. "Thank you for the clothes!"

The door to the office was unlocked. Alyssa pulled her wand out from the folds of her dress and pushed the door open with her foot. It swung open with a painful groan, and from the opening she could see that the office was a mess, with papers covering the floor and Zane laying across his desk.

"Zane! Zane, are you okay?"

She stepped across the room while sweeping her wand back and forth, searching for an intruder. She was scared, and her heart thumped in her chest. Alyssa stood over Zane, one hand extending her wand and the other shaking him awake. "Zane!"

His eyes fluttered for a moment before he opened them and focused on her. "Alyssa?"

Zane rolled over and slipped off the desk. He hit the floor with a large thud, then groaned as he worked to stand. She put her wand away and helped him. "What happened?"

"I needed to lay down..."

He glared at the corner, then picked up one of his shoes and threw it. "Shut up!"

Zane was angry, and his wild eyes made him look unhinged. He turned and started adjusting his clothes, but try as he would, the wrinkles wouldn't come out. She put a gentle hand on his shoulder. "What's wrong?"

He leaned against the desk and held his face in his hands. "It's complicated. More complicated than I thought possible. I thought I was crazy, but now I *wish* that's what was wrong with me."

"Start from the beginning."

He looked her in the eyes, and she could see the pain he carried. She listened intently as he explained what had happened since she left. Alyssa waited until the end of his story before speaking. "I have never heard anything like this. I don't even know where to begin."

"Could it be some type of possession?"

She shook her head. "Nobody has ever proven a case of possession, be it ghost or demon." She looked into his eyes and, for the first time, saw fear. "This isn't something I have studied and I don't know any experts that have, either." Alyssa gripped his hand and squeezed comfortingly. "But I will help."

He looked up from the floor. "Help? How?"

"The Institute is the center of knowledge in the Empire. There might be something or someone there who can fix this."

He extended his hand. "Thank you for your help. It might not be worth much, but I will offer my assistance in anything you need."

"You are already helping me, Detective Vrexon."

Zane's face was stern. "I will pay you back. I promise."

CHAPTER 25

The Brew was clean at last. Fex set the broom to the side and sat on his stool overlooking the room. His room—and not just that damn closet.

Fex had been afraid when he first looked at Vana's letter. Full ownership, along with all merchandise. He had already reached out to a cousin of a cousin who could paint the window. His dream of the Gnomen Brew was finally within reach.

As he surveyed his spoils, Vana's voice played in Fex's head, reiterating her desire to find Dennis's murderer.

"Hello, nephew." Dex stood in the doorway, his black clothes covered in ash.

Fex jumped down from his stool and rushed over to his uncle. "Uncle Dex, how are you?"

"I am well. Is it true that you—"

"Own the Brew?" Fex nodded excitedly. "Yes!" He gestured with his hands and spun in a circle to display the room. "I am the sole owner."

A smile crept over Dex's face, one of the few genuinely happy expressions he had seen from his uncle. "So that woman was guilty. I just knew humes couldn't be trusted."

"No, she's innocent."

Fex watched as the smile fell away from his uncle's stunned face. He realized that his fist was balled and his jaw clenched. Fex was angry. Not at his uncle, but at himself. "Sorry uncle, but it's not that way."

His uncle looked around. "Is there a place where we can sit?"

Fex led his uncle into the workshop and grabbed two stools. Both sat at the edge of the table. His uncle scratched his head. "So, what happened?"

Fex pulled from his jacket the packet of paper that contained the letter and deed. With a limp hand, he pushed it over to his uncle. Dex sat quietly as he read through the papers, line by line, page by page. When he finished, he folded it and handed it back to his nephew.

The old gnome shook his head. "I have never seen anything so generous."

Fex could see the mixture of emotions in his uncle's face. Fex knew what his uncle thought of humans, but what sat in front of him was something that completely opposed his world view. "Can I get you a drink, uncle?"

The old gnome nodded. Fex jumped down and made tea. While it brewed, his uncle asked, barely above a whisper. "Have you considered whom to hire as apprentices?"

Indecision slammed into him like a wave rocking a pier. "I haven't put a lot of thought into it."

His uncle traced the names on the table as he said them. "There is Dan, Bil, and Gil on your mom's side. Then there's Jil, Del, and Fel on your dad's, but those are just the boys. Then there's Lil, Uil, Eal…"

Fex's mind wandered from the conversation as his uncle went on with names from both sides of the family. He couldn't focus on them. Instead, Fex thought about Vana, sitting by herself in her father's room. The kettle whistled, pulling Fex back to reality.

His uncle poured drinks for both of them and took his seat. "So, who do you think would be good?"

"Good for what?"

"Your apprentice." Dex looked at his nephew, concerned. "What is bothering you?"

Fex sighed and stared into his drink. "I feel guilty."

His uncle eyed the packet and sipped from his drink. "Did you get this through illegal means?"

Fex shook his head. "No. I feel guilty over not helping her find Dennis's killer."

"So what?"

"So what? Lady Zel gave me everything I could ever ask for, but I didn't help her with what she wanted most."

His uncle set his glass down. "Then why are you here?"

"What?"

"Why are you here?"

His uncle put a finger into Fex's chest and spoke sternly. "A gnome shouldn't leave things unfinished. We are—"

"Better than that." Fex nodded his head. "You're right." He jumped from his seat and grabbed his coat, hastily shoving the wand into a pocket. "I have somewhere I need to be. If you'll excuse me..."

Dex was already at the door. He smiled and bowed. "I hope to discuss your future apprentice later."

Fex barely remembered to lock the door to his new shop before rushing off.

z

ZANE WAS IMPATIENT as Alyssa read. "Have you heard from your grandfather?"

Alyssa nodded her head and pulled a piece of paper from the window. "Yes. He was able to set up another archmages' board meeting for this evening. He will speak on our behalf."

"We need to go back to The Institute?"

Alyssa nodded. "There is evidence there, and we need to confront Tatius-Lasome to find out what's wrong with him."

"What do you mean?"

She looked away in thought. "It was as if he was someone else last time we were there. He was short and sharp during the hearing, but he has always been so calm and long-winded. If we can, we need to talk to him."

Zane scratched his head. He wished this case was a simple robbery gone wrong. "Could he be under a charm like I was? Or maybe that is how Tatius-Lasome really is, and he just puts on a show most of the time."

"Tatius-Lasome is an archmage. If he didn't suspect anything, maybe someone could enchant him. If he isn't being controlled, then he has played me for years. Maybe we should take a look in his office, too."

Zane smiled. Alyssa had changed so much in so little time. "Do we have any other allies we can rely on?"

"Agwen. I think he will help us. He must be aware of what is going on."

A knock drew their attention. Alyssa placed the slip of paper on the desk and crossed the room. The door opened and she welcomed the guest.

" Mister Fex! Please come in."

Fex thanked Alyssa and marched in, his whole body radiating resolve. Zane could see heavy bags under his eyes as the gnome looked for a chair. Alyssa pulled one out as though she was Zane's secretary. "Have a seat."

Fex took the chair with a nod. "Detective, I want to help."

"Help?"

Fex yawned, one small hand covered his mouth. "Yes. Whatever you need in this case, I want to help."

Alyssa and Zane brought him up to speed, including their plan for the board meeting. Fex nodded and asked a simple question. "So, you're saying that the archmage Tatius-Lasome is acting suspicious?"

Alyssa handed him a glass of water. "Yes."

Fex sipped on the drink. "How likely is it that someone could have impersonated him?"

Alyssa's face sagged into worry. "What are you getting at? He is an archmage inside The Institute. For an outsider to get in would be not just unlikely, but virtually impossible."

The gnome set the cup down on the table. "Right, right. May I come with you both?"

Zane looked to Alyssa. "Would that be okay?"

"I see no reason why not. We may need the extra help."

Zane checked the condition of his wand and holstered it as they prepared to leave for The Institute. Fex watched, then did the same, loading his spell wicks. Then they traveled in silence, all aware that the most dangerous part of their ordeal was soon to come.

As they approached The Institute, Fex ran up to a courier and sent him on his way.

"What was that about?" Zane asked.

Fex smiled. "Helping, hopefully."

Shadow cackled from a dark corner of the street.

At the doors of The Institute, the guards stopped them and pointed to both Zane and Alyssa. "We have been given strict orders not to let you in."

Alyssa stepped forward. "We are here for a board meeting. Word should have been sent to you from Archmage Benedictus-Lasome."

One guard slammed the butt of his spear down. "An archmage *has* given us orders. He has said that you are not allowed. I am sorry, but we cannot go against the order of an archmage."

"An archmage? But you take orders from Central Hall, not from any one archmage."

The guard suddenly looked confused. One of them rubbed his forehead. "Central Hall? Yes. But the archmage..."

The other guard spat on the ground and leveled his spear. "You are under arrest for attempting to charm a guard."

Zane stepped in front of Alyssa, his cane outstretched as a weapon. "You will do no such thing!"

Both guards froze and crumpled to the ground as the doors burst open. Archmage Benedictus-Lasome stepped out slowly. "Sorry for the wait. I keep finding more people charmed. My guess is it's the same spell that was used on Zane." The old man shook his head. "This is a problem that reaches much farther than I expected. But we're about to get to the bottom of it. Are you ready?"

Zane and Alyssa made eye contact, and he found a mixture of emotions: Fear, excitement, and hopefulness. She nodded, and he did the same.

Fex tugged his jacket tight. "I will catch up. I need to wait here."

Alyssa started to argue. "These halls move and shift constantly. Without a guide you will never—"

Benedictus-Lasome stopped her. "No time, dear. The board has already been called together." He tossed a compass to Fex. "This will lead you to me."

Zane's stomach turned as archmage Benedictus-Lasome unlocked a nearby door that led them to the boardroom. He once more stood looking up at the rows of archmages.

Alyssa stepped forward. "Archmages, thank you for seeing us again. I believe we have new information that will show—"

Tatius-Lasome slammed the floor with his iron staff. "You have no authority to speak here. You are neither an archmage nor professor now. You're not even a student. You have no connection to The Institute, and I dismiss this meeting."

Principal Arch-Lasome stood up. "Wait a moment, you don't hold that power."

Zane watched as Alyssa bit her lip in frustration. Benedictus-Lasome spoke up. "You might try to dismiss them, but you can't get rid of me that easily. I have brought forth information showing that large amounts of The Institute's property has been stolen."

Tatius-Lasome stood and glared down at them. "That may be, and by no means do I look to deny you the right as an archmage to bring this forward. But I must ask that Alyssa and the detective be escorted out. Now."

⌐

ALYSSA TRIED TO argue but was drowned out by Arch-Lasome. "Let's leave it to a vote."

The crowd grumbled and the vote proceeded with a unanimous decision to expel both Zane and Alyssa from the chamber. The head of the archmages stood up at the end of a count. "It is decided, then. You two shall be escorted to a holding room. If it is seen as necessary, we will call you back."

Two students, a boy and girl, came to escort them. Alyssa recognized one of them.

Frame.

"Hello again," Alyssa said. "How is your study on transmutation of human cells coming along?"

Frame looked confused. "What study, ma'am?"

Alyssa narrowed her eyes. "Don't you remember? You ran those tests for me. I signed poly-hair over to you."

"I am sorry, but I think there is some confusion. We've never met."

Alyssa gave a strained smile and pulled out her glasses. They were cracked, but they would work. With a single mumbled eldritch word, she could see that an arcane charm buzzed around the heads of the students. She closed her eyes for a moment and felt the layout of the building. The path to the waiting room was not this way.

She took a deep breath. "Zane, do you trust me?"

"Yes."

Without responding, Alyssa spoke an eldritch word and Frame's body froze and her forward momentum carried her to the floor. The male student turned to them and Alyssa could feel him trying to form words. They were lost in the air as Zane caught him in the jaw with the head of his cane. The young man slumped to the floor.

Zane nodded to Frame. "Will she be, okay?"

"Yes. She's frozen, but it will wear off. What about him?"

"Nothing that a healing brew and dentist won't patch up. Now what?"

Alyssa's senses were already seeking a path through the building. "Remember what I said about seeing Tatius-Lasome's office?"

He nodded. "Lead the way."

The halls twisted and turned, and Zane leaned harder on his cane as they went.

"Are you all right?" Alyssa asked.

He nodded and waved her onward. The two raced through the shifting rooms until they stopped in front of Tatius-Lasome's office door. It was locked. Zane pulled his wand out of its holster, but she stopped him. She knew the door to an archmage's room might not respond well to wand fire. Instead, Alyssa spoke an eldritch word and the lock simply clicked in response.

That was too easy, she thought. *No counter charms or spell weaved to stop us.*

But they were working under a time crunch, so Alyssa pushed open the door despite her trepidation.

The sight that greeted them turned her stomach. Tatius-Lasome sat behind his desk, his head slumped down and twisted unnaturally to the left. The putrid smell of death attacked her.

But he had just expelled them from the meeting. How could he be sitting there, a rotting corpse.

Alyssa tried to say something but stopped as Zane raised a finger to his mouth. The detective walked around the desk, pulled off his glove, and inspected the wizard's neck.

"It's broken. Like someone crushed it."

Her legs grew weak, but she found her strength and managed to remain standing. It was yet another death and there had been so much killing over the last few days. "Can you check his desk? Last time I saw him, I had left the department's finance ledger on his desk."

Without a word, Zane carefully sorted through the mess of papers. "Sorry, I don't see anything like—"

A cough from behind Alyssa cut him off.

She turned and recoiled from a staff with glowing runes pointed at her face.

FEX PACED BACK and forth in front of the large metal doors of The Institute, only stopping once to check on the unconscious guards. He fidgeted and looked up at the clear sky of the courtyard. He couldn't remember the last time he'd seen the sun, and he decided to take a vacation in the country when he could get away from the shop. His shop.

Fex shook off the thought and continued to worry about Vana. *The boy should have reached them by now*, he thought.

The doors were like the gaping maw of some great beast, the halls inside seeming to shift every time he looked away. Finally, Vana Zel, dressed in black and white robes and a thick veil that flowed to her chest, entered the courtyard with a host of armed men. Flanking her were Evan and Giles.

Fex raced down to the bottom of the steps to meet them. Vana's authority radiated from her, and none that followed seemed to question it. Fex bowed, not like a servant, but a subject. "Thank you for coming so quickly."

Vana knelt beside him. "No, I thank you for this opportunity."

She stood and turned to Giles. "Take half the men and guard the steps. No one enters until I come back."

He bowed with a smile. "Yes, Lady Ironbark."

Lady Ironbark? Fex caught Evan's scowl at the title. As if reading his mind, Vana answered the question. "The will of my father has been read, and I have been named head of the clan. All that the Ironbark's own, I own. All the family's responsibilities are my responsibilities."

Fex took pleasure in learning that Vana had inherited everything from her father. He imagined, with a smile, Evan's sullen face when the will was finally read.

Vana turned to her brother. "Evan, you will follow me into The Institute?"

His scowl never left his face, but he bowed. "Of course, Lady Ironbark."

She pointed to the great doors. "Lead the way, Fex."

The funhouse of a building that was The Institute dampened Fex's mood, but he would not be deterred. He used the compass to find a large room with several older men sitting in rows above him. He recognized Benedictus-Lasome on the ground floor with him.

One of the other men called out. "Who are you? Where are the guards?"

Fex took a deep breath. "I would like to introduce you to Lady Vana Zel, head of the Ironbark family, and her escort."

The gnome stepped to the side as Vana strode into the chamber, followed by Evan and his men, each with a sword and wearing a leather jerkin, the sleeveless vests accentuating their massive arms.

Vana's voice was clear and loud. "I am here to find my husband's killer."

Tatius-Lasome stood in a panic, iron staff in hand. "Who do you think you are? Don't you see we are busy?"

"As has been said, I am Vana Zel. I'm sure you are already

aware—"

"So, what, you silly woman?"

Benedictus-Lasome coughed. "Tatius-Lasome are you forgetting?"

Tatius-Lasome laughed and wheeled around to face the old wizard. "Forgetting what?"

Benedictus-Lasome pointed to Vana, with a slight chuckle. "Vana Zel is the widow of Dennis Zel. The man who was murdered. The man Alyssa claims *you* hired. Solving this crime is the root cause of our last two meetings."

Tatius-Lasome swallowed hard and waved his hand dismissively. "Of course I know that."

Vana stood graceful and aloof as ever. "Mister Tatius-Lasome, will you please come down here? I wish to ask you a question of a... delicate nature."

The archmage snorted in disdain. "You and your bullies are not welcome here."

Vana repeated her request and Tatius-Lasome repeated his answer. Benedictus-Lasome sighed. "Why not have Lady Zel's guards stand to the side? If you're afraid, that should fix the issue. If it's only her, there should be nothing to worry about."

Tatius-Lasome jerked forward, cold sweat on his face. "No, I—"

"This has been a mess, Tatius-Lasome," said Principal Arch-Lasome, who looked tired and frustrated. "I have already been forced to undo much in the way tampering and political grandstanding." He leaned over, his eyes narrowing. "If you going down there would resolve things faster, then you will go down there. Understood?"

Tatius-Lasome nodded and reluctantly descended the stairs. Vana ordered her brother and guards to move to the wall and wait. Fex stood by Benedictus-Lasome, his hand in his jacket, gripping his wand.

Tatius-Lasome crossed the room slowly, his face pale and covered in beads of sweat.

His hand was tight around his iron staff.

CHAPTER 26

Alyssa froze, her eyes locked on the figure in the doorway pointing a glowing staff at her face.

Agwen.

He wore a pained expression as he closed the door and reached into his pocket. Agwen used what looked to be Tatius-Lasome's keys to open a direct door to the basement. Alyssa's mind struggled to process the scene in front of her, to understand why Agwen was holding Zane and her at staffpoint and forcing them into the Fey department's basement.

She glanced over her shoulder and studied Agwen's beet-red face, which was shattered and lined with cracks of worry. Even his hood was down, revealing his ears. She hadn't seen them before. They were thin but not as long as those of others of Fey descent.

"Down the stairs. Keep your eyes up and straight ahead," Agwen commanded.

Zane raised his hands and took the lead, followed by Alyssa and Agwen. They descended the staircase in silence. At the last step, Alyssa dared to turn her head back. The racks of the basement loomed over her now, like the dark walls of a tomb. Before she knew what she was doing, she was speaking.

"Why are you doing this?"

It sounded like Agwen missed a step. He clearly hadn't expected this and there was almost relief in his voice. "I have been stealing money from the department for a long while. There are so many rare texts left by the Fey, and I could never get enough funds from The

Institute to purchase them. After pinching a little here and there, the fools ended up paying for them anyway. I was able to cover it up at first, but I eventually needed money to cover what I'd taken, so I started selling some of the artifacts to the Red Tusk."

What he said explained why the ledgers were off when she had looked at them. The account had been emptied and filled over and over. "So that's why you never wanted us to hire anyone new?"

"The more money the department used, the more the budget needed adjusting. More adjustments lead to more questions. So few students ever come to us, it never seemed to matter. A few charms here and there to alter memories and—"

"How does Dennis fit into this?" Zane's voice was stern as he cut Agwen off.

Alyssa looked over to the detective, startled by how hard and cold his expression was.

A loud sigh came from behind. "I had some outsider, claiming to be representing Evan Zel of the Ironbark family, threatening me. He said he would go public with my connection to the Red Tusk gang. All he asked of me was to keep Dennis out of The Institute. Simple enough. I moved some paperwork around and charmed some others so that he would only be sent to our department, where I would easily keep him out. But then"—Alyssa heard him take in a big gulp of air before continuing—"you and Tatius-Lasome had to let him in, didn't you? Couldn't accept things as they were. So, I hired the shapeshifter, paid him with that damn dagger, and now look where we are!"

Zane snickered. "How *did* we get here?"

Agwen's voice was weak and unsure, as if he questioned his own actions. "I... I didn't mean for anything like this to happen, but I had to keep it a secret, you must understand. Then that damn freak used the dagger and dropped it. It tried to be subtle, then it tried attacking, but in the end, nothing was enough to get the dagger back. By then, the number of people connected to all this had grown, so I needed more people to disappear. That is when the shapeshifter got in touch with Red Tusk for help of a more… direct nature."

Alyssa jumped at the shattering of glass as Agwen swung the staff in rage. "That assassin did it without asking me! But when I heard that the guards thought it was a gang war, I asked them to play it up." He became more aggravated with every breath.

"Who pushed me into the Dream Sphere?" Alyssa asked.

There was shame in Agwen's voice. "I did… I'm sorry about that, but you were getting too close, having Tatius-Lasome look over the books. I intended to let you out later, after I had covered all my tracks, but you both know too much now."

They turned the corner of a familiar row.

"Speaking of…" Zane said as they walked up to the sphere, which sat open and waiting, like an old friend expecting a hug.

"No," Alyssa said. "Please don't—"

"I am sorry, but these were your choices. I have modified the Dream Sphere. You two will dream and never feel death's sting when it comes. You will pass on in total bliss." Agwen leveled his staff at them. "Or I can shoot you in the back and stuff you inside it."

The runes on the staff hummed. "It's up to you."

⌐

TATIUS-LASOME'S STAFF boomed with every step. Fex found the walk odd, like someone pretending to need a crutch.

The archmage stopped short of Vana. "Well, here I am. What questions do you have?"

Fex was close enough to notice that Vana sniffed the air harder and harder as she stepped closer to Tatius-Lasome. "What do you know about Dennis?"

"That he had been interviewed for a position but was denied."

Vana nodded. "Yes, but that is very little. Everyone should know that. What else was on his file?"

Tatius-Lasome shrugged nervously. "I don't know. I see a lot of files."

Vana stopped sniffing.

"You killed my Dennis."

The room broke out into hushed debate. The head of the assembly silenced everyone. "Those are strong accusations," Arch-Lasome said. "Do you have any proof of this?"

Something in Fex snapped, and without thought he pulled the wand and fired it. Tatius-Lasome lifted one arm. It inflated, ripping his sleeve as it made a meaty shield.

A stunned silence fell over the room.

Tatius-Lasome dropped his iron staff, standing a little taller and straighter than before. "I promise I can explain all of this." The voice had changed, as if the archmage's body was now hollow.

Benedictus-Lasome cried out. "He is an imposter!"

Tatius-Lasome yelled out, but his voice was now younger and stronger. "I can explain!"

The crowd of archmages burst into yelling. Fex couldn't make out anything that was said as they argued. The shapeshifter charged toward a nearby door, but Evan and his men gave chase. The door flashed and repelled the creature, and it turned to see Vana. Its screeches sounded like metal scraping over metal as its limbs grew into massive lumps of fleshy hammers. The shapeshifter leaped forward toward Vana, arms outstretched.

Then Eldritch words rained down on the shapeshifter and its form began bending under an invisible weight. Evan and his men took their chance and charged it in with their swords, assaulting the creature with heavy blows. Sprays of blood covered the floor with each hack as the creature cried out in pain.

The shapeshifter leaped at Vana. "I am not going to die like this!"

Vana raised her arms, which pulsed and grew as hair streaked across them and her hands expanded into claws. A loud clash filled the air as their limbs slammed into each other. She kicked the shapeshifter back, her own guards frozen, watching.

"Do you know what you took from me?" Vana shouted, though there was little need as the archmages had fallen silent.

She slashed the shapeshifter across the chest, blood splattering across the floor. The creature raised an arm to block another swipe of Lady Zel's massive claw.

"Do you know *who* you took from me?"

Fex lowered his wand as tears filled his eyes. *Dennis.* The memory of his master washed over him.

The shapeshifter's arms turned into wings and it attempted to fly away.

"No!" Vana grabbed one of the creature's shrinking legs, and with a primal cry she slammed the shapeshifter into the floor. Fex flinched at the sound of shattering bone.

The shapeshifter's body spasmed on the floor, its voice hollow and weak. "Mercy. Please, have mercy—"

Vana stood over the creature. "No. This is for my Dennis."

She slammed one claw deep into the shapeshifter's chest as her guards rushed back and formed ranks around her. Vana seemed to shiver while removing her claw from the lifeless body on the floor.

Fex walked closer to comfort her, and was perhaps the only one who noticed tears rolling down past her veil.

ZANE SAW FEAR in Alyssa as she looked toward. "Please, can't we just talk—"

"Don't turn around!"

Zane had felt the kind of fear gripping Alyssa, but he had learned how to deal with it.

Shadow, who is the staff pointed at?

Oh, are you talking to me now?

Just answer me!

"I said move," Agwen shouted.

Shadow's voice responded quickly.

It's pointed at you, right hand on the runes.

Zane needed Agwen to get closer. "Is this really what you want to do? Isn't she a friend?"

He started to turn but stopped short when the wooden end of the staff pressed against his back. "I told you, don't turn around!"

Agwen's voice sounded ragged, and heavy. Alyssa was pale, her lips pleading for him to stop. Fear fought for control of Zane's body, but he breathed out, releasing the tension.

The staff pressed harder into his back. "I said move, de—"

Agwen never finished the word *detective*. Zane spun left, swiping with the cane in his left hand. The weight of the cane connected with the staff, and he parried it away. A blast erupted from the staff's tip, ripping Zane's coat. He pressed forward, jamming his cane against Agwen's body as the wizard tried to level his staff again.

The detective kicked out at the weapon, causing it to fire off another random blast as Agwen dropped it. A shelf collapsed, filling the floor with scattered trinkets and magical items. Zane shuffled through them as he moved to secure his footing, but Agwen slipped on one of the items as he swung the staff around.

Agwen spoke an eldritch word. The air rippled and Zane was shoved back. The atmosphere seemed to fill with electricity as the archmage uttered word after word. Zane braced himself.

Alyssa stepped forward, placing herself between them. She matched her former friend word-for-word and added wand fire to the mix.

But she was not an archmage, and her voice quickly grew weak from the spell duel. Her wand emptied of wicks quickly, and she tossed the wand at Agwen.

Zane had been given enough time to recover, so he pulled out his own wand and started firing it. Wand fire erupted in the air against an invisible barrier the archmage had thrown up in response. When Zane's wand ran out, Agwen picked up the staff, its runes again humming with power. Zane charged forward and tossed his own wand, but it bounced off the barrier. Zane flicked his cane through the air at Agwen.

The archmage laughed as the wooden cane also bounced off the barrier. "Resorted to throwing things now have we?"

Zane lunged forward.

Agwen's face went from smug to scared as the sword hidden inside his cane flashed in the light.

Jweal, the Fey smith who made it for Zane, had not been happy to see such a superb weapon leave his shop.

The blade seemed to sing as it passed through the air and buried itself deep into Agwen's chest. The archmage cried out as a blast from his staff went wide. Zane knew he had pierced the man's lung. The Fey's eyes burned hot like two small suns, then turned to black holes as he grabbed Zane's collar. Blood bubbled from his mouth.

"I will not die alone!"

Zane couldn't look away from the two orbs of Agwen's eyes. He could hear Alyssa and Shadow's voice as distant sounds. Fatigue and exhaustion took over as his breathing became increasingly shallow.

The world faded to the same black as Agwen's eyes.

ALYSSA'S HANDS SHOOK as she watched Agwen and Zane drop to the floor. She slid to a stop next to the detective and listened as his breathing faded.

Agwen pulled himself to the nearest cabinet, Zane's sword still sticking through him. Alyssa left Zane's side and stopped Agwen's crawl. "What did you do?"

"I used Fey magic to cause him to go into a deep sleep," he explained between coughs and gurgles of blood, a cruel smile spreading across his pale face. "The deep sleep of death." Agwen spat blood onto the floor. "He overpowered my charm during that trial, and so I threw everything I had left at him."

Alyssa looked deep into Agwen's eyes and found them black as burned wood. She waved one hand confirming his blindness.

With the archmage incapacitated, Alyssa rushed back to Zane's side. His breathing was almost gone, and she had only the slightest idea of what might save him. She started to speak in a musical language that quickly turned into a song.

The artifacts on the wall vibrated, and Alyssa closed her eyes and focused as Agwen yelled out.

"Stop! You're going to kill us all!"

A quiet voice in her knew he was right. Her attempt at Fey magic was causing all the relics around her to act up, which may cause a deadly explosion. At that thought, Alyssa remembered her parents' death and the grief that attempted to overcome her. The song weakened, and she opened her eyes to look at Zane.

She gritted her teeth, pausing the spell. *Not again, I am not a child!* Her grief became determination, and Alyssa tossed all her strength into the spell. Her words seemed to bounce off the shelves and the vibrating relics added to the song. The air filled with light, and when she touched Zane's head. Light poured into his eyes.

The room fell silent, and Alyssa thought she had failed until Zane gulped for air. Then he sat hacking as if something sat in his lungs.

Alyssa smiled and hugged him tight. "I thought you had died." She only let go when Zane patted her on the back.

"I don't understand what happened," he said, "but I owe you."

She turned to Agwen, who laid in a pool of his own blood. *He got what he deserves.* Then, she shook her head. She couldn't just let him die. Not if there was another way.

Alyssa turned to Zane. "Do you have any way to save him?"

He looked confused and raised one eyebrow. "You want to help him?"

She nodded.

Zane pulled out a bottle with golden liquid and stared at it before sighing and handing it to Alyssa. "Pull the sword free and then pour it in the wound and in his mouth."

Alyssa nodded and went to work. With the blade laying off to the side and the wound covered, she poured the golden liquid down Agwen's throat. But it wasn't liquid.

She was pouring in life.

With each ounce, Agwen's body reanimated, and soon he was taking greedy drinks.

Zane pulled his iron manacles free and handed them to Alyssa. "Make sure to handcuff him. We don't want him getting away."

Alyssa smiled and forced the restraints onto her former friend. When he'd had enough of Zane's life-giving elixir, Agwen spit the old blood out of his mouth. "Why did you save me?"

She frowned at the question.

"Because I'm better than you."

CHAPTER 27

F ex scurried back and forth, setting up his new displays. A new
stack of shatter-resistant bottles were freshly filled and ready for
sale. His cousin had checked each one to ensure their quality. Fex was
going to be more cautious than last time.

He had walked past Atom's old shop that morning. The Fountain's
windows and the door were boarded up, already tagged by local
gangs. He felt bad about Atom's condition. His shop was ruined along
with what little reputation he'd had.

But the man was still alive.

The Brew's doorbell rang.

"Sir, a man named Zane is here." Jefferson looked cleaner and
happier than he had while working across the street. "Should I let him
in?"

Fex smiled. "Please do."

The boy nodded and opened the door wide. "Master Fex will see
you."

Zane limped in on his cane and inspected the room. "The shop
looks good," he said dryly.

The gnome beamed with pride. "Thank you. I should hope so. This
place has gone through a lot in just a few days."

"Is this what it looked like when Dennis worked here?"

Fex explained the differences and enjoyed remembering those early
days. "On the whole, it's mostly the same. By the end, I was making
most of the decisions for the shop."

Zane's eyes seemed to glaze over as if he was watching something far away. Fex gave the detective his time for whatever closure he was seeking.

Until his cousin Jil—Fex was pretty sure that was her name—came out from the back. "Master Fex, I have the next batch done just like you said."

She glanced at Zane, then bowed and stepped back into the workshop. Zane gestured in her direction. "You have two apprentices?"

"Yes."

"The boy outside looks like the one who worked at Atom's shop."

Fex chuckled. "Yes, Jefferson. I felt sorry for him. The kid seemed good natured, so I offered him a job."

"And the other one?"

"One of my cousins. My uncle recommended her." Fex held up a hand as he remembered something. "Wait a moment please."

The gnome went into the workshop and brought back a crate filled with potions. "This is for you. My way of saying thank you for helping Vana and finding Dennis's murderer."

Zane placed the box under one arm with a warm smile. "Thank you, Fex. I wish you well."

Fex smiled back at the human, who he was proud to call a friend.

"Same to you."

Z

ALYSSA COLLECTED THE last of her ruined clothes after having returned the borrowed ones to Mrs. Mose. Though her old pieces were little more than bloody shards, they were secrets of The Institute. She took one last look around and hoped that she had cleaned it to Zane's satisfaction.

A sigh slipped across her lips as she stepped out into the office. The detective stood pointing out the carving to some carpenters. "I need this replaced."

"Sir, that looks really good. Are you sure you want it removed?"

"Yes."

Alyssa approached them and bowed politely. "Please, excuse us. I need to speak with Mr. Vrexon alone."

The two men nodded and stepped into the hallway. "We will contact you later, sir."

Zane leaned on his good leg. "How are you?"

"Good."

Zane seemed uncomfortable as unasked questions hung in the air between them. She felt like a balloon about to burst until breaking the news. "I have been offered the job of Dean of my old department."

Zane's face betrayed his surprise. "Oh, well, that is good. Congratulations." He stepped over to his desk and started to collect some money. "It isn't much, but I can buy you lunch to celebrate. How about noodles, just like at the beginning of the case."

"You didn't let me finish," she said. "I didn't take the position."

Zane stopped and turned back to her. "What? Why?"

"I need some time away from The Institute. The memory of that place is … complicated. The years I spent there are tainted. I don't know if I will ever go back."

He cleared his throat. "What are you going to do then?"

Alyssa smiled and looked out the window. "I don't know... maybe I'll explore the city. Though, if you are in need of an assistant, I could be of help."

He smiled. "I can't offer you much in the way of pay."

She laughed and shook her head. "That is all right. I have years' worth of money saved. I have already picked out an apartment that my grandfather recommended. I am about to collect my stuff from my old room at The Institute."

Zane scratched his head. "Well then, I guess I'll see you around."
She smiled wide.

"I think you will, Detective Zane."

ZANE SAT BEHIND his desk holding his flask, filled with Fex's elixir. The first potion of The Gnomen Brew. He looked at the freshly repaired wall, reflecting on the events of the last few days of the case. Fex had his own shop. Vana had gotten her revenge. , and Alyssa... He didn't know about what she'd gotten out of it all, but she seemed happy.

A knock at the door pulled Zane back to the present. He set his flask back on his desk. "It's open."

Vana stepped in, her robes gliding across the floor as she walked. Her black veil was now replaced with a thin white one. It was elegant and gave her an ethereal look.

Zane stood up and offered her a chair. "I am surprised to see you. I thought that you might have left town."

She took the seat with the trained grace of a noble. "I wished to pay you in person."

"You didn't have to—"

"Yes," the word came out harsh. "I did."

Vana set an envelope on the desk. It was thinner than Zane had hoped. As if sensing his disappointment, she continued. "It might have been a step too far, but I paid your rent for the next six months." Her face looked towards the flask that laid out in the open. "I can recognize a person struggling with a demon."

Shadow laughed from his corner, and for a moment Zane felt like his checks matched the creature's eyes. "Thank you so much for that consideration."

He hated to admit it, but she had done the best thing possible for him. Otherwise, he would have spent the money on more brew. He sighed and accepted his fate. "How did you know?"

Vana pointed to where her nose would be beneath the veil. "I could smell it on your breath and your body. You are in bad shape." She shuffled uncomfortably in her seat. "I would even say that you need to quit, but addiction is hard, from what I've seen."

He grimaced and looked to change the subject. "So, what will happen to you now?"

"I am now the head of the Ironbark clan. There is a carriage downstairs waiting to take me to my homeland."

Zane raised an eyebrow. "Are you going to raise a rebellion with your brother?"

She laughed. "What a question. If I were, should I leave you behind to tell?" Her veil shifted, and Zane imagined her smile. "No, I am going there to bring my people together, to strengthen our bonds with the empire. Hopefully breathe life back into those old clans."

She looked back to the flask. "Did Fex send you home with a gift?"

"Yes, he sent me a crate of healing brew. In case I get hurt, of course."

"Of course."

"He said you gave him the shop. That must have hurt."

"I didn't need it, and my Dennis always said he wanted Fex to have it once he was a State Mage. Fex deserves it. I was worried he may not make it, but without Atom around he'll make Dennis proud." Vana took a deep breath, likely to stave off tears. "So, how is that woman, Alyssa Benedictus?"

"She was offered the position of Dean of her old department, but she turned it down."

Zane looked out the window. The Institute had paid him, but he considered it hush money. Perhaps she'd considered her job offer with the same cynicism.

"I see," Vana said. "After everything she went through, I was unsure if she would return or move on."

Zane shrugged. "It seemed that she had mixed feelings. But, in the end, she said she needed time away from The Institute."

Vana was silent for a moment. "And what of that awful archmage, Agwen?"

"He has disappeared to the disciplinary halls of The Institute. What they do to him will be far worse than any jail ever could." He tried to read her reaction, but couldn't divine one through her veil. "Is that satisfactory?"

Zane could imagine how conflicted her mind and heart must have felt. When she finally spoke, it was slow and methodical.

"I killed the creature that murdered my husband, and everything else seems to have worked itself out." She stood and started toward the door but stopped short. "But if that archmage ever comes within reach of me…"

She didn't need to finish. Zane pitied Vana. It weighed heavily on him, but the words wouldn't form. "I hope you are safe in that old country of yours. And if you ever need anything, let me know. Dennis had asked me to look out for you."

Vana opened the door and gave a noble bow. "I often wonder if he had an idea of what was about to happen. Either way, thank you for everything you have done for me, detective. Be safe."

With that, the door closed, and the case came to an end. Rarely had everything wrapped up so neatly. He stood and watched from his window as she got into her carriage and rode away. It had been a long week and he needed a break, but Zane had things to do. He pulled out some paper and started to write down everything he could remember about Shadow, then turned to face his special guest. Though he couldn't see it, he could feel it grinning. *What... I mean, who are you? Really?*

Shadow's voice slid from the corner, cutting off his thoughts. *You have customers coming.*

He sighed and set down his pen, smiling despite himself.

"We're open!"

ACKNOWLEDGMENTS

I have many to thank for the creation of this book.

My wife, who patiently listened to me ramble through the plot as I adjusted and fine-tuned the story.

Charles D'Amico, who took a risk on a no-name author with nothing but a story in hand and a dream in mind.

My aunt and grandmother, who took time out of their days to help me edit my book.

Brandon Biggers, my first editor. Thank you for putting up with my constant checkups and questions.

Ricky Treon and Chelsea Kolterjahn, who polished this story till it shined.

Without all of you, this book would never exist. Thank you.

JORDAN REED

For more great titles from Blue Handle Publishing authors, visit BlueHandlePublishing.com or follow us on Twitter and Instagram **@BlueHandleBooks**

Follow our Founder Charles D'Amico **@Charles3Hats** on all platforms

Authors on Instagram

Leslie Liautaud
@author.leslie.liautaud

Jordan Reed
@author.jordan.reed

Andrew J Brandt
@andrew.j.brandt

Ray Franze
@TheHeightsNovel

CPSIA information can be obtained
at www.ICGtesting.com
Printed in the USA
BVHW032149020523
663443BV00009B/76/J

9 781955 058100